J Verres

Luther

An Historical Portrait

J Verres

Luther
An Historical Portrait

ISBN/EAN: 9783337126810

Printed in Europe, USA, Canada, Australia, Japan

Cover: Foto ©Raphael Reischuk / pixelio.de

More available books at **www.hansebooks.com**

LUTHER.

AN HISTORICAL PORTRAIT.

BY

J. VERRES D. D.

Burns and Oates.

London.
GRANVILLE MANSIONS
ORCHARD STREET W.

New-York.
CATHOLIC PUBLICATION
SOCIETY.

1884

Generatio praeterit, generatio advenit.
Si radit una haeresis, mox surgit alia, quia
diabolus non dormit, neque dormitat!

Luther. Wittenb. V 271.

Contents.

Ad Lectorem.

It will be said that this book comes post festum. It does, but the festum caused the book. The way in which on the occasion of the 4th. centenary of Luther's birth the „Reformer" was spoken of by almost all shades of Protestants showed clearly that the real Luther is little known in this country. The bulk of the sermons, speeches, lectures and newspaper articles delivered or written in praise of him made it evident that most of the speakers or writers derived their knowledge of him not from his own works, but from old legends or from admiring biographies, or perhaps from the tiny, tidy, revised and expurgated editions of the Tabletalk which were to be had at the railway bookstalls. Some friends suggested to me the idea of drawing a portrait of the Prophet of Wittenberg from his own works. The prospect of having to devote many months to going through his voluminous and frequently disgusting books was anything but cheerful, but I resolved to carry out the idea, in the hope of contributing a little towards vindicating historical truth.

It will seem that there is a prima facie argument against the book I now present to the public, it will supposed that it has been written in a party spirit. I have honestly tried to avoid being influenced in that way and to overcome the great temptation connected with my task, viz. to write a satire; I have honestly striven to put aside those feelings which naturally fill a Catholic in presence of a man, who has reviled and hated and cursed the Catholic Church more than any other mortal being ever has done or ever can do, and I hope not to have lost sight for a moment of the commandment: Thou shalt not bear false witness. It has been my intention to write *about* Luther, not *against* him. If the result is not favourable to him, it is not my fault. Though at the risk of having my intention misunderstood, I have made a point of giving Luther's own words on all the subjects that had to be touched. Wherever I have said anything of my own, I may confidently leave is to the reader to judge from the accompanying quotations whether or not my statements are groundless.

The reader must not expect to find here a complete life of Luther. To follow him step by step, this may be left to his admirers, to whom of course even the most trifling incident in the „Reformer's" life is of the greatest importance. My object was different; I wished to faithfully describe Luther's character and work or rather to let him describe it himself and to let him express his own views on the most important subjects.

It will also be said that this book contains many objectionable things. It does, but those things are not mine. If now and then the reader should cry out: Shame! I answer: Yes, shame indeed, but upon whom? I have not studiously picked out the worst sayings of Luther, and I should have to protest against the supposition, as if I had tried to secure for my book a sort of meretricious interest in that way.

On the contrary, the worst sayings of Luther have been excluded, nor have any of the passages quoted been admitted without due deliberation or without the approbation of friends, on whose judgment I can rely. Many Englishmen know in a general way that the „Reformer" was in the habit of using „rather hard words", as it is mildly put, but few know how far he was capable of going.

When on the occasion of the Luther celebration the Archbishop of York chose to speak about the corruption of Rome, which, he said, Luther found to be „the centre of infidelity and paganism", why did he not in confirmation of his words read to his hearers just a few pages of the Prophet's book against Popery, where that corruption is so glaringly painted? True, that in all probability his congregation would have risen and walked out of S. Michael's after hearing half a page and that there would have been the danger of driving some of them into Popery by reading such a detestable libel against the same. But it might have been a good thing to give just an idea of what is euphemistically called Luther's „robust Christianity", though the „Catholic slanderers" (of whom Mr. Köstlin speaks) call it ribaldry and filth.

Of this „robust Christianity" we shall have to give some specimens. It is of no use whatever to be satisfied with general phrases about Luther's style. People want proofs and we must give them. When in November 1883 the Right Rev. Dr. Bewick applied to Luther the epithets *foulmouthed* and *scurrilous,* the Presbyterians of Newcastle on Tyne strongly denounced such „pulpit Billingsgate" as they called it. If they had ever seen a few pages of Luther's own works, (not of the railway bookstall tabletalk), they would have known on what side the Billingsgate is. The reader will have occasion to judge whether or not the expression of Bishop Bewick was too hard. To arrive at a just estimate of Luther's character without taking into account his style, which was part of his nature, is an impossibility.

It need hardly be said, that this book was never intended for a lady's boudoir or for a nursery.

I have taken all possible care to ensure the accuracy of the references, so as to give to everybody the chance of verifying the quotations. The reader will excuse if, considering the great number of them, some errors should have crept in.

It will be noticed that also on doctrinal points I have quoted from the Tabletalk, though not on any point exclusively from this source, and perhaps it will be thought that in so doing I have laid myself open to objection. It has been urged that, the Tabletalk not having been written by Luther himself, but having been compiled from the notes of persons who were in the habit of listening to him, no body would go to a book of this sort for evidence on a man's teaching. But, salvo meliori judicio, I think that the Tabletalk is a most important book. If we cannot trust to it, to get a proper idea of Luther's views, let no Englishman depend on Boswell for a faithful expression of the views of Johnson. Luther's disciples hung on their master's lips with greater devotion than the scottish laird on Johnson's. Like Boswell they have even recorded sayings, in which it is impossible to discover anything striking, mere platitudes. The reliability of the book appears also from the fact, that Lauterbach, whose notes are the chief source of it, put down his reminiscences day after day, as they were fresh in his memory. If the Tabletalk were in opposition to Luther's own books, we could not trust to it, but this is far from being the case. On the contrary, the official teaching of Luther finds further familiar illustrations in the Tabletalk, and the Tabletalk shows how seriously Luther meant even the most startling things which he said as „Evangelist".

As a German I wish to use this opportunity to protest against an assertion which recently has been made ad nauseam in English books and pamphlets and newspaper articles, viz. that Luther is the national hero of Germany. He is nothing of the kind. Let it be said that he is the hero of the Protestant part of that nation. But there are 26,000,000 of German Catholics in the German Empire and in Austria i. e. nearly half of the Germans in Europe. Are they to insignificant a fraction, so worthless a lot of parias, that a man may be made a „national" hero without their concurrence?

Vale!

Caverswall,
Stoke upon Trent.

J. Verres.

Chapter I

The intellectual, religious and social state of Germany before Luther.

Germania fuit; et nunquam erit quod fuit.
Luther. De Wette V. 451.

The character of a prominent man, — prominent
whether for good or for evil — cannot be properly un-
terstood and estimated without a knowledge of his time
and surroundings. Such knowledge is especially necessary
with regard to Luther, for, in order to make his figure
stand out all the more strikingly, many of his admirers
have thought it necessary to paint the background as
dark as possible. Even Protestants begin to see and to
acknowledge, that the legendary Luther and the real
Luther are totally different persons. Holtzmann(¹) speaks
of a „Luthermyth, in the formation of which theological
prejudices and — at least unconscious — falsification have
played a great part", and Maurenbrecher protests against
„the *deeply rooted nonsense,* which until recently has been
offered to the public as Luther's *history".* (²)

If we were to believe the admirers of the „Reformer",
we should have to suppose that, before he appeared and
before the light of his „Evangelium" began to shine, darkness covered the whole of Germany, that crass ignorance
and gross superstition where the characteristic signs of

(¹) Quoted by Germ. 63.   (²) Studien und Skizzen, Leipz.
1874 p. 207.

the time, that misery and poverty were the common lot
ot the bulk of the population, that the clergy were a mass
of ignoramuses and villains, that especially the monasteries were sinks of iniquity. Such are the ideas, which
from „popular" books the greater part of the English public derive. The average Englishman cannot think or speak
of the state of Christendom before the „glorious Reformation" without a feeling of loathing.

It is not the object of these pages, to write a pane-
gyric of that age, but to put before the reader plain, duly
authenticated historical facts, from which he will be able
to form a judgment for himself. We shall have to call
the reader's attention to many things showing that bright
side, which has been studiously ignored, but we shall also
point out the real and great evils and abuses, which caused misery to the people, weakened the empire and
brought disgrace upon the Church of God.

Some of the most prominent writers of the 15th century, not only Germans, but also distinguished members
of other nations, speak of the state of Germany at that
period with genuine enthusiasm. According to Aeneas
Sylvius (afterwards Pope Pius II) no other nation has been
favoured by God so much as the Germans, who excel all
others in strength and power, whose country is like a
garden, whose towns are adorned with the most magnifi-
cent Churches and public buildings; the people live most
comfortably, a great number possess extraordinary wealth
— the kings of Scotland would be glad to have a house
like that of a well-to-do citizen of Nürnberg! — the population of the Italian free republics are nothing better than
slaves, whilst the Germans enjoy perfect freedom. (³)

(³) Liquebit nunquam fuisse
Germanici nominis eas vires aut
opes, quales sunt hodie. (Schardii
op. I. 449.) Agros ubique cultos
videmus, novalia, vineta, viridaria,
violaria, pomaria rustica et subur-
bana, aedificia plena deliciis, villas
amoenissimas, arces in montibus
sitas, oppida muris cincta, splen-
didissimas urbes (Ibid. 451.) (Co-
loniâ) nihil magnificentius, nihil or-
natius tota Europa reperies. Tem-
plis et aedibus nobilis, populo insignis, opibus clara (Ibid.) Quis
(Norimbergae) aspectus! quae majestas! quod decus ab extra visen-

This was written in 1458, but fifty years later matters had greatly changed; we shall point out the causes in the proper place.

The intellectual life of the country received an extraordinary impulse from the newly invented art of printing. The whole population was benefited by it in an extraordinary way. It was especially the clergy, that welcomed this new art as the best means to further the religious instruction of the people. (⁴) If we remember what imperfect appliances had to be used for a considerable time, it is truly astonishing to see how rapidly the art spread. Falkenstein (⁵) gives a list of more than a thousand printingfirms, which were established before the end of the 15th century. Most of the printers were Germans. During that period Mainz possessed 5, Ulm 6, Basel 16, Augsburg 20, Cologne 21 printing establishments. (⁶) More than a hundred German printers settled in different towns of Italy, where Schweynheim and Pannartz had set up the first presses in the Palazzo Massimi and at Subiaco. How great an activity was displayed by the followers of the new art, may be gathered from the fact, that the firm of Koburger in Nürnberg published, before the year 1500, more than 200 large works. (⁷) This „art of arts and science of sciences", as the Carthusian Werner Rolewink calls it, was especially made use of, to further the glory of God through the religious instruction of the people. Few have spoken of it more enthusiastically, than Jacob Whimpheling, justly famed for his great erudition and piety. „As formerly the Apostles went out, so now the disciples of this holy art go out from Germany into all countries; their

tibus, quis intus nitor platearum! quae domorum munditiae! Quot ibi civium aedes invenies regibus dignas! Cuperent tam egregie Scotorum reges, quam mediocres Nurnbergae cives habitare (Ibid. 456.)

(⁴) „Magnum quoddam ac pene divinum beneficium collatum est universo terrarum orbi a Joanne Gutenberg." Wimpheling, Epit. rerum Germ. c. 65. in Schardii tom I.

(⁵) Gesch. d. Buchdruckerkunst, Leipz. 1840.

(⁶) Janssen I. 11.

(⁷) Hahn, Die Koburger, Leipz. 1869 p. 90 seqq.

printed books are like heralds of the Gospel, preachers of truth and science." „The books we print in Germany, are mostly noble productions, which further the glory of God, the salvation of souls and the instruction of the people." (8)

The prayerbooks, hymnbooks, catechisms, books of meditation etc., which were printed at that time and still exist, may be counted by the hundred. If we examine those publications, we do not find in them a vestige of all the nonsense, which is so often supposed so have form- ed the religion of the Catholic people in those days, but in simple, clear and correct words the very same doc- trine is expressed, which the Catholic Church teaches in our own days and always will teach. To give those books into the hands of the people in our days, nothing more would be required, than to alter the spelling. Over- critical minds might be scandalized by the tales of miracles, which frequently occur in those old publications. But it must not be thought that the people were expected to believe such histories, as they would have to believe ar- ticles of faith. The author of the „Selenfürer", (Guide of souls) says distinctly: „Thou needest not believe all the miracles, which thou readest in pious books; the miracles of the Bible are real miracles, and there are many other creditable miracles which the Saints wrought through God, but mind, many of them are set before thee only by way of illustration. (9)

It may be well, to test some of those books on one or another important point. Many Protestants are still under the impression, that an indulgence is equivalent to the sale of the forgiveness of sins, that consequently the use of indulgences necessarily demoralized the people. Let us see, how the devotional books of the 15th century

---

(8) MS. „De arte impressoria", quoted by Janssen I. 16.

(9) Du breuchst nit all wunder zu gleuben, die du lesest in from- men büchern, die wunder der Schrift sint warhafte wunder, und es gibt vil glaubhaffte wunder auch sunsten, die dy lieben heyli- gen wurkten durch Got; aber wisz, vile sint dir nur zum exempel er- zält.

explain this particular point. *They contain the invariable Catholic doctrine.* The „Selenfürer" says: „Know, that an indulgence does not forgive sins, but only remits the punishment thou hast deserved. Know, that thou canst not gain an indulgence as long as thou art in sin, until thou hast confessed and truly repented, and resolved to do better for the future; without this, it will do thee no good." ([10]) The „Summa Joannis" (1480) explains, that *he* only can gain an indulgence, who truly repents of his sins; „if a man were in mortal sin, he would not gain the indulgence, for it is not given to sinners. ([11])

It is also frequently supposed, that the Catholics had almost lost sight of the infinite merits of Christ and trusted too much, if not entirely, in their own works. Let us see, whether the devotional books of the 15th century encouraged anything of this kind. The „Kerstenspiegel" (Mirror of Christians) says: „Man must direct his faith, his hope and his charity towards God and not towards any creature." The „Selenwurtzgertlein" (Garden of the Soul) gives instructions how to prepare people for death. Let them be exhorted: „You must put all your hope and trust in nothing but the merits and the death of Christ. ([12]) Let the dying Christian say: O merciful Lord Jesus. I put thy painful death between thy sentence and my poor soul. ([13]) Let him be asked" whether he firmly believes, that he cannot be saved, except through

---

([10]) Wisz das der ablasz nit sunden vergibt, sondern allein straffen nachlässt die du verdienet hast. Wisz, das du keinen ablasz haben kannst, wann du in sünden bist und nit gebichtet hast, und geruwet hast wahrhafftiglich und dich hertziglich bessern wilst, sunsten hilft dir alles nit.

([11]) „wann wer der mensch in todsünden, so empfing er den ablasz nit, wann er wird nit den sündern gegeben." Cfr. the explanation given by Geiler von Keiserberg (in „Christenlich bilger-schafft", Basel 1512) an indulgence is „verzyhung der zitlichen pin, die einer schuldig würd zu bezalen nach worem rüwen und bicht." Hasak 431. See also Hasak 60. 62. 165. Everywhere we find the same correct explanation.

([12]) so soltu alle deyn hoffnung und getruwen auf nirgent anders setzen, dan auf das verdienen und den tod Jhesu Christi.

([13]) deinen so schmertzlichen tod setze ich zwischen deyn urteyl und meyn arme Seel.

the bitter sufferings and death of Christ. ([14]) In the „Geistl. Streit" (Spiritual Combat) we find these words: „I know that we have a merciful God, I will die trusting in his mercy and goodness, not in my own good works." ([15])

Luther says ([16]) that under the Pope neither the decalogue, nor the Our Father, nor the Creed was taught, nor was it considered necessary to know them. We advise his admirers to see the beautiful explanations of the ten commandments given by Nider (1474) ([17]), in the „mirror of sinners" (Augsb. 1470 ([18]) in the „buch der X gepot" (Venedig 1483) ([19]), in „der selen Trost" (Augsb. 1483)([20]), „der ewigen wiszheit betbüchlein" (Basel 1518)([21]); or the explanations of the Lord's prayer in „Hymelstrasz" (Augsb. 1501) ([22]), „der beschlossen gart" (Nürnb. 1505 ([23]), in „Keisersberg Pater Noster" (Strassb. 1515). ([24]) In the excedingly rich devotional literature of Germany, before Luther's time, the Creed, the Sacraments, the Mass, the necessity of grace, the meaning of the invocation of Saints, etc. etc. are explained not only with the greatest theological precision, but also in the best popular way. The necessity of sincere sorrow for sins, of amendment of life, of purity of heart, of the love of God is urged everywhere, whilst superstition is mercilessly attacked. ([25]) All the writers and preachers appear to be very well versed in Holy Scripture and in the Fathers, their books abound with quotations from both. There is nowhere an

---

([14]) „ob er ungezweyfelt glaube das er nitt ewigklichen behalten und selig werden mög, dann durch das bitter leyden und sterben Jhesu Christi." Hortulus animae. Strassb. 1509.

([15]) For further proofs see Hasak 70. 143. 151. 152. 367. That „our salvation depends entirely on the merits of Christ" as the Schatzbehalter" (Treasury) Nürnberg 1491 says, is *invariably* the doctrine laid down in all the Catholic books of the period.

([16]) Lauterb. 151.

([17]) Hasak 11.
([18]) Ibid. 42.
([19]) Ibid. 67.
([20]) Ibid. 105.
([21]) Ibid. 541.
([22]) Ibid. 281.
([23]) Ibid. 309.
([24]) Ibid. 469.
([25]) See the examination of conscience in the „Beichtspigel" Leipz. 1495 ap. Hasak 192. To readers who take an interest in this branch of literature we cannot recommend Hasak's book too warmly.

attempt at vain oratorical flights; they go straight to the
point, and, what is just as important, their words evidently
come from the heart and go straight to the heart of the
hearer or reader. We only wish that in our own time
more sermons were preached in that good old style.

Before the year 1500 there existed already 59 editions
of the „Imitation of Christ“ in different languages; of the
Epistles and Gospels, with explanations, *more than 50 editions* in the different German dialects. ([26]) Must not such
a supply have supposed a very large demand? And can
the Germans before Luther have been so brutally ignorant in religion, as sometimes they are said to have been?

Luther's admirers maintain that one of his greatest
claims to immortality is founded on his having given to the
people the word of God, the Bible. Such is the opinion
even of men who may boast of the best education and
who occupy high positions in ecclesiastical and political
life in this country. ([27]) Is there any truth in the statement, that „Luther fetched the Bible out of its hidingplace“,
or is it only an old and fondly cherished fable? The reader will be able to judge from facts.

Nobody will expect, that a copy of the Bible should
have been found in every house, before the art of printing was invented, at a time, when a whole Bible, written, with infinite labour, on parchment, represented a small
fortune. Even after the invention of the new art, for a
considerable time, a mighty foliovolume, containing the
whole of the Scriptures, was not within the reach of
everybody indiscriminately. But everything that could
be done, was done, to promote the reading of the Bible,
long before Luther. Before the year 1500 the Bible had
been published in Latin almost a hundred times ([28]) and

([26]) The full titles of 38 of them
ap. Alzog, d. deutschen Plenarien,
4 seqq.

([27]) See the sermon of the
Archb. of York at S. Michael's.
Nov. 1883. About the same time

M[r]. Forster M. P. expressed the
same opinion in his speech at
Bradford.

([28]) Catalogue and description
of the different editions ap. Kau-
len, Gesch. der Vulgata p. 304 seqq.

yet it is said, that not even the Clergy were acquainted
with it! But how can it be said, that it was rigidly withheld from the laity, when we find that, apart from numerous editions of various parts,([29]) there existed of the
whole of the Bible, before Luther's time fifteen complete
versions in High-German, besides five others in German
dialects?([30])   When we find, that many of those versions
went through a great number of editions, that, for instance,
Amorbach in Basel printed the Bible nine times within
ten years, Koburger in Nürnberg fifteen times before the
end of the 15th century?([31])

In the very first lines of his introductory chapter to
the „Narrenschiff" (printed for the first time in 1494) Sebastian Brant says: that the whole country is full of Bib-
les and other books concerning salvation.([32])

So far from keeping the Bible out of the reach of
the people, the Clergy did their best, to make the faithful read it.   The author of a devotional book([33]) says:
Whatsoever Holy Church teaches, whatsoever thou hearest
in sermons, or hearest or readest in other instructions,
whatsoever is written in spiritual books, all thy hymns in
God's praise, all thy prayers for thy soul's salvation, all thy
sufferings in troubles and adversities, all this ought to move
thee, to read with piety and humility the Holy Scriptures,
as they are now translated into the German tongue, and
printed *and scattered far and wide in exceedingly great
numbers, either in parts or as a whole;* thou mayest have

([29]) An account of them ap.
Alzog l. c. p. 65.

([30]) The Catalogue is given by
Kehrein, Gesch. d. deutschen Bibel-
übersetzung, p. 34 seqq., who also
gives the full text of 33 different
German versions of the 5th chapter of S. Matthew, beginning with
Ulfilas. Nine of the old versions
of the Bible are in the British Mu-
seum, eight in the University library
of Freiburg i. B. Cfr. Alzog l. c. 25.

([31]) Janssen I. 16.

([32]) Alle Land sind jetzt voll
                  heiliger Schrift
Und was der Seelen Heil
                  betrifft:
Voll Bibeln, heiliger Väter
                  Lehr,
Und anderer ähnlicher Bü-
                  cher mehr.

As the original of the Narrenschiff
is not within my reach, I quote
from Junghans' edition in modern
German, Leipzig.

([33]) Himmelstür 1517.

them now for little money." The author of the Explanation of the Gospels (Basel 1514) says, that his object
has been to excite the people to the reading of the Holy
Scriptures, especially of the four Gospels, „whose power
and truth is above all books". He continues: „Therefore
I advise every sensible man, to read always the Holy
Scriptures, that he may know God, his Master and Creator, for the grace which man may receive from God through
the reading or the hearing of the Bible is infinite ... There
is no care, no trouble so great, but in reading the word
of God, and in taking it to heart, thou wilt find consolation through the grace of the Holy Ghost." A similar
exhortation exists in the preface to the German Bible printed in Cologne before 1480 (³⁴) and in „Ein sond'lich nutz-
lich und trostlich buchlen" (Leipzig 1508) we find the following prayer recommended to those, who are reading
the Bible: „O Lord Jesus Christ, help me that I may understand what I am reading and that I may faithfully
follow it in my life." (³⁵)

That great care was taken to instruct the people in
the truths of Religion from the pulpit, is evident from the
ecclesiastical laws on this point and from the testimony
of numerous contemporary writers. The parishpriests are
reminded of their duty to preach to the people every
Sunday by the Diocesan Synods of Bamberg (1491), of
Basel (1503), of Meissen (1514), numberless benefices were
founded for the maintenance of priests, who had to devote all their time and energy to preaching, (³⁶) the faithful were warmly exhorted to hear the word of God, and,
where necessary, they were even threatened with ecclesiastical punishment in case of negligence. It seems that the
assistance at the sermon was considered as a very grave
obligation, binding under a mortal sin. The faithful were
reminded, to examine themselves on this point, when preparing for confession, fathers of families and masters were

---

(³⁴) Alzog l. c. p. 65.
(³⁵) Hasak.

(³⁶) Janssen I. 31 gives a long
list of such places.

reminded of their duty to see that those under their care
fulfilled this obligation. (37)

Joannes Cochlaeus tells us in 1511, that in Nürnberg
the Churches were always full during the sermon, „even
when sermons are preached in thirteen different places at
the same time. (38) The whole practice of the Church was
in harmony with the words of Ulrich Surgant" Exceedingly great is the profit to be derived from a good sermon of a pious and prudent priest, who loves God and
the salvation of souls. For no word is above God's word,
and God's greatest blessing flows down upon the preacher
and upon all those who listen to him in humility."

Very significant is also the fact, that numerous col-
lections of sermons on the principal truths were published
over and over again. (39) Of the sermons of John Herold,
a Dominican Friar, 41 editions existed before the year
1500. (40) Besides the regular sermon, there was also a
catechetical instruction for the whole congregation. „It is
a praiseworthy custom, which has been introduced by
many pious priests in villages and towns, to explain in
the mornings or afternoons the articles of faith and the
commandments to both young and old, and to examine,
how they understand them. In this way the sermons are
further explained, as also the tables with the commandments, with the intruction for confession and the others,
that are hung up in the Churches. (41)

The faith of the people naturally found its expression
in ecclesiastical hymns. Wackernagel, a strict Protestant,
and an authority in the history of German literature, says
of the period preceding Luther: „No other nation in Christendom possessed so large a treasure of sacred hymns
or such a beautiful poetical expression of faith. (42) Al-

(37) In 1497 Count Oettingen
made known to his servants, that
those who would not hear the sermon on Sundays or holidays, would
receive notice ... „dem werd uff-
gesagt." Janssen I. 29.
(38) Ap. Otto, p. 48.

(39) A number of them ap. Janssen I. 30.
(40) Hain, Repert. bibliogr.
(41) Selenfürer.
(42) Das deutsche Kirchenlied,
Leipz. 1867.

ready in the year 1148 i. c. more than 300 years before
any one dreamt of Luther, the Provost Gerho of Reichens-
berg wrote in his explanation of the Psalms: „The whole
world exultingly sings the praises of God, also in the ver-
nacular tongues, this is especially the case amongst the
Germans." That the hymn-singing had not been forgotten in the following centuries is evident from the fact, that
there still exist more than thirty German ecclesiastical
hymnbooks, printed before Luther's apostasy, and that,
to speak of only one feast of the Church, there still exist
about a hundred Christmas-hymns of those days. [49] Many
of the hymns which are sung nowadays in the Catholic
Churches of Germany, were known and were sung in the
14th and 15th centuries. Nay, Luther himself says: „Under the Pope they used to sing fine hymns."

Though education was not as common in the 15th
century as it is now, though there were neither School-
boards, nor Revised Codes, it would be a great mistake
to suppose, that the schools were neglected. Every town
and almost every village boasted of its school. Religious
education was urged above everything, but the parents
were exhorted to have their children instructed also in
reading and writing, and the children, to respect and reverence the masters who imparted knowledge to them.
Sebastian Brant gives, in his celebrated „Narrenschiff"
amongst the fools a place also to the man, who neglects
to have his children instructed. [44] But it was evidently
not so much the object of the schools, to cram the children with all sorts of useless knowledge, as to make them
good men and good Christians.

How the schools were attended, appears from the
fact that even in small towns like Xanten and Wesel there
were four or five schoolmasters; and how these were re-

---

(49) Meister, d. kath. Kirchenlied. Freib. 1862.

(44) Weil man der Kinder Zucht
         nicht will,
     So trifft man Catilinen viel.

Es stände besser um man-
                ches Kind,
Gäb man ihm Lehrer wohl-
                gesinnt.
                Chapt. VI.

spected is shown by the salaries they received, which,
considering the value of money at that time, were not
inconsiderable. In Goch, for instance, the schoolmaster
had 8 florins a year, besides his house and the schoolpence,
whilst the townclerk's salary amounted to only 5 florins.

Let us pass on to intermediate education. Without
hesitation or fear of contradiction we may state, that in
the 15th century Germany possessed more Grammarschools,
than England possesses at the present day. ([45]) The elder
humanists, who did not, like most of their successors,
despise the literature of their own country, and who combined the love of the old classics with the most devoted
love of the Church, developed an extraordinary activity
in establishing schools. Prominent amongst them were the
members of the brotherhood founded by Gerhard Groote,
who possessed schools over the whole of the Empire, including Holland and Flanders. At Zwolle they had at
one time 800 students, at Alkmaar 900, at Hertogenbosch
1200, at Deventer more than 2000! The great Cardinal
Cusanus who had been their pupil, was amongst their
greatest friends, likewise the Popes Eugen IV and Pius II.
The city of Cologne possessed eleven Grammarschools
connected with its eleven Collegiate Churches. ([46])

During the 15th century the German Universities were
perhaps more flourishing, than |they are now. There were
seven old established ones (Cologne, Vienna, Prague, Heidelberg, Erfurt, Leipzig, Rostock); during the fifty years
from 1456—1506 nine new ones were founded, Greifs-
walde, Basel, Freiburg, Ingolstadt, Treves, Tübingen,
Mainz, Wittenberg, Frankfurt a. O. Almost all of them
were founded by the Popes, who assigned to them a certain income out of the Churchproperty to secure their
existence; the clergy too, largely contributed towards the
funds. ([47]) The students at almost every one of the dif-

([45]) In Germania tot fere sunt   ([46]) Janssen I. 54.
academiae, quot oppida. Erasmus.   ([47]) Prantl, Gesch. der Ludw.
Opp. III. 689.   Max. Universität, München 1872.

ferent Universities were counted by the thousand. Vienna
alone had at one time 7000. A. D. 1451 the number of
fresh students inscribed on the rolls of the Vienna University was 751; more than half of them came from the
Rhine (⁴⁸). According to a very moderate calculation the
number of University students in the whole of Germany
during the second half of the 15th century cannot in any
year have been less than 20,000. The number of eminent
men, whose minds were formed at the Universities and
who adorned their country with their piety and learning
is so great, that we can only mention a few of them.
Werner Rolewink († 1502), a Carthusian monk was famous
not only for the holiness of his life, but also for the theological depth of his lectures on S. Paul's Epistles, professors as well as students thronged the hall, to listen to him.
At the same time his historical works met with the greatest success; one of them was published thirty times within
18 years. Rudolf Agricola († 1483) was celebrated as un-
surpassed in classical knowledge. (⁴⁹) Jacob Wimpheling
(† 1528 at the age of 78) acquired great fame by his numerous pedagogical writings, which were scattered over
Germany in 30,000 copies. Geiler von Keisersberg († 1510),
a most extraordinary genius, preached for years in Strassburg Cathedral, with such success, displaying such profound knowledge of theology, of the human heart and of
the wants of his time, that few preachers have ever equalled him. Trithemius, the famous abbot of Sponheim († 1516)
was acknowledged to be the most universal genius of his
age and one of the greatest ornaments of the Church.
To avoid prolixity, we will only add the names of Gabriel
Biel, the theologian, Ulrich Zasius, prominent in jurisprudence, Regiomontanus, the pioneer of astronomical science,
Johann von Dalberg, the zealous Bishop of Worms and
learned Maecenas of all learned men, Cochlaeus and Eck,

(⁴⁸) Kink, Gesch. d. Univ. Wien.
1854.
    (⁴⁹) Cujus ingenium et eruditio-

nem et summam morum innocen-
tiam ipsi Itali laudaverunt. Wimpheling, in Schardii tom I. 389.

who afterwards became so famous through their opposition to Luther. But prominent above all his contemporaries appears the grand figure of Cardinal Nicolaus, called Cusanus from the name of his native village Cues (on the Moselle) († 1464) a genuine Catholic Reformer, who in the true spirit of Christ „began to do and to teach", ([50]) who preached even more with his example, than with his word. He displayed a most astonishing activity over the whole of Germany, teaching, exhorting, reforming, punishing, presiding over Provincial Councils and superintending the training of the Clergy. Trithemius calls him „an angel of light and peace". ([51]) Eminent in every branch of science, he used all his influence, to advance learning; his ardent love of his country is proved by the plan, which he drew up for the political reform of the Empire. He was the first to suggest the idea, afterwards carried out by Maximilian, of dividing the Empire into regions for the better administration of the country.

The extraordinary thirst for knowledge which, principally after the invention of the art of printing, distinguishes the 15th century, is found also amongst the female sex. We will here mention the Benedictine nuns Aleydis Raiskop, of Rolandswerth ([52]) Richmondis van Horst, of Seebach (near Dürkheim) and the ornaments of the city of Nürnberg, Charitas Pirkheimer and Apollonia Tucher, all famous for their classical knowledge. ([53])

We have seen that the printing press amply provided the German people with spiritual books, but secular literature for their instruction and amusement was not ne-

---

([50]) Acta App. I. 1.

([51]) Wimpheling (Epit. rer. Germ.) praises in Cusanus „doctrinam omnifariam, eloquentiam singularem, ingenium perspicacissimum. ... Cardinalatum doctrina et virtutibus meruit. In Schardii tom I. 388.

([52]) This lovely island in the Rhine, a few miles above Bonn, is now called Nonnenwerth.

([53]) F. Binder's „Char. Pirkheimer" (Freib. 1873) gives a most interesting description of the highly developed intellectual life in the convents of Nürnberg, also of the sufferings their inmates had to go through, when the storm of the Reformation broke out.

glected. We can hardly suppose that the masses of the
people became acquainted with the many large chronicles
which appeared before the year 1500; the common people
want something more interesting and exciting. This was
offered to them and eagerly read by them in the popular
talebooks about heroes and knights, giants and fairies,
adventures and travels. Of such popular books in prose
or verse a great number are still in existence, and many
of the stories they contain, for instance, the stories of
Melusina, of Fortunatus, of Eulenspiegel, the celebrated
fool, and of his practical jokes, form even now the de-
light of the German youth. „Everybody", says the „Selenfürer", „wishes to read and to write, this is praiseworthy and desirable if the books are good, but not, if
they are bad and excite to luxury and impurity. Such
are many talebooks; thou must not read them". But comparatively speaking, the number of objectionable books
of this class in very small.

We must devote here a few words to a book, to
which we have already referred above, the „Narrenschiff"
or „Ship of fools", published by Sebastian Brant in 1494.
In a very short time it became the favourite book of the
nation. In it the author fearlessly, but with the greatest
humour, lashes the follies of his age. In 115 chapters all
the fools to whom he assigns a place in his ship, whether
of the clergy or of the laity, the backbiter, the miser, the
gambler, the drunkard, the adulterer, the glutton; the
proud, the improvident, the fashionable, the boasting, the
idle, the lying fool — all have to pass muster, and each
one has his folly and weakness put before him in the
most telling manner. Goodhumouredly the author finds
also a place for himself in the same ship. Throughout
the work it is evident, that scoffing was not Brant's object, but the serious endeavour, to further the welfare of
his countrymen. His book would never have had such
an enormous success and become so popular, if everybody had not recognized in it a true and outspoken

friend. Geiler von Keisersberg called id „the mirror of
salvation". (⁵⁴)

Towards the middle of the 15th century Germany
was perhaps the richest country in the world. Poverty
was almost unknown even amongst the lower classes; the
country abounded with natural resources, masses of grain
were exported, the mines furnished a great quantity of
metals, especially silver, the greater part of the commerce
of the world was in the hands of Germans. (⁵⁵)

„Very little money" says Macchiavelli (⁵⁶) „leaves Germany, for the people are satisfied with what their country produces, but a great deal of money comes to them
from others, who buy the fruits of their industry, . . . at
the same time there is an abundance of natural produce."
And Whimpheling says: „Germany was never so rich and
splendid, as it is in our days; this is owing to the unre-
mitting industry of her citizens, of those who work with
their hands and of those who follow commerce. The
peasants too have become rich." (⁵⁷) A great number of
the peasants owned the land they tilled, especially along
the Rhine and in the South, and as generally the land was
not divided amongst the children after the father's death,
but descended to the eldest son, the stability of the smaller possessions was well secured. There were no serfs,
except in a small part of the North East, among the
Wends, where civilization made but slow progress; the
Empire acknowledged the principle of absolute personal
freedom.

Many of the peasants were of course tenants under
large owners, noblemen, monasteries and Churches, but
their rights and duties were well defined in the so called
„Weisthümer", documents, which as Grimm says (⁵⁸) bear

(⁵⁴) Brant's son said about it:
Wenn man es gründlich hatt' er-
      kannt,
Würd es das Schiff des Heils ge-
      nannt.

(⁵⁵) The »Buch der Croniken,
1493« gives a glowing description
of the wealth of the country.
(⁵⁶) Opere IV. 153.
(⁵⁷) De arte impr.
(⁵⁸) Rechtsalterthümer IX.

a splendid testimony to the free and noble nature of the old German law. The tenants paid their rent partly in kind, partly by personal labour (Frohndienst). Curiously enough, in some cases the personal labour was demanded only nominally. There is one instance, in which the tenants were bound to perform a dance before the landlord.([59]) During the performance of the Frohndienst the tenant received an ample supply of food, such as „red wine, beef and ryebread", in some cases he was rewarded in the evening with a loaf, wich reached, when he was sitting, „from his knee to his chin". The abbey of Prüm gave to the tenant, who had been carting, „plenty to eat and to drink, two kinds of bread, two kinds of meat and two kinds of wine". The still existing regulations of many large farms show us that the wants of the common labouring man were carefully attended to, but the master expected from his workmen strict observance of their religious duties.([60])

The wide connexions and the great influence of the German merchants during the period we are speaking of, is well known. The ships of the northern cities sailed to Russia, Scandinavia, England, Scotland, France, Spain, Portugal and Italy. To Englishmen it will be interesting to learn, that sometimes in one year from 6 to 700 vessels left the port of Danzig with corn for England, whence they generally returned with a cargo of English woollen · manufactures. The regulations, which were drawn up for the conduct of the sailors show the common character of the period: „Ora et labora." Religion still pervaded life in all its parts.

Cologne, Frankfurt and Nürnberg became the centres of the commerce of almost the whole western world. Of

---

([59]) Maurer, Fronhöfe III. 306.
([60]) Blavignac (quoted by Janssen I. 339) gives the result of his researches into the condition of the working classes toward the end of the 15th century in the words: Le travail des ouvriers était bien plus avantageusement rétribué au moyen-âge que de nos jours.

the latter town Wimpheling says: „The riches that flow into it are almost beyond conception."([61])

But it is the common voice and the common complaint of the best men of the period, that the riches of Germany proved anything but an unmixed blessing. Few could have loved their country better, than Wimpheling did, few therefore felt more bitterly that state of corruption, which began to set in. His words deserve to be quoted at length. „Riches cause many dangers, as we see every day with our own eyes. They cause excessive luxury in dress, gluttony, and what is just as pernicious, the desire to possess more and more. This eagerness makes man worldly and ends in the contempt of God, of the Church and of her commandments. The evil appears in all conditions of life, also amongst the clergy there is much luxury, especially amongst the clergy of noble birth, who have no cure of souls and who try to equal the rich merchants in gormandizing. The least touched by the evils of the time are those peasants and artisans, who still follow the old simple customs, and those parishpriests in the towns or in the country, whose greatest care is the salvation of the souls of their parishioners — thanks be to God, the number of such priests is not small — als of those monasteries, which faithfully observe their rules and do not possess too much property. But the evil is worst, where there is too much commerce, where too much profit is easely made, where always fresh wants are invented and have to be satisfied. Such commerce is rather a doubtful blessing."

The extravagance in dress became so enormous, not only in the towns, but also amongst the peasantry, that in many places the magistrates thought it necessary, to make laws against it, lest the people should ruin themselves.([62])

([61]) A most interesting and minute description of the state of Nürnberg at the beginning of the 16th is given by Cochlaeus, ap. Otto 44 seqq.

([62]) The 4th chapt. of the Narrenschiff is very instructive on this point.

„It is hardly credible", says the author of „a Christian exhortation" (Eyn christlich ermanung) how foolish and changeable the fashions have become, and what precious clothing men and women put on their corruptible bodies." Janssen[63] calls our attention to the fact, that just in those parts of the country, where some time afterwards the revolt of the peasants began, in Franconia, Bavaria, Alsace etc. the peasants had been richest and had been led to ruinous extravagances through their money. Sebastian Brant complains[64] that „nowadays a peasant is no longer satisfied with ticking for his coat, but he must have fine cloth from Leyden or Malines, and it must be slashed, and puffed up with other colours, and adorned with fur; the peasants have too much money, they wear goldchains and silks; the wife of a townsman stalks about more proudly, than a countess would do". The board of the German peasantry in our days is very simple indeed, the average English workman would probably turn up his nose at it, but it was quite different in the 15th century. A writer of the beginning of the following century says, that during his father's time every peasant had plenty of meat every day, that on feastdays the tables bent under the load of dishes and everybody drank wine like water. That gluttony was a fruitful mother of other sins, especially of sins of impurity, is as much as may be expected. From the sermons of Geiler von Keisersberg and other preachers we see that such sins were not unfrequent, at least in the towns. We say „not unfrequent", for the corruption cannot have been anything like universal. In 1502 Wimpheling was able to say[65] that „Germany is distinguished „feminarum pudicitià — honesto vestium usu." He also adds: Sunt demum Germani sacrosanctae Christi religioni deditissimi et observantissimi."

The growing extravagance of the people was one of the causes, which made usury most flourishing. The

[63] I. 185.
[64] Narrenschiff, chapt. 82.

[65] Epit rer. Germ. Conclusio ap. Schardii tom I.

2*

money-changing business — a most important one in the
15th century through the incredible multiplicity of the
coinage in different cities and principalities — was almost
exclusively in the hands of the Jews, who, true to their
traditions, shunned manual labour as much as possible and
monopolized the moneymarket for a long time. That, as
a rule, they were guilty of the most heartless extortions,
cannot be denied; the bitter complaints of the most respectable contemporary writers are too frequent, and the
fact, that the Jews at times demanded and received interest at the rate of 32, 43, 52 and even $86^2/_3$ per cent.
shows, that the people, who fell into their hands, had
very little chance of ever regaining independence. The
popular indignation, fostered by the common belief, that
the Jews were also guilty of the most horrid blasphemies
and practices against Christian faith, burst out more than
once in cruel persecutions, and the Jewish usurers were
forcibly expelled from many towns and territories, from
Speyer, Mainz, Augsburg, Würzburg, Erfurt etc. The
much calumniated Popes, for instance Innocent IV and
Paul II, raised their voice against such acts, through which
the innocent and the guilty suffered alike. Trithemius (De
Judaeis) did his best, to make his infuriated countrymen
look at the matter in the proper light. Though he strongly
protests against aliens domineering over Germans, and
domineering not through honest exertions, but through
robbery, he also strongly protests against the most extravagant charges being believed without proper proofs and
against people taking the law into their own hands. Very
different from his is Luther's language, as we shall see
later on. With the expulsion of the Jews the evil was
not remedied, unfortunately many Christians followed in
their footsteps. The preachers and satirists of the time
dit not omit to expose the practices of such „Juden-Chri-
sten“ to public execration. ([66])

([66]) See Narrenschiff, chapt. 93.

What was the state of the ecclesiastics at that time? We have heard already that the clergy did not remain untouched by the corruption that set in.

Unfortunately the lives of a considerable number of priests and monks and Bishops were not in harmony with their calling. Various causes concurred, to produce this lamentable effect. Some of the lower clergy were so poor, that they had to recur to unworthy means to raise their incomes, others were far too rich and squandered their money in feasts and sports and worldly dress. ([67]) The worthy Bishop of Augsburg, Friedrich von Zollern, was made fun of at the diet of Nürnberg A. D. 1487, because he appeared in episcopal dress. ([68])

Another most deplorable abuse was this, that frequently the younger sons of noblemen were preferred to benefices, though they had neither vocation to the priesthood nor the knowledge necessary for the discharge of their sacred duties; sometimes even political motives decided an appointment. We know of one Archbishop that he was unable to read a latin letter, of another, that he never celebrated Mass. The nobility scandalously monopolized some of the Cathedralchapters and even Convents. The plurality of benefices was another source of evil, as it only fostered luxury and extravagance amongst those who had intruded into the sanctuary.

In many of the monasteries the rules were neglected and the spirit of the order was forgotten. Religious men, like Joannes Busch, who, full of zeal for the purity of the Church and full of holy indignation at the scandals they had to witness, tried to introduce a reform, found themselves in more than one case baffled by the obstinacy of unworthy monks.

([67]) Omnes (praelati) principum more equos canesque alunt et histrionesparasitosquenutriunt, neque sine magno comitatu esse volunt. Nec tu aliter quam in aulis regalibus apud praelatos convivia instrui videbis. Aen. Sylvius, ap. Schardii I. 466. However we shall see, that the „omnes" cannot be taken in a strict sense.

([68]) He wrote to Geiler: „Omnes archiepiscopi et episcopi incedunt, ut vix fistulatores et ipsi inter se discerni possint."

The best men of the age, Geiler von Keisersberg,
Trithemius, Wimpheling and others had the courage to
raise their voices against the existing abuses and fearlessly
demanded that the glory of God and the salvation of
souls should become again the object of ecclesiastical
administration, not selflove, nor the care to provide for
poor noblemen. Brant, too, bitterly complains, that
„many have the care of souls, to whom nobody would
entrust the care of cattle, who know as much about the
administration of the Church, as a donkey knows about
music.“ ([69])

But whilst the accusers of the Catholic Church and
admirers of Luther dwell with a certain predilection on
this sad picture, they ought not to forget that a sweeping
condemnation of the whole Clergy of the time, low and
high, secular and regular, would not only be a great mistake, but also an enormous injustice. Let us hear once
more the opinion of Wimpheling, who cannot be accused
of partiality, who points out evils, wherever he finds them.
„God knows“, he says, that I am acquainted in the six
rhenish dioceses with many, nay with numberless parishpriests amongst the secular clergy, who possess great
knowledge for their duties and live pure lives. At Cath-
edrals and Collegiate Churches I know distinguished
prelates, canons and vicars, not a few only, but many,
who are men of unblemished character, full of piety, liber-
ality and humility.“ „Every day we see a greater number of learned men, who enter upon the cure of souls.“
Nor must is be forgotten, that thousands of monks and
nuns withstood all the temptations, which the „Reformation“
threw in their way and proved faithful to their vows and
rules at a time, when apostasy would no longer have called down execration upon them, but would have secured

([69]) „Seelsorg sieht man trei-
ben die,
Denen man vertraute kaum
ein Vieh:
Sie wissen so viel vom
Kirchenregieren.
Als des Müller's Esel kann
quintiren.“
Narrenschiff. chapt. 73.

to them the applause of the majority, that thousands preferred to be driven from their quiet homes and to face
bitter want and persecution, that many even gladly preferred death to apostasy.

If a number of prelates disgraced their high pastoral
office by their ignorance or worldliness or vices, others
adorned their sees with their piety and learning and wisdom, the names of many of them are still gratefully remembered by every friend of true ecclesiastical Reform.([70])

We beg to be allowed to make here a general remark
about the abuses in the Church, on which the friends of
Luther's „Reformation" so frequently insist. No Catholic
can or will deny the existence of great and scandalous
abuses at the end of the 15th and the beginning of the
16th century. Catholic historians point them out as sharply
as Protestants do, and all Catholics deplore them even
more sincerely than Protestants *can* do. But how their
existence can be appealed to, to justify the apostasy of
Luther, we fail to see. There has never been a time,
when the Church has been entirely free from scandals.
The human element in the Church makes this impossible.
Though a Divine institution, the Church is not composed
of Angels, but of men living in the flesh; though offering
to all the means of sanctification, she cannot force anyone to be holy. Until the last day she will have to
struggle with the evil, which is to be found in the individual souls, nor can she expect to be victorious in the
case of every individual.([71]) But if „it is necessary, that
scandals should come", we cannot be astonished, that under the influence of a thousand circumstances sin and
scandal should be more flourishing at one time, than at

([70]) A list of more than thirty
most worthy German Bishops and
Archbishops of the period we are
speaking of, with short biographi-
cal sketches, will be found in
„Kirche oder Protestantismus?"
Mainz 1883. p. 139 seqq.

([71]) A. D. 1538 *Luther* said:
„Valeant illi, qui Ecclesiam plane
puram et purificatam habere volunt. Hoc est plane nullam velle
Ecclesiam." Lauterb. 192.

another. It is just at those times, that the divine vitality
of the Church appears all the more strikingly. Whenever
the members of the Church have been in special want of
a Reform, God has raised up Reformers, not such, as
have thought it their first duty to put up an Altar against
the Altar, but who have worked *in* the Church and *with*
the Church. Of such Reformers, of men like S. Charles
Borromeo, S. Vincent of Paul, S. Philip Neri, S. Francis
of Sales and others the Church may justly be proud.
Their principle was the same, which Egidius of Viterbo
proclaimed at the opening of the 5th Lateran Council:
„*Homines per sacra immutari fas est, non sacra per homines!*“ ([72])

But Rome itself? But the Popes? In the minds of
some people the whole seems to turn on this question.
An Anglican Prelate wrote to the author: „I fear you
have undertaken a heavy task, against all historians, in
undertaking to defend the condition of Rome.“ These
pages will show whether we mean to defend more than
can be defended without prejudice to historical truth.

We do not deny that unworthy Popes have disgraced
the venerable see of S. Peter. But in the name of logic and
of common sense, we protest against the inferences drawn
from that fact. Sixtus IV, Innocent VIII, Alexander VI
were not men, „whose memory is in blessing“. Luxury,
or sin, or worldliness, or political intrigues or nepotism
have cast a slur on their names for ever. Therefore —?
Does it follow that Luther was right in revolting against
the Pope? Has no unworthy king ever disgraced the
throne of England? Did the facts, that Charles II. kept
a number of mistresses, and excelled most of his contemporaries in licentiousness, and shed the blood of those,
whom he knew to be innocent, on the scaffolds, did these
facts give to his subjects the right to refuse allegiance?
No student of English history will deny, we think, that

([72]) Hard. Conc. IX. 1576.

more than once this country, like all others, has been disgraced by the most shameful administrative abuses. Would therefore any demagogue have the right, to unfurl the standard of revolt, and to take the law into his own hands? An old established authority, which for its claims does not depend on the personal character of its representatives, cannot submit to have its legitimacy tested by that character.

Paint the Popes as black as you like, make every one of them ten times worse than the worst of them has been — it must be a grand institution, which under such heads has yet weathered the storms of nineteen centuries, whilst every other power of the world has gone to pieces.

But if we refuse to have the Papal power judged by the personal character of some Popes, is it not unjust on the part of Catholics to urge Luther's personal character against *his* claim?

We beg our readers to bear in mind, that whenever a man comes forward who claims for himself an extraordinary mission, we expect him to be able to produce his credentials. Luther claims to be God's special messenger *to reform the Church of God,* which as he says, had fallen into an abyss of error and corruption. Where are his credentials? Does he first reform himself? His most devoted admirers will not consider him to be a pattern of virtue. If S. Peter or S. Paul or any other of the Apostles had come forward, to convert a pagan world to a religion, whose very essence is humility, purity 'and charity, and if they had been as little reformed themselves as Luther was, we think the heathen would have justly answered: „Medice, cura teipsum" and the world would still be pagan. Let not the reader think, that we are making unfounded charges, we shall have a portrait of Luther drawn by himself. The worst of the Popes has never ¡abused his authority *to teach sin and to advise it.* We shall *prove* that Luther has done so.

Moreover we would beg of those, whose knowledge of
the Catholic Church seems to consist only in the knowledge
of the unworthiness of some Popes, to make themselves
acquainted with the virtues and merits of the infinitely
greater number of worthy successors of S. Peter. We need
not go back to very remote times, we need not show how
much men like S. Leo the Great and S. Gregory the Great
have done for the benefit of the whole world and for the
advancement of Christianity and Christian civilisation. Must
the faults of Sixtus IV and Alexander VI make us forget
the virtues and zeal and labours of Martin V, of Eugen IV,
of Nicolaus V, of Pius III?

Let us return to the state of Germany. There still
remain a few circumstances to be explained, which helped
to prepare the coming religious and social revolution; for
the two are most intimately connected. For some considerable time the influence and power of the Emperors,
who, according to the original idea of the Empire, were
to represent the highest secular power on earth, had been
on the wane; the smaller princes, formerly mere vassals,
steadily rose in power and were at last almost independent.
The weak policy of Frederick III more and more confirmed
the powerful houses of Saxony, Hessen, Würtemberg etc.
Often enough ¡it happened, that where the Emperor had
a right to command, he was obliged to beg and depended
more or less on the whims or interest of his vassals. In
some cases the financial embarassments of the Emperor
could only be relieved at the cost of his power. It is
well known, that Friedrich von Zollern, the Burggraf of
Nürnberg, became Markgraf of Brandenburg in return
for the money he had advanced to Sigismund, who was
unable to repay it. It was the policy of the petty princes,

to have Emperors, of whose power and resources they
had no reason to be afraid. ([73])

The free cities, such as Cologne, Strassburg, Speyer,
Nürnberg, Aix-la-Chapelle etc., though frequently at logger-
heads with the Emperors, when their privileges were in the
least threatened, proved, as Macchiavelli says, „the nerve
of Germany." True, they were jealous of the growing
power of the princes and found it to be their own interest,
to check this evil as much as possible, but by so doing
they upheld the old principle on which the organization of
Germany was built up, viz. selfgovernment. Their citizens
were far from being mere shopkeepers and artisans; every
citizen was proud of his right to carry arms and knew
well enough how to handle them. ([74])

The power of the smaller noblemen was greatly broken
through the revolution, which the invention of firearms
had produced in the art of war. Personal valour ruled
no longer the destinies of battle, as it formerly had done.
With their influence the nobility also lost in great part
the sense of honour, which had formerly distinguished
the knighthood. The same men, who were bound by the
rules of knighthood to protect the oppressed, frequently
became oppressors and robbers. One of the worst of
these ruffians was Götz von Berlichingen, quite a different
man from what Göthe has made of him in his drama.
Frederick, Markgraf of Brandenburg told his noblemen,

([73]) Est et alia major ratio, quae
vestrum imperium comminuit et
ad nihilum rediget, nisi occurre-
tis. Pluralitatem principum philo-
sophi abhorrent, vos ea gaudetis.
Nam quamvis Imperatorem et regem et dominum vestrum esse
fateamini, precario tamen ille im-
perare videtur: nulla eius potentia
est: tantum ei paretis, quantum
vultis: vultis autem minimum.

Aeneas Sylv. ap. Schardii
tom I. 465.

Era desiderio inveterato in tutta
Germania, che la grandezza degli
imperatori non fusse tale, che gl'
altri fussero costretti ad obedirlo.
Guicciardini, Istoria d'Italia 7.

([74]) Aeneas Sylvius (l. c. p. 461)
speaks very highly of the military
accomplishments of the German
citizens and of the extraordinary
riches of their military stores. Vettori, in the relation of his travels
in Germany, says that everywhere
the practice at the target, with
crossbow or rifle (chi colla balestra,
chi collo schioppetto) was a favourite occupation.

that as long as they spared the merchants' lives, he would not object to their putting their hands into the pockets of the same. ([74a])

Unfortunately the laws of the Empire allowed feuds. There were, it is true, certain restrictions; for instance, that no feud should be lawful, except, if the challenger had tried in vain to obtain justice before the proper tribunals, nor without sending an open challenge before beginning hostilities, that on certain days of the week all hostilities should be abandoned, that certain persons and properties should never suffer by them etc. But these restrictions were far from being sufficient barriers to quarrelsome and revengeful spirits. ([75]) We can understand better why so many feuds broke out, which sometimes were carried out in a most barbarous way, when we add that it was often difficult to obtain justice. The Emperor was the highest representative of the law and he was expected, personally to deliver sentence in the cases which were taken before his court. But the Emperor had no fixed residence, he moved about from town to town, from province to province; who could have followed him everywhere? Besides, some writers of the 15th century bitterly complain that at the courts of Sigismund and Frederick III justice had become venal. ([76])

Amongst the bulk of the population the administration of the ordinary civil and criminal cases was fortunately in a far better state and, as a rule, very expeditious. How very expeditious at times, appears from a fact mentioned in Müller's Annales Saxonum, ad annum 1470. A man, who had stabbed another man to death, was arrested, tried, condemned and beheaded on the day of the murder. The administration of justice was practically in the hands of the people, who, though not trained lawyers, knew

---

([74a]) Janssen II. 230.

([75]) Discordiae inter vos crebrae, et assidua bella grassantur, ex quibus rapinae, incendia, caedes et mille malorum emergunt genera. Aen. Sylv. l. c. p. 465.

([76]) Cfr. Janssen I. 453.

the simple laws and customs which had to guide them in
their decisions, and who, as contemporary writers affirm,
were well aware of the dignity of the law, and of the
sacred character of their duties. Every blameless man
was eligible as juryman (Schöffe) and was allowed to act
as advocate. All proceedings were public.

No greater blow has ever been inflicted on the Germans
as a nation than the abolition of this palladium of liberty.
We come to one of the principal causes of the terrible
revolt of the peasants in mentioning the forcible introduction into Germany of the Roman Law. A greater
opposition can hardly be imagined, than that which exists
between the old Germanic law and the Codex of Justinianus. The spirit of the former may be summed up in
these words. God alone is the fountain of right, therefore the law has to be an expression and application of
God's will; the powers that be, are not supreme, but
have to conform to a superior law. On the other hand
it is the distinctive character of the Codex of Justinianus,
that the ruler is the fountain of right — quod principi
placuit, legis habet vigorem. In the former the law follows
the right, in the latter the right follows the law. The
Roman law was in favour of absolutism. Already Frederick Barbarossa, influenced and aided by his crafty
Chancellor Reinald von Dassel, had claimed to be the
successor of the Roman Emperors and therefore, like
them, he had claimed that supreme authority, from which
all rights emanate. But it was only at the end of the
15th century, that such ideas began to prevail. As the
younger humanists had no taste for the rich national literature, but were only in raptures about the beauties of the
old classical writers, so the German students, who had
heard lectures on the Roman Law at the famous University of Bologna, came back to their own country with
an utter contempt for the national institutions. Only too
easily did they find in the princes eager listeners to the
doctrines of absolutism they expounded. „Quod principi

placuit, legis habet vigorem." This was „good tidings"
for those, who had the power in their hands. Doctors of
Imperial Roman Law soon occupied a conspicuous place
in the courts. The smaller princes were not slow in
perceiving that, what might be advantageous to the Emper-
or, was just as advantageous to themselves, or even more
so, and did their best to outrun him in the race. It is
an honour to Germany, that its people deeply resented
the importation of that foreign plant, which was so little
suited to their soil and that with all their power they resisted its introduction. But their efforts were fruitless;
A. D. 1500 the Codex of Justinian was introduced. ([77])
The ideas and regulations of the Roman law, which knew
nothing of free peasants, nor of the relations existing between a German landlord and his tenants were forcibly
applied to a state of things utterly different from that,
for which they had been originally intended. The peasantry
found themselves deprived of rights, which they and their
forefathers had enjoyed without contradiction from time
immemorial. The rights of shooting, of common, of wood,
of streams, of pastures, everything was usurped by the
dukes and barons and counts, by all who claimed some
petty sovereignty. Another and perhaps worse effect was
this, that the administration of justice was taken from
the people and was transferred to the hands of a new
caste, of the lawyers. The people, used to simple and
patriarchal ways, did not understand, nor could they be
expected to understand, the finesses of the Code of Justinian, which, complicated in itself, became more hopelessly
complicated through the sophistical and hairsplitting explanations of the Glossatores. The nation found itself
suddenly under the necessity of supporting a new and

([77]) The much calumniated
Popes proved also in this particular
point the true friends of the people.
They perceived, that though some
parts of the Roman Law might be
a benefit to any nation, nevertheless, as a whole, it was not in harmony with true Christian civilization. Hence Alexander III. forbade
the study o fit to the monks, and
Honorius III. extended the prohibition to all priests.

large class of people, who only too frequently made it their business to feed on the marrow of the country and to protract a lawsuit as far as possible. All over the country there was an outcry against the innovation and especially against its hateful representatives, the lawyers. [78] This outcry is echoed in the writings of the best patriots of the period. [79] The common people however frequently wreaked their vengeance in a more practicel way.

Though the study of science, favoured by the facilities which the art of printing offered, made such enormous progress and benefited so many classes of the people, the period we are speaking of, offers a sad spectacle in the aspirations and endeavours of the younger school of humanists. They were, not only conspicuous by a foolish contempt for the language and literature of their own native country [80] and an extravagant worship of the ancient classics, but they did their best to undermine the faith of the nation. Most conspicuous among them are two men, to whom we must devote a few words, Erasmus of Rotterdam and Ulrich von Hutten.

The early years of Erasmus resemble in many details those of Luther. Brought up under many hardships, he became an Augustinian monk, but soon left the monastery, which he had entered without vocation. A deep hatred against monasticism characterized him all through life, as is the case with many apostates, who throw all the blame on institutions, of which they had never been fit to be members. A brilliant genius, a great wit, an indefatigable reader, a perfect master of the most perfect latin diction, Erasmus directed all his accomplishments towards what he called a Reform of Theology; in reality it was nothing but the introduction of rationalism into Religion. Though

---

[78] A. D. 1497, The knights of Bavaria complained: Illi juris professores nostrum morem ignorant, nec etiam si sciant, illis nostris consuetudinibus quicquam tribuere volunt. Ap. Janssen I. 484.

[79] See Brant's Narrenschiff, chapt. 71.

[80] Erasmus proudly said, that he knew no modern language, his own native tongue not excepted!

in later years an opponent of Luther, in the controversy about the freedom of the human will, Erasmus has perhaps done more than any other man, to prepare Luther's way. Whilst declaring that he would never separate himself from the Catholic Church, he not only attacked the authority of the successors of S. Peter, but also the Mystery of the Blessed Trinity and other fundamental truths. His treatment of Holy Scripture is at times shameful;([81]) the supernatural character of its books is almost entirely set aside. What Erasmus did in his „Encomium Moriae" for the world at large, that he unfortunately repeated for the youth in particular in his „Colloquia familiaria". Everything connected with the Church becomes in them the object of cynical mockery; that especially monasticism is not spared, we may expect from an unfrocked monk. This book was scattered in thousands of copies; in the preface to the second edition Erasmus says: Rapitur et teritur manibus studiosae juventutis. We can therefore easily imagine that his remarks about pilgrimages, his advice to the „virgo μισογαμος" who wishes to become a nun, his absurd description of what is going on in monasteries,([82]) and similar things did a great deal, to lower religious orders and religion in general in the estimation of the rising generation. It was not only his classical style, which caused Erasmus to be so generally admired, but his very tendency found a ready response in the hearts of those, who saw in the existence and power of Christianity the greatest obstacle against the reestablishment of pagan licentiousness. Erasmus was almost adored.([83]) His disciples made it their special study, to carry out his principles, perhaps much farther, than he ever intended. The writings of Eobanus Hessus, Mutianus, Crotus Rubianus and others abound with the most horrid blasphemies and

---

([81]) See Drummond I. 200.

([82]) In the „Exequiae Seraphicae" he describes how refractory monks were buried alive. Cfr. Maria Monk!

([83]) Mutianus said of him: Erasmus surgit super hominis vires. Divinus est. et venerandus religiose, pie, tamquam Numen!

obscenities. But one of this new pagan school was yet
to exercise a more direct fatal influence on the destinies
of Germany, Ulrich von Hutten. Though now and then
he did something to save appearances and played himself
out as a friend of the „Evangelium“ or of „Reformed
Theology“, he had completely thrown religion overboard,
and the brilliant gifts, which nature had bestowed upon
him, became only weapons to attack Christianity.

The Archbishop of Mainz, Albrecht von Brandenburg,
a prelate, who unfortunately had been raised to the see of
S. Willegis for no other merit but his noble birth and who,
at least in his younger years, cared for little besides music
and worldly pomp, was proud to become the Maecenas
of literary men like Hutten and eagerly fed on the vile
flattery, with which they abundantly supplied him. The
archiepiscopal court of Mainz became the rendezvous of
all, who conspired to the ruin of the Church. The infamous „Epistolae obscurorum virorum“ show best, what
sort of man Hutten was.[84] We shall meet him again in
connexion with Sickingen and Luther.

We must not conclude this short historical sketch
without a word about Maximilian, who since A. D. 1493
occupied the royal throne. He was far different from
his indolent father Frederick III.[85] At a period, when by
the changed aspect of the world the old knighthood was
doomed to extinction, it seems as if in Maximilian all virtues and perfections, that ever distinguished a knight, had
been united for a last effort. In person the type of manly
beauty and valour, intrepid and untired in the dangers and
exertions of the chase and the battlefield, ever jealous of

---

[84] Hutten died of a shameful
disease, of which he left a description in classical Latin. Münch, the
editor of his works, says: (III. 231.)
That this is a tribute which great
men like Hutten have to pay to
inferior nature, to as to be reminded of the fact, that they are tied
to the dust!

[85] Wimpheling's estimate of
Frederick's character is far too
mild. „Imperator pacificus, quietus, admirandae patientiae et man-
suetudinis.“ Schardii tom. I. 390.
We wish he had possessed a little
less of his wonderful »patientia et
mansuetudo.“

the honour of his country, openhearted, sincerely pious, condescending to the very poorest of his subjects, heartily entering into the merry sports of the people — as such „Kaiser Max" still lives in the memory of his nation, and there is at the present day no schoolchild in Germany, but will be able to speak of him and of his adventures. But his greatest admirers will not say that he was fit to cope with the enormous difficulties, which at that period beset the representative of the supreme power. Though full of the best intentions, he had not the necessary tenacity of purpose, to carry them out in all cases. Like many goodnatured men, he was only too apt, to judge others from himself, he trusted too easily to the promises of the princes, who on more than one occasion shamefully deserted him and, in the most unpatriotic way, preferred their own selfish ends to the welfare and honour of their whole nation.

Let us sum up the state of Germany at the end of the 15th and the beginning of the 16th century. The imperial power was weak, and the petty princes did their best, to weaken it still more. Part of the clergy, secular and regular, were unworthy of their calling and were therefore despised by the people. The study of science had made immense progress, but the endeavours of the younger humanists were directly opposed to faith. Luxury with its accompanying vices had corrupted a part of the nation, the introduction of a foreign code of laws had ruined and embittered another. Though, as Macchiavelli tells us „there was still much honesty and religion in Germany", there was all the material for a great conflagration. It only wanted a man, to throw the firebrand into it, and that man appeared in the person of Martin Luther.

Chapter II

Luther before his apostasy.

Terrore et agone mortis subitae circumval-
latus vovi coactum et necessarium votum.
Luther. Wittenb. II. 484ᴿ.

Martin Luther (or as he first spelled his name, Luder)
was born Nov. 10th 1483 of rather poor parents [1] in the
little town of Eisleben, in the present Prussian Province
of Saxony, a few miles West of Halle. The character of
the future „Reformer“ finds to a certain extent its explanation in the far too strict treatment dealt out to him in
his own home as well as at school. Though he seems to
have been very fond of his parents in afterlife, it appears
from his own relation that they were extremely severe
and punished him cruelly even for trifling offences; so
much so, that on one occasion he ran away from home. [3]
The schoolmaster too seems to have used the rod with
anything but discretion; at least Luther says, that, when
a boy, he was flogged fifteen times in the course of one
morning. [4] In a fiery character such treatment could
only lay the foundation to that stubbornness which after-

[1] For particulars about Luther's family see Jürgens I. 13 seqq.
Köstlin I. 21 seqq. About his father Seckendorf (I. 18) says: Pater
operarius erat metallicus, qui in fo-
dinis Mansfeldensibus tunc celeber-
rimis victum commodius quam domi
invenit, ita ut ... fodinas ipse ac-
quisiverit et magistratus ibi gesse-
rit, vitae integritate omnibus carus.

[2] Without any comment of our
own we will only notice Carlyle's
words about Luther's birth: „It
leads us back to another birth-
hour, in a still meaner environ-
ment, eighteen hundred years ago.“
(On heroes and heroworship.)

[3] Tischr. II. c. 20. § 69. Cfr.
Jürgens I. 151.

[4] Tischr. l. c. §. 155.

wards became one of the leading features of the man; naturally enough it did not increase the eagerness for study, in fact Luther says that at that time he learnt nothing at all.

At the age of 14 he was sent to the school of the Franciscan Friars at Magdeburg, soon after to the Grammarschool at Eisenach. Though not of absolutely poor parents he, like many other students of the same time, had to get the means of subsistence by singing in the streets.(⁵) He was freed from such cares, when Frau Cotta, a wealthy young lady, had pity on him and took him into her house. Luther never forgot her generosity; 40 years afterwards he took care of her son, then a student at Wittenberg.(⁶) In Frau Cotta's house he began for the first time to enjoy life; with great ardour he practised music. There also it was that he became first acquainted with the saying, which had so great an influence on him in later years, that there is no dearer thing on earth, than the love of a woman.

„Es gibt kein lieber Ding auf Erden,
Denn Frauenliebe, wem sie kann zu Theil werden."(⁷)

At the age of 18, according to the wish of his father, he began to study jurisprudence at the University of Erfurt, but philosophy had greater charms for him and in this branch of science he took his degrees in 1503 and 1505. As Baccalaureus he was the 30th amongst 57 candidates, as Magister the 2nd amongst 17. The study of the latin Classics was another favourite occupation. His Virgil and Plautus were the only books he took with him to the monastery. Luther was on his way to become an excellent Professor, when unfortunately he resolved to become a monk. We say *unfortunately*, and for a very good reason. To religious life we may justly apply the

(⁵) „Ich bin auch ein solcher Partekenhengst gewest und habe das Brod vor den Häusern genommen, sonderlich in Eisenach." Erl. 17, 414. Cfr. Jürgens I. 276.

(⁶) Jürgens I. 276.
(⁷) He wrote this verse on the margin of his Bible to the text Prov. 31. 10. („Who shall find a valiant woman?")

words of S. Paul about the priesthood, that „no man takes the honour to himself, but he that is called by God. (Hebr. IV. 4.) That Martin Luther was not called by God to this state is evident enough from the circumstances. The sudden death of a friend who was killed in a fray([8]) made an awful impression upon him; a tremendous thunderstorm, in which he found himself one day outside Erfurt filled him with fear and terror. It was there and then, that he made „a forced vow" in honour of St. Anne, to become a monk. ([9]) In vain did his friends who were sorry to lose a merry companion beg of him to give up his hasty resolution; at a supper party to which he had invited them, he took leave of them. With tears in their eyes they accompanied him to the door of the Augustinian monastery.

Why did not Luther explain to his Superiors that his was only „a forced vow"? Being such, it was certainly not binding, nor would the Augustinians have admitted him, if they had known it to be a forced vow. If Pitt in his „Life of Luther" ([10]) says that, though forced, a vow would be considered by the Church as binding, he only reveals his ignorance of the Church's doctrine on this point. Every manual of Catholic Theology would have shown to him, that a calm deliberation is absolutely required for the validity of a vow. During the year of the Novitiate Luther had time not only to reflect on the duties which at the profession he would have to take upon himself, — duties which were carefully explained to him by his superiors — but also on the obligation he thought himself to be under, of becoming a monk. The door of the monastery was open to him at any moment, to return into the world. The forms observed at the profession of

---

([8]) Mathesius says: „Da ihm sein gut Gesell erstochen."

([9]) Neque enim libens et cupiens fiebam monachus, multo minus vero ventris gratia, sed terrore et agone mortis subitae circumval-latus *voti coactum et necessarium votum*. Wittenb. II. 484n. („Ein gezwungen und gedrungen Gelübde." Walch XIX. 1809.

([10]) Leipzig 1883.

the Augustinian monks show clearly, how carefully the
Superiors, the novicemaster and the Prior, had to ascer-
tain the purity of motives in the postulant „for the Lord
forbids that a blind being should be offered up to him"
(with allusion to Levit. XXII. 22). After the repeated official enquiries about his motives: „Utrum vi vel metu
faciat professionem" Luther solemnly declared that he
would take the vows as an Augustinian monk „at his own
desire, freely, not influenced by force or fear" (sponte,
libere, non vi, non metu.)(¹¹) It was only after this declaration that he was admitted to the profession. If all
the while he was under the impression that his vow to
become a monk was only a „forced" one, did he act honestly in making the above declaration?

It does not say much for the prudence of his Superiors, that he was ordained priest in a very short time
(April 1507), soon after the year of his novitiate was over.
On the occasion of his first Mass his father who had been
exceedingly angry with him on account of his entrance
into religious life, was prevailed upon to assist and was
seemingly reconciled to his son. But even on that day
he said at the dinnertable, when the young monk tried to
pacify him: „Hast thou never heard that obedience is due
to parents? You, learned masters, have you not read in
the Scripture that father and mother have to be honoured?" (¹²) A letter written by Luther to invite a priest of
Eisenach to his first Mass is the earliest document we
have of him; it shows how high an opinion he had of the
sacerdotal office and dignity. (¹³) But whilst celebrating
his first Mass he was tormented by the idea of his unworthiness and was on the point of leaving the altar. (¹⁴)

(¹¹) The whole formula of the profession ap. Germanus 58.

(¹²) Jürgens I. 696.

(¹³) Cum itaque gloriosus Deus et sanctus in omnibus operibus suis infelicem me, quin et omnibus modis indignum peccatorem, tam magnifice exaltare, inque sublime suum ministerium sola et liberalissima sua misericordia vocare dignatus sit, ut tantae divinae bonitatis magnificentiae (vel quantulumcunque poterit pulvis) gratus sim, creditum mihi officium implere omnino debeo.
De Wette I. 3.

(¹⁴) Jürgens I. 694.

The terrifying idea he had of God spoilt even the happiness of that day. According to his own words he used to say Mass with terror (Entsetzen). This will account in great part for his fearful hatred of the Mass in later years.

The cowl does not make the monk. The truth of the old proverb appeared again in Luther's case. Though he says of himself: „I was a serious monk and led a modest and pure life" ([15]), he did not possess that humility, obedience and docility, through which alone a religious, who by his vow has given himself into the hands of his Superiors as God's representatives, can expect to find peace of heart. The state of his mind whilst a member of the Augustinian monastery at Erfurt not only throws a light on many events of the following years, but accounts even for many of his peculiar doctrines. From one extreme it is easy to fall into the other.

Even during the merry days of his University life melancholy and sadness had at times befallen him, ([16]) now it returned with greater force. Was it the fault of the state of life which he had chosen? Perhaps inasmuch as he had chosen it without due deliberation. But if he had been humble enough to follow the admonitions of his superiors, his troubles would have disappeared. Luther wanted to have his own way. With all the energy that his impetuous character was capable of ([16a]) he made up his mind to be a good monk, nay, a great Saint. But the way he chose was utterly wrong; he wished to arrive at perfection through his own exertions, through

---

([15]) Erl. 48. 306.

([16]) Köstlin. I. 59. This author tries to explain that sadness by the idea, which through the religious instruction he had received in his earliest years, Luther had formed of God, as merely a „formidable judge". „Noone taught him the *love* of God." As this seems to be an insinuation against Catholic doctrine, we are bound to protest against it. In Catholic families the children are taught to *love* God as well as to *fear* him. The documents collected by Hasak show that also in the „dark" ages the *love* of God was not forgotten.

([16a]) „When first I became a monk, I would have stormed heaven." Jürgens I 576.

his own works; he forgot the words of Christ: Without
me you can do nothing. When Köstlin says([17]) that the
Catholic teaching drove Luther to such extravagances, he
probably has of that teaching the same wrong idea that
Luther had([18]). Protestants are frequently under the impression that Catholics trust too much, if not entirely, in
their own good works. Some of them will be incredulous,
if we describe Luther's state of mind at that time as
thoroughly uncatholic. Yet, such it was. Speaking of
that period, he called himself a „praesumptuosissimus justitiarius," he said that he trusted not in God's, but in his
own justice. Here was Luther's great mistake; but it
would be an equally great mistake to suppose that the
Catholic Church taught him anything of the kind. If
the reader will look once more at the quotations we
have given in the preceding chapter from popular books,
he will see that a Catholic was not expected to become
a praesumptuossimus justitiarius. „Many times have I
made myself ill and have almost killed myself with fasting.
I faithfully observed the rules. (This was *not* always
the case, as will appear from his neglecting the Divine Office) I put before myself particular tasks, I had
my own particular ways. The Seniors in my rule objected to singularity and they did well. Most abominably I persecuted and murdered my own life by fasting
praying and watching and exhausted myself beyond my
power".([19]) The task of becoming a saint merely in that
way was impossible, nay absurd. But when this truth began

([17]) I. 69.

([18]) Köstlin would do well to
inform himself a little better about
a few more points concerning Catholic dogma and practice. He gives
(I. 73) as „a form of absolution"
a translation of the prayer said by
the priest *after* absolution has been
given, and from this prayer as representing the form of absolution
he argues against the Catholic doctrine about justification. This mistake of Köstlin is probably owing

to the fact that he has blindly believed his master, Dr. Luther, who
quotes the same prayer and argues
from it in the same way in his
Commentary in Galatas (Wittenb.
V. 314B.) But the „Reformer" had
no excuse whatever. He *did* know
that the form of absolution consists in the words »Ego te absolvo
etc.", words, in which merits on
the part of the penitent are not
mentioned at all.

([19]) Jürgens I. 577.

to dawn upon the young monk's mind, it only plunged him
into deeper sadness, and that God, who in his eyes was
a tyrant, whom even the greatest mortifications could not
propitiate, became an object of hatred to him. How deplorable his state of mind was, appears from his own
word: „I felt such enmity against Christ, that whenever
I saw his image, representing him on the cross, I cast
down my eyes and I had rather have seen the devil.“
Staupitz, his Superior, consoled him sometimes by calling
his attention to the infinite merits of Christ, but on the
other hand he must have done Luther a great deal of
harm by the repeated remarks, that, to judge from his
interior troubles, God had evidently chosen him for a
great work. Greater humility was not the effect.([20]) Even
after Staupitz had severed all connection with his former
pupil, Luther was grateful to him. As late as 1545
he said, that he ought to be „a damned, ungrateful, papistical ass, if he did not remember bis late master“.([21])
In his tabletalk he says that on one occasion his confessor
told him: You are foolish; God is not angry with you, but
you are angry with God.([22]) That confessor must have
been a shrewd man, who knew how to say a great deal
in a few words. Luther would have done well, to listen
to him. He said afterwards that it was „a dear, great
and glorious word, though it was uttered before the light
of the Evangelium came.“ Köstlin too seems anxious to
make of that confessor a sort of unconscious Protestant, he
calls him „a true Christian in a monk's cowl.“ ([23]) But
we beg to say that his excellent advice was thoroughly
Catholic.

Scrupulosity with its distinguishing feature, stubborn-

([20]) „Tum ille (Staupitius): Ne-
scis, Martine, quam tibi illa tenta-
tio sit utilis et necessaria; non
enim temere te sic exercet Deus,
videbis quod ad res magnas geren-
das te ministro utetur. Aeque ita
accidit. *Nam ego magnus (licet
enim hoc mihi de me jure praedi-*

care) factus sum doctor. De Wette
IV. 188.
([21]) Köstlin I. 81.
([22]) Gott ist nicht zornig auf
dich, sondern du bist auf ihn zornig. Tischr. II. c. 3. § 83.
([23]) I. 77.

ness and selfwill, and wild efforts to be perfect. alternating with despair brought Luther almost to the verge of madness. A regular observance of the rule became under the circumstances an impossibility; the recitation of the Divine Office, one of the principal safeguards of the life of a priest, was frequently omitted for weeks; and strange efforts to make up for the omission were resorted to; the state of the mind naturally produced restlessness and sleeplessness, and in return the state of the body had its effect on the mind. (24) Luther was unhappy not because he was a monk, but because, though being a monk exteriorly, he never entered into the spirit of his rule or of his Church. A reaction was inevitable, and his mind, not accustomed to selfcommand, went as far as possible to the other extreme. He who formerly had trusted too much in himself, perceiving the absurdity of such confidence, entirely despaired of it and threw himself too far upon God's mercy, so far in fact, as to renounce even the cooperation with God's grace and to expect salvation without any action on his own part. But a full explanation of this new „Evangelium" of Luther must be reserved for a separate chapter.

In 1508 Luther was called by Frederick of Saxony to the chair of philosophy at the newly founded University of Wittenberg. It was through Staupitz, on whose judgment the Elector greatly relied, that he received this appointment. He lectured on Aristotelic philosophy at the University as well as in the monastery, and at the same time he was obliged to begin his activity as preacher — not without much fear and anxiety.

After three years' work of this kind he had to make a

(24) A Bavaro refertur, Lutherum in monasterio tanta cum assiduitate legisse et scripsisse, ut aliquando multis diebus recitationem horarum caanonicarum, ad quam obligatus erat, omiserit; ut vero conscientiae satisfaceret ... cubiculo sese inclusisse, et quae per unam, duas imo tres quandoque septimanas prae studii assiduitate neglexerat, cibo et potu abstinentem recitasse, eumque in modum se macerasse, ut aliquando quinque septimanis somno caruerit et pene in mentis deliquium inciderit. Seckend. I. S. § 8.
Luther considered the Office as a „torture". Tischr. I. 479. 485.

journey to Rome on some business of his order. This event, it is commonly thought, greatly helped to develop his „reformatory ideas"· He is said to have been thunderstruck with the wickedness and impiety of Rome and of Italians in general. We have said above that not only in Rome but also in many other parts of Christendom there was at the beginning of the 16th century an extraordinary amount of sin and scandal, and that unfortunately the Clergy too were infected with it. The scandalous life of Alexander VI had naturally borne its fruit also amongst the Ecclesiastics of the lower ranks. However it was a good sign, that after his death, in 1503, the Cardinals, ashamed of him, did their best to secure to the Church the blessing of a better and worthier head; but Pius III, a man of great zeal and piety and a friend of a thorough Ecclesiastical Reform, died after a Pontificate of only one month. His successors, Julius II and Leo X, though far better men than Alexander VI, were unfortunately of too wordly a turn of mind and too much wrapped up in political affairs, to give due attention to the requirements of the Church. Whilst acknowledging the evil which existed, we beg to be allowed to doubt about its extent, and especially to have a doubt about the accuracy of the statements made by Luther at a time, when fury against Rome had taken the place of former respect. If nowadays a man, armed with his Bädeker or Murray which are brimful of information, „does" a country in a few weeks' time, we would hardly grant him the right to set up as a judge of that country and its inhabitants. Luther was in Rome not more than four weeks, a great part of this short time was taken up with his business and with sightseeing, ([25]) consequently there was very little time left for studying the character of the Romans; he did not know the language of the country.([26]) With priests and monks he may have conversed in latin, but he had not the means to become acquainted with the

---

([25]) Köstlin. I. 106.
([26]) This appears from the in-

accurate bits of Italian, wich are found here and there in his books.

people. Besides, if Luther had found such inexpressibly
horrid wickedness in Rome, how is it, that we hear nothing from him about it immediately after his return? Jürgens says: (27) he *may* have spoken of these things to his
friends. He *may*, yes, but did he?

In all the „Reformer's" works we have found only a
few things connected with Italy and Rome, for which in
later years he had a kind word. He greatly admired the
hospitals on account of their comfort, cleanliness and attention to the wants of the sick, (28) he praised the sobriety
of the people and acknowledged the promptness of the
proceedings of the Roman Rota. (29) But for the rest the
tales he tells about Rome and Italy, especially in the tabletalk, many years after he had been in Rome, are mostly
such, as to prove in him either an extraordinary credulity,
if he believed them himself, or an extraordinary want of
veracity. Of course we hear again from him the alleged
scandalous history of Lucrezia Borgia, (30) and the absurd
old fable about the female Pope Joanna, (31) though *not*
as a fable; we are expected to swallow the assertion that
a Council decreed, that no Cardinal was to keep *more*
than five concubines, (32) that from a pond near an old
Roman Convent 6000 children's skeletons were fished
up. (33) (Luther piously adds: „Such are the fruits of celibacy!") We are told about the brutish ignorance of the
Italian priesthood as manifested in answers like these:
How many Sacraments are there? *Three!* Which are
they? *The holy water brush, the thurible and the cross!* (34)

(27) II. 349.

(28) Optimi cibi et potus in
promptu, ministri diligentissimi,
medici doctissimi, lectus et vestes
mundissimi ... Huc concurrunt
honestissimae matronae, quae to-
tae sunt velatae; ad aliquot dies
serviunt pauperibus quasi ignotae
et dein iterum domum redeunt
... Haec ego vidi Florentiis.
Lauterb. 104.

(29) Nihil laudabat, nisi consistorium et curiam Romae. Ibid 9.

(30) See on this point Roscoe'
Life of Leo X.

(31) Tischr. II. c. 4. § 19. The
well known allegorical statue of a
female person is in his eyes a sufficient proof. See about this fable
Döllinger, Die Papstfabeln des
Mittelalters, München 1863.

(32) Tischr. II. c. 4. § 21.

(33) Ibid. c. 20. § 182.

(34) Lauterb. 193.

Let not the reader imagine that such things were told at Luther's table merely as bad jokes; they were meant seriously, as evidently appears from the pious conclusions, which the Prophet of Wittenberg drew from them, also when they were told by others. Here is a specimen. On 9. May 1538 Frederick Mecum speaks about superstition and tells the company, how a pious German pilgrim was persuaded by his confessor in Rome, to *buy* of him a most precious relic, viz. a leg of the ass, on which Our Lord rode into Jerusalem. Proud of his treasure, he returns home, but on his journey he meets four more Germans, who as it turns out, have also each of them bought as a relic a leg of the same animal, which therefore must have had five legs. Luther answers: This the Italians used to boast of, that they cheated the barbarous Germans. But by the grace of God Germany now feels and sees the malice. ([35]) Wherever Luther mentions the Italians, he has almost always something bad to say against them. They are ignorant and superstitious, ([36]) intriguers, ([37]) proud, ([38]) profane and disciples of Epicure, ([39]) immoral ([40]) etc. etc.

Let the reader judge for himself whether a man who is capable of telling or believing absurd stories like those we have mentioned, can be looked upon as an impartial witness, or whether the sweeping condemnation ([41]) which

---

([35]) Rt. Lutherus: Haec fuit gloriatio Italica, Germanos barbaros ita illudere. Sed dei gratia Germania sentit et videt malitiam. Lauterb. 77.

([36]) Italia est nihil aliud quam superstitio, qui sine verbo Dei et praedicatione tantum in superstitionibus vivunt *et ita neque resurrectionem carnis, neque vitam aeternam credunt.* Lauterb. 16. — Magna est Italorum caecitas et superstitio, qui plus timent S. Antonium et Sebastianum quam Christum, propter plagas. *Ideo* si quis vult locum aliquem servare, ne eo mingatur italico more, sicut canes, imaginem

S. Antonii ignea cuspide eo pingeret, quae imago omnes depelleret micturos. Ibid.

([37]) Lauterb. 13.

([38]) Ibid. 17.

([39]) Ibid. 48.

([40]) Ibid. 53. He calls their impurity „satanica"!

([41]) Rome, he says (Tischr. II. c. 54. § 1.) was at one time sanctified by the blood of the martyrs, but now „hat der Teufel seinen Dreck, den Papst, drauf —". It is almost amusing to see what things Luther is capable of believing about the Popes. Here is a specimen of it. In 1545 an anonym-

after many years he pronounces, can be considered reliable.

The same interior struggles which Luther had carried with him across the Alps, were still harassing him, when he reentered the Wittenberg monastery. His scrupulosity and the feeling of dissatisfaction arising from his false idea of sanctity, had not disappeared. But he resumed the study of Theology, took his degree as Doctor in 1512 and began to lecture on the Epistles of S. Paul and on the Psalms. Some years before the question of indulgences arose, his teaching had been an object of suspicion to careful observers. In a public disputation in 1516, of which at his own request he was appointed moderator or president, and under his auspices, the following thesis was defended: „Man sins when he does that which is in

---

ous writer (see Seckend. III. 32. § 128) published a pamphlet „on the fidelity of Popes" in which Hadrian IV and Alexander III were charged with horrid intrigues against Barbarossa. Luther wrote the preface (Walch XIX. 2445) in which he recommended the book, not without saying some elegant things about the Popes, „who from being most holy Fathers have become most hellish Fathers" (this is one of his favourite jeux de mots) „and in whatever part of hell they may be, they will want no furcloaks" Behold the wickedness of one of them! When Barbarossa was waging war against the Turks, Alexander III tried to get rid of him. „Therefore he sent out a painter, who was to paint the Emperor's portrait secretly, without his knowledge, and with colours, so that is should be a faithful likeness, from which everybody might know him. And the painter did so with all care. This same portrait of the poor betrayed Emperor the Pope did send to the Sultan and exhorted him in a letter, to see how he might by

craft and treachery get hold of the Emperor and execute him, otherwise there would be no peace from him. The Sultan was glad of this advice etc. etc." Barbarossa is really caught whilst bathing in a river in Armenia and is taken before the Sultan, who from the portrait sent by the Pope knows him at once, though Barbarossa declares he is only the Emperor's groom. „And the Sultan produced the portrait and the Pope's letter" etc. etc. etc. (l. c. 2476.) Such stuff Luther recommends as *history*, but everything is welcome to him for his purpose. We will also notice that in *one* column (2447) of Luther's introduction (and the columns in Walch's edition are small and the type is large) the Pope receives the following titles from „the dear man of God": Unflätiger Wanst (dirty paunch), fauler Bauch (lazy belly), garstiger Balg, schnöder Sack, lästerlicher Bube, Gottesverächter, grosser grober Esel, Tölpel, Knebel, Rülze, Filz, Range, Klotz, Ploch, unvernünftiger Narr, Teufelslarve, Putze, Bestie, Barbar.

his own power."(42) Another thesis denied the freedom
of the human will when destitute of grace.(43) In the
following year he proposed for another disputation the
thesis: „It is not true that the will of man can decide for
either side; the will of man is not free, but captive,(44)
and in his lenten sermons of the same year he warned
against „the vain talkers who have filled all Christendom
with their words and have from the pulpits seduced the
people with their teaching that one may have a good
will, a good intention and a good purpose."(45) Here we
have already some of Luther's peculiar dogmata. Whilst
he was exteriorly a member of the Catholic Church, his
teaching was already in direct opposition to hers. Martin
Pollich, the Rector of the University of Wittenberg is
said to have expressed his opinion of Luther in the words:
This friar has deep eyes and strange fancies (wundervolle
phantasias).(46) If he said so, the events justified his
words.

<hr />

(42) Homo quando facit quod in
se est, peccat, cum nec velle aut
cogitare ex se ipso possit. Wittenb.
I. 50n.
    (43) Voluntas hominis sine gra-
tia non est libera, sed servit, licet
non invita. Ibid.
    (44) Opp. lat. I. 315.
    (45) Erl. 21. 192.
    (46) Jürgens II. 261. Köstlin I.
98. — Seckendorf (I. 8. § 8.) quot-

es from the first sermon of Mathesius the following words attributed to Pollich: „Iste monachus
omnes doctores turbabit, novam
doctrinam proponet, totamque
Romanam reformabit Ecclesiam."
Probably Lord Beaconsfield was
not the first man in the world,
who thought that prophecying
after an event had taken place, is
a safe thing.

Chapter III.

Luther and Tetzel.

„As truly as Our Lord Christ has redeemed
me, I did not know what an indulgence was."
Luther. Walch XVII. 1704.

If what we have said in the preceding chapter
about Luther's theological or rather heretical views could
still leave any doubt about the real cause of his apostasy,
such a doubt would be finally dispersed by his own words
in a letter which he wrote to Tetzel, shortly before the
latter's death, and in which he distinctly said, that his
antagonist's activity as preacher of the Papal Indulgence
had nothing whatever to do with the religious revolution.
„The child has quite a different father." ([1]) Though it is
evident enough, that the controversy about indulgences
was to Luther the *occasion*, to give for the first time greater
publicity to the particular views, which he had formed,
and to transfer his revolutionary activity from the lecture-
hall to a wider sphere, it cannot be supposed that the
work of the Wittenberg „Reformer" took its rise from
the same question. Luther would have broken sooner or
later with the Church and would have dragged others
with him, if no Indulgence had been promulgated or if
Tetzel had never been born.

On the occasion of the Luther Centenary we have
heard again so much from Protestants about Indulgences

([1]) sondern hab das Kind viel einen andern Vater.
De Wette-Seidem. VI. 18.

and about Tetzel, or rather so much against both, that we are obliged to appeal to the good old principle: Audiatur et altera pars.

As it is not at all our intention, to write here a dogmatic treatise, we shall not enter into a theological discussion of the arguments, on which the Catholic doctrine on Indulgences is based. We are quite satisfied, if Protestants will be fairminded enough, to accept their notions on this point not from the representations, which, either through ignorance, or through malice, — we trust, through ignorance only — are given by the adversaries of the Church, but from the Church herself; if they will listen to the protest, which Catholics are bound to make against carricatures of their faith. In the folio-volumes of dogmatic writers and in the penny Catechism intended for the school-children, in the religious instructions of the 15th century and in the instructions given in our own days, there is the same invariable doctrine, without a vestige of all the nonsense, which ignorance or bigotry have tried to smuggle into our Creed. — „An Indulgence is a remission, granted by the Church, of the *temporal punishment*, which often remains due to sin, *after its guilt has been forgiven.*" That an Indulgence is the sale of the forgiveness of sins, (²) even of sins to be committed in the future, or that it can be gained without sincere repentance and without the firm purpose of amendment of life, these are fancies, in which the excited imagination of a No-Popery man

---

(²) Sometimes Protestants think, (for instance Hase, Handbuch der protest. Polemik p. 401) they can prove, that an indulgence is considered as equivalent to the *forgiveness of sins*, from the expression „remissio omnium peccatorum", which occurs in the Papal Bulls. We answer in the words of S. Augustine (contra duas epistolas Pelag. l. 3. c. 6. n. 16) „They ignore that already in Holy Scripture the word peccatum is used in different meanings". It will be only fair not to suppose another meaning in this word, than that, in which the Church declares she uses it when speaking of indulgences, viz. as equivalent to the punishment due for sin, in which sense it occurs II Macch. XII. 46. We refer the reader to Benedict XIV. De Synodo Dioeces. XIII. 18, Ferraris, Biblioth. s. v. „Indulgentia", Perrone, de Indulg. n. 37; II. v. d. Clana, Protest. Polemik. Freib. 1874. p. 66.

may revel, but Catholics protest against the supposition
that such is their Creed.

But is there not the fact, that people had to pay for
an Indulgence? There is the fact, that an alms for a
charitable purpose was one of the *conditions* required for
the gaining of an Indulgence. We are not trying to extenuate an objectionable practice, but we give its original
and only legitimate meaning, which has been distorted by
Non-Catholics, so as to make the practice appear objectionable. An Indulgence has never been sold; if the Church
were to consider it as a marketable good, she would be
guilty of Simony.

The infinite merits of Christ are the treasure, in which
the Church trusts for the forgiveness of sins and of the
punishment due for sin, but man has to do something on
his part too. He, who by his sins has dishonoured God, has,
as a sort of compensation, to do something special to
honour him. Even after the guilt of sin has been taken
away, man may still be liable to some temporal punishment.
This he may either entirely or partly avoid by additional
endeavours to do his best for God's honour; and he will
be all the more successful, if, in view of such honest endeavours, the Church benignantly opens to him the treasure of divine merits, which is entrusted to her keeping.
It seems superfluous to say, yet Luther's unfair attacks
on the Catholic doctrine about justification make it advisable to say, that the supernatural value of good works
is entirely based upon that intimate union, which exists
between Christ and the members of his mystical body.
„I am the vine, you are the branches."

We merely state these points of Catholic doctrine,
without entering into an explanation of the proofs.

Those works, which, in addition to true repentance
and to the firm purpose of amendment, the Church makes
a condition for gaining an Indulgence, whether they are
special prayers or mortifications, or alms, are always such,
as directly or indirectly tend to the glory of God. Con-

tributions towards the building of Churches, Convents and Hospitals were justly considered as good works, which, combined with the above mentioned essential conditions, the Church was able to reward with an Indulgence. The building of the very monastery, in which Luther resided at Wittenberg, and which afterwards became his own private property, had been begun in 1502 with the alms collected in that way. ([3])

When Frederick, surnamed the Wise, intended to build a bridge over the Elbe, at Torgau, but was unable to find the necessary means, he obtained from Innocent VIII an Indult, in virtue of which all, who contributed to the same object the twentieth part of a rhenish florin, were, for one lent, to be freed from certain laws of abstinence. ([4]) This was not really an Indulgence, it was merely the commutation of one good work into another, of abstinence into charity. It was considered as a work of charity, to facilitate the wayfarer's progress, and, under the circumstances, as a work even more advisable, than abstinence.

The objection, that through the demand of an alms as a condition for gaining an Indulgence, those that were not rich enough to give alms were unreasonably and unjustly excluded from a spiritual benefit, has nothing whatever to stand on. The principle was this: Let he, who can, give an alms: he who cannot, need not, but may do other good works which are in his power. This appears clearly from the official instruction, given by Archbishop Albrecht of Mainz and by Arcimboldi, the commissaries of Leo X's Indulgence, to the preachers they sent out. „They (the preachers) shall not dismiss anybody without participation of God's grace; for the mere building (of St. Peter's) is not of greater importance, than the salvation of the faithful. Those, who have no means, may substitute prayer and fasting in the place of alms; for the kingdom of heaven must be open to the poor as well as

to the rich." ([5]) The conscientiousness of this instruction
is also proved by the clause, that a wife, who has no
means of her own, and who meets with opposition from
her husband in the matter of almsgiving shall be allowed
to substitute special prayers. ([6]) True repentance, contrition of heart and a firm purpose of amendment appear as
absolutely necessary conditions in the instructions of both
the Archbishop of Mainz and of his subordinate Tetzel.
Luther said in afteryears, ([7]) that according to Tetzel, no
repentance was required, that man might gain an indulgence without any contrition. Kemnitz coolly repeated
this assertion. ([8]) The text of Tetzel's instruction shows
that it is a *calumny*.

We are accustomed to hear that the promulgation of
indulgences was caused by avarice, that it was a convenient way of getting at people's pockets. If this were
the case, it is more than probable, that Indulgences would
not be promulgated without a prospect of a pecuniary
advantage, — cessante causa, cessat effectus. Alms, given
by the faithful at their own discretion, frequently form
even nowadays a condition for the gaining of an Indulgence, but who will say, that in this way a priest finds
himself richer by the sum of one halfpenny? Yet every
priest will gladly welcome and gladly announce to his flock
the news, that the Vicar of Christ has opened the treasury of the Church.

That now and then the promulgation of an Indulgence
was made use of by unprincipled Ecclesiastics for their
own selfish ends, we do not deny. Hieronymus Emser,
who is certainly no friend of the Lutheran Reformation,
complains, that some of the preachers look more to the
money, than to confession and repentance. ([9]) The letter

([5]) Ibid. 194.

([6]) Ibid. 195.

([7]) Tischr. II. c. 4. § 85. Er
(Tetzel) schrieb, dass der Ablass
nütze wäre, wenngleich ein Mensch
nicht Busse thäte, ohne alle Reu
und Leid.

([8]) Exam. Conc. Trid. IV. q. 144.

([9]) Wider das unchristenliche
Buch Luther's an den tewtschen
Adel.

of Albrecht of Mainz d. d. 13. Dec. 1517, in which he exhorts Tetzel, to see that for the future (hinfürder) his subordinates shall be in all things „honest, modest and acting in the spirit of their office" ([10]), naturally makes us suppose that at least some of them had disgraced their office. But how this can be urged against Indulgences in general, is indeed a puzzle. If such logic is legitimate, we can prove many startling things. From the fact, that a soldier deserts from the ranks, we shall prove that the army is an abomination,. and from the fact, that lately many Bankmanagers have bolted with the contents of the cashbox, we shall prove that a Bank is an immoral institution. But this is exactly Luther's logic, when he says, that, even if Indulgences were legitimate, they ought not to be tolerated on account of the abuses. ([11]) Of course, when he speaks of the scandalous state of things in his own Church, he remembers and urges the old principle: Abusus non tollit usum. ([12]) Again, in his abominable „Hans Worst" he argues against the Catholic Church in this really astounding way: There are abuses in it, *ergo* it is not the right Church, ([13]) and: Your Church is in want of a Reform, *ergo* it is not the right Church. ([14]) A few pages farther on, when he speaks in favour of his *own* Church, he finds out, that the scandals existing in it say nothing against it.([15]) Such indiarubber principles are extremely convenient.

Whatsoever may be urged against one or another unprincipled priest or friar, we must say that Tetzel has been calumniated. If in this chapter we try to vindicate his honour, we are not merely making a digression; the way in which Luther has treated his antagonist, helps us to understand better the „Reformer".

Nothing is easier, says Erasmus, than to fix any crime

---

[10] Gröne 199.

[11] Opp. lat. 28. 231.

[12] Erl. 21, 138. 26, 275. Cfr. De Wette II. 133. Quid hoc ad

doctrinae puritatem, quod mali male utuntur?

[13] Walch XVII. 1692.

[14] Ibid 1693.

[15] Ibid. 1700.

on any man; and no lie is too big, but will find believers
amongst the prejudiced. ([16]) Protestant history has made
of Tetzel a hateful carricature. He is represented as the
embodiment of monkish ignorance, greediness, fanaticism
and immorality. He is credited with the saying, that „as
soon as the money is dropped into the box, the soul
jumps out of purgatory." Of him the Archbishop of York
said lately, that „he offered *immunity from crimes and
sins for money payment*, warranting his ware with the
confidence of a huckster." ([17]) He has been accused of
adultery and is said to have been condemned to death
for the same crime. All sort of villainous tricks are fathered upon him. The most absurd fables have been
warmed up again. For instance, that a nobleman, having
purchased from Tetzel *an indulgence to rob*, waylaid him
and took his money; against which proceeding there was
of course no remedy. *„An indulgence to rob!"* We know
of an indulgence to commit sin in general, but it was not
given by Tetzel, it was granted by „the dear man of
God", „the Ecclesiastes of Wittenberg", Dr. Martin Luther.
„Pecca fortiter, sed fide fortius."

    How some „historians" have treated Tetzel, is shown by
the words of Hofmann, who in 1844 thoughtlessly copied Vogel and Hecht, giving however many of their *on dit's* as
facts. He remarks, that the word attributed to Tetzel: „So-
bald der Groschen etc." though many differ about it, is nevertheless the most appropriate to represent the spirit of the
age. In other words, he wishes to represent that spirit in
a certain light, and in order to prove his assertion, he
makes use of that assertion as proved. ([18]) Many of the
tricks ascribed to Tetzel are some centuries older and are
to be found almost verbatim in the „Pfaff Amis" (written

([16]) Nihil facilius, quam quod-
vis crimen in hominem fingi. Nihil autem his temporibus tam im-
pudenter fingi potest, quin inven-
iat plurimos, qui arrideant ob insania partium studia. Epp. p. 771.

([17]) Sermon at S. Michael's,
York, Nov. 14th 1883. See York-
shire Herald Nov. 15.

([18]) See Hermann p. 18.

before the year 1300), ([19]) others are found in the Deca-
meron! Also Walch gives all those fables as Gospeltruth. ([20]) It is truly astonishing, that men, who justly
enough always want stringent proofs for historical facts,
should display such largehearted credulity for things, which
directly or indirectly tend to the dishonour of the Catholic Church. Wherever *history* reveals villainy, whether in
high places or low, we mean frankly to acknowledge the
fact, but *history* knows nothing about the things which
make Tetzel's name execrable.

John Tetzel was born at Leipzig about the year 1460;
when he died in 1519, during the famous Leipzig disputation, he was about 60 years old. ([21]) Even Vogel, whose
life of Tetzel ([22]) reveals the bitterest party feeling, says
that he was „neither an idiot, nor a stupid friar, nor a
donkey," ([23]) nor could he have excelled in ignorance,
since in 1487 he occupied the sixth place among fifty-five
candidates for the baccalaureatus in Philosophy. ([24]) The
order of S. Dominic, which he entered, and for which he
was eminently fit through his great eloquence, has no
reason to be ashamed of him. Ordained priest shortly
before the end of the century, he began to appear in
public and very soon acquired a great name on account
of his oratorical gift. ([25]) — At Dresden, Pirna and Leipzig
he was publicly received by the authorities with the
greatest honours; the Churches were not large enough to
admit the crowds that flocked together to listen to the

([19]) Lindemann, Gesch. d. deutschen Literatur. Freib. 1873. 160.

([20]) Walch XV. 442 seqq.

([21]) A. D. 1482 he entered the
University in the same town. One
of his professors was the celebrated Wimpina, who afterwards taught
theology for many years at the University of Frankfurt a. O., until his
death in 1521.

([22]) Leipz. 1717.

([23]) Er war kein Idiot, kein fra-
terculus ignobilis, auch kein unge-
lehrter Tropf, kein Esel. p. 44.

([24]) Gröne 3.

([25]) Hecht, the title of whose
work: Disputatio de vita J. Tetzelii,
nundinatoris sacri (1707, publ. again
at Wittenb. 1717) sufficiently indi-
cates the line he follows, says:
Maxime vero propter eloquentiae
laudem, magnam nominis apud ple-
bem, ut plerumque fieri solet, auctoritatem consecutus magis clares-
cere coepit.

words of the celebrated friar. ([26]) Frequently he was compelled to address the people in the open air.

In 1514 Leo X issued a Bull, granting an Indulgence to all, who should contribute towards the rebuilding of S. Peter's Basilica in Rome. Whether this was opportune, or, as Roscoe thinks ([27]) inopportune, is not necessary to discuss in this place. ([28]) We are satisfied, if Protestants with allow us to think that the Pope had the power to do what he did, and that a contribution towards the erection of a worthy temple in the centre of Christanity was a well spent alms, the giving of which the Church might reward with a spiritual benefit, provided always that the essential condition (true repentance) should be fulfilled. But we fully agree with Protestants, that the administration of this Indulgence was not free from blame. That part of the money, which came in, was given by the Pope to his sister Maddalena, may safely be classed amongst the fables invented or repeated by Paolo Sarpi, as Roscoe acknowledges. But there is a dark spot on the history of this Indulgence viz. that transaction, which granted part of the money to Albrecht of Brandenburg, Archbishop of Mainz. ([29]) When in 1514 this prelate was

---

([20]) Gröne 17.

([27]) „The time at which he resorted to such an expedient is no additional proof of that prudence and that sagacity which all parties have so liberally conceded to him." Roscoe, Leo X. ch. XV.

([28]) Ma quell' edificio materiale di San Pietro in gran parte rovinò il suo edificio spirituale: perciocchè a fin d'adunar tanti milioni di scudi quanti ne assorbiva il lavoro immenso di quella chiesa, convenne al successore di Giulio far ciò donde prese origine l'eresia di Lutero, che ha impoverita di molti più milioni d'anime la chiesa.
Pallav. I. 29.

([29]) The accession of Albrecht and the state of his court during the first years of his Episcopacy are one of the sad examples, which show that a Reform was really wanted, such a Reform as was carried out by the Council of Trent. At the age of 23 the young nobleman had been created Bishop of Magdeburg and Administrator of Halberstadt, which offices he retained also after his election to te see of Mainz. In his younger days he gave a great deal of scandal by his worldliness and his connexion with the younger humanists, especially Hutten. Leo X complains in a letter to Albrecht: „eum (Hutten) circumspectionis Tuae familiarem esse." Though he is inclined to think, that Hutten's virulent books against the Church have been published without the Archbishop's knowledge: „(pene cogit)

raised to the See of St. Willegis, he promised to the Chapter that he himself would pay the Pope the sum of 20,000 rhenish florins, which was the tax for the Pallium. This sum, enormous for the time, had been paid already twice within the preceding ten years (1504 and 1508) and had naturally embittered the minds of the people. Though it is evident that pecuniary means are necessary for the administration of the Church-government, every Catholic is sincerely glad, that nowadays the money is not got by such means; the voluntary contributions, called Peter's Pence, show clearly enough that the Catholics do not wish their spiritual head to suffer from want.

Albrecht was obliged to borrow the above mentioned sum from the famous banking house of the Fuggers at Augsburg; and to free himself from his financial difficulties, he demanded and obtained from the Pope permission, to repay the money out of the sum, which was expected to come in through the promulgation of the Indulgence. This was certainly an unworthy transaction, in extenuation of which nothing can be urged except the fact, that, at least indirectly, also the sum assigned to Albrecht was applied to Church purposes. Practically the whole transaction amounted to this: the palliumtax was remitted in favour of the archdiocese of Mainz, and was paid out of the contributions of all Germany. But it would have been better, if this had never been done.

The Cardinal Archbishop of Mainz, jointly with the Guardian of the Franciscan Friars, was named Commissary of the Indulgence for Saxony and the North of

res ipsa, credi ante oculos tuos, in aede tua, a tuo domestico et familiari non potuisse edi tantum scelus in apertum te ignorante." (Hutteni opp. ed. Münch. III. 568.) In his answer to the Pope Albrecht says that he can do nothing against Hutten," qui se munitissimis arcibus in hunc usque diem continet", but „cavi, ne quis ejusmodi contumeliosa et in diminutionem auc-
toritatis sanctae sedis Romanae scripta venderet, aut emeret sub meis dioecesibus". Ibid. 570. Fortunately Albrecht disappointed in the end the hopes of the „Reformers". A great change took place in him, and he worked hard in later years for a true ecclesiastical reform. (See Hennes, Albr. von Brandenburg, Mainz 1858.)

Germany. Tetzel, whose eloquence was well known, was
chosen as the preacher. The instruction which he and
his subordinates received, ([30]) is perfectly correct, nor is
there anything in it, to which a Catholic would not subscribe nowadays. However, the clause that during this
Indulgence all others should cease, caused many difficulties
to Tetzel; for some priests and monasteries were selfish
enough merely to take into consideration the losses which
their churches or institutions would suffer for some time
in consequence of it. How far Luther may have been
influenced by such a motive, or by his superiors, on whom
this motive may have had some effect, we are not in a
position to decide. Another motive can hardly be denied
to have greatly influenced him, viz. that petty rivalry,
which at times existed between different religious orders
and regularly produced more or less deplorable effects.

Tetzel was a Dominican, Luther an Augustinian;
Tetzel was a Scholastic, Luther was on the side of the
humanists, some of whom were his intimate friends (amongst
others Crotus Rubeanus, one of the authors of the infamous
Epistolae obscurorum virorum). The Dominicans had just
lost their cause in the famous Reuchlinian controversy,
Luther looked upon this as a triumph of his own party. ([31])
An opportunity of humbling the Dominicans once more,
may naturally be supposed to have been welcomed by
their rivals. But the principal cause of Luther's attack
has to be sought in the theological opinions, which he
had formed before. His onslaught was not so much directed against the *abuse* of Indulgences; the very doctrine

([30]) Instructio summaria pro
subcommissariis, poenitentiariis et
confessoribus in executionem gratiae plenissimarum indulgentiarum
subdeputandis et ordinandis. Ap.
Hecht, Vita Tetzelii.

([31]) Luther tried to identify his
cause with that of Reuchlin, he
called him „praeceptor vere mihi
venerabilis". In 1518 (14 Dec.) he
wrote to him: Eram ego unus eorum, qui tecum esse cupiebant,
sed nulla dabatur occasio. Eram
tamen oratione et voto semper
tibi praesentissimus, De Wette I.
196. But why Reuchlin should
have found a place on the Luther-
monument at Worms, is more than
we can understand.

of the Catholic Church on this point was no longer re-
concilable with his view on the efficacy of faith. In fact
he had become a heretic for years before he openly renounced his allegiance to the Church. ([³²]) His superiors
seem to have had no idea of the revolution, which had
taken place in his mind, at first they considered the whole
matter merely as a dispute about points which, without
prejudice to faith, might be considered as debatable.
Staupitz wrote in this sense to the Elector, saying. That
Luther had come forward, „nil asserens, nil disputans,
non in fide, sed in opinionibus scholasticis." ([³³])

Tetzel was preaching at Jüterbogk, a few miles from
Wittenberg, when on the eve of All Saints' day A. D. 1517
Luther affixed his 95 theses to the door of the Schlosskirche. When we consider that in those theses he is still,
comparatively, guarded, and that the custom of publicly
challenging others to learned disputations was rather
prevalent in those days, we cannot find here that act of
heroic courage over which still many of the „Reformer's"
friends are wont to go into ecstasies, nor do we think
that Luther himself was in the least conscious, of how far
the stone which he set a rolling would grow into an
avalanche. ([³⁴])

([³²]) It is most interesting to see how Luther, when still a Catholic, describes the pecularities of a heretic. It is in many points exactly his own portrait in later years. In the theological lectures on the Psalms which he delivered as Professor in the years 1513—1516, and which have been published for the first time by Seidemann in 1876 (2 voll. Dresden) we meet with the following: „The principal sin of heretics is their pride." (I. 133). „In their pride they insist on their own opinions." (I. 413.) „Frequently they serve God with great fervour and they do not intend any evil; but they serve God according to their *own* will." (II. 283.) „Even when refused, they are ashamed to retract their errors and to change their words." (I. 250.) „They think they are guided directly by God." (II. 101.) „The things which have been established for centuries and for which so many martyrs have suffered death, they begin to treat as doubtful questions." (II. 132.) „They interpret (the Bible) according to their own heads and their own particular views and carry their own opinions into it." (I. 10.) Ex ore tuo te judico!

([³³]) Gröne 31.

([³⁴]) The title of the theses is as follows: Amore et studio elucidandae veritatis haec subscripta themata disputabuntur Wittenbergae Praesidente R. P. Martino

Though, as we remarked, Luther is still, comparatively, guarded, he puts forward opinions, which show clearly enough that he means to go straight against the Catholic Doctrine. The 6th thesis, for instance, implicitly denies the power of the keys, for it maintains that the Pope can only *declare* a sin to be forgiven by God;[35] the 36th maintains that through true contrition a Christian is freed from all guilt and punishment.[36] This is evidently in contradiction with the 44th, where it is admitted, that through an indulgence a man may be freed from punishment.[37] The 66th thesis speaks not of abuses, but says of Indulgences in general, that they are nets to catch money with,[38] but the 71st says anathema to him, that would reject Indulgences altogether.[39] However the words are vague, inasmuch as „veritas“ may be differently construed.

To a Catholic mind some of these theses appear at once erroneous, some are admissible, others are dubious. When we take into account the contradictions, the obscurities, the want of theological precision we meet in them, we can believe Luther, when in one of his later books (Wider Hans Worst) he solemnly declares, in two different places, his ignorance on the object of the dispute. *„As truly as Our Lord Christ has redeemed me, I did not know what an Indulgence was.“*[40] This is rather a poor compliment for a Professor of Theology to pay

Luthero, Eremitano Augustiniano, artium et S. Theologiae Magistro, ejusdem ibidem ordinario Lectore. Quare petit, ut qui non possunt verbis praesentes nobiscum disceptare, agant id literis absentes. In nomine Domini Nostri Jhesu Christi. Amen. Wittenb. I. 51.

[35] Papa non potest remittere ullam culpam, nisi declarando et approbando remissam a Deo etc. Ibid.

[36] Quilibet Christianus vere compunctus habet remissionem

plenariam a poena et culpa, etiam sine literis veniarum, sibi debitam. Ibid. 51n.

[37] (Homo) per venias non fit melior, sed tantummodo poenâ liberior. Ibid. 52.

[38] Thesauri indulgentiarum retia sunt, quibus nunc piscantur divitias virorum. Ibid. 52n.

[39] Contra veniarum apostolicarum veritatem qui loquitur, sit ille anathema et maledictus. Ibid. 52n.

[40] Walch XVII. 1704.

to himself, nor can it be considered as very prudent, that a man should talk about things which he does not know. But when Luther continues that „no one else knew it either“, we do not agree with him, since Tetzel soon showed his perfect theological knowledge of the subject. If Luther was really ignorant in the matter, he had plenty of opportunities of learning the unadulterated teaching of the Church.

„The Liberator“ — as now he began to call himself — „Martinus Eleutherius“ ([41]) sent his theses to the Archbishop of Mainz. In the letter which accompanied them we notice that another of his later fundamental errors is first hinted at, viz. the *exclusive* value of the Bible as the rule of faith, „Nowhere has Christ commanded to preach Indulgences.“ ([42]) He also throws out a distinct threat, in case that the Archbishop, as Commissary of the Pope, should not withdraw his instruction „lest some one might arise to refute them (the preachers) and the book, to the dishonour of your Highness. ([43]) He also complains of abuses, of which, he says, the preachers have been guilty, but he says nothing with regard to Tetzel's person. Many years afterwards, in his „Hans Worst“, he puts, *from hearsay* the most horrid blasphemies into the mouth of his antagonist. They are so horrid, that we cannot reproduce them here. ([44]) Luther's words contain a *calumny*, as the antitheses of the Dominican amply prove. How could a man express himself, as Tetzel does in the antitheses, if he had really preached such blasphemies? The public would have risen against him and would have annihilated him with their testimony. But the „Hans Worst“ was written in 1541, at a time, when Luther had become perfectly blinded by what cannot be called but *rage*. The

---

([41]) De Wette I. 73. 75. 76 etc.
([42]) Nusquam praecepit Christus indulgentias praedicari.
        Wittenb. I. 93.
([43]) Ne forte aliquis tandem consurgat, qui editis libellis et illos et

libellum illum confutet, ad vituperium summum Illustrissimae tuae Sublimitatis. Ibid.
    ([44]) Walch XVII. 1704. cfr. Lauterb. 67.

reader will find by and by that this expression is not too strong.

The theses were rapidly spread over Germany; as Luther says, without his consent, for as yet he would not have them considered as final assertions, [45] though as we shall see, he had fully made up his mind not to retract. As they were so pointedly directed against Indulgences and against the preachers, it was impossible that Tetzel should leave them unnoticed. He published and publicly defended at the University of Frankfurt his 106 antitheses. Those who like to represent him as a bigotted blockhead, including Luther, have said — without giving any proof — that his old Professor Wimpina was the real author. [46] This is after all a great compliment to Tetzel, for his theses are distinguished by theological correctness and preciseness of expression. Some of his assertions represent only opinions of the school, but from the tout ensemble it is evident, that he thoroughly understood the doctrine of the Church. [47]

It has been stated and thoughtlessly repeated also by Catholic writers [48] that Tetzel in his capacity as Inquisitor publicly burned Luther's theses. There is absolutely no proof for it. If it had been done, the „Liberator" would have eagerly made use of the fact, not only to throw it into the teeth of his antagonist, but also to excuse with it the *fact*, that his Wittenberg students burnt

---

(45) ... deinde viderem. disputationes meas latius vagari, quam volueram, atque passim non disputabilia, sed asserta acciperentur. De Wette I. 112. — Non fuit consilium neque votum eas evulgari (theses) ... sunt enim nonnulla mihi ipsi dubia, longeque aliter et certius quaedam asseruissem aut omisissem, si id futurum sperassem.   De Wette I. 95.

(46) The reasons why Wimpina cannot be considered as the author of the antitheses see ap. Gröne 75. seqq.

(47) This is also the opinion of Pallavicini: „In esse (conclusioni) mostrossi egli buon teologo; perchè con pochissime parole ... discoprì l'equivocazioni di Lutero (I. 36.) and of Hefele, who says: „Whosoever has read Tetzel's antitheses, must needs confess, that this man understood very well the difficult doctrine about Indulgences. Tüb. Quartalschr. 1854. 631. The antitheses are printed Wittenberg I.

(48) V. gr. Riffel I. 70.

the antitheses of Tetzel. But nowhere does he mention it or hint at it; his silence is the best proof that the whole thing is only an invention. Nor does Mathesius, the most devoted admirer of Luther, allude to it when speaking of Tetzel. He would not have passed it over in silence.

In a letter to his friend Lang (d. d. 21. March 1518) Luther relates at length [49] how the students of Wittenberg got hold of some hundreds of copies of Tetzel's antitheses, partly by force, and publicly made a bonfire of them. This was done without his knowledge and consent, and in letters to other friends, he expresses his grief, that he should have been thought capable of such an act. [50] But that he was pleased with this demonstration in his favour, is credible enough.

It would tire the reader, if we were to mention here all the polemical writings, which were published by both sides, we must be satisfied with a few general remarks. Luther took care to transplant the discussion from the school into the masses of the people. This he did especially in his „Sermon vom Ablass und Gnade", [51] and in the „Freyheit des Sermons D. Martin Luther's". [52] It became more and more evident that a reconciliation would not be possible, except if the whole Church were to throw herself at the „Liberator's" feet and to acknowledge that he was the only legitimate teacher.

Whilst many learned men and many of the Ecclesiastical authorities looked upon the whole matter as a mere schooldispute, Tetzel was shrewd enough to see to what extremes Luther would be driven by his tenets. In his

[49] De Wette I. 98.

[50] Miror quod etiam credere potuisti me fuisse auctorem concremationis Positionum Tetzellinarum. — Letter to Jodocus. De Wette I. 119. Haec inscio Principe, Senatu, Rectore, denique omnibus nobis. Certe mihi et omnibus displicet illa gravis injuria homini a nostris illata. Sum extra noxam, sed timeo quod totum mihi imputabitur. Letter to Lang. But it is difficult to think that the authorities should have known nothing about it, when, as Luther says in another letter (De Wette I. 98) it was done „praemissa intimatione et convocatione, ut si quis vellet adesse conflagrationi etc.

[51] Walch XVIII. 533 seqq.

[52] Ibid. 564 seqq.

reply to Luther's „Sermon vom Ablass und Gnade he says: „On account of those articles many will despise the authority and power of the Pope and the Roman See ... *Everybody will want to explain Holy Scripture according to his own liking.*" ([53]) It became all the more necessary to clear up the situation, the more Luther entrenched himself in his private judgment. The Indulgence became a matter of quite secondary importance, the principal question was now this: Is Luther to teach the Church and the Head of the Church, or vice versa?

Considering Luther's style which showed how firmly he had made up his mind not to give way, it hardly speaks in favour of his honesty, that on Trinity Sunday A. D. 1518 he addressed to Leo X a letter expressing in almost abject terms his devotion to the Holy See and his astonishment that he should be supposed to deny its power. ([54]) He knew perfectly well what his stubbornness had to expect from the supreme authority. In order to blunt the weapon before it could strike him, he had already preached a sermon about excommunication, in which he said that a greater merit could not be imagined, than to fall under an unjust sentence of excommunication. ([55]) Of course, the decision whether such a sentence would be just or unjust, would lie entirely with him.

Luther received the order to appear within 60 days in Rome, and to answer there for his conduct. Once

---

([53]) Walch XVIII. 561.

([54]) Auditum audivi de me pessimum ... ut qui auctoritatem et potestatem clavium et summi Pontifices minuere molitus sim ... *Horrent aures et stupent oculi* ... Disputationes enim sunt, non doctrinae. Yet he adds: *Revocare non possum* ... Quare, Beatissime Pater, prostratum me pedibus tuae B. offero cum omnibus quae sum et habeo. *Vivifica, occide, voca, revoca, approba, ut placuerit;* vocem tuam ut vocem Christi in te praesidentis et loquentis agnoscam.

Wittenb. I. 100B — 101B. — Also in the letter in which he asks Staupitz to send his theses to the Pope he seems astonished that „Suavissimi homines, crassissima astutia instructi ... fingunt summi Pontificis potestatem laedi meis disputationibus. (Ibid 100.) But *before this* he had written to the Bishop of Brandenburg: „Non quod eorum bullas et minas timeam." (Ibid. 99B.)

([55]) Excommunicatio injusta nobilissimum meritum est. Ibid. 63B.

more his want of honesty appears from a letter, in which he asks his friend Spalatinus to obtain for him the *favour*, that the Elector of Saxony would *refuse* him safeconduct and so furnish him with an excuse for not obeying the summons.[56] Leo X, who had been informed by the Emperor Maximilian about the real state of things,[57] saw that it was necessary to bring the matter to an issue, but he consented that Luther should appear at Augsburg before the Cardinal Legate Cajetanus.[58] Germanus justly remarks[59] that Luther's conduct on this occasion is indeed a riddle.

On the day on which he appeared before Cajetanus, he wrote to Melanchthon that he would rather perish than recant,[60] before the Legate he declared his submission to the Roman See,[61] but added that he would not retract, except his opinions were *proved* to be erroneous.[62] Before a public Notary he drew up an instrument, in which

---

[56] Id visum est amicis nostris tum doctis tum bene consulentibus, ut ego apud Principem nostrum Fridericum postulem salvum (ut vocant) conductum per suum dominium. Quod ubi mihi negaverit, sicut scio mihi negaturum, justissima fuerit mihi exceptio et excusatio non comparendi in Roma (sic enim loquuntur). Si ergo velles et meo nomine apud illustrissimum Principem impetrare rescriptum, quo mihi salvum conductum negaret, et meo mihi periculo committeret, si vellem ire: optime mihi consuleres. De Wette I. 133.

[57] Quibus (auctoribus) nisi Beatitudinis Vestrae ... auctoritas legem finemquae imposuerit, brevi non solum imperitae imponent multitudini, sed et principum virorum sibi auram et favorem in mutuam perniciem comparabunt. Letter of Maximilian to Leo X. from Augsburg 8. Aug. 1518. Wittenb. I. 203.

[58] Thomas de Vio, called Cajetanus from his native town Gaëta,

born in 1469, famous in his youth through a public disputation with Pico della Mirandola, was one of the worthiest Ecclesiastics of the time. His great learning, sincere piety and spotless life are acknowledged also by Protestants (Herzog's Realencyclop. II. 493). He died in 1534. Luther speaks of him at times very respectfully. See Wittenb. II. 208.

[59] p. 68.

[60] Ego ... vado immolari, si Domino placet. Malo perire et quod unum mihi gravissimum est, etiam vestra conversatione dulcissima carere in aeternum, quam ut revocem bene dicta et studiis optimis perdendis occasio fiam. De Wette I. 143. Wittenb. I. 207.

[61] Lutherus rogavit ut responsum una cum obtestatione promptissimaque sua voluntate ad Pontificem Maximum transmitteretur. Wittenberg I. 207b.

[62] Si certis et veris rationibus convinceretur. Ibid. 208.

he solemnly declared his *absolute* submission to Rome. ([63])
Then he absconded and appealed in a letter to Cajetanus([64])
as well as in a public document affixed to the Church-
door by a Notary ([65]) „a Papa male informato ad Papam
melius informandum." Again, after his flight, he wrote to
Cajetanus through a friend, asking forgiveness for any
words that might be supposed hostile to the power of the
Pope, ([66]) and in a few weeks' time appealed from the
Pope to the Council. ([67])

One more attempt was made by Rome to settle the
matter without coming to extremes. Carl von Miltiz, a
German by birth, who had spent many years in Rome,
was chosen for the purpose. Though of pleasing man-
ners, he was not the man to carry out a work of this
sort. He possessed neither the energy nor the straightforwardness that were required. The interview he had with
Luther at Altenburg in the beginning of the year 1519
produced no result, but once more the latter adressed, on
the 3? of March, a letter to Leo X, in which he repeats
that no retractation will take place, yet it overflows with
expressions of the greatest loyalty and most perfect submission. ([68])

([63]) Ego Frater Martinus Lutherus Augustinianus, protestor me colere et sequi sanctam Romanam
Ecclesiam in omnibus meis dictis
et factis, praesentibus, praeteritis
et futuris. Quod si quid contra
vel aliter dictum fuit vel fuerit,
pro non dicto haberi et habere volo.

([64]) (Dignetur tua Paternitas ...)
hanc meam abitionem et appella-
tionem pro mea necessitate et ami-
corum auctoritate paratam boni
consulere. Nam eorum vox et ratio mihi insuperabilis est haec:
Quid tu revocabis? Numquid tua
revocatione nobis legem fidei statues? Damnet Ecclesia prius, si
quid damnandum est, et ejus tu
judicium sequere, non illa tuum
sequatur judicium, atque ita victus
cedo. Wittenb. I. 216n.

([65]) Ibid. 217—219.
([66]) Grône 153.
([67]) The appellatio a Papa ad
Concilium Wittenb. I. 231—232n.
([68]) In the exordium of this letter he calls himself: „Ego faex
hominum et pulvis terrae." „Cum
resistentibus et prementibus adver-
sariis scripta mea latius vagentur,
quam unquam speraveram, simul
profundius haeserint plurimorum
animis, quam ut revocari possint
... Istud revocare nihil fieret, nisi
Ecclesiam Romanam magis ac magis foedare et in ora omnium hominum accusandam tradere . . .
Nunc, Beatissime Pater, coram
Deo et tota creatura sua testor,
me neque voluisse neque hodie
velle Ecclesiae Romanae ac Beatitudinis tuae potestatem ullo modo

A fortnight before (20. Febr.) he had written to Scheurl: „I have often said, that hitherto I have only been playing. Now at last we shall have to act seriously against the Roman Pontiff and against Roman arrogance." ([69])

Ten days afterwards (13. March) he writes to his friend Spalatinus: „I will whisper into your ear, I do not know whether the Pope is the antichrist himself or his apostle." ([70])

We must mention here once more the name of Miltiz, on account of a letter which he wrote to Pfeffinger (1. May. 1519), and in which he speaks of Tetzel as a liar and cheat and charges him with immorality. ([71]) Whereas Cajetanus had treated Luther's affair in a straightforward and honourable way, though unsuccessfully, Miltiz followed quite another line. He stooped to flatter the Augustinian friar, and tried to disarm him by throwing the greater part of the blame on Tetzel, ([72]) nor did he shrink from making, in the above mentioned letter, statements, which were intended as a sop for Luther's party. ([73]) The value of his assertion will appear from the following facts. Miltiz declares he will write to the Pope about Tetzel and obtain judgment against him. After his report

tangere aut quacunque versutia demoliri. Quin plenissime confiteor hujus Ecclesiae potestatem esse supra omnia nec ei praeferendum quidquam sive in coelo sive in terra, praeter unum Jhesum Christum Dominum nostrum. Wittenb. I. 235ᴮ. These are very diplomatic expressions; whilst they make Luther appear as a most loyal son of the Church, they leave his private judgment undisturbed.

([69]) Saepius dixi, hucusque lusum esse a me. Nunc tandem seria in Romanum Pontificem et Romanam arrogantiam agantur. De Wette I. 230.

([70]) Verso et decreta Pontificum pro mea disputatione et (in aurem tibi loquor) nescio, an Papa sit

Antichristus ipse vel apostolus ejus: adeo misere corrumpitur et crucifigitur Christus (id est veritas) ab eo in decretis. De Wette I. 239.

([71]) „wann seine Lügen und Schalkheit ist mir zu Massen offenbar worden ... auch hat er II Kinder." ap. Gröne 198.

([72]) Là dove il Cardinale avea mantenuto almeno il decoro della Sedia Apostolica ... il Miltiz che s'avviſì a parlargli conforme d'umiliazione e di timore, sofferse di riceverne anche in iscritto risposte ignominiose al pontefice. Pall. I. 53.

([73]) Seckend. (I. 62) bases his relation exclusively on this letter of Miltiz.

has reached Rome, Leo X speaks of Tetzel in a very
friendly way. [74] From this it is evident, that either Miltiz was unable to substantiate his charge, or that he omitted to report scandalous enormities to the proper authority; in this latter case he was a traitor to the cause he
had to represent, and such a character can not be relied
upon. The mean begging letters of Miltiz, [75] from which
it appears that he was open to bribery, speak very strongly against him, and if Miltiz really made those remarks
about the Papal power, which are attributed to him, this
would be an additional proof that Leo X was very unfortunate in his choice of an ambassador. [76]

As to Tetzel's character, he is accused of having committed adultery, when at Innsbruck. For this crime, it is
said, he was condemned to be drowned in a sack, and
was rescued only through the intercession of the Elector
Frederick. We can follow Tetzel from place to place,
from his entry into the Dominican order until his death;
there is not the slightest proof that he has ever been at
Innsbruck, nor do the archives at Innsbruck, which Evers
searched for the purpose, contain the slightest allusion to
the said trial and sentence. [77] But the place may be a
matter of minor importance. Let the reader answer for
himself the following questions: If Tetzel had committed
this crime and had been on the verge of dying a felon's
death,

1) Would Luther have been the man, to despise such
   a ready and sharp weapon against his antagonist?
2) Would the University of Frankfurt a. O. have
   allowed Tetzel to take his degree?
3) Could Tetzel have been chosen to extraordinary
   public offices of the greatest importance?
4) Would the magistrates and population of Leipzig, *where he is said to have been imprisoned for*

---

[74] Gröne 170.
[75] Hermann 28.
[76] But even Seckendorf says

(I. 63) Id quod serio an joco scrip-
tum sit, mihi non satis liquet.
[77] Evers I. 255.

his atrocious crime, have received him afterwards
with a public procession and with the greatest
rejoicings? ([78]) Credat Judaeus Apella!
In the beginning of 1519 Hermann Rab, the Provincial of the Dominicans bitterly complained, in a letter to
Miltiz, of the calumnies which were set afloat against
Tetzel. He could not have done so, if Tetzel had been
a notorious criminal. The great preacher, wounded by the
rude treatment he had received at the hands of Miltiz and
deeply affected by the religious revolution which he had
been the first to foresee, retired to his monastery at Leipzig, where he died, more of a broken heart than of anything else. It is an honourable trait in Luther's character
that he tried to console his dying antagonist, ([79]) but the
consciousness that he had repeated some of the slander-
ous statements of Miltiz against Tetzel may have had something to do with it.

([78]) A full vindication of Tetzel's
character will be found in Gröne,
201 seqq. At Leipzig the tower
used to be shown, „where Tetzel
was imprisoned." The Leipziger
Tageblatt, which is anything but
friendly to Catholics (29. May 1879),
calls attention to the fact that the
said tower was built only in 1577
i. e. almost 60 year after Tetzel's
death. The same protestant paper
protests against the common fables which cast a slur on his name
and praises his learning and piety.

([79]) Quem ego ante obitum literis benigniter scriptis consolatus
sum ac jussi bono animo esse, nec
mei memoriam metuere.
                          ap. Gröne 176.

Chapter IV

The Leipzig Disputation.

Male disputatum est.
Luther. De Wette I. 287.

Dr. Joannes Eck, Vicechancellor of the University of Ingolstadt, an eminent genius and a man of great erudition, had been for some time a personal friend of Luther, but when the latter's revolutionary tendencies became evident, he sacrificed this friendship to his most sacred convictions. Not only did Luther himself speak of him very highly, ([1]) but even after the Leipzig disputation, where Eck had been victorious, Melanchthon praised his genius ([2]) and Christopher Scheurl acknowledged his „dexterity, knowledge, erudition“ etc. ([3]) If afterwards Luther called him „Dr. Porcus Eccius“ ([4]) or „homo imperiosus, imo impudens et impudicus,“ ([5]) or an „ass in theology ([6]) this change of opinion is easily explained with the rancour caused by his own defeat at Leipzig.

Eck had criticised Luther's neoteric doctrine in a work entitled „Obelisks,“ which was intended for the hands

([1] Insignis veraeque, ingeniosae eruditionis et eruditi ingenii homo, et quod magis urit, antea mihi magna recenterque contracta amicitia conjunctus. DeWette I 96.

([2]) apud nos magnae admirationi plerisque fuit Eccius ob varias et insignes ingenii dotes. Ap. Janssen II. 87.

([3]) Ibidem.
([4]) Wittenb. VII. 456.
([5]) Lauterb. 190.
([6]) Wittenb. I. 297.

of his own Superior, the Bishop of Eichstätt; but when,
through unknown causes ([7]) it had been made public,
Luther answered in his „Asterisks", ([8]) and defended the
teaching laid down in this book in a disputation at Heidelberg, April 26. 1518. In this disputation the question of
Indulgences was not touched at all, but the absolute corruption of human nature, the want of freedom in the human
will and justification by faith alone were urged. ([9])

Carlstadt (Andreas Bodenstein) now entered the arena
by the side of Luther and challenged Eck to a public
disputation. Eck did not expect much good from it and
the event proved that he was perfectly right in this opinion. But to avoid it, would have been considered as a
confession of ignorance and fear, and when Luther earnestly begged of him to accept the challenge, ([10]) he
consented, chosing Leipzig out of the two Universities
offered to him by his antagonist. At the sight of Eck's
theses Luther, who had first despaired of having an opportunity of taking a personal part in the conflict ([11]) made
up his mind to do so in spite of all obstacles, and
announced his intention in a public letter to Carlstadt,
which is brimful of invectives against and contempt for
Eck. ([12]) But if his antagonist, jointly with the Elector,
had not interceded for him with the Senate of the Uni-

([7]) Riffel I. 73.

([8]) Asterisci Lutheri adversus obeliscos Eckii Wittenb. I. 145B.

([9]) Conclusio 3%: Opera hominum, ut semper speciosa sint, bo-
naque videantur, probabile tamen
est, ea esse peccata mortalia. (Ibid.
141B.) Conclusio 13%: Liberum arbitrium post peccatum, res est de
solo titulo, et dum facit quod est
in se, peccat mortaliter (Ibid. 143).
Conclusio 25%: Non ille justus est,
qui multum operatur, sed qui sine
opere multum credit in Christum.
(Ibid. 144B.)

([10]) Eccius noster a me tenta-
tus Augustae, ut cum Carlstadio
nostro Lipsiae congrederetur pro
componenda contentione, tandem
obsecutus est. De Wette I. 216.

([11]) He complains several times
that Cajetanus had refused him permission for a public disputation.
Ibid. 185. 276

([12]) DeWette I. 249. It is note-
worthy that in this letter Luther
acknowledges that it is no longer
a question about Indulgences. He
complains that Eck „stultas quaesti-
ones de indulgentiis paene ex orco
revocat".

versity, he would not have been admitted to the disputation. ([13])

The disputation which was to begin on the 27th of
June 1519 drew a great number of people to Leipzig
Eck was there first. ([14]) Luther came accompanied by
many friends; two hundred armed students of Wittenberg
formed his bodyguard. The combativeness of these members of the new militant Church was so great that a civic
guard had to be formed for the maintenance of order in
the streets and in the hostelries. ([15]) The Bishop of Merseburg, to whose diocese Leipzig belonged, had forbidden
the disputation in public placards, which however were
torn down by the order of the magistrates. ([16])

The 26th of June was devoted to fixing the conditions to be observed throughout the conflict. Partly on
this day, partly after the disputation it was arranged:

1) That all proceedings should be taken down verbatim by public notaries.

2) That the Universities of Paris and Erfurt should
   deliver judgment.

3) That neither party should publish the Acta before the sentence of the judges should be known.

The first condition was objected to by Eck, who did
not wish to be hampered in his speech by the necessary
regard for the pens of the writers. But this was overruled. ([17])

To the second condition Luther objected, for he
knew well enough, what the judgment would be. ([18]) He

([13]) Riffel I. 143. Cfr. Lauterb.
190. Eccius . . . mihi Lipsiae coram Duce Georgio publicam fidem
et salvum conductum impetravit
ut cum eo disputarem. Protestant
authors have frequently said that
Luther was dragged into the disputation against his will. Janssen
(II. 83 Nota) fully refutes this assertion.

([14]) Köhler (p. 52) says that Eck
took part in the Corpus Christi pro-

cession, clad in a chasuble, and that
*in this way he meant to express his
confidence of victory!* Risum tenea-
tis amici!

([15]) Evers IV. 366.
([16]) Ibid. 367.
([17]) Luther represents this in his
own way: Voluit potius Eckius noster sine notariis, meris et liberis
clamoribus rem agi.
                    Wittenb. I. 294.
([18]) See Köstlin I. 257.

insisted that at least *all* professors of *all* faculties should have a vote in the question, not Theologians only. However this objection too was overruled, and his remark to Spalatinus, that he meant to reserve his right of appeal, shows how little a satisfactory result could be expected from the whole affair.

The third condition was after the disputation infringed by the Lutherans. The excuse given by Melanchthon ([19]) for this step, that, as thirty notaries were present, the proceedings would anyhow have soon been published is very flimsy. They had given their word and ought to have kept it.

After a solemn High Mass in the Church of S. Thomas and the singing of the „Veni, Sancte Spiritus" the disputation was opened in one of the halls of the Castle (the Pleissenburg) which had been decorated for the occasion. Carlstadt insisted on opening the battle, ([20]) but did certainly not gain any laurels. The remarks which Luther made about him almost twenty years afterwards, that he only made himself ridiculous, that he was most unfortunate in his argumentation and slow of perception, ([21]) need not be charged to the enmity, which at that time existed between the two men. During the week that Carlstadt remained in the arena it was the common impression, that he manifested confusion, want of erudition, of memory, of confidence, of coolness; defects which appeared all the more striking when compared to the vast knowledge, great dialectic power, precise language

---

([19]) Wittenb. I. 242B.

([20]) Noluit mihi Lipsiae primas partes disputationis concedere, ne ei praeriperem honorem, cui tamen libenter favebam. Luther ap. Lauterb. 190. In the famous interview at the „Black Bear" at Jena Luther threw this at Carlstadt's head. „I punished you at Leipzig, when you were so conceited and wished to be the first to dispute." Carlstadt:

„Ah, Doctor, how can you say so? You know that when I was disputing, you were still uncertain whether they would admit you or not ... But you must always talk in that way, to make sure of your own glory." Walch XV. 2429.

([21]) Er legte schannde fur ehr ein zu leipzig, quia est infelicissimus disputator, horridi et hebetis ingenii. Lauterb. l. c.

and self command of Eck. ([21a]) Luther says ([22]) that Carlstadt was all the more to be blamed, as he had such a pleasant subject (materiam omnium jucundissimam). It is difficult to agree with him in this, for the points which Carlstadt had undertaken to defend, the want of freedom in the human will and the absolute corruption of human nature, were not at all apt to excite any enthusiasm in the bosoms of the hearers. In his answer Eck clearly established the Catholic doctrine, defending it against both extremes, against Pelagian presumption and Lutheran despair; showing that, though man is unable to bring forth any fruits of eternal life or even to prepare himself for his salvation without the help of God, yet he is not what Carlstadt tried to make of him, a block of wood, but able, as to resist, so to follow divine grace.

The disputation about the power of the Roman See, which was reserved for Luther, ([23]) was certainly a „more pleasant" matter, since the revolutionary sympathies of many of the hearers could be counted upon. We can imagine with what eagerness everybody looked forward to the 4th of July, when the first personal encounter between Eck and Luther was to take place. ([24]) In the „Protestatio", with which the latter introduced his remarks, he alluded to Tetzel, expressing his regret that the Dominican Friar should be absent. ([25]) But Tetzel was on his deathbed in the very town of Leipzig and expired either

([21a]) Köstlin (I. 262) acknowledges in Eck „great bodily and mental vigour", but thinks that his own glory was a higher object to him than the matter in dispute. Such assertions ought to be *proved*. If Köstlin (269) quotes Luther, we must hesitate to consider a man as utterly selfish on the testimony of his avowed enemy. Throughout the disputation Eck's words show his genuine love of the Church, which he so ably defended.

([22]) Lauterb. l. c.
([23]) Mihi vero ultimas Eccii propositiones de Primatu Papae et Joanne Hus impugnandas reliquit. Ibidem.
([24]) The acta are printed Wittenb. I. 242—291.
([25]) Doleo etiam eos non adesse, quos maxime oportuit, qui cum et privatim et publice toties me crimine haereseos profanarunt, nunc, cum instet cognitio causae, se subtraxerunt, haereticae pravitatis inquisitores dico. Ibid. 242.

before the disputation was over, or at least within a few days after its end.(²⁶)

The reader will not expect us to follow every step of the disputants or to mention every pro and contra urged by either side. Let us suppose that the arguments of Catholic Theologians with regard to the Primacy of S. Peter and of his successors are sufficiently well known, though it cannot be said that Luther understood them well. It will be sufficient for our purpose, if from the Acta we notice those views advanced by him, which must be considered as so many steps on his way to complete heresy.

Luther still acknowledged some sort of Primacy, but merely as an honorary distinction, which conferred no supreme power on S. Peter.(²⁷) Only as far as the Western world is concerned, will he admit that Ecclesiastical unity is owing to the authority (whatever this authority may be) of the Roman See; but this fact does not prove the supremacy of the same See over the whole of the Church; otherwise it would follow that Jerusalem, being the Mother of all Churches, would be the supreme Church.(²⁸)

To the argument urged by Luther, that Christ is the head of the Church, Eck most properly answered that this is not denied by any Catholic,(²⁹) but that this truth is in perfect harmony with the other, that Christ may have a Vicar on earth. But to this Luther replies with the curious argument: The Church is a Kingdom of *faith,*

(²⁶) Gröne 175.

(²⁷) Hoc sane fateor, Apostolum Petrum fuisse primum in numero Apostolorum, et ei deberi honoris praerogativam, sed non potestatis. Aequaliter electi sunt et aequalem potestatem acceperunt. Ita et de Romano Pontifice sentio, quod honoris praerogativâ ceteris debeat anteferri, salva cujusque aequali potestate. Wittenberg I. 246ᴮ.

(²⁸) Revera etiam Romana ec-

clesia orta est ex Hierosolymitana, haec est matrix proprie omnium Ecclesiarum. Sed nec valet consequentia: ex Romana Ecclesia orta est sacerdotalis unitas, ergo ipsa est caput et domina omnium prima, alioqui insuperabiliter concluderet, Hierosolymitanam esse caput et dominam omnium. Ibid. 244.

(²⁹) Nemo hoc negare praesumit, nisi qui Antichristus est.

Ibid. 244ᴮ.

ergo the head of the Church must be invisible. When he
further says that Christ must not be *shoved out* of the
militant Church into the triumphant one, we perfectly
agree with him, but we do not know that Catholics have ever
made such an attempt. ([30]) Luther's forte, interpretation of
the Bible according to his own head, appears in his explanation of the text: Thou art Peter etc. The rock is not Peter,
but faith, and as faith is the same throughont the whole
Church, no special power can be attributed to Peter. ([31])
If the Fathers have thought that Peter himself was the
rock, they must have been mistaken, or they must have
meant something else. ([32])

Some of Luther's arguments are such as not to give
one a very grand idea of him as a theologian, they are
simply unworthy of any thinking man. He says for instance, that if Peter had been the foundation of the Church,
the whole Church must be supposed to have tumbled
down with him at the words of a servant maid. ([33]) He
supposes here two things as held by Catholics, which
Catholics certainly do not hold, viz. that every act of
Peter was formaliter an act of the head of the Church, and
that, at the time of the event alluded to, Peter was already
constituted head of the Church. But Christ had merely
said: *I will* build my Church etc.

The proceedings of the day on which Luther made
the above mentioned remark (5. July) served greatly to

([30]) Prorsus audiendi non sunt
qui Christum extra Ecclesiam mi-
litantem trudunt in triumphantem,
cum sit regnum fidei, *hoc est* quod
caput nostrum non videmus et tamen habemus. Ibid. 243B.

([31]) ... aut (petra) significat
fidem (quod verum est); iterum
eadem est fides omnium Ecclesiarum. Ibid. 249.

([32]) Sancti Patres, quando Petrum appellant petram, hoc loco
vel humana patiuntur, vel aliquem
alium sensum habent; de quo non
pronuntio. Ibid. 251.

([33]) Si Petrus esset fundamen-
tum Ecclesiae, lapsa fuisset Ecclesia ad unius ancillae ostiariae vocem, quam tamen nec portae infer-
orum expugnare poterunt. Ibid.
Luther seems to have thought a
great deal of this joke (it can hardly be called by any other name)
for he repeated it also in a sermon
he preached during the time of the
disputation. (Evers IV. 391.) But
he must have become ashamed of
it; he omitted it in the edition of
the same sermon published in 1520.

clear up the situation. In the morning he strongly protested against the supposition that he was favourable to
the schism of the Hussites. „May God forgive him (Eck)
for representing me as their patron . . . The Bohemians do
wrong, that by their own authority they separate themselves from our unity, *even if they should have divine
right on their side.*" ([34])

But there was a great surprise in store for the hearers.
When at 2 p. m. the disputation was resumed, Luther
openly defended some of the heresies of Huss. It can
hardly be supposed that within that short space of time
he had changed his opinion, but he found it opportune to
speak out more openly than he had done before. Though
formerly he had denounced the „Bohemians" in very
violent language,([35]) that sympathy which makes all revolu-
tionaries akin, had drawn him towards the followers of
Huss and had made the latter look with the greatest hopes
towards Wittenberg, where teachings, in many points identical with their own, were developed. Eck's statement,([36])
that the Hussites offered up public prayers for Luther's
success, and that secretly some of them were present at
Leipzig, contains in itself nothing improbable and is confirmed by letters of some Bohemian leaders to Luther.
From the letter of Wenzel Rosdalowsky (Rosdialovinus)
d. d. 17th July we learn, that on that day all about the
Leipzig disputation had already been made known at
Prague through „Jacobus quidam organarius." ([37]) If some

([34]) Primum diluam contumeliam, quod me egregius D(ominus)
D(octor) insimulat Bohemicae fac-
tionis studiosum et plane patronum.
Parcat ei Dominus! . . . Nunquam
mihi placuit nec in aeternum pla-
cebit quodcunque schisma. Inique
faciunt Bohemi quod se auctoritate
propria separant a nostra unitate,
etiamsi jus divinum pro eis staret,
cum supremum jus divinum sit charitas et unitas spiritus. Wittenb. I.
250. The Acta have the remark:
D. Martinus petiit Eckium, ne ve-

lit impingere tantam contumeliam,
ut eum Bohemum faceret, quia sibi
semper invisi fuissent, ideo quod
ab unitate dissentiant. Ibid. 251.

([35]) Erl. 40, 15—17. Wittenb.
I. 43n.

([36]) Evers IV. 406.

([37]) Riffel I. 152. Walch XV.
1627. Luther says of these letters:
Exhortantur autem me ad constan-
tiam et patientiam, esse hanc theo-
logiam puram quam doceo.
De Wette I. 341.

of the sect were present at Leipzig, Luther's change is
easily explained. It was not his interest, to make enemies or to alienate from himself a powerful party which
was already in open conflict with the See of Rome. The
remarks he had made in the morning were apt to produce
such an effect, hence it was necessary to smooth them
down. If Eck had mentioned the Hussites *in order* to
make Luther express himself in unmistakable terms on
this subject, it would be difficult to find such an action
unfair, though Köstlin calls it a „snare." ([38])

When in the afternoon of the 5th of July Luther declared, that though he did not approve of the schism,
he acknowledged many of the articles of Huss to have
been unjustly condemned, especially the one about the
Church and the Primacy of the Roman See, ([39]) Duke
George indignantly exclaimed:" „Das walt' die sucht!"
His attack on the authority of the Council of Constance
Luther tried to veil the next day by saying that probably the articles in question had not been condemned,
but falsely inserted as having been condemned. ([40]) If
at the beginning of the disputation there had been the
faintest glimmer of a hope of reconciliation, it would certainly have disappeared from the moment, that he advanced such theories. However the disputation lagged on
until the 14th July; indulgences, penance and purgatory
furnished additional matter. But since we have heard

([34]) I. 270.

([39]) Hoc certum est, inter articulos Joannis Hus vel Bohemorum
multos esse plane Christianissimos
et evangelicos. quos non possit universalis Ecclesia damnare. Velut est
ille et similis, Quod tantum una est
Ecclesia universalis.   Haec enim
agentibus impiissimis adulatoribus
inique est damnata. (Let the reader remember that in the opinion
of Hus the Church consisted only
of predestinated souls.)   Deinde

ille: Non est de necessitate salutis credere Romanam Ecclesiam
esse aliis superiorem, sive sit Wickleff, sive Huss, non curo. Scio quod
salvati sunt Gregorius Nazianzenus,
Basilius Magnus etc. et tamen hunc
articulum non tenuerunt!
          Wittenb. 251b.

([40]) Crederem hos et similes articulos non fuisse ibi damnatos,
sed ab aliquo impostore interser-
tos. Ibid. 254b.

Luther put forward his theory about Church and Pope, we need not follow the disputants any farther.

To us it seems that Eck most ably and satisfactorily answered; but considering what sort of an antagonist he had to deal with, how much Luther insisted on his own interpretation of the Bible, (⁴¹) how decidedly he rejected the authority of the Fathers, it might have been better to oppose him more on general grounds and with a priori arguments.

Which of the two was the conqueror? Of course this is a question, on which the parties of both disputants almost always have had and will have their own opinion. The very fact that the disputation took place, and without any definite result, seems to be a conclusive proof of the absolute necessity of a supreme judicial power in religious matters. Protestants ought not to forget, that if Luther had the right, not to find in the Bible a proof of the power of S. Peter and of his successors, Eck had just as much right to find the same there, for private judgment ought to be granted to him too by those, who establish it as a principle. But from the existence of two diagonally opposed opinions, which are equally legitimate it would follow either that the truth cannot be arrived at, or that it is of no importance to know what the truth is.

Luther did certainly not consider himself as the conqueror. Anything but satisfied (⁴²) he had left Leipzig before the final act. He complained about the honours be-

---

(⁴¹) As Eck did not agree with Luther's interpretation of the Bible, he became „sacrarum literarum inanis disputator". (Letter to Spalatinus Wittenb. I. 294B.) Luther adds that he does not mean to play himself out as alone possessing knowledge of the Bible, but he thinks he must know more about it, than Eck „qui sacras literas vix a limine salutavit". Almost the *first* study of Eck was the Bible, and he studied it so assiduously, that *when ten years old,*

he knew the greater part of it by heart. See Wiedemann p. 5. It was at this same age that he was qualified to enter the University of Heidelberg.

(⁴²) Letter to Spalatinus: ut intelligere possis disputationem illam fuisse perditionem temporis, non inquisitionem veritatis. Deinde Eckium Eckianosque simulare in gloria aliud et aliud sentire in conscientia. Wittenb. I. 294.

stowed upon his antagonist by the University men and the coldness shown to himself. ([43]) He thought that on the whole the disputation had not been good and promised to publish his „Resolutiones" again([44]) and threatened that Eck's triumph would not last long.([45]) We are confirmed in our opinion of Eck's success, more than by anything else, by the fact that Luther and his party treated him with scorn and insults. It became a favourite pastime with them, to make all sorts of contemptuous puns about his name. Not only Erasmus, but even Melanchthon, whom Köstlin calls „a man of a tender Christian mind"([46]) (of whose tenderness we shall see some specimens) joined in this unworthy sport. ([47]) Here are a few names which Carlstadt gave to the man who had exposed his ignorance: „Geckius, asinorum parens; asinus tardissimus; ad nates es caedendus fustibusque eges, asinus es ad lyram (Carlstadt had learnt this from Luther); dignus in cujus natibus decem virentes scopae moriantur, bestia, caprarum petulantissima."([48]) [But we are still in the beginning of the glorious Reformation, the style will be found to improve in the course of time.] Weapons like these are always sus-

---

([43]) Lipsienses sane nos neque salutaverunt, neque visitarunt ac veluti hostes invisissimos habuerunt; illum comitabantur, adhaerebant, convivabantur, invitabant, denique tunica donaverunt et shamlotum (camelotto) addiderunt, cum ipso spatiatum equitaverunt, breviter quidquid potuerunt, in nostram injuriam tentaverunt. (Löscher III. 203.) The fact that Eck was considered by the Leipzig University as conqueror and honoured accordingly. was considered by the „Liberator" as a personal insult.

([44]) Quia male disputatum est, edam Resolutiones meas denuo.
De Wette I. 287.

([45]) Interim tamen ille (Eck) placet, triumphat at regnat, donec ediderimus nos nostra. Ibid. Nat-urally he will not allow that Eck has proved anything. „Quantum in Eckio fuit, fere nullus scopus tactus est." (Wittenb. I. 294.) He adds: Ita me Deus amet, fateri cogor, nos esse victos clamore et gestu, hoc est, eckiana modestia, sic enim ipse vocat. — Many years ago we saw a Protestant Churchhistory, written for the students of a Prussian Gymnasium, where the whole of the Leipzig Disputation was described in the words: „Eck was declared conqueror, because he shouted the loudest (Weil er am sehrsten schrie)." This is a very convenient way of writing history.

([46]) I. 271.

([47]) See Evers IV. 269.

([48]) Wiedemann 362.

picious.   Luther charges Eck with vanity,([49]) hypocrisy([50])
stupidity([51]) and drunkenness.   Seidemann accuses him of
immorality.([52])   Köstlin says([53]) that after the disputation
Eck remained in the town for nine days, „enjoying mani-
fold sensual pleasures, for which he had notoriously a great
susceptibility.“   Would Mr. Köstlin be good enough to
prove this? — On the 10th of Febr. 1541 Eck died at
Ingolstadt, and as eyewitnesses assure us([54]) he died as
piously and as well prepared as any Christian could wish
to die, but his adversaries persecuted him even after the
tomb was closed over him.   Luther exulted,([55]) Veit Dietrich wrote that Eck had died like a beast, intent on drink
and on money,([56]) Melanchthon, „the tender Christian
mind“ composed an Epitaph:

Πολλα φαγων και πολλα πιων και πολλα κακ’ ειπων
’Εν δε ταφω εκτος γαστερ εθηκε ετην.

Multa vorans et multa bibens, mala plurima dicens
    Eccius hac posuit putre cadaver humo.

At Ingolstadt there is an inscription on Eck's tomb, which
represents better the value of the man:

Fortiter in Christi castris hic vivus agebat,
    Magnus doctrina, maximus ingenio.

([40]) Aperuit oculos suos Satan
et servum suum Joannem Eckium
insignem Christi adversarium ex-
stimulavit indomita gloriae libidine.
Luther's letter to Leo X. Wittenb.
II. 2.
    ([50]) See Note 42.

([51]) Eckius ad rem theologicam
— ονος προς λυραν. Wittenb. I. 297.
([52]) Die Leipz. Disput. p. 53.
([53]) I. 269.
([54]) Wiedemann 352.
([55]) Ibid. 354.
([56]) Ibid. 355.

Chapter V

From Leipzig to Worms.

Che la diritta via era smarrita.
Dante, Inf. I.

The Leipzig disputation produced a long and bitter controversy; numberless polemical pamphlets were published by the friends of either party. Melanchthon described the proceedings at Leipzig in a letter to Oecolampadius. Eck complained, not only because he considered this as a breach of the agreement entered into; but also on account of personal attacks made against him. Luther imitated the example of his friend[1] and moreover published his „Resolutiones" [2] in which he defended again the theses he had maintained at Leipzig.

Miltiz tried once more to make peace with Luther; the two met (8. Oct. 1519) at Liebenwerda. The Augustinian promised to submit to the decision of the Elector-Archbishop of Treves, Richard von Greiffenklau,[3] but when called upon to set out for Treves, refused, denying that he had ever consented.

The Universities to which the arbitration on the Leipzig disputation had been entrusted, never gave judgment. But the Universities of Cologne and of Louvain, the former in August, the latter in November 1519 condemned

[1] De Wette I. 284.
[2] Wittenb. I. 298 seqq.

[3] De Wette I. 343.

Luther's theses together with several of his books. ([4]) In return Luther poured out his vial of wrath over them. ([5]) In connexion with this we may notice here at once the pamphlet, which he published two years afterwards as an answer to the condemnation of his writings by the University of Paris. His peculiar style appears in it to grow towards perfection. No matter how learned or how generally respected either private persons or public bodies are, the moment they oppose Luther, they become a mass of dunces, fools, asses and villains. Here is a specimen: „In its upper part, called the faculty of theology, the University of Paris is from the top of the head down to the soles of the feet, snowwhite of the true, last, antichristian chief heresy, a mother of all errors in Christendom, the greatest spiritual whore the sun shines upon and the real backdoor of hell .... Paris is the largest brothel of the true Antichrist, the Pope." ([6]) Is a calm discussion of religious matters possible where such language is used? Here is another specimen of Luther's controversial logic at the same period. Augustinus von Aleveld, a Franciscan of Leipzig, maintains that the Church cannot exist without a head, just as little as a secular community can. Luther ridicules this argument by saying: If so, we shall have likewise to conclude: As a corporal community cannot exist without women, we must also give to Christendom, lest it should perish, one corporal and common woman — das wird je eine weidliche Hure seyn müssen!" ([7])   Can

---

([4]) The sentence of the Doctores Lovanienses is expressed in the following words: Librum et tractatum doctrinaliter condemnamus tamquam communitati fidelium nocivos, verae et sanae doctrinae adversos et de medio tollendos censemus, ignique cremandos, et autorem ipsum ad revocationem et abjurationem supradictorum cogendum. Wittenb. II. 37ʙ. The Colonienses say: praefatum librum tantis scandalis, erroribus haeresibusque ab olim damnatis refertum etc. Ibid. 38ʙ.

([5]) In his Responsio l. c.

([6]) Walch XVIII. 1142. Cfr. Ibid. 1144: Ja lieben Esel, man lasse euch auf dem Polster sitzen und Lampreten fressen! wenn euch denn der Bauch gurret und einen — lasset, so dringt uns dahin es sei ein Artikel des Glaubens.

([7]) Walch XVIII. 1205.

logic maintain its place where ribald jokes are passed off
for arguments?

Before we direct our attention to the steps which
„Eleutherius" was about to take and which were to lead
to that formal, complete and definite rupture with Rome,
which up to the present day divides Germany into two
hostile encampments, we have to consider a very important item in his calculations, how far he knew himself to
be backed by powerful friends. Early in 1520 he tried
to secure the help of Charles V, who had succeded his
grandfather Maximilian. In his letter he adresses the young
Emperor in words breathing the greatest humility and represents himself as the innocent victim of persecution. ([8])
Invain, he says, he has offered to be silent, invain has he
proposed conditions of peace, invain has he asked to be
taught better. ([9]) Of Luther's desire to be taught we have
not a very great idea, and our readers know by this time
what the „conditions of peace" amounted to, viz. that the
Church should commit suicide. Luther also tried to make
the Bishops of Mainz and of Merseburg favourable to his
cause. The answers he got were very different. We fully
agree with him that the letter of Archbishop Albrecht was
thoroughly „unepiscopal". ([10]) This prelate said that as
yet he had had no time to read Luther's books or even
to look at them (vel obiter videre). It fills one with shame
to hear him complain that people should dispute about
frivolous opinions and questions, such as the power of the
Roman Pontiff, whether it be based on divine or human
right, about the freedom of will and similar trifling and
useless questions *with which a good Christian has little to
do!* ([11]) Far more dignified and worthy of a Bishop was

([8]) Tertius jam finitur ferme
annus, ex quo patior sine fine iras,
contumelias, pericula et quidquid
adversarii excogitare possunt mali.
Wittenb. II. 44b.

([9]) Frustra silentium offero,
frustra pacis conditiones propono,

frustra erudiri meliora postulo.
Ibid.

([10]) Walch XIX. 657.

([11]) Non sine ... vehementi
displicentia in dies intelligimus, a
quibusdam professoribus pro fri-
volis suis opinionibus quaestiun-

the answer of Adolph of Merseburg. In a few words he
protested against the hostile and presumptuous tone of
Luther's books and exhorted him to use his talents for a
better purpose. ([12]).

In a letter dated 3. May 1520 Eck announced to a
friend that soon a Papal Bull of excommunication would
be published against Luther. The „Reformer" had been
expecting this for a considerable time, and the nearer it
approached, the more did he find comfort in the friendship of certain persons, on whom he was able to rely in
any case. His natural allies were the humanists, who for
years had prepared his way by reviling the Clergy, high
and low, secular and regular, by exaggerating the existing
evils and undermining spiritual authority. ([13]) No wonder
that Luther felt himself drawn towards them and did
his best to confirm the friendship even at the cost of a
great deal of flattery. ([14]) They did their best for him in
return. The Elector Frederick of Saxony began to be-
friend Luther more openly, after he had received Erasmus'
„axiomata pro causa Lutheri." ([15]) They spread the „Liberator's" books in enormous numbers([16]) and sang his
praises in unmeasured terms. Amongst his friends at that
time were men like Willibald Pirkheimer and Albrecht
Dürer who were hoping for a real Reform, without wish-

culisque, ut puta de Romani Pontificis potestate, an scilicet de jure
divino humanove sit, deque libero
arbitrio atque multis aliis his similibus nugamentis non admodum
ad vere Christianum perinenti-
bus ... acerrime digladiari.
  Wittenb. II. 47.
([12]) Potuisti pro insigni indus-
tria tua, meo quidem judicio, pro
his scribere saluti caritatique pro-
culdubio commodatiora, quod et
hortor, jurgiis et opprobriis hujusmodi spretis et posthabitis.
  Ibid. 49.
([13]) Otto, 118.
([14]) See letter to Erasmus: Quis
enim est, cujus penetralia non pe-

nitus occupet Erasmus, quem non
doceat Erasmus, in quo non reg-
net Erasmus? etc.
  De Wette I. 247.
([15]) Amongst these axiomata we
find: Bullae saevitia probos animos offendit, ut indigna mitissimo
Christi Vicario. — Qui Lutherum
impetunt ea inducunt, quae nullae
piae aures ferunt. Wittenb. II. 121.
([16]) Luther made the amplest
use of the press. Though written
with regard to a particular book,
his words may be applied in a
more general sense: „Jam obstetri-
cantibus praelis pario."
  De Wette I. 408. 412.

ing to break with the Church, and stood by him until
his work appeared in its real character from the fruits it
bore. But the greater part of his admirers among the
humanists were men who cared little about religion or
put on a religious mask when it served their purpose. ([17])
Foremost amongst them was Ulrich von Hutten, a fiery
character, an accomplished scholar and an unprincipled
libertine. Hutten's great friend was Franz von Sickingen,
who on his own accord waged cruel war against all who
had the courage or the misfortune to oppose him and
whose armed bands of hired robbers and assassins devast-
ated the country. Par nobile fratrum! And these were
the men who, more than others, petted and encouraged
and protected Luther. Sickingen was preparing a revolution on a large scale; popular opinion credited him even
with aspirations to the imperial crown, the religious dis-
turbance would only make it easier to him to carry out
his ambitious plans. Hence he offered his protection to
the monk, who as his admirers proudly say „shook the
world.“ Hutten writes to Luther that Sickingen offers
him hospitality and will defend him against all enemies. ([18])
In the same letter he encourages Luther to persevere:
„They say thou art excommunicated. How great, o Luther,
how great art thou, if this is true!“ ([19]) The offer of protection was gratefully accepted and Luther expressed his
absolute confidence in Sickingen. ([20]) When in addition to
this he received the assurance that Sylvester von Schaum-
burg (or Schauenberg) was ready to put a number of
armed knights into the field for him, he used the words of

([17]) Strauss, Ulr.v.Hutten II. 52.

([18]) ... adversus omnis generis
inimicos defensurus strenue. Hoc
ter aut quater jussit ad te scrib-
erem. Hutteni opp. III. 576.

([19]) Ferunt excommunicatum te.
Quantus, o Luthere, quantus es, si
hoc verum est, ... Tu confirmare
et robustos esto, nec vacilla.
Ibid. 575.

([20]) Scripserat ... Lutherus, se
plus confidentiae erga illum (Sickingen) gerere. majoremque in eo spem
habere, quam habeat in ullo sub
coelo principe. Cochlaeus (de ac-
tis et scriptis Lutheri) ap. Kampschulte II. 74.

Caesar at the crossing of the Rubicon „Jacta est alea." ([21])
„Sylvester von Schauenberg und Franz von Sickingen *have
freed me from the fear of men.*" ([22]) We have never
heard of S. Peter or S. Paul waiting for such news.

Luther felt that he was safe, a fate like that of Huss
or Hieronymus of Prague was out of the question. There
was nothing to prevent him from completing the rupture.
With greater confidence was he now able to repeat what
he had said in his answer to Prierias, the Magister
sacri Palatii: „Farewell, thou unhappy, lost, blaspheming
Rome." ([23])

His most important books of the year 1520 are an
appeal „to the Christian nobility of the German nation" ([24])
and the „Babylonian Captivity." ([25])

In the former Luther proclaims for the first time the
universal priesthood. He declares he means to pull down
the three walls, behind which the Romanists are entrenched.
— The first wall is the priesthood as attributed to a certain
caste. This is nothing but usurpation. Every Christian,
„everybody that has crawled out of the baptismal font"

([21]) A me quidem, jacta mihi
alea, contemtus est Romanus furor
et favor: nolo eis reconciliari nec
communicare in perpetuum.
          De Wette I. 466.

([22]) Jam securum me fecit Sylvester Schauenberg et Franciscus
Sickingen ab hominum timore. De
Wette I. 469. — Sickingen per Huttenum promittit tutelam mihi contra omnes hostes. Idem facit Sil-
vester de Schauenberg cum nobi-
libus Franciscis cujus literas pul-
chras habeo ad me. Ibid. 475. —
Hutten literas at me dedit ingenti
spiritu aestuantes in Romanum
Pontificem, scribens se jam et literis et armis in tyrannidem sacer-
dotalem ruere. Ibid. 486.

([23]) Nunc vale infelix, perdita
et blasphema Roma, pervenit ira
Dei super te sicut meruisti in
finem ... Relinquamus ergo eam,
ut sit habitatio draconum, lemurum,

larvarum, lamiarum, et, juxta nomen suum, confusio sempiterna,
idolis avaritiae perfidis, apostatis,
cynedis, priapis, latronibus, simoni-
bus et infinitis aliis monstris ad os
plena, et novum quoddam Pantheon impietatis. Wittenb. I. 189.
— It is in this same controversy
with Prierias that we meet for the
first time with an outbreak of Luther's *rage*. „Si fures furca, si la-
trones gladio, si haereticos igne
plectimus, cur non magis hos magistros perditionis, hos Cardinales,
hos Papas, et totam istam Romanae Sodomae colluviem quae Ecclesiam Dei sine fine corrumpit omnibus armis impetimus et *manus
nostras in sanguine istorum lava-
mus?* Ibid. 195.

([24]) An den christl. Adel deut-
scher Nation. Walch X. 296 seqq.
([25]) De Captivitate Babylonica
Ecclesiae. Wittenb. II. 66B. seqq.

is a priest. For the sake of order there must be ministers, but they receive their power from their flocks.
With the pretended dignity of the Roman priesthood also
all their privileges fall to the ground. The clergy will
have to be entirely under the power of the secular authorities, just as they get their shoes and coats made by secular workmen. — The second wall is the Bible as interpreted by the Pope, who claims for himself the exclusive
right to judge of its meaning. For the future the word
of God shall be free. As everybody is a priest, everybody has a right to teach and to judge of Christian doctrine. The mind illumined by faith determines the meaning
of the Scriptures. — The third wall is the pretended exclusive power of the Pope to summon a Council. It is
the secular authority that has this right and this duty,
let the Pope protest as long as he likes. The next council
will have to rid the Germans for ever of the „Roman
robber" and from his „abominable and diabolical regime."

In the existing evils and abuses, which we have not
omitted to point out, there was quite enough to embitter
many minds, but when Luther threw in his wild exagger-
ations, the picture became such as to stir up the deepest
hatred in the masses, who from his words looked upon
themselves as the downtrodden victims and serfs of the
Pope. At the same time Luther threw out some hints
which were calculated to secure the friendship of the
nobility, for he proposed that the Cathedral Chapters
should remain untouched, for the benefit of the younger
sons of noblemen. The mention of a „Primate of Germany" was a bait for Albrecht, Archbishop of Mainz.

The other Book, the „Babylonian Captivity" was in
preparation when the Bull of excommunication against
Luther arrived in Germany, but was published before this
document reached Wittenberg. ([26]) We have tried in vain
to find in this book that which Köstlin ([27]) praises so much,

(²⁶) Köstlin I. 368.   (²⁷) Ibid. 369.

the „luminбus explanation"· and „the thorough acquaintance
with the arguments of the adversaries." If the biographer's
acquaintance with the same is not greater, it is not very
great.

Luther begins by excusing himself, that, only two
years ago, he has still held the belief in Indulgences and
defended them; he begs of all who possess his writings
on this subject, to burn them and to believe for the future
that Indulgences are „iniquities of the Roman flatterers." ([28])
Now he knows better and is sure that the Papacy is
nothing but Babylon. ([29]) The whole force of the book
is directed against the seven Sacraments; for the time he
will allow only three: „Baptism, Penance and Bread." ([30])

With regard to the Eucharist he insists that the laity
should receive it under both kinds. Until then they were
excluded from this „not by the Church, but by the tyrants
of the Church, without the consent of the Church, i. e. of
the people of God. ([31]) „If one kind can be denied to
them, they might with the same right be deprived of a
part of baptism or of penance." ([32]) Luther does not yet
reject the Mass altogether, but under his hands it becomes
a quite different thing from what the Catholic Church believes it to be. The Mass is, according to him, nothing but
a divine promise of the remission of sins. ([33]) „Behold, o
man," says Christ, „ . . . out of mere charity I promise to
thee by these words (accipite et manducate etc.) without
any merit on thy part, the remission of all thy sins and
everlasting life. And that thou mayest be sure of this
my irrevocable promise, I shall deliver up my body and
shed my blood, confirming my promise with my death
and leaving to thee both as a sign and memorial of my

([28]) Indulgentiae sunt adulator-
um Romanorum nequitiae.
                Wittenb. II. 66ᴜ.
([29]) Scio nunc et certus sum,
Papatum esse regnum Babylonis.
Ibid.
([30]) Principio neganda mihi sunt

septem Sacramenta et tantum tria
pro tempore ponenda: Baptismus,
Poenitentia, Panis. Wittenb. II 68.
([31]) Ibid. 69.
([32]) Ibid. 68ᴜ. Is this perhaps
the „luminous explanation"?
([33]) Ibid. 72ᴜ, 73ᴜ.

promise." The Mass, says Luther, is only ¦the use of
a Sacrament," but it cannot be a sacrifice, since a sacrifice
is offered up, whilst in the Mass we only receive a promise. But a thing cannot at the same time be received
and offered up, nor can it be given and received by the
same person. ([34]) Though Luther defends the real presence,
he denies the transsubstantiation, ([35]) which he represents as
an invention of Aristotelic Philosophy.

When he proceeds to Baptism, he pours out a long
prayer of thanksgiving that at least this Sacrament has
remained unadulterated under all the abominations of Popery. ([36]) But alas! „Whereas Satan has not been able
to abolish the practice of baptism of children, he has managed to extinguish (the thought of) it in adults, so that
nowadays hardly anyone remembers, much less glories,
that he has been baptized, since so many other ways have
been found out to receive the forgiveness of sins and to
go to heaven." ([37]) This is especially the fault of the
Pope, „the man of sin and the son of perdition," ([38]) „the
source and author of all superstitious," who has done everything to promote monkery, but not to make Christians
proud of their baptism. And yet what riches does baptism
contain! „*A Christian or baptized man cannot, even if
he would, lose his salvation by any number of sins, except
if he refuses to believe. No sins can condemn him, except
the want of faith.*" ([39])

But Penance has been treated more shamefully by the
Papists. In their religion people have to look for salvation to the tyrannical power of the Pope! whilst Christ does
not speak of power but of faith! There is no *power* in
the Church, but only *ministry*. ([40]) Moreover the sorrow
for sins is wrongly urged! „Take care not to trust in
thy contrition or to attribute the remission of sins to thy

([31]) Ibid. 76. Does this perhaps
show „a thorough acquaintance
with the arguments of the adversaries"?

([35]) Ibid. 66.

([36]) Ibid. 77.
([37]) Ibid. 77B.
([38]) Ibid. 81.
([39]) Ibid. 78.
([40]) Ibid. 83B.

sorrow." ([41]) The words of Christ: „What you shall loose on earth etc." are said to every Christian. ([42]) — Of Luther's attacks on the other Sacraments we will only notice, that he proclaims again the universal priesthood and makes the „ministry" dependent on the commission given by the people. ([43]) Later on we shall have occasion to speak of his views on matrimony as expressed in this book.

In June 1520 Leo X issued the Bull „Exsurge Domine," in which 41 propositions of Luther were condemned and he himself was declared excommunicated, should he not recant within the space of 60 days. No doubt it was a great mistake that for Saxony the publication of this document should have been entrusted to Eck. He felt the difficulty himself, but had to give way to the express command of the Pope. ([44]) Eck's strong opposition to Luther made him appear in the eyes of the „Reformer's" friends as a personal enemy, and the hostile feeling which existed against him made the document which he brought with him all the more hateful. On 21st of September the Bull was published at Meissen, a few days later at Merseburg and Brandenburg. ([45]) In Leipzig Eck was insulted and threatened by a number of Wittenberg students. ([46]) The Universities of Wittenberg and Erfurt refused to receive the Bull, in many places it was torn to pieces. ([47])

It is difficult to understand why Köstlin ([48]) should call the style of the Bull bombastic or why he should find in it, with Luther, impious pride and pious hypocrisy. His assertion that the doctrine on justification by faith alone was not condemned by the Pope, because he had

([41]) Ibid. 84. Once more, is this perhaps „thorough knowledge of the arguments of the adversaries"? or even of the Catholic doctrine?
([42]) Ibid. 85.
([43]) Quid si cogerentur admittere, nos omnes esse aequaliter sacerdotes quotquot baptisati sumus? sicut revera sumus, illisque solum ministerium, nostro tamen consensu, commissum. Ibid. 89ʙ.
([44]) Wiedemann 153.
([45]) Ibid.
([46]) Ibid. — Riffel I. 235.
([47]) Wiedemann 156 seqq. Cfr. Janssen II. 111.
([48]) I. 379.

not the courage to condemn it,([49]) we will notice here, without making any comment. We give a part of the Bull which shows the Pope's feelings and a part of what may be called a Bull of Luther in juxtaposition, to enable the reader to judge of the style.

<table>
<tr><td>Leo X.</td><td>Luther:</td></tr>
</table>

Leo X.	Luther:
„Imitating the clemency of God, who does not wish the death of the sinner but that he should be converted and live, and forgetting all the insults which until now have been heaped upon us and upon the Apostolic See, we have resolved to make use of the utmost clemency and to do everything in our power that he (Luther) . . . may return from the above mentioned errors, that we may receive him like the prodigal son with benignity into the bosom of the Church. We therefore from our very heart exhort and conjure Luther and all his adherents by the bowels of the mercy of God . . . that they will desist from disturbing the Church's peace, unity and truth . . . If they obey . . . they shall find in us the affection of fatherly love" etc. ([50])	„Thus say I, Doctor Martinus Luther, Our Lord Jesus Christ's unworthy Evangelist: this article (justification by faith alone) shall remain untouched by the Roman Emperor, by the Turkish Emperor, by the Tartar Emperor, by the Persian Emperor, by the Pope, by all the Cardinals, Bishops, priests, monks, nuns, kings, princes, lords, by all the world and all the devils, and may they have the fire of hell on their heads, and not a word of thanks. Let this be mine, Doctor Luther's final decree, through the Holy Ghost, and the true holy Evangelium. ([51]) Sic volo, sic jubeo, sit pro ratione voluntas. ([52])

([49]) Ibid 381.
([50]) Wittenb. II. 62, 62b.
([51]) Erl. 25, 76.
([52]) Walch XXI. 314.

Miltiz had one more interview with Luther at Lichten-
berg (11. Oct. 1520) where the latter promised to write a
humble letter to the Pope. [53] How the Nuntius could
still entertain any hope to settle matters in a friendly way
is difficult to understand. If Leo X himself expected that
Luther might be brought back to obedience, the letter
which the „Reformer" wrote to him, must have completely
undeceived him. [54] The fact that the latter addresses
the Pope now with the words „Your Holiness," now with
the insultingly familiar „My Leo," „My good Leo" is significant. He declares that he has no illwill against or
thinks badly of the Pope's person, [55] but pities him, for
he is like a lamb among wolves, like Daniel in the lions'
den, like Ezechiel among scorpions. [56] He appeals to the
example of S. Bernard, when he presumes to tell the Pope
what his Curia is like. It is, he says, more corrupt than
Babylon and Sodom. „At one time the holiest of all, the
Church of Rome is now the most licentious den of robbers,
the most shameless brothel, the kingdom of sin, death and
hell. [57] Eck, Cajetanus and Miltiz get each a share of
his wrath. It is *their* fault of course, that peace has
not been established. „I have always offered peace and
wished for it." [58] Retractation is impossible. [59] „The
word of God must not be fettered. . I will not suffer the
laws of interpreting the word of God." [60] But „lest I

---

[53] Riffel I. 167. Köstlin I. 383.

[54] This letter is printed Wittenb. II. 1 seqq. (where however
the date is given wrongly as April
6th) also ap. De Wette I. 497.

[55] Köstlin (I. 384) says that
Luther nowhere speaks badly of
the person of Leo X. In the
Tischr. II. c. 20 § 138 there is a
most infamous charge against „Pope
Leo" and there is nothing to show
that Luther did not mean Leo X.
It would be indeed surprising if
this Pope had escaped from that
flood of venomous personal remarks which the „man of God"

poured out over all who were not
of his party. Erasmus, Emser, Eck,
Carlstadt, Cochlaeus, Witzel, Agricola and a hundred others had each
their ample share of it.

[56] Wittenb. II. 1 b.

[57] Ibid.

[58] Ibid. 2 b.

[59] Verbum deserere et negare
nec possum nec volo. Ibid. 1 b. —
Palinodiam ut canam, beatissime
Pater, non est quod ullus praesu-
mat. Ibidem 2 b.

[60] Leges interpretanti verbi Dei
non patior. Ibid.

should come with empty hands, Holy Father, I bring with me a little book dedicated to thee." This was his pamphlet „on Christian liberty" which accompanied the letter.

Before this remarkable document could reach Rome, Luther renewed (17. Nov.) before a notary and witnesses, his appeal from the Pope to the future Council, denouncing Leo X in the strongest terms ([61]) and calling upon all princes, to oppose „the incredible madness of the Pope". Hutten edited the Bull with a number of sarcastic notes. ([62])

The 10th of December 1520 witnessed an exciting spectacle which was to announce to the world, that Dr. Martin Luther had no more to do with the Pope. The students of Wittenberg, who had been invited by public placards, assembled at one of the towngates, where one of the Professors erected and lighted a pile. Then the new Evangelist stepped forward and threw the books of Canon Law and the recently published Papal Bull into the fire saying: „As thou hast saddened the holy of the Lord, so may eternal fire sadden thee." ([63]) Some books of Emser and Eck, likewise the Summa Angelica shared the same fate.([64]) On the day following this autodafe he lectured to the students (felici patrii sermonis elegantiâ, as Melanchthon([65]) says) on the abomination of Popery.

([61]) He appeals a praedicto Leone 1) tamquam ab iniquo, temerario tyrannicoque judice, 2) tamquam ab erroneo, indurato, per Scripturas sanctas damnato haeretico et apostata, 3) tamquam ab hoste, adversario, antichristo, oppressore totius sacrae Scripturae, 5) tamquam a blasphemo superbo contemptore sanctae Ecclesiae Dei et legitimi Concilii. Wittenb. II. 52. It would seem from this, that Luther's admirers have very little reason to be scandalized at Leo X's Bull.

([62]) Wittenb. II. 54 seqq.

([63]) Quia tu conturbasti sanctum Domini, ideoque te conturbet ignis aeternus. Wittenb. II. 129.

([64]) Luther issued a kind of Encyclica in which he announced „omnibus Christianae veritatis cultoribus et studiosis" what had happened. „Ego Martinus Lutherus, dictus Theologiae Doctor, notifico in universum omnibus, mea voluntate, consilio et opera ... exustos esse Pontificis Romani libros et nonnullorum ejus discipulorum." Ibid. 125. — He wrote to Staupitz: Exussi libros Papae et Bullam primum trepidus et orans, sed nunc lactior quam ullo alio totius vitae facto. De Wette I. 542.

([65]) Wittenb. II. 129.

„This burning does not say much; it would be better, if the Pope himself i. e. the Papal See could be burned. And if you do not from your very hearts renounce Popery, you cannot save your souls." ([66])

And Melanchthon, the „man of a tender Christian mind" adds: „That Luther's words were true, noone can doubt, except those that are more stupid, than a block of wood, as indeed the Papists are to a man." ([67])

We acknowledge the compliment.

([66]) Ibid. — Cfr. De Wette I. 522: Impossibile est enim salvos fieri qui huic Bullae aut faverunt aut non repugnaverunt. Even De Wette says in a note: This is rather strong.

([67]) ... nisi trunco sit stupidior, cujusmodi sunt papastri ad unum omnes. Wittenb. l. c.

Chapter VI

Luther at Worms.

„This man will never make me a heretic."
Charles V.

Marino Caracciolo and Hieronymus Aleander, both men of unblemished character, of ability and learning, and both afterwards as Cardinals ornaments of the Church,([1]) were sent out by Leo X as Papal Legates, to end if possible the religious disturbances in Germany, for wich purpose they were to secure the cooperation of the Emperor Charles V. Whilst Caracciolo's task was more of a political nature, Aleander played a prominent part in the negotiations concerning Luther. That on account of his exertions he should have received a bad name with the Protestant party, is not more than would be expected. The „Reformer" gave a good example. He called Aleander a Jew, who however could not be called a Pharisee, as he did not believe in the Resurrection; he charged him with avarice, vainglory, voluptuousness etc.([2]) Curious, that everybody who did not join Luther had those vices!

Hutten was lying in ambush for the legates, but to his greatest grief he missed them, a misfortune which also his friend Luther greatly deplored.([3]) As the intention of Hutten is so frankly acknowledged, we need not suppose

([1]) See Freib. Kirchenlexicon (2nd edit.) I. 470, II. 1930.
([2]) Walch XV. 1583.
([3]) Gaudeo Huttenum prodiisse,

atque utinam aut Marinum aut Aleandrum intercepisset! Letter to Spal. De Wette I. 523.

that the repeated warnings which Aleander received even
at Worms were merely based on fancies. He frequently
complains of the dangers to which he is exposed.([4]) In a
letter to Eobanus Hutten says that if the legates have escaped, it certainly is not *his* fault. ([5])

The legates were the bearers of a Papal Breve to the
Elector Frederick of Saxony, whom they met at Cologne.
In this document the Pope accuses himself of having been
so far too lenient with Luther, ([6]) but as the latter's pride
cannot be cured by charity, ([7]) severity has become necessary, and Frederick is exhorted to do everything in his
power to supress the new heresy. Balan gives the original
text of this Breve from the Vatican Archives; that which
is printed in Luther's works, ([8]) is a spurious concoction.
Leo X does *not* demand, that Luther should be sent to
Rome as a prisoner, ([9]) on the contrary, Aleander was to
offer him safe conduct in case that he should express a
wish to be heard in Rome. ([10]) The Elector who strongly
inclined to the side of Luther and whom, as we have seen
above, Erasmus confirmed in this favourable opinion by
his „axiomata," got rid of the legates by various excuses,
v. gr. that the effect of the appeal ought to be waited for,
that Luther had not been sufficiently convicted of heresy

([4]) Casulano ben mi consiliò
che guardasse come io andasse
per camino, perchè auribus suis
havea udito da Hutteno, che cer-
cava farmi gran dispiacere. Balan
25. — Communi omnium rumore
circumfertur che Hutten con li
suoi conjurati me cercano am-
mazzar e sono avisato . . . che io
me guardi, che a gran pena la
scaparò di questa Germania.
                          Ibid. 31.

([5]) Ap. Janssen II. 172.

([6]) nos . . . diutius esse passos,
quam forsitan pastoralis curae vi-
gilantia postulabat: sed ea spe esse
passos, quod illum ad poenitentiam
converti . . . optavimus. Balan 1.

([7]) Vicit malum virus superbiae
omnem charitatis medicinam.
                          Ibid. 2.

([8]) Wittenb. II. 51.

([9]) The Pope is made to say:
Nobilitas Tua . . . Lutherum capi,
captumque ad nostram instantiam
custodiri curet et studeat.
                          Ibid. 51 B.

([10]) The Instruction sent to
Aleander says: Si Martinus vellet
hodie ad romanam Curiam venire
et ibi audiri, paratus est S^{mus} D. N.
juxta formam bullae dare sibi plen-
issimum salvum conductum et li-
bentissimum eum audire. Balan. 9.

7

etc.([11])   His approval of the burning of the Papal Bull
soon showed how those excuses were meant.

On January 28th 1521 Charles V opened the Diet of
Worms which has become so famous. He had commanded
Frederick to bring Luther with him; but the Elector
began to fear for the safety of his protégé and wished
to keep him back. When however Luther's opinion was
asked, he declared that he was ready to appear, and
that even illness would not prevent him from obeying
the summons. „For it is certain that, when the Emperor
calls us, God calls us. But if they should use force, as
probably they will" (we doubt very much that Luther was
under any apprehension of this sort) „we must put the
matter into God's hands." For the sake of the Emperor
he hopes that his blood will not be shed, for has not
Sigismund been most unfortunate ever since the execution
of Huss?([12])   When about a month afterwards in a letter
to Frederick he expressed again his readiness to go to
Worms if he should be granted safeconduct,([13]) he knew
already, as appears from a letter to Spalatinus,([14]) that
Charles V had revoked his command. The reason of this
change was that the period of 60 days allowed by the
Bull of Leo X had elapsed,([15]) and the burning of this
same document must have convinced the Emperor, that
all endeavours for reconciliation would be futile.([16]) As
the obstinacy of the Wittenberg monk could no longer be
doubted, another Bull was issued (3. January), in which
he was definitely declared a heretic and the interdict was
put on all places where he should sojourn. Of course
Luther called this a „Satanissima Bulla;" at the same time
he expressed his joy, that in virtue of it he might consider

([11]) The Elector's answer Wittenb. II. 122.
   ([12]) De Wette I. 535 (29. Dec.
1520).
   ([13]) „sufficiente securitate et libero securo conductu contra omnem vim". Ibid. 551 (25. Jan. 1521).

([14]) Cum dolore legi novissimas
Caroli literas revocatorias prioris
instituti. Ibid. 544 (16. Jan 1521).

([15]) Riffel I. 257.

([16]) Janssen II. 149.

himself freed from all papal laws, but he did not yet throw off the monk's cowl or leave the monastery. ([17]) Also afterwards he seems to have been proud of being excommunicated. „By the grace of God," he wrote in the autumn of 1521, „I am in the Pope's excommunication and greatest disgrace." ([18])

The antipapal feeling at Wittenberg found vent in a demonstration of the students at the time of Carneval. Masks representing the Pope and his Court were carried about; they were first destined to be drowned, but a general hunt after them through the town was found to be more exhilarating. Luther called this, in a letter to his friend Spalatinus, very witty. ([19]) With this same letter he sent a little pamphlet, which was calculated to strengthen his authority amongst the people and to obviate the effects of the Bull. It is an instruction to penitents, ([20]) to whom absolution might be denied on account of their persisting in reading the books which were forbidden by the Pope as heretical. Luther advises such penitents to convince the confessors of the injustice of the refusal, to remind them that the Bull is absolutely worthless etc., and if all this has no effect, to give up Sacrament, Altar, priest and Church. ([21]) The „ipse dixit" is stamped on every line of this pamphlet.

In a letter to the Elector Frederick, Luther once more declares in those vague terms which he had used before and the meaning of which entirely depended on his own interpretation, that he was ready „to honour the Roman Church

---

([17]) Ab ordinis et Papae legibus solutus sum et excommunicatus autoritate Bullae: quod gaudeo et amplector, nisi quod vestem et locum non relinquo.
De Wette I. 568.

([18]) Der Schreiber (ist) ein verachtet und vordampte Person. Ich bin von Gottis Gnaden in des Papsts Bann und allerhohisten Ungnaden, dazu in grossem Vormaledeyen und Hass seiner lieben Junger.
De Wette II. 98.

([19]) Juventus nostra his diebus bacchanalibus nimis ludicre Papam personatum circumvexerunt sublimem et pompaticum ... festivo valde et arguto invento.
De Wetfe I. 561.

([20]) Dr. M. L.'s Unterricht an alle Beichtkinder. Walch XIX. 1007.

([21]) lass fahren Sacrament, altar, pfaf, Kirchen. Ibid. 1012.

in all humility, so as not to prefer to her anything in heaven
or on earth, except God and God's word, „therefore I am
willing to retract those points, the error of which is proved
to me." (²²) Five days later he writes to a friend *how* he
is going to retract: „Whereas formerly I called the Pope
the Vicar of Christ, I now recant and say: The Pope is
the adversary of Christ and the apostle of the devil." (²³)

It was principally owing to the exertions of Frederick
of Saxony, that many members of the Diet wished to
have Luther once more examined. The fact that the
highest authority in the Church had delivered its sentence
was not yet sufficient. Luther, it was urged, must not be
condemned without having been heard or without having
a chance of defending himself. (²⁴) It was Aleander's duty
to oppose such ideas which, after the supreme tribunal
had spoken, were absolutely irreconcilable with the principle
of authority on which the Church is based, and he dis-
charged his duty in an admirable way. He first published
(13 Febr.) the above mentioned Papal Bull which finally
condemned Luther's teaching as heresy, and a in most
effective speech explained the real meaning of this new
heresy and the revolution which it was apt to produce also
in the nation; he demanded that the only remaining means
should be resorted to, viz. that according to the existing
laws Luther should fall under the ban of the Empire. It
is greatly to be regretted that we have not the original
text of this speech; Aleander never wrote it down, he
says that he had little time to prepare himself. (²⁵) The

(²²) De Wette I. 575.

(²³) Papam prius dixi esse Christi
vicarium, nunc revoco et dico: Papa
est Christi adversarius et apostolus
diaboli.   Ibid. 580.

(²⁴) Naturally Luther was very
much pleased with such news. He
wrote to Staupitz: Wormatiae nihil contra me adhuc actum, etsi
miro furore mihi moliantur mala.
Spalatinus scribit tantum favoris
Evangelio esse istic, ut me inaud-

itum et inconvictum damnari non
speret. De Wette I. 556. — The
Elector kept up his courage. Princeps e Wormatia scripsit ad me ut
intelligam, non esse adhuc rem in
nido Papistarum. Ibid. 569.

(²⁵) Habui horationem per forse
tre hore et più, nella qual ancor-
chè io havesse havuto pocco spatio
a pensarci ... me trovai con la
grazia di Dio sì in ordine, che an-
corchè dicesse assai in tre hore,

speech as reported by Pallavicini [26] is based on other
documents emanating from Aleander, [27] but may be considered to contain the substance of the legate's remarks.
According to Seckendorf [28] Aleander calumniated Luther
or distorted his meaning, by accusing him of having
taught the articles on universal priesthood, the want of
freedom in the human will etc. But we have shown before,
that this was perfectly correct. Aleander's speech produced
a great effect, [29] especially in the Emperor and the Spanish
Grandees who were present, but some of Luther's noble
allies expressed their displeasure. [30]

The action of Charles V with regard to Luther shows
that he thoroughly understood his position, much better
than many of his predecessors. We must not lose sight
of the idea on which the Empire was based. It was the
Emperor's duty not only to remain faithful to the Church
himself, but also to protect the Church, and at his coron-
ation Charles had taken a solemn oath to that effect.
Empire and Church had to go hand in hand to promote
and consolidate the „Civitas Dei" on earth. From the
time of Constantine, Theodosius and Justinian the universally acknowledged principle, that the divine truth had
been deposited by the Son of God with his Church, made
heresy a crime not only in the eyes of this Church, but
also a crime against the Christian Empire. „Each heretical doctrine of the middle ages," says Döllinger," [31] either
clearly contained revolutionary principles or led to them
i. e. the more they would have prevailed, the greater a
political and social revolution would have taken place.
The gnostic sects, the Kathari and Albigenses, sects which
after all caused the hard and inexorable laws of the middle

harrei certo possuto dirne ancor
quatro. Balan 56.

[26] I. 75 seqq.
[27] They are given by Balan
69. 87
[28] Lib. I. 37. § 91.
[29] Köstlin I. 423.
[30] „me faceano di brutti visi".

Aleander ap. Balan 57. The legate says that he is considered to
have spoken „apte et apposite ad
causam et feliciter"; in his own
opinion „mediocriter et non omnino infeliciter. Ibid. 56.
    [31] Kirche und Kirchen, 51.
Cfr. Hamb. Briefe I. 55.

ages against heresy and which had to be put down in
bloody wars, were the Socialists and Communists of the
time. They attacked matrimony, family and property. If
they had been victorious, the world would have relapsed
into barbarism and pagan licentiousness."

If the „Reformers" themselves in word and practice
considered heresy as a capital crime, ([32]) Charles V cannot
be blamed for protecting the unity of the Church without
coming to such extremes.([33]) He acknowledged that real
grievances existed([34]) and promised to write to the Pope for
their speedy suppression, but he insisted that such complaints about persons and administration should not by any
means be mixed up with matters concerning faith. ([35]) Disputation with Luther, he continued, was out of the question,
as he was finally condemned by the proper ecclesiastical
authority. If Luther came to Worms, he would only have
to answer the question, whether he confessed to have written
the books condemned by the Holy See; if he refused to
recant, he would have to expect punishment according to the
existing laws of the Empire, but only *after the expiration of
the safeduct.* The result of the deliberations was, that Luther

([32]) In 1521 Bucer said in the
pulpit that Servetus had deserved
the most ignominious death; everybody knows that this man was really burnt as a heretic by command of Calvin. The „man of a
tender Christian mind", Melanchthon, wrote about this execution:
„Pium et memorabile ad omnem
posteritatem exemplum." Corp.
Ref. 9, 133. For further examples
of „tolerance" on the part of the
Reformers see Hergenröther, Kath.
Kirche und christl. Staat, Freib.
440 seqq.: and Kirche oder Protest. 60 seqq.

([33]) Aleander praises the Emperor's disposition. Caesar ha il
meglior animo, che homo nascesse
già mille anni e se lui non fusse
tale, certo le cose nostre per pri-
vati affetti sarebbero molto intri-

cate. Balan 27. On the other side
Luther pities the Emperor. From
the Wartburg he writes about him
to Spalatinus: Carolum impeti bel-
lis nihil mirum, nihilque unquam
habebit prosperum, et cogetur ali-
enae impietatis poenam solvere;
infelix juvenis, quod veritatem
Wormatiae malis consultoribus in
faciem sic repudiarit.
                De Wette II. 30.

([34]) So did Aleander, who in
his report to the Vice-Chancellor
begs of him „per l'amor di Dio"
to see that the existing abuses are
abolished. Balan 33.

([35]) Sù Maestà respose prudenter
che le querele di Roma lui non
voleva che se mescolassero con la
cosa di Luther, che toccava la fede.
Ibid. 73.

should be summoned to Worms, not for the sake of
disputation, but that he might declare whether or not he
meant to submit to the Church. Aleander justly remarked
that, considering the man's character, this step would prove
absolutely useless, for an angel from heaven would not
make him change his opinion. Already before the opening
of the Diet the legate had said that all such hope was
only a „phantasia." (³⁶)

Caspar Sturm, the imperial herald, was despatched to
Wittenberg to summon Luther and to hand over to him
the safeconduct. (³⁷) The „Reformer" started on the 2nd
of April. Was his obedience to the summons really an
act of a most extraordinary heroism? It would have been,
if death or imprisonment had awaited him at his journey's
end, but he travelled under the protection of the Emperor,
who had given his word of honour, that he should freely
come and freely return; his friends Hutten and Sickingen
were only a day's journey from Worms with their armed
bands, ready to pounce upon the town; at the Diet Frederick of Saxony was as busy as possible to spread Lutheran principles and to protect Lutheran interests. Under
these circumstances it was a very cheap boast of Luther,
that he would have gone to Worms, „if there had been
as many devils as there were tiles on the roofs" (³⁸) and
that he was prepared „to jump into the mouth of Behe-
moth". Of this fact of appearing before the Emperor and
the Diet he remained proud all his life, boasting of it
numberless times. He must have felt all the more keenly
the bitter words which Münzer threw into his teeth, that the
only real danger at Worms had been from his noble friends,
should he have disappointed them. „For the fact that you
have appeared before the diet, thanks are due to the German nobility, whose mouths you had so well smeared with

---

(³⁶) Ibid. 26.
(³⁷) This document is to be
found in latin ap. Balan 120; in
German ap. Köhler 328.

(³⁸) De Wette II. 139. Walch
XVI. 14.

honey. They thought that your preaching would bring
in Bohemian presents, convents and monasteries, which
you promise to the princes. If you had wavered at Worms,
you would have been killed by the nobility." ([39])
At Erfurt Luther was received by the University with
the greatest honours; Crotus, the Rector, praised him in
a bombastic speech. ([40]) On the day following his arrival
he preached in the Augustinian Church; his sermon, though
professedly about justification, was spiced with invectives
against the Pope and the clergy. ([41]) The consequence
was, that on the day after his departure (he started for
Gotha on the 8th of April) the mob attacked the houses
of the clergy and did great damage, whilst their inhabitants barely escaped personal illtreatment by a precipitate
flight. ([42]) Nothing was done by the Magistrates to punish
the tumultuants. At Reinhardsbrunn Luther exhorted his
host „to say an Our Father for Our Lord Christ, that
His Father would be propitious to him, for if His cause
is safe, mine also is won". ([43]) From Frankfurt he addressed a letter to Spalatinus, who as chaplain to Frederick was already at Worms, announcing his coming in
spite of the devil who, he supposed, was trying to keep
him back through illness. ([44]) On the 16th of April he
made his entry into Worms, where he was received by
the people partly with enthusiasm, partly with curiosity.
His friends had done their best to stir up the feelings of
the masses, in whose eyes it was not difficult to represent
Luther as a hero; ([45]) with them his violent and abusive
language went farther than volumes of theological argu-

([39]) Riffel I. 600.
([40]) Kampschulte II. 96.
([41]) Erl. 17, 98 seqq. see Kampschulte II. 97.
([42]) Ibid. 106 seqq.
([43]) Ratzeberger 50.
([44]) Venimus, etsi non uno
morbo me satan impedire molitus
sit. Intrabimus Wormatiam invitis
omnibus portis inferi et potestatibus
aeris. De Wette I. 586.

([45]) La plebe fertur praeceps ad
dicta aliorum et si lassa trasportare.
Balan 32. Cfr. Luther's own words
directed against the Anabaptists:
When the mob hear big sounding
invectives, they are persuaded and
believe at once without asking
for reasons. Walch XVII. 2685.
But it was to this that he owed
in great measure his own success.

ments would have done. A press had been set up at
Worms for the purpose of scattering his writings,([46])
numerous portraits represented him with a halo round his
head, or with a dove, the symbol of the Holy Ghost,
above him.([47]) Aleander also mentions one woodcut, where
Luther with a book and Hutten with his hand on the sword
were put together with the inscription: „The defenders of
Christian liberty.“ ([48]) Hutten sent several letters from the
Ebernburg, Sickingen's stronghold, to assure his friend of
his ardent admiration; he would not, he said, shrink from
anything.([49]) His ruffianly character appears also from the
„Invectivae“ which he published against the legates. In
the plainest words he threatened Aleander with murder.([50])

On the day after his arrival (17. April), Luther appeared for the first time before the Emperor and the members of the Diet. Joannes ab Acie (von Eck), the official
of the Archbishop of Treves, put two questions to him
1) whether he acknowledged himself the author of certain
books put before him, 2) whether he was willing to retract.([51]) To the first question Luther answered in the af-
firmative, as to the second he demanded time to deliberate. This latter reply caused general surprise; to his
friends because it seemed to imply some wavering on his
part; to his opponents because, knowing for what purpose

([46]) Li Lutherani ogni dì pio-
veno nuovi libri sì in Alemanno
come in latino, et tenono qui uno
impressore, dove mai avanti fù più
tal mestieri, nè si vendono altri
libri qui, che de Luther. Balan 99.

([47]) L'hanno depento da nuovo
con la colomba in capo et la croce
di nostro Signore, et in altre im-
agini con la diadema irradiata.
                                        Ibid. 40.

([48]) Heri in un medesimo folio
vidi la immagine di Luther con
un libro in mano et la imagine
di Hutten con la mano alla spata,
et sopra era in belle lettere: Chris-

tianae libertatis propugnatoribus
M. Luthero, Ulrico ab Huten.
                                        Ibid. 103.

([49]) Equidem atrocissima omnia
concipio. Wittenb. II. 182B.

([50]) Omne adhibebo studium, ut
qui furore, amentia, scelere, ini-
quitate gravis accessisti, vita inanis
hinc efferaris. Hutten, Opp. IV.
244. Caracciolo gets the following
compliment: Omnium qui unquam
furati sunt hic, furacissime! omnium raptorum violentissime, omnium impostorum vaferrime, astut-
issime, iniquissime. Ibid. 250.

([51]) Acta comparitionis Lutheri
in Diaeta Wormatiensi.
                                        Balan. 175.

he had been summoned, he might be expected to have
prepared his answer. However, a day was granted to him
to make up his mind, and when on the afternoon of the
18th he appeared for the second time, he showed much
more confidence and courage than on the preceding day
and declared both in German and in Latin, that a retractation was impossible on his part, except if he should be
convinced of his errors from evident reasons or from the
testimony of Holy Scripture. He added: „Gott helff mir.
Amen." The other words attributed to him: „Hier stehe
ich, ich kann nicht anders" are not in the „Acta", nor in
the reports published by the Lutheran party immediately
after the Diet, though they are in the Wittenberg Edition
of 1546. After all it matters very little, whether he said
them or not, for that which he certainly said, sufficiently
expresses his final determination not to give way to authority, but to consider himself supreme judge in religious matters, especially with regard to the sense of the
Bible. ([52])

The Emperor issued a decree (19. April) in which he
gave expression to his own faithful adherence to the Catholic Church and commanded that Luther should leave
Worms under the imperial safeconduct, but should not be
allowed to preach on his way. But Frederick of Saxony
did not give up his endeavours for his protégé. At his
instigation the members of the Diet sent (20. April) a
memoriale to Charles, asking him to allow another conference with the monk, who perhaps might be convinced
of his errors, this would also, they added, stop the mouths
of the people, who otherwise would say that Luther had

([52]) Nisi convictus fuero testimoniis scripturarum aut ratione
evidenti ... et victus sim scripturis a me edoctis et capta conscientia in verbis Dei, revocare
neque possum neque volo quidquid, cum contra conscientiam
agere neque tutum neque integrum
sit. Balan 183. — This text seems
to be much more intelligible than
that wich appears in the Wittenberg Edition (II. 173) and which
is quoted by Seckendorf (Lib. I.
41. § 154) and translated by Köstlin (I. 452) „victus sum scripturis
a me adductis, captaque est conscientia in verbis Dei, revocare neque possum neque volo."

been condemned unheard; at any rate it would be an act of charity.([53]) Charles allowed for this purpose three days, and after their expiration another two days. But all endeavours of the Elector Richard of Treves, of Cochlaeus and other theologians proved fruitless, as might have been expected. Luther departed under the protection of the Emperor, but when his safeconduct came to an end, he was under the „Reichsacht", the ban of the Empire.

([53]) affinque le dict Luther ne puist dire que les articles esquelz il a erre ne luy aient este proposes, affin aussy que le commun peuple que ignore ces choses icy ne estime que ledict Luther ait este condamne sans estre ouy.

Balan 189.

Chapter VII

Luther and the Bible.

Scriptura „per sese certissima, facillima,
apertissima, sui ipsius interpres".
Luther. Wittenb. II. 100.

Scripturas sanctas sciat se nemo *degustasse*
satis, nisi qui centum annis cum Prophetis ...
Christo et Apostolis Ecclesias gubernarit.
Idem Luther. Tischr. I. c. 1. § 10.

On the 26th of April Luther left Worms, apparently to return to Wittenberg. In spite of the prohibition of the Emperor he preached at Hersfeld and at Eisenach; in the former place he was solemnly received by the abbot, ([1]) in the latter the parishpriest protested invain. By this act Luther really lost the right to the safeconduct, but he excused himself by saying that he had not consented to the condition, and if he had, he would not be bound by it, as it was sinful. ([2])

In order to protect him from the consequences of the imperial decree, Frederick of Saxony had devised a plan to put him into a safe place, but by unknown people and apparently by force, so that his own name should not suffer. This plan had been communicated to Luther and

---

([1]) Senatus intra portas nos excepit ... (abbas) in monasterio suo pavit nos laute. De Wette II. 6.

([2]) Isenaci praedicavi, sed timido parocho et notario testibusque praesentibus coram me protestante ... Ita et Wormatiae forte audies per haec a me solutam fidem, sed non est soluta. In mea enim potestate non erat ea conditio, ut verbum Dei non esset alligatum, nec pepigi in eam, et si pepigissem, quia contra Deum fuisset, servanda non fuisset. Ibidem.

to a few of his friends before they left Worms. (^{3}) During the journey he wrote from Frankfurt to Lucas Cranach,
the painter: „I shall have to be secreted somewhere, but
I myself do not know yet where." (^{4}) When therefore on
the 4th of May, near Altenstein, a small band of horsemen
attacked the party, (^{5}) he was able to whisper into friend
Amsdorf's ear: „Be of good heart, they are our friends." (^{6})
Apparently yielding to force he mounted the horse offered
to him and allowed himself to be conducted to the Wartburg which was not very far distant. This arrangement,
though providing for his safety, was not quite to his liking, as he would have preferred to push on his revolutionary work publicly and amongst the masses. (^{7}) To
ensure his incognito he put aside the monk's cowl, donn-
ed the dress of a knight and allowed his hair and beard
to grow. (^{8}) The castle which three centuries before had
been graced with the presence of one of the most amiable
Saints that ever lived, S. Elizabeth of Thüringen, now harboured for then months „Squire George" (Junker Jörg)
under which name Luther was known to those about
him. (^{9}) His life on the Wartburg seems to have been a
curious mixture of idleness, (^{10}) despair, (^{11}) temptations, (^{12})
a little hunting (from which he took an opportunity to

(^{3}) Seckend. Lib. I. 42. § 96.
(^{4}) De Wette I. 588.
(^{5}) Ratzeberger 53.
(^{6}) Köhler 96.
· (^{7}) Letter to Melanchthon: In-
vitus admisi. Verebar ego ne aciem
deserere viderer ... Nihil magis
opto, quam furoribus adversarior-
um occurrere objecto jugulo. De
Wette II. 1. — Letter to Agricola:
Ego mirabilis captivus qui et volens
et nolens hic sedeo; volens quia
Deus ita vult: nolens quia optem
in publico stare pro verbo. Ibid. 4.

(^{8}) Ita sum hic exutus vestibus
meis et equestribus indutus, comam
et barbam nutriens, ut tu me dif-
ficile nosses, cum ipse me jam
dudum non noverim.
De Wette II. 7.

(^{9}) His letters are dated: Ex
monte, ex Pathmo mea, ex loco
peregrinationis meae, in regione
avium, inter volucres de ramo
suaviter cantantes etc.

(^{10}) nunc sum hic otiosus. De
Wette II. 3. — Octo jam dies sunt
quod nihil scribo neque oro, neque
studeo, partim tentationibus carnis,
partim alia molestia vexatus.
Ibid. 22.

(^{11}) nescio an, quia vos non
oratis pro me. Deus a me aversus
sit.   Ibid.

(^{12}) ... cum ego hic insensatus
et induratus sedeam in otio, proh
dolor parum orans. nihil gemens
pro Ecclesia Dei: quin carnis meae
indomitae uror magnis ignibus:
summa, qui fervere spiritu debeo,

make some pious reflexions on the diabolical snares of the Pope) ([13]), a great deal of good feeding, ([14]) work ([15]) and rage. ([16]) Some of his most venomous pamphlets were written on the Wartburg, against Latomus of Louvain, ([17]) the University of Paris ([18]) the Pope, ([19]) and against monastic vows. A more important work was his translation of the New Testament.

Though only in 1534 he published the whole of the Scriptures translated by him, some remarks about the „Reformer" in connexion with the Bible may not be out of place where we see him launch part of it.

It has been shown above, in the introductory chapter, that nothing could be more unfounded than the statement made frequently by Luther himself([20]) and more frequently repeated by his admirers, that before him the Holy Scriptures were unknown to the people. But as he declared the Bible to be the *only* rule of faith, it was of course his interest to promote still farther its circulation among the masses; moreover, a translation emanating from his pen was sure to be a success, as he was becoming more and more popular. Finally, the version which he gave, containing so many arbitrary additions and changes in

---

ferveo carne, libidine, pigritia, otio, somnolentia. Ibid.

([13]) DeWette II. 44: The hounds killed a hare which he intended to keep alive; sic saevit Papa et satan, ut servatas etiam animas perdat, nihil moratus *meam* operam. Denique satur sum ejus venationis, dulciorem arbitror, qua jaculis et sagittis ursi, lupi, apri, vulpes et id genus magistrorum impiorum confodiuntur.

([14]) Ego otiosus hic et crapulosus sedeo tota die. DeWette II.6.

([15]) Ego hic otiosissimus et negotiosissimus sum. Hebraica et Graeca disco et sine intermissione scribo. Ibid.

([16]) In his letters the Duke of Saxony receives the title: Porcus Dresdensis, the legates: galeriti

upupae (De Wette II. 7. 9), the Canon Law is „Papae excrementa venenosa" (Ibid. 20) etc.

([17]) Rationis Latomianae pro incendiariis Lovaniensis scholae sophistis redditae Lutherana confutatio. Wittenb. II. 223 seqq.

([18]) We have given a specimen of this production above, page 83.

([19]) He published a satirical commentary to the Bulla Coenae under the title: „Bulla vom Abendfressen des allerheiligsten Herrn des Papstes" (Walch XV. 2127), exceedingly rich in invectives and slang.

([20]) 22. Febr. dicebat (Lutherus) de insigni et horrenda caecitate Papistarum. Nam ante 30 annos nullus legit Bibliam, eratque omnibus ignota. Lauterb. 36.

favour of his „Evangelium", would only help to make the same „Evangelium" more acceptable to the people. That his translation surpasses those which had been published before him in the perfection of language, nobody will deny, but this is here a matter of less than secondary importance. As amongst Protestants he is so universally looked up to as „the hero of the Bible" it may be well to examine a little his claim to such a title. Let us put the question: Has he treated the Bible i. e. the word of God, as it deserves to be treated? The well known Bunsen says, that Luther's translation, though showing everywhere his genius, is the most inaccurate of all and wants correction in at least 3000 places, ([21]) but let the reader judge for himself from some facts.

. If we were to collect all the selfcontradictions of Luther (N. B. not of Luther *before* versus Luther *after* his apostasy, but of the „Reformer" versus himself) we might fill a goodsized volume.([22]) Though he stuck to his fundamental teachings until death, (not however without the most harassing and excruciating doubts), he either admitted or rejected other points, just as it suited him at the moment. If we take for instance his opinion of the early Fathers of the Church, we generally find that he has nothing but contempt or imprecations for them. „One might just as well strain milk through a coalsack, as expect truth from the Fathers";([23]) to Hieronymus he assigns unhesitatingly a place in hell.([24]) But when the controversy with the „Sacramentarians" broke out and when against them Luther had to prove that Christ is really present in Holy

---

([21]) Nippold, Bunsen, Leipz. 1871. III. 483.

([24]) Some of the most glaring of them will be found in Arndt, Blumenstrauss aus Luther's Werken. Berlin. — Arndt, formerly a Lutheran minister, was led back to the Catholic Church through the study of the „Reformer's" works; so was Evers.

([23]) Wenn das Wort Gottes zu den Vätern kömpt, so gemanet mich's gleich, als wenn einer Milch seiget durch einen Kolsack, da die Milch muss schwarz und verderbet werden. Tischr.

([24]) De servo arb.
                    Wittenb. II. 516b.

Eucharist, he appealed to the Fathers without saying anything about a coalsack; on that occasion he called them
„the dear Fathers". (²⁵)

In a similar way he was able to speak about to Bible
in an anything but respectful manner, whenever he found
it difficult to get over some texts, which his opponents
urged against his „Evangelium". „The Papists insist much
on the Scriptures (this is a very valuable concession!) ...
but I do not care for that. I trust in Christ, who is truly
the Master and Emperor of the Scriptures. I do not care
for all the sayings of the Bible, if you were to bring forward ever so many more of them against me. I have on
my part the Lord and Master of the Bible." (²⁶)

It would be a great mistake to suppose that Luther
was the man to take up the Bible with an unprejudiced
mind and calmly to examine whether his „Evangelium"
was contained in it or not. There was *first* his doctrine,
that doctrine which, as he proudly said, he would not
have judged even by Angels (²⁷), and *then* the Bible had
· to be made to appear favourable to it. For instance: He
intends to prove his „Evangelium" from S. Paul's Epistle
to the Romans, but first he takes care to instruct his readers how they must understand the words contained in it,
on which the meaning of that Epistle depends: law, sin,
grace, faith, justice, flesh, spirit etc. viz. in his own, Luther's, sense. (²⁸) With such trickery everything can be
proved from the Bible.

(²⁵) Letter to Albr. von Brandenburg. Walch XX. 2088.
(²⁶) Wittenb. I. 147.
(²⁷) Erl. 28, 144.
(²⁸) Primum natura vocabulorum et tropi Apostoli nobis diligenter scrutandi et observandi sunt.
Ante omnia, quid sibi Paulus his
et id genus vocabulis velit: lex,
peccatum, gratia, fides etc. Alias,
quantum vis legas diligenter, opem
omnem luseris. Wittenb. V. 96.
After determining the meaning of

each of the above words of S. Paul
in his own sense, he continues:
Nisi in eum modum accipias haec
vocabula, neque epistolam hanc
Pauli, neque ullos alios libros Divinae Scripturae intelliges. Pro-
inde sive Hieronymus sit, sive Augustinus, sive Ambrosius, sive Origenes, breviter quicunque tandem
sint scriptores, nihil te moveat
auctoritas hominum, sed tamquam
pestem fuge omnes. Ibid. 98.

· But Luther went much farther than this. He presumed to judge whether a book belonged to the Bible or not, merely from its appearing favourable or unfavourable to his teaching. S. James denies the sufficiency of faith for salvation, saying: „Faith without works is dead"; this is enough for Luther to reject the whole Epistle of S. James, to call it a straw-epistle and to declare that he will not admit it into his Bible. (²⁹) Even with regard to the books of the Bible which he means to admit, he makes a great distinction as to their interior value, according as they seem more or less favourable to the „Evangelium". „As John writes little about Christ's works, but very much about his teaching, and as on the other hand the other three Evangelists relate many of his works, but few of his words, John's Evangelium is the right, choice, chief Evangelium and is to be far preferred to the three others. Thus also S. Paul's and S. Peter's epistles are far above the three Gospels of Matthew, Mark and Luke." (³⁰) The Apocalypse is distasteful to him: „As to the Revelation of John, let everybody please himself . . . I find many things defective in this book, which make me consider it neither apostolic nor prophetic . . . The Apostles did not concern themselves with visions." (³¹)

Nor did Luther shrink from positive falsifications of the sacred text, to make his „Evangelium" more•plausible. S. Paul says: „The law worketh wrath" (Rom IV. 15) Luther puts in a word of his own, translating „The law worketh *only* wrath". (³²) Again S. Paul says: „By the law is the knowledge of sin" (Rom. III. 20) and again Luther puts in a word of his own, translating: „By the

(²⁹) . . . eine recht stroherne Epistel. Dieser Jacobus thut nicht mehr denn treibet zu dem Gesetz und seinen Werken und wirft unördig eines ins andere. Introd. to the New. Test. of 1522. Luther's disciples followed his example in this matter. Althamer said of S. James: mentitur in caput suum; Palladius called the epistle: Scopae dissolutae, Bugenhagen said it contained impium argumentum.

Döll. III. 359.

(³⁰) Walch XIV. 104.
(³¹) Introd. to the New. Test.
(³²) In the editions published after 1530 the „only" is omitted. See Döll. III. 140.

law is *only* the knowledge of sin." This little word *only*
changes the whole meaning of the texts. If there, it would
represent S. Paul as favourable to the peculiar teaching of
Luther, which will be more fully explained in another place,
that the commandments were not given by God that we
should keep them, but that we should see the impossibility
of keeping them.

In the same third chapter of the Epistle to the Romans
S. Paul says: „We account a man to be justified by faith,
without the works of the law." The whole Church had
always understood this text as referring to the laws of
Moses about purifications, ceremonies, sacrifices, circumcision etc., to the specifically Judaic laws, against the ad-
option of which the Apostle was at times obliged to warn
the newly converted Christians. But Luther makes the
text appear favourable to his „Evangelium" by inserting
the word *alone* and making S. Paul say: „We account a
man justified by faith alone." (alleyn durch den glawben).
The answer he gave when a storm of indignation arose
on account of this arbitrary addition, is most characteristic
of him and deserves to be quoted at length: „If your
Papist grumbles about the word *alone*, answer him at once:
Dr. Martin Luther will have it so and says that a Papist
and an ass are one and the same thing. *Sic volo, sic jubeo,*
sit pro ratione voluntas. For we shall not be the disciples
and pupils of the Papists, but their masters and judges;
we too for once will glory and protest against those asses' heads. As S. Paul glories against his mad saints, so
will I glory against these my asses. Are they doctors?
So am I! Are they learned? So am I! Are they preachers? So am I! Are they theologians? So am I! ...
And I will glory further. I can explain Psalms and Prophets, they cannot. I can interpret, they cannot. I can read
the Bible, they cannot ... I am only sorry that I have
not put in also the word *any*, so as to make it read:
„without *any* works of *any* law"; this would have expressed it better still. Therefore it (the word *alone*) shall

remain in my New Testament, and if all Papistical asses
should go mad and frantic, they will not get it out
again".(³³)

Luther's teaching, that the justification of man does
not consist in an interior renovation and regeneration of
the soul, but that man, whilst his sins remain inhering in
him, has them *covered over* with the merits of Christ and
is thus *reputed* just before God, without *being* just, led
him to another falsification. The Apostle says (Rom. III.
25. 26.): „Whom (Christ) God has proposed a propitiation,
through faith in his blood, to the showing of his justice
for the remission of former sins, Through the forbearance
of God, for the showing of his justice in his time; that
he himself may be just and *the justifier of him*, who is
of the faith of Jesus Christ.“ (³⁴) If God is not only just
in himself, but also makes others just, as the Apostle here
says; if the very justice of God overflows as it were into
the soul of man (cfr. facti consortes divinae naturae),
Luther's teaching of a merely *reputed* justification appears
in all its weakness. Hence Luther begins to knead the
text in the mould of his preestablished opinion and behold!
it comes out showing S. Paul a true Lutheran! „The
shewing of his (God's) justice“ becomes in both verses
„*the offering of justice which is reputed as such before
him*“(³⁵) i. e. the justice of God, of which the lutheranized
S. Paul speaks, is not God's *own* Divine justice, but it is
the „güldene Gnadenrock“, „the golden coat of grace,“
viz. the merits of Christ which are put on our shoulders
to *hide* our sins. But then there still remains the expression
of the Apostle, that God himself „is just and the justifier of

---

(³³) Walch XXI. 314 seqq.

(³⁴) For the sake of convenience
we give here the original text:
Quem proposuit Deus propitiati-
onem per fidem in sanguine ipsius,
ad ostensionem justitiae suae *(εἰς
ἔνδειξιν τῆς δικαιοσύνης αὐτου)* propter remissionem praecedentium de-
lictorum. In sustentatione Dei, ad

ostensionem justitiae ejus *(πρὸς
τὴν ἔνδειξιν τῆς δικαιοσύνης αὐτου)*
in hoc tempore: ut sit ipse justus,
et justificans eum qui est ex fide
Jesu Christi. *(εἰς τὸ εἶναι αὐτὸν
δίκαιον καὶ δικαιοῦντα τὸν ἐξ πίστεως
Ἰησοῦ.)*

(³⁵) Damit er die Gerechtigkeit
die vor ihm gilt, darbiete.

him who is of the faith of Jesus Christ." Once more Luther,
who is equal to any occasion, puts in a word of his own:
„that he *alone* may be just and the justifier etc." If the
word *alone* is in the text, the whole import of the sentence
falls on it, and the question *in what way* God is the
justifier appears to be of no importance. It would show
what *God* is and does, in opposition to *others;* as the text
stands in the original, it shows that God *is* just and *makes*
others just. — Luther tells us: They cannot interpret, but
I can. Indeed, he can!

Against the epithet „just" as applied to man he had
a great antipathy; wherever it is applied by inspired writers,
it is always a strong protest against his teaching that man
could not really be or become just, not even through the
action of divine grace. Hence, wherever this word is
applied to man in the Bible, we find Luther performing
another legerdemain. In the place of „just" he quietly
puts „pious" (fromm), which of course is milder in itself
and would not signify that state of the soul, which the
Church expresses by the word „justice." When therefore Moses says: Noah was a *just* man, (³⁶) Luther says:
Noah was a pious man; where S. Luke calls Zachary
and his wife „just before God," (³⁷) Luther improves
upon the inspired writer by calling them „pious". (³⁸)
In the Tabletalk too (³⁹) he says that it is one of the
Popish errors to translate *justus* and *justitia* with *just* and
justice, when the real meaning of the words is *pious* and
piety. „Sic volo, sic jubeo," and we papistical asses have
to be quiet.

Döllinger very properly observes (⁴⁰) that in his explanation of the Bible Luther is the most enigmatical
character. His violent interpretation of texts, to make

(³⁶) Gen. VI. 9.
(³⁷) Luke I. 6.
(³⁸) Similarly with regard to
S. Joseph (Matth. I. 16), Simeon
(Luke II. 25), Cornelius (Acts X.
22). Already before his open rup-

ture with the Church he said: Justicia, germanice: fromkeit." Wittenb. I. 66в.
(³⁹) Tischr. I. c. 13. § 68.
(⁴⁰) III. 156.

them appear in harmony with his own teaching, his arbitrary explanation of the meaning of words makes one sometimes disbelieve one's eyes. He finds his fundamental dogma about the efficiency of faith in places, where no other mortal man can see it; and wherever a text inculcates the necessity of good works for salvation, a decision ex cathedra without entering into the reasons, or some rude and opprobrious names thrown at the heads of the Papists are deemed a sufficient solution of the difficulty.

One of his most curious attempts to get over such difficulties, contained in S. Luke, is the following. Luther supposes that at the time of the Apostles the Evangelium, being still in all its brightness, not having yet been dirtied by the Pope or the devil, was preached, especially by S. Paul, exactly as 1500 years afterwards he preached it himself, with the same effect however which he, the „Reformer“, unfortunately was obliged to witness, viz. that the people, joyful at the good tidings of salvation by faith alone, neglected good works altogether. Hence — we are told by him — S. Luke, S. James and others had to insist again on good works, and as it happened, they did this in such a way, as to make them appear necessary for salvation! (⁴¹)

When Luther tells us that „with S. John the *keeping of the commandments* is the same as *believing*“ (⁴²) and that in general in Holy Scripture *to do* means *to believe* (⁴³), we might justly expect some proof for such a startling assertion. But Luther says so, and he knows how to interpret — ergo! The words addressed by Our Lord to the youth: If thou wilt enter into life, keep the commandments (Matth. XIX. 17) seem to have sorely perplexed the „Reformer.“ In one place he calls them *obscure* (⁴⁴) and thinks that, being obscure, they cannot be urged against the *clear* words of Holy Scripture to the contrary, in another place

(⁴¹) Walch XI. 1995 seqq.
(⁴²) Walch IX. 1047.
(⁴³) Walch VIII. 2106.

(⁴⁴) Luther's ungedr. Predigten ed. Bruns. See Döll. III. 169.

he advises Christians to trust in Christ, no matter what
the Bible says, (¹⁵) finally he has the courage to represent
Christ as having spoken to the youth ironically. This is
how he puts it in his own vulgar way: „Do this. This is
only a jest or irony. Just as if Our Lord had intended
to say: tomorrow morning you will do it, yes, over the
left!" (⁴⁶) This last interpretation is in harmony with his
general conception of the idea of Divine laws, a point
which will be more fully explained in another place.

The prophetic words of Christ (Matth. XXIV. 24)
about false prophets that are to come before the end of
the world, have been treated by the Evangelist of Wittenberg in a way which deserves to be mentioned here. His
amazing assertion, that before him, almost from the time
of the Apostles, the whole Church had been buried in the
darkness of error, he tried to defend by saying that there
was nothing impossible or incredible about it, for *Christ
had foretold that state of things.* Where? He quotes the
above mentioned text. „The argument of the asses of
Paris (the Sorbonne) and of the papistical sect of hogs
falls to pieces" before this text, where Our Lord clearly
says: They (the false Christs) shall seduce many, so that
even the elect shall be led into error. (⁴⁷) „The Papists
are always urging this against us: Should so many holy
men and doctors have erred? They do not see that these
words (Matth. XXIV. 24) give them a knock on the head,

(⁴⁵) Quodsi adversarii Script-
uram urserint contra Christum,
urgemus Christum contra Script-
uram. Nos dominum habemus, illi
servum; nos caput, illi pedes seu
membra, quibus caput oportet dominari et praeferri.
                    Wittenb. I. 387.
    (⁴⁶) Thue das, ist nur eine
Schwankrede oder Ironie.   Als
wenn unser Herr hätte sagen wol-
len· Morgen früh wirst du es thun;
ja, hinter sich!
         Wittenb. (Germ.) I. 158.
    (⁴⁷) Corruit hic argumentum

Parrhisiensium asinorum et papisticae sectae porcorum, quo a mul-
titudine et sanctitate arguunt.
Christus solvit argumentum a mul-
titudine dum dicit: Et seducent
multos, ita ut electi in errorem
duci possint. Argumentum vero
a sanctitate solvit eodem, quod
electos seducendos praedicit. Nihil ergo rudientes asini agunt dum
dicunt, Ecclesiam non fuisse tanto
tempore derelictam, nec ignorasse
quae Lutherus sese scire promittit.
Wittenb. II. 318 (De votis mon.)

so as to make them reel. What shall we answer? There
are the words, perfectly clear, we must believe them." (⁴⁸)
Yes, indeed we must believe the words of Christ. But
why does Luther maim the text? Why does he suppress
the words on which its meaning depends and which show
that Our Lord said quite the contrary of what his self-
made „Evangelist" makes him say? „In so much as to
deceive *(if possible)* even the elect." Twelve times does
Luther quote this text (⁴⁹) and twelve times does he suppress that allimportant parenthesis. And this man is the
„hero of the Bible"!

In one sense it is true that Luther was the first to
give the Bible to the people, but whether this is a merit,
is another question. He constituted everybody, man or
woman, young or old, learned or unlearned, wise or foolish, absolutes judges of the meaning of the Bible. However he sowed the wind and reaped the whirlwind. As
far as it was in his power, he did away with the living
authority of the Church, he based his system exclusively
on Holy Scripture as understood by him. It was only
just, that he should grant to others the same right which
he claimed for himself; but when he did so, he little
thought how soon the weapon would be turned against
him. As long as the revolutionary party acknowledged
him as their leader, *the Bible was clear and easy to understand,* as soon as others had the courage to differ from
him, the Bible became *the most difficult book,* and nobody
was to be presumptuous enough to explain it, except, of
course, Dr. Martin Luther, „by the grace of God Evangelist of Wittenberg".

If Holy Scripture, he says in his book against Erasmus, is obscure or ambiguous, why should it have been
given to us? (⁵⁰) And he quotes a number of texts from
the Psalms and Prophets (v. gr. Praeceptum Domini luci-

(⁴⁸) Walch XI. 2511.
(⁴⁹) Döll. III. 199.
(⁵⁰) Si Scriptura obscura vel
ambigua est, quid illam opus fuit
nobis divinitus tradi?
       Wittenb. II. 474.

dum, illuminans oculos), to prove that the word of God
must be clear. But such superficial interpretation may be
met with other texts: Revela oculos meos, Da mihi intel-
lectum, Faciem tuam illumina etc., which show that something is required for the understanding of the Bible.(⁵¹)
„They lie, he says, who maintain that the Pope is the
judge of the Scriptures. Pardon, Squire Pope, I say: he
who has faith, is a spiritual man and judges of all things
and is judged by nobody. And if a simple miller's girl,
nay, a child nine years old, has faith and judges according to the Evangelium (i. e. if they only agree with Luther!) the Pope owes obedience and ought to throw himself at their feet if he means to be a genuine Christian.
And this is likewise the duty of all Universities and learned
men and sophists."(⁵²)   If anyone maintains — so Luther
says in the Tabletalk — that we want the interpretation
of the Fathers or that the Scripture is obscure, you shall
answer: This is not true, there is no clearer book on
earth, than the Holy Scripture; compared to all other
books it is like the sun compared to all other lights.(⁵³)

The principle of private judgment in the interpretation
of the Bible was eagerly taken up by the Reformer's followers, and almost immediately Protestantism was split
into numberless sects. Though they contradicted each
other on every conceivable point, they had all the same
right, and if the principle of private judgment is legitimate,
all the different sects were equally true. The religious
anarchy became such, that in 1576 J. Andreâ, a Lutheran
minister, complained that it would be difficult to find one
Church, were even the minister and his clerk would agree
in their Creed.(⁵⁴)   But already during Luther's lifetime

(⁵¹) See Becanus, Man. Contro-
vers. Patavii 1713, 9 seqq.
    (⁵²) Walch XII. 1959. Carlstadt
carried out this idea in a practical
way. He went into the houses of
the poor and unlearned and asked
them to explain the Bible to him.
Köstlin I. 519.

(⁵³) Cfr. Wittenb. II. 100: Scriptura „per sese certissima, facillima,
apertissima, sui ipsius interpres.

    (⁵⁴) Oratio de stud. sacr. litt.
Tubingae 1577.

the consequences of the principle which he had proclaimed were such, as to plunge him into the deepest despair
and, at times, to make him add to his already existing
exceedingly rich stock of slang, to be used against his
own children. „How many doctors have I made by preaching and writing! Now they say: Be off with you! go
to the devil! Thus it must be. When we preach, they
laugh; when we promise them the grace of God, they —
— —; when we get angry and threaten them, they mock
us, snap their fingers at us and laugh in their sleeves." (⁵⁵)
That power and authority, to which he had laid claim so
many times, he saw slip away from under his hands, for
according to his own principle every new head of a sect
claimed as much authority to be supreme judge of the
meaning of the Bible, as Luther himself had. *Therefore
the Bible became a difficult book.* The man who had said
that the judgment about doctrine belonged not to the pastors, but to the flock, who had proved the existence of
this right with the words of Christ: Beware of false prophets, very soon had to complain most bitterly: „There is
no smearer (Sudler), but when he has heard a sermon or
can read a chapter in German, makes a doctor of himself
and crowns his ass and convinces himself that he knows
everything better than all who teach him." (⁵⁶) „When we
have heard or learned a few things about Holy Scripture,
we think we are already doctors and have swallowed the
Holy Ghost, feathers and all." (⁵⁷) „This one will not hear
of baptism, that one denies the Sacrament, another puts a
world between this and the last day; some teach that Christ
is not God, some say this, some say that; there are about
as many sects and creeds, as there are heads. No yokel
is so rude, but when he has dreams and fancies, he thinks
himself inspired by the Holy Ghost and must be a
prophet." (⁵⁸) „Noblemen, townsmen, peasants, all classes
understand the Evangelium *better than I or S. Paul,* they

(⁵⁵) Walch VII. 2310. (⁵⁷) Walch V. 472.
(⁵⁶) Walch V. 1652. (⁵⁸) De Wette III. 61.

are now wise and think themselves more learned than all
the ministers." (⁵⁹) „Ah! Dear Lord God! we cannot understand Holy Scripture so easily, though we study it with
all diligence." (⁶⁰) Two days before his death Luther
wrote: „Let nobody think he has had a sufficient taste of
the Scriptures except a man who for a hundred years has
ruled the Church with the Prophets, with John the Bapt-
ist, with Christ and the Apostles." (⁶¹) Had he been one
of that choice number? And yet, on the strength of his
own „taste" of the Bible he had torn thousands and thousands from the Church!

„What will be the consequences — asked Carl von
Bodman — of the lutheran principle about the interpretation and authority of the Bible? He rejects one or another book as not apostolic, as spurious, because it does
not suit him; others will reject other books for the same
reason, in the end people will not believe in the Bible at
all and will treat it like a profane book." (⁶²) Everybody
that knows a little of the present state of Protestantism
in Germany, knows also how completely this prophecy
has been fulfilled. Luther himself too was depressed by
the gloomy outlook that opened before him. „As long
as the men who in our time diligently teach the word of
God are alive, and as long as those live, who have seen
and heard me, Philip Melanchthon, Dr. Pomeranus and
other pious, faithful and upright teachers, things will be
tolerable. But when these are gone and their time is past,
what a fall there will be! We have something like it in
the book of Josuah and of the Judges: There arose others
that knew not the Lord and the works which he had done
for Israel." (⁶³) On the 27th of June 1538 Luther and Me-

(⁵⁹) Walch XIV. 1360.
(⁶⁰) Tischr. II. c. 5. § 46.
(⁶¹) Scripturas sanctas sciat se
nemo degustasse satis, nisi centum
annis cum Prophetis, ut Elia et
Elisaeo, Joanne Baptista, Christo
et Apostolis Ecclesias gubernarit.

Hanc ne tu divina Aeneida tenta,
sed vestigia pronus adora. Wir
sind Bettler (we are beggars) hoc
est verum. Tischr. I. c. 1. § 10.
(⁶²) Quoted by Janssen II. 200.
(⁶³) Tischr. I. c. 1. § 7.

lanchthon spoke at table about what the future would bring:
„There will be the greatest confusion. Nobody will allow
himself to be led by another man's doctrine or authority.
Everybody will be his own rabbi; hence the greatest scandals will arise." [64]

Who had opened the floodgates? Who, but Martin
Luther, the „Evangelist"?

[64] Multa dicebant gementes de futuro saeculo, quod multos habiturum sit magistros. Erit maxima confusio. Nullus alterius doctrina neque auctoritati se regi permittet. Es wirdt cyn ieder sein Rabbi sein wollenn ... Et hinc maxima orientur scandala et dissipationes ... O utinam nostri Principes et Status concilium et concordiam aliquam doctrinae et caerimoniarum constituerent, ne quilibet sua temeritate erumperet ad multorum scandala.   Lauterb. 91.

Chapter VIII.

The „Evangelium".

Nisi ignoraveris legem, et in corde tuo
certo statueris, nullam esse legem et iram
Dei, sed meram gratiam et misericordiam
propter Christum, non potes salvus fieri.

Lutheri Comment. ad Gal.
Wittenb. V. 273B.

As soon as you understand this, I will say·
Dear Doctor, you are a learned man. S. Paul
and myself have not managed it yet.

Idem Lutherus. Tischr. I. c. 12. § 52.

Before we see Luther reappear in public, to super-
intend the organization of his new Church and to take up
arms against his new adversaries, the ranters, we must cast
a glance at the gift he brought with him, viz. his „Evangelium", which was to renew the face of the earth. Though
with regard to minor points he frequently changed his
opinion, the substance of his teaching remained the same
throughout his whole life. Hence in explaining this system
we need not restrict ourselves to the writings which he
had published before 1522.

As Luther thought that in his dogma about justification he had found a remedy for the unhappy state of his
soul, he gave it the short name „Evangelium", i. e. „the
good tidings",[1] and under this name it easily insinuated

[1] Etymologically the word „Gospel" would not, of course, express the same meaning; we shall therefore use the word „Evangelium".

itself to the people. The facts, however, proved, that
great numbers embraced the „Evangelium“, because it announced to them not simply liberty, but licentiousness.
Let Luther himself explain his system.

In his writings he frequently opens to the reader the
innermost recesses of his soul. We cannot help pitying
him, when we see him in the most fearful struggles; but
the fact, that the ideas he struggled against were entirely
the creatures of his fancy and not teachings of the Catholic Church, is in itself a sufficient answer to those who
maintain that the corrupt teachings of that same Church
forced him to set up as a Reformer. The love of God
as of a loving Father had been entirely unknown to him,
to him God had been *only* the fearful avenger of sin; the
justice of God had been equivalent to the manifestation
of his wrath. „The word *God's justice* used to sound
formerly in my heart like a thunderclap . . . for I thought
God's justice to be the same thing as his fearful anger,
wherewith he punishes sin. I felt sincere enmity against
S. Paul, when I read that the justice of God is made
manifest in his Evangelium.“ (²) Might not Luther have
heard from his masters and superiors — if he had been
inclined to listen to them — that God is equally just in
rewarding, and that his mercy is infinite? „My case was
this: Though I lived as a holy and blameless monk, I
found I was a great sinner before God . . . and had not
sufficient confidence to propitiate God with my own merits.“ (³) But did the Church never condemn Pelagianism?
„Therefore,“ he continues, „I did not love at all that just
and angry God, who only punishes sinners, but *I hated
him*, and in my heart I was seriously angry with him, saying many times: Is it not enough that God heaps upon
us, poor miserable sinners and condemned to death by
original sin, all sorts of troubles and afflictions in this life,
besides the terrors and threatenings of the law? Must he,

(²) Tischr. II. c. 12. § 85.   (³) Walch XIV. 460.

through his Evangelium, cause us still more afflictions and
sufferings?" (⁴)

Luther's utterly wrong and *uncatholic* idea, that he was
expected to propitiate God with his own works exclusively,
caused him to be at times not only severe but cruel to
himself in the observance of his monastic rules. „If ever
a monk has gone to heaven through his monkery, I should
have gone there. If it had lasted longer, I should have
killed myself with praying, watching, reading and other
work." (⁵) It is clear enough, that with the hopeless task
before him he never enjoyed a moment's peace, but felt
despair growing in his heart. There was only one way
for him to feel once more happiness and peace, viz.
humbly to accept the teaching of the Church, that bids
us put all our trust in the infinite merits of the Precious
Blood of Christ and fulfil our duties with the help of
that divine grace, which is continually offered to us. But
Luther was not the man to take advice, his whole life
shows that he was a most selfwilled man, who would not
look to anyone for guidance but himself.

When the reaction set in, it was to be expected that
a man like Luther would go as far as possible to the
other extreme. As the task he had put before himself,
became more and more odious, as its impossibility and
absurdity appeared more and more clearly, he declared
that human nature was absolutely incapable of doing
any good, that the work of salvation belonged to God
alone, to the exclusion of even the slightest cooperation of man, that man had only to remain passive under
the action of his Redeemer. He says that this change in
his belief was wrought by reflecting on the words of
S. Paul: „The just man liveth by faith." „Here I felt

(⁴) Ibid.
(⁵) In his Comment. ad Gal. he
says: Plus inedia, vigiliis orationi-
bus et aliis exercitiis corpus ma-
cerans, quam omnes illi, qui hodie

tam acerbe oderunt me ... Tam
diligens et superstitiosus eram, ut
plus oneris imponerem corpori,
quam ut sine periculo sanitatis
ferre poterat. Wittenb. V. 291.

immediately that I was born to a new life and that the gates of paradise were wide open to me."(⁶)

According to the new „Evangelium" which Luther announced, the nature of man is, through the sin of the first parent Adam, so thoroughly corrupted, that good actions have become absolutely impossible. It is now the nature of man, to commit sin; he cannot help it. „Sin is in us not a work or an action, but it is our nature."(⁷) Let a man do his best; to be good, still his every action is unavoidably bad, he commits a sin, as often as he draws his breath.(⁸)

This corruption extends also to the intellect, which is so absolutely blind to all heavenly truth, that every thought of the mind is necessarily an error. „Whatsoever is in our will, is bad, and whatsoever is in our intellect, is sheer error and blindness. Therefore man has for divine things nothing but darkness, error, maliciousness, evil will and obtuseness."(⁹) Even involuntary temptations, which arise from human weakness, concupiscence itself, is, according to Luther, a sin.(¹⁰) He declares, it is necessary to paint the corruption of man in the darkest poss-

(⁶) Preface to Opp. lat.

(⁷) Walch XI. 2793.

(⁸) In how material a way Luther explains the corruption and sinfulness of the very nature of man, appears from his explanation of the Psalm Miserere. With regard to the words „Ecce enim in iniquitatibus etc." he says: Totam humanam naturam ceu uno fasce complexus addit (Psalmista): In peccatis conceptus sum. Non enim de operibus quibusdam, sed de materia simpliciter loquitur et dicit: Semen humanum, massa illa, ex qua formatus sum, tota est vitio seu peccato corrupta. Materia ipsa est vitiata, lutum illud, ut sic dicam, ex quo hoc vasculum fingi coepit, damnabile est. Quid vis amplius? Talis sum ego, tales sunt omnes homines. Ipsa conceptio, ipsa augmentatio foetus in utero, antequam

nascimur et homines esse incipimus, est peccatum ... Non dicit: mater mea peccavit, cum conciperet me, neque dicit: ego peccavi, cum conciperer, sed de ipso rudo semine loquitur et pronuntiat id peccato plenum et massam perditionis esse. Wittenb. III. 518.

(⁹) Wittenb. (Germ.) I. 100.

(¹⁰) Moses dicit: Non concupisces, ut repetit Paulus. Concupiscentia igitur peccatum est. Contra, principium fidei Parrhisiensis et Lovaniensis Sodomarum, cum suo Papa, est hoc: Concupiscentia non est peccatum, sed poena et infirmitas, et cum caro concupiscit adversus spiritum, non est peccatum. Licet ergo secundum decalogum Papae sanctissimi sanctissimum, concupiscere sine peccato, et Moses mentitus est dicens: Non concupisces. De Missa abrog. Wit-

ible colours, that God may be all the more glorified.([11])
Natural benevolence is mere hypocrisy, for by nature man
hates and must hate his neighbour. „By nature I cannot
utter a friendly word or make a friendly sign, and if I
do, it is only hypocrisy; the heart at least remains full
of venom."([12])

So corrupted is the nature of man according to Luther,
that it can never be regenerated; even God's all-powerful
grace makes no attempt at cleansing it from sin; sin remains in the souls, also of the just, for ever; only, that
God does not look at the sins, but covers them over with
the merits of Christ, if we make them our own by faith.
„This is the effect of faith: it makes *that our filth does
not stink before God*"([13]) Here then we have the meaning
of „justification." Christ has suffered for our sins and
has fulfilled the law of God for us. We have only to
believe in him and, by believing in him, to take hold as
it were, of his merits, and to put them on like a cloak.
If we do that, we are saved. „If thou wishest to fulfil all
the commandments, and to get rid of concupiscence and
sin, believe in Christ."([14]) All that man has to do, is, to
remain passive; he must never attempt to do *anything*
himself for his salvation. This would be presumption.
He must remain like the pillar of salt, like a block of
wood or a stone.([15]) „To be a Christian means to have
the Evangelium and to believe in Christ. This faith brings
forgiveness of sins and divine grace, it comes solely through
the Holy Ghost, who accomplishes it through the word,

tenb. II. 277B. This is not the
only place in Luther's works, where
this piece of sophistry is to be
found.

([11]) Ut justificatio, quantum
potest fieri, magnificetur, peccatum
est valde magnificandum et ampli-
ficandum. Wittenb. I. 391B. (thesis
28). Cfr. Döll. III. 34 and Wittenb. V. 290B.

([12]) Walch XI. 1821.

([13]) Wenn mein Hänsichen or

Lenichen in den Winkel —, dess
lachet man, als sei es wolgethan.
Also macht auch der Glaube, dass
unser Dreck nicht stinkt vor Gott.
            Walch XIII. 1480.

([14]) Walch XIX. 1212.

([15]) Wittenb. (Germ.) III. 162.
Cfr. In Gen. c. XIX. (Nürnb. 1550.
fol. CXXIIB, seqq. In spiritualibus
et divinis rebus, quae ad animae
salutem spectant, homo est instar
statuae salis, in quam uxor patri-

without any coöperation on our part ... Man remains passive and suffers to be acted upon by the Holy Ghost, just as clay is shaped by the potter."([16]) „A Christian is absolutely passivus." ([17]) This passiveness, which Luther demanded on the part of man, for salvation, led him farther on, to the denial of the freedom of the human will. But this particular point will have to be reserved for a separate chapter.

That through such teachings Luther found himself in direct opposition to Moses, as the representative of God's commandments, is evident. But he not only acknowledged this opposition, but urged it as far as possible. This he does especially in his Commentary on the Epistle of S. Paul to the Galatians. In this epistle he thought he had found so much to confirm his teaching about justification, that it became his favourite book; he called it his „affianced bride." „Epistola ad Galatas est mea epistola, cui me despondi. Est mea Catharina de Bora." ([18]) In his Commentary he expounds the very essence of his system, viz. the irreconcilable opposition between *Law*

archae Loth est conversa, imo est similis trunco et lapidi, statuae vita carenti, quae neque oculorum, oris aut ullorum sensuum cordisque usum habet.

([16]) Tischr. II. c. 15. § 1.

([17]) Tischr. II. c. 16. § 19. Est mere passiva justitia. Ibi enim nihil operamur aut reddimus Deo, sed tantum recipimus et patimur alium operantem in nobis, scil. Deum. (Wittenb. V. 272.) Ista est justicia coelestis et passiva, quam non habemus, sed ex coelo accipimus; non facimus, sed fide apprehendimus. (Ibid. 273.) Nihil ergo facimus nos? nihil operamur ad hanc justitiam consequendam? Respondeo: *Nihil*, quia haec justitia est: prorsus nihil facere, nihil audire, nihil scire de lege aut de operibus. (Ibid. 273b. cfr. 278.)

([18]) Döll. III. 36. — The larger commentary on this Epistle (Wittenb. V. 269b. seqq.) may be considered as his chief theological work on his „Evangelium". It is rather tiresome, on account of the endless repetitions, especially on the meaning of the „law", and the endless declamations on „the blindness of the Papists." We find in it ad nauseam another thing, of which Luther is extremely fond, viz. coupling his own name with that of S. Paul, and finding S. Paul's courage, teaching, suffering etc. reproduced in himself. Throughout this book Luther facilitates his work of arguing against the Catholic doctrine on justification by persistently representing it in a false light, by asserting again and again, that Catholics expect their salvation only from their own works. What has to be thought of the following? „Si Papa nobis concesserit, quod solus Deus ex mera

and *Evangelium.* He knew that this was something entirely new, but the principle of Lirinensis „Quod semper,
quod ubique, quod ab omnibus" could not restrain a man
like Luther. It was just like him, to say that from the
time of the Apostles he was the first man, to discover
the truth. He — unjustly enough — *thought* that perhaps S. Augustine, as the only exception, might have had
an idea of his, Luther's, Evangelium. ([19])

According to the „Reformer" the *law* is the sum
total of all the moral duties of man, of those duties, which
— this must not be forgotten — man is absolutely incap-
pable of fulfilling. Hence the law creates in man anything
but the love of God, in fact, it naturally leads to the
hatred of the lawgiver — „Lex summum odium Dei affert."

To this law is opposed the *Evangelium,* which tells
man not what he must do, but what Christ has done for
him, and what he has to make his own by faith. „The
Evangelium does not preach what we must do or omit, . . .
but bids us open our hands to receive gifts, and says:
Behold, dear man, this is what God has done for thee,
for thy sake he has made his Son assume human nature.
This believe and accept, and thou shalt be saved. The
Evangelium only shows us the gifts of God, not what we
have to give to God or to do for him, as is the wont of
the law." ([20]) „Law is what we have to do, Evangelium
what God is willing to give. The former we cannot fulfil, the latter we receive and apprehend by faith." ([21])
„The Evangelium is *good tidings* . . . it is not a sermon
on works of ours. He who says that the Evangelium

gratia per Christum justificet peccatores, non solum volumus eum
in manibus portare, sed etiam ei
osculari pedes. *Quia vero hoc impetrare non possumus,* vicissim su-
perbimus in Deo ultra omnem modum . . . Maledicta sit humilitas,
quae hic se demiserit . . . Deo dante.
mea frons durior erit fronte omnium." Wittenb. V. 299n.

([19]) De hoc legis et Evangelii
discrimine nihil legitur in libris
monachorum, canonistarum, schol-
asticorum, imo nequidem veterum
Patrum: Augustinus aliqua ex parte
illud discrimen tenuit ac indicavit.
Hieronymus et alii ignorarunt.
                                    Ibid. 358n.
([20]) Walch III. 4.
([21]) Tischr. I. c. 12. § 7.

demands works, necessary for salvation, is a liar." ([22]) „That
the law should have been abolished, so that it can no
longer condemn the faithful, was just as necessary, as
that is should have been given." ([23]) „The law and the
Evangelium are two quite contrary things, which *cannot
be in harmony with each other by the side of each other.*" ([24])
The law is one of the three mouths of the infernal Cer-
berus, the other two are sin and death. ([25])   When we
hear Luther speak about this opposition between law
and Evangelium with such extraordinary boldness, it is
astonishing, to hear him frequently say that he himself
cannot sufficiently realize it.   „There is no man on earth,
who can properly distinguish between the law and the
Evangelium."   In this same place Luther goes so far as
to say, that even the man Jesus Christ, when in the
garden of Gethsemane, suffered from such ignorance!
He continues: „I thought I knew it, because I have written
about it so much, and for so long a time, but . . . I am
still far from it." ([26]) „Someone complained that he was
unable to distinguish between the law and the Evangelium.
Luther answered: yes, if you knew that, you would be a
great doctor.   And he got up, took off his biretta and
said: As soon as you know that, I will say to you: Dear
Doctor, you are a learned man. *S. Paul and myself have
not managed it yet.*" ([27]) „If I could only well distinguish
between the two, the law and the Evangelium, I would
tell the devil at all hours that he might — — — —" ([28])

This is however not the only point, on which Luther
speaks ex Cathedra, without feeling sure of it himself.
We have seen above, ([29]) that he disputed about indulgences
without knowing what they were; and about his whole
sola-fide system he confessed: „I wonder how it is, that
I cannot learn this doctrine myself, when all my pupils

([22]) Ibid. § 39.
([23]) Ibid. § 41.
([24]) Ibid. § 16.
([25]) Ibid. II. c. 1. § 129.
([26]) Ibid. I. c. 12. § 19.

([27]) Ibid. § 52. Cfr. § 68, where
the above mentioned expression
about Christ is also repeated.
([29]) Ibid. II. c. 1. § 15.
([40]) page 60.

boast, that they have it at their fingers' ends."(³⁰) In one
place he tries to explain his inability by saying: „If God
were to give us a strong, unwavering faith, we should be
proud, perhaps we should despise him,"(³¹) in another(³²)
he supposes that the remnants of papistical belief in him
cause the difficulty and congratulates his young students on
their freedom from that leaven.

Not to distinguish between the law and the Evangelium would mean to make „a satanic and infernal confusion," such as the Pope has made,(³³) yet, also in his
Commentary in Galatas does Luther speak dozens of times
of the enormous difficulty which this distinction presents
to the mind of man, *especially when the voice of conscience
makes itself heard.*(³⁴) „He who knows how to distinguish between the law and the Evangelium, may thank
God and may consider himself as a theologian." „I and
others like me hardly possess the first elements of this
art."(³⁵) With what despair does this man cling to everything, which looks like an argument to confirm himself in
the belief, that he believes his own „Evangelium!" „We
possess the knowledge of this matter, for we can teach
the same, and this is a sure sign, that we ourselves possess
it. For nobody can teach others, what he does not know

(³⁰)   Rebenstock,   Colloquia,
medit. etc. II. 125.

(³¹) Tischr. I. c. 12. § 52. (Cfr.
S. Petr. V. 9: Fortes in fide!)

(³²) Wittenb. V. 321.

(³³) Ibid. 304B.

(³⁴) Etiamsi probe discamus et
teneamus eum (articulum), tamen
nullus est, qui eum perfecte ap-
prehendat, aut pleno affectu et
corde credat. Wittenb. V. 278B.
O, qui hic bene distinguere nosset,
ne in Evangelio legem quaereret,
sed id ab illa tam longe discerneret,
quam distat coelum a terra! ...
In agone conscientiae et in ipsa
praxi hoc certo statuere, est diffi-
cile etiam exercitatissimis. Ibid.

292n. Qui bene novit discernere
Evangelium a lege, gratias agat
Deo et sciat se esse theologum.
Ego certe in tentatione nondum
novi, ut deberem. Ibid. 304.

(³⁵) Ego et mei similes vix te-
nemus hujus artis prima elementa.
Et tamen seduli sumus discipuli
in ea schola, ubi ista ars discitur.
Ibid. 367. Cfr. 312 and 381 B. Novi
enim in quibus horis tenebrarum
nonnunquam lucter. Novi quoties
ego radios Evangelii et gratiae
veluti in quibusdam densis nubi-
bus subito amittam. Novi denique
quam versentur ibi in lubrico etiam
exercitati et qui pedem firmissime
figunt. Ibid. 290.

himself." ([³⁶]) Yet in „the time of temptation" all such arguments are useless! „In tentatione senties Evangelium rarum, et econtra legem assiduum hospitem in conscientia." ([³⁷]) But why? Whence this extreme difficult y nay almost impossibility of understanding the very first article of Lutheran faith, that article on which everything depends?

Luther acknowledges that man hears within his heart a voice, which reproaches him with his sins and which threatens him with the judgment of God. But *he calls it the voice of the devil,* who tries to cheat man. „Such is human weakness and misery, that in the tremblings of conscience and in the danger of death we look to nothing but our works, our worth and the law, which, in showing us our sins, reminds us of a badly spent life." ([³⁸]) „In the struggle of conscience the devil is wont to frighten us with the law, to object to us our consciousness of sin, a badly spent life, the wrath and judgment of God, hell and eternal death." ([³⁹]) „The devil — for he is wont to come under the name of Christ — transforms himself into an angel of light. Therefore we must learn to distinguish carefully. . . . Christ from the lawgiver, that, when the devil comes under the appearance of Christ, and under his name tires us, we may know that it is not Christ, but the devil." ([⁴⁰]) If Christ appears as an angry lawgiver or judge, demanding an account of the past life, this is a sure sign that the devil is trying to cheat you; for Christ cannot appear like that, he has nothing but mildness for us. ([⁴¹]) But what is to be done, when man cannot help feeling terrified at the thought of God's tribunal? Then, Luther says, man must persuade himself that he has no-

---

([³⁶]) Ibid. 290.
([³⁷]) Ibid. 304 B.
([³⁵]) Wittenb. V. 272 B.
([³⁹]) Ibid. 274.
([⁴⁰]) Ibid. 321 and 321 n. Cfr. 382: (Diabolus) mirus est artifex seducendi homines.

([⁴¹]) Si Christus specie irati judicis aut legislatoris apparuerit, qui exigit rationem transactae vitae, certo sciamus, eum furiosum esse diabolum, non Christum. Ibid

thing to do with the law, and that *no sins can condemn him* ; nay, let him, so to say, boast of his sinfulness and thus take the weapon out of the devil's hands." When the devil rushes at thee and tries to drown thee in the floods and the deluge of (thy) sins . . . answer: Why dost thou wish to make a Saint of me, why dost thou expect justice in me, who have nothing but sins and most grievous sins?" ([42]) In fact, what would be the use of Christ, if the law and our transgressions of the law could still terrify us? Therefore „when the conscience is terrorstricken on account of the law, and struggles with the judgment of God, do not consult reason, or the law, . . . act exactly, as if thou hadst never heard of the law of God." ([43]) „Answer: There is a time to live, and a time to die; there is a time to hear the law, and a time to despise the law . . . Let the law be off, and let the Evangelium come." ([44])

But always does Luther come back to the extreme difficulty — and a very intelligible one — of calming one's conscience in that way. „The reason and nature of man does not remain firmly in the embrace of Christ, but falls now and then back again into the thoughts about law and sin." ([45]) „These things are easily said, but blessed the man, that would know them well in the struggle of conscience, blessed he, who, when . . . the law accuses and terrifies him, could say: What does it matter to me, that thou, o law, makest me out to be guilty, that thou provest so many sins against me? . . . I am deaf, I do not hear thee, thou talkest to a deaf man, I am dead to thee." ([46])

([42]) Wittenb. V. 281 B.

([43]) Omnino sic te geras, quasi nunquam de lege Dei quidquam audieris, sed ascendas in tenebras ubi nec lex nec ratio lucet, sed solum aenigma fidei, quae certo statuat, se salvari extra et ultra legem, in Christo. Ibid 303 B.

([44]) Ibid. 304 B.

([45]) Wittenb. V. 305.

([46]) Haec dictu sunt facilia, sed beatus qui ista probe nosset in certamine conscientiae, hoc est, qui irruente peccato et lege accusante ac terrente posset dicere: Quid ad me, quod tu lex me agis reum, quod convincis multa peccata me commisisse. Imo quotidie

However, in spite of all difficulties, man *must* stifle that voice! It is a question of life and death! „If you do not ignore the law, if you are not sure in your heart, that there is no law, that there is no wrath of God, but only grace and mercy through Christ, *you cannot be saved.*" ([47]) If you do not send away Moses with his law . . . and, in those tremblings and terrors apprehend Christ, who has suffered etc. for your sins, *it is all over with your salvation.*" ([48]) „The decalogue has no right, to accuse and to terrify the conscience, in which Christ reigns through grace, for through Christ those laws have become antiquated." ([49])

The only safeguard in those struggles is, according to Luther, the remembrance, what place the law occupies in the religion of Christ, and for what purpose it *now* exists. Mind then, the law cannot condemn a Christian, who has not observed it. For the *only* purport of the law is this, *to show to man, that he is a sinner*, to terrify him in that way, and so to make him throw himself upon Christ. ([50]) Man is naturally inclined to think a great deal of himself and of his works. To crush „this horrible monster and stiffnecked brute" of pride, God wants a great and strong hammer, ([51]) i e. the law, for *the law re-*

adhuc multa committo. Hoc nihil ad me, jam surdus sum, non audio te, ideo surdo narras fabulam, quia tibi sum mortuus. Si autem omnino mecum vis disputare de peccatis, vade ad carnem et membra. servos meos, illus crudi, exerce et crucifige. Mihi vero conscientiae, dominae et reginae, ne sis molesta. Ibid. 315 n. In a letter to Agricola Luther acknowledges that it is almost impossible to man to abandon the idea of good works being necessary for salvation „ita operum opinio nobis incorporata, agnataque et innaturata est". De Wette III. 197. This was said to pacify Agricola, who from some expressions in the Order for the visitation of Churches, was afraid, that Luther was softening down his Sola-fide Evangelium.

([47]) Ibid. 272 n.
([48]) Ibid. 359.
([49]) Ibid. 396 n.

([50]) Lex ostendit tantum peccatum, perterrefacit et humiliat, atque hoc modo praeparat ad justificationem et impellit ad Christum. Ibid 307. Legis proprium officium est, nos reos facere, humiliare, occidere, ad infernum deducere, et omnia nobis auferre. sed eo fine, ut justificemur etc.
Ibid. 367 B.

([51]) habet opus Deus ingenti et forti malleo scil. lege. Ibid. 358 n.

veals to man his absolute inability of keeping it. This same
idea (to which we shall be obliged to return when speaking of Luther's controversy with Erasmus) is explained
also in his „Sermon on the liberty of Christians." „The
laws have been given only, that man should see in them
the impossibility of doing good, and that he should learn
to despair of himself ... For instance, the commandment:
Thou shalt have no bad desires, proves that we are all
sinners, and no man may be without bad desires, let him
do, whatever he likes. From this he learns to distrust
himself and to look elsewhere for help to be freed from
bad desires, and to fulfil through someone else the law,
which he himself is incapable of fulfilling ... As soon as
man begins to learn and to feel, from the laws of God,
his own incapacity ... he becomes thoroughly humble
and annihilated in his own eyes.(^{52})

Of course, Luther says, the law has to be preached,
and as far as social and political affairs are concerned,
it has to be preached, as if there was no promise or
grace.(^{53}) But beware of allowing the law to have any influence on your conscience, for then the law would become
„a sink of heresies and blasphemies." (^{54})

It cannot be said, that Luther's explanation of the
necessity of the law (as far as he admits it at all) is too clear:
The body with its members, he says, has to be subject to the
law, it has to carry its burden like a donkey, but leave the
donkey with its burden in the valley, when you ascend
the mountain. For the conscience has nothing to do with
law, works, earthly justice.(^{55}) We want indeed the „light
of the Evangelium," to understand this, and in this light
the meaning is: Keep the law, by all means; but if you

(^{52}) Walch XIX. 1212.
(^{53}) Wittenb. V. 272 b.
(^{54}) Si permiseris legem in conscientiam dominari ... nihil aliud
est lex quam omnium malorum,
haeresum et blasphemiarum sen-
tina.   Ibid.
(^{55}) Si agatur de fide, seu con-

scientia, excludatur prorsus lex et
relinquatur in terra ... Conscientia perterrefacta sensu peccati, sic
cogitet: Jam agis in terra, ibi asinus laboret, serviat et portet onus
sibi impositum i. e. corpus sit cum
membris suis subjectum legi. Cum
autem ascendis in coelum, relinque

do not, you need not be troubled in your conscience, for the transgression of the law cannot possibly condemn you.

Against Moses, who so very frequently and so very strictly insists on the keeping of the law, Luther nourished feelings, which verge on personal hatred. To him Moses is the incarnation of everything, that can torment the soul, he calls him by the most opprobious names and denounces him to Christians as a most dangerous man. Not only that Moses „who has been given to the Jewish nation only, has nothing to do with us gentiles and Christians,“ ([56]) but, „if you are prudent, send that stammering and stuttering (balbum et blesum) Moses with his law far away from you, and be not influenced by his terrific threats. Look upon him with suspicion, as upon *a heretic, excommunicated, damned, worse than the pope and the devil.*“ ([57])

„I will not have Moses with his law, for he is the enemy of the Lord Christ... We must put away the thoughts and disputes about the law, whenever the conscience becomes terrified and feels God's anger against sin. Instead of that it will be better to sing, to eat, to drink, to sleep, to be merry in spite of the devil. ([58]) No greater insult can be offered to Christ, than to suppose, that he has come to give commandments, to make a sort of Moses of him. ([59]) Only the mad and blind Papists do such a thing. ([60]) Christ's work consists in this: to fulfil the law

---

asinum cum sarcina in terra. Nihil enim conscientiae cum lege, operibus et terrena justitia. Ibid. 304. Patiatur sane (Christianus) legem dominari corpori et membris ipsius, non item conscientiae. Ibid. 305. Cfr. 317 B.

([56]) Walch XX. 203.

([57]) Ilic simpliciter sit tibi suspectus ut haereticus, excommunicatus, damnatus, deterior papâ et diabolo, ideoque prorsus non audiendus. Comment. in Gal. Almost

the same words occur. Tischr. I. c. 12. § 15. Nay, Luther went so far as to say: To the gallows with Moses.

([58]) Tischr. I. c. 12. § 17.

([59]) Ibid. § 66.

([60]) Tanta fuit Papistarum dementia et caecitas, ut ex Evangelio legem charitatis, ex Christo legislatorem fecerint.

Wittenb. V. 292 B.
Christus et Moses nullo modo conveniunt. Ibid. 370.

for us, not to give laws to us, and to redeem us. ([61]) „The
devil makes of Christ a mere Moses." ([62])

That faith, to which Luther ascribes the power of
saving man, must not be understood to be equivalent
to *fides*, in asmuch as this word expresses the submission
of the mind to the revealed truth, it is identical with
fiducia, it is, as he explains, „that confidence, by which
man trusts not in his own merits or his own worthiness,
but in Christ." ([63]) That such confidence in Christ, through
whom alone we can expect salvation, is absolutely necessary, the Catholic Church teaches plainly enough. But
Luther declares that this *fides* is sufficient. We find this
teaching fully set forth in his explanation of the Prophet
Isaias. ([64])

Man must look upon his sins, we are told there, not
as his own, but as the sins of Him, on whom God has
laid them. Christ has come to atone for the sins of the
world, he has taken them upon himself as his own, and
man has no more to do with them, except to persuade
himself, that they are no longer his own. ([65]) This faith
in Christ justifies man before all works and without any
works, ([66]) but if even the least work were to enter into

([61]) Evangelium docet, Christum
non venisse, ut ferret novam legem
et traderet praecepta de moribus.
                                    Ibid.

([62]) Walch VIII. 58.

([63]) Walch XII. 710.   Glauben
heisset, auf Gottes Barmherzigkeit
gewiss bauen. Tischr. I. c. 11. § 13.
Fides est fiducia constans miseri-
cordiae Dei ergo nos, in corde
vivens et efficaciter agens, qua
projicimus nos toti in Deum et
permittimus nos Deo.
                        Wittenb. V. 97 B.

([64]) Wittenb. IV. 261 seqq.

([65]) Quod si Christianus peccata se habere sentit, aspiciat ea
non qualia sunt in sua persona,
sed qualia sint in illa persona, in
quam a Deo sunt conjecta ... Sic

fiet ut habeat purum et mundum
cor ... Dices enim: peccata mea
non sunt mea, quia non sunt in
me, sed sunt aliena, Christi vide-
licet, non ergo me laedere poterunt ... Neque Christianismus
aliud (est) quam perpetuum hujus
loci exercitium, nempe sentire, te
non habere peccatum, quamvis
peccaris, sed peccata tua in Christo
haerere. Ibid. 262.

([66]) Haec fides sine et ante
charitatem justificat. Wittenb. V.
310. Fides non respicit charitatem.
Non dicit: quid feci? quid peccavi?
quid merui? Ibid. 296 n.   Promis-
siones novi Testamenti nullam ad-
nexam habent conditionem, neque
exigunt quidquam a nobis.
                                Ibid. 393 B.

it, faith would lose is justifying power. ([67]) Whatever S. Paul may say about the necessity of the theological virtue of charity, how emphatically soever he may tell us, that, if we had faith enough to move mountains, but not charity, we should be nothing (I Cor. XIII.), Luther tells us that charity has nothing whatever to do with justification, for charity has to be classed under „works." If charity were the necessary „form" of faith, i. e. if only faith manifesting itself in the loving observance of God's laws could justify, then this charity would become the chief thing ([68]) and this is, according to Luther, an accursed and damnable opinion. ([69])

Sanctifying grace, as understood by the Catholic Church, i. e. that real purity of the soul from at least mortal sin, which is owing to the cleansing power of the blood of Christ, does not find a place in Luther's system. ([70]) According to him the soul of the just, or rather that soul which is reputed just, can be considered as pure only in this sense, that „its filth does not stink," but the filth of the sin remains in it for ever, ([71]) only it is *covered over* with the merits of Christ. We make those merits our own, in the same way, that Christ has made our sins his own. ([72]) The following passage will explain this: „God cannot se in us any sin, though we are full of sin,

---

([67]) Nisi fides sit sine ullis, etiam minimis operibus, non justificat, imo non est fides.
Jen. I. 522.

([68]) Si charitas est forma fidei, ut ipsi nugantur, statim cogor sentire, ipsam charitatem esse principalem et maximam partem Christianae religionis, et sic amitto Christum. Wittenb. V. 346 B.

([69]) Pereant sophistae cum sua maledicta glossa et damnetur vox ista: Fides formata, ac dicamus constanter: ista vocabula, fides formata, informis, acquisita etc. esse diaboli portenta, nata in perniciem doctrinae et fidei Christianae, ad blasphemandum et con-

culcandum Christum et ad statuendam justitiam operum.
Ibid. 347 B.

([70]) Christianorum justitia reputative tantum justitia est, non formaliter. Ibid. 264.

([71]) Homo Christianus simul justus et peccator, amicus et hostis Dei est. Ibid. 335 B.

([72]) And Christ has made our sins his own to such an extent, that, as the Prophets had foreseen, he became „omnium maximus latro, homicida, adulter, fur, sacrilegus, blasphemus etc. quod nullus unquam major in mundo fuerit! Ibid. 348 B. We find this idea still further developed in the following:

nay are sin itself, inside and out, body and soul, from the
top of the head to the soles of the feet, but he only sees the
dear and precious blood of his beloved Son, our Lord Jesus
Christ, wherewith we are sprinkled. For this same blood
is the golden garment of grace (der güldene Gnadenrock)
which we have put on, and clothed with which we appear
before God, so that he will not and cannot look upon us
differently, than though we were his own dear Son himself,
full of justice, holiness and innocence." ([73]) The consciousness of thus having our sins covered over, and of being
free from all exertions for our salvation will produce the
greatest peace of mind and heart. ([74]) Luther praises his
„Evangelinm" as giving man the absolute certainty of salvation, whereas under the Papacy the most monstrous
thing was the uncertainty about the same point. ([75]) There
is, according to him, nothing in the whole world, which
can make us unhappy, except the want of faith, and this
is infact the only sin, through which a Christian can lose
eternal life. „You see how rich a Christian or baptized man is, who, *even if he would*, cannot lose salvation
by any number of sins, except if he refuses to believe.
No sin can condemn him except the want of faith." ([76])

Christus, dum offeretur pro nobis,
factus est peccatum metaphorice,
cum peccator ita fuerit per omnia
similis, damnatus, derelictus, con-
fusus, ut nulla re differret a vero
peccatore, quam quod reatum et
peccatum quod tulit, ipse non fe-
cerat. Wittenb. II. 270. Omne
illud malum, quod post actum
peccati in nobis est, scilicet *timo-
rem mortis et inferni*, sensit et
tulit Christus. Ibid. 270 B. Quid
ergo dicemus? Simul Christum
summe justum et summe peccatorem? simul summe mendacem et
summe veracem? simul summe
gloriantem et summe desperantem?
simul summe beatum et summe
damnatum? Nisi enim haec dixe-
rimus, non video quomodo a Deo
derelictus sit. Wittenb. III. 369 B.

([73]) Walch VIII. 878.

([74]) Comment in Gal. De du-
bitatione. Wittenb. V. 376 B. Ut
conscientia laeta obdormiat in
Christo sine ullo sensu legis, peccati et mortis.

([75]) In quo (papatu) si etiam
omnia salva essent, tamen istud
monstrum incertitudinis superat
omnia monstra.   Ibid. 379 B.

([76]) Ita vides, quam dives sit
homo Christianus, sive baptizatus,
qui, etiam volens, non potest per-
dere salutem suam quantiscunque
peccatis, nisi nolit credere. Nulla
enim peccata eum possunt damnare, nisi sola incredulitas.
Wittenb. II. 78 (De Capt. Babyl.)

Such views necessarily led Luther to the denial of
another Catholic dogma, viz. that of the power of the
keys. Absolution, in the Catholic sense of the word,
could find no place in his system. In his own way he
expressed his opinion in the words: „The Pope ought to
be hanged, with his keys round his neck." ([77]) The forgiveness of sins (or rather the covering over) is merely the
fruit of the apprehension of Christ's merits, but this apprehension is an entirely private act of every particular
individual, for which no priest is required. The power
of the keys is then reduced to this: Faith forgives sin,
the want of faith retains them. You may go to another
person for absolution and a very good thing it is, but it
only means, that another Christian will remind you of
the power of faith; if you can manage to persuade yourself of this point privately, you do not want assistance.
We find this doctrine of Luther developed in the 8th of
a series of sermons, which he preached against Carlstadt.
(A. D. 1522.)

„I will not have secret confession taken away, I
would not give it up for the treasures of the whole
world . . . No one knows how much it can do, except
he, who has frequently to fight the devil. Long ago I
should have been conquered and strangled by the devil,
if confession had not preserved me . . . Now, whosoever
is fighting against sins and desires to get rid of them and
to hear a sure word of consolation for the quiet of his
heart, let him go and and accuse himself secretly of his
sin to a brother and beg absolution and a word of consolation. If he gives you absolution and assures you, that
your sins are forgiven, that you have a gracious God
and merciful father, who will not impute to you your
sins, believe his word and the absolution gladly and be
persuaded, that God speaks to you through the mouth
of your brother. But he, who has a strong and firm

([77]) Döll. III. 74.

faith in God and is sure that his sins are forgiven him,
may omit this confession and confess to God alone.([78])
Whenever therefore a „minister" gives absolution, it is
only a more solemn way of announcing the „Evangelium,"
but the act in itself is not more efficacious through the
character of the person. „A child or a woman may say
to me: Be of good heart, I announce to thee the forgiveness
of sins, I absolve thee."([79]) „Christ has given to every
Christian the power and the administration of the keys."([80])

A very important point still remains to be explained,
viz. the connexion, in Luther's system, between faith and
good works. That, according to him, good works have
nothing whatever to do with salvation, will be evident from
what we have said above. For salvation is exclusively
the work of God, under whose action man has to remain
passive like a block of wood, or like a lump of clay in
the potter's hand. We have spoken before more fully
about Luther's treatment of the Bible, but we may mention
here the way, in which he gets over the words of Our Lord:
„Then will he (the Son of man) render to every man according to his works"([81]) Luther does here what he does in so
many other places. His doctrine is not be judged by the
Bible, but the Bible has to be interpreted so as not to clash
with his doctrine. To avoid the difficulty, manifestly contained in the above words, he tells his disciples, they must
deny, that this text has anything to do with justification ([82]).
It only means, he says, that on the day of judgment Christ
will compensate man for the unjust persecutions he may
have suffered in this world.

The only place then, which Luther assigns to good
works in his system, is that of natural, necessary, spontan-

([78]) Walch XX. 59. 60.

([79]) Walch XI. 1040.

([80]) Wittenb. (Germ.) VII. 355.

([81]) Matth. XVI. 27.

([82]) Nostri monendi (sunt) ut
locos hujusmodi, ad justificationem
non pertinentes, negent ad causam

justificationis pertinere et in hoc
fortiter stent et perseverent ...
Ile urges again the difference between law and Evangelium and
continues: Hac distinctione stante
et concessa, sequitur necessario,
quod omnia dicta et allegata de
operibus et praemiis pertineant ad

eous fruits of faith. Whatever is said in the Scriptures about good works, has to be understood in this way: that man does not become good through them, but that by them he is proved to be good.([83]) As soon as man has faith, he becomes a „good tree“, and a good tree cannot help bearing good fruit.([84]) He explains this further by saying, that to *command* good works to the faithful, would be just as senseless, as to command a man to be a man, or a woman to be a woman,([85]) and that „he must be a fool, who would give to an appletree a law, to bear apples, and not thorns“,([86]) since it is the nature of the appletree, to bear apples. But the good actions of the faithful are not good, because they have any interior value, but merely because he that is acting pleases God by his faith.([87])

If faith naturally and necessarily produces good works, we should hardly expect Luther to say in another place: „Those who do *not* believe, we cannot *get away from the works*, and those who *do* believe, we cannot get *to* them“.([88]) But this latter remark was caused by the fearful consequences of his Evangelium, which afterwards we shall hear him describe. There must have been amongst his followers very few that possessed any faith, if, what he says, is true, that: as faith is the only tree, which produces good works, bad works entitle us to the conclusion, that faith is wanting“.([89]) But may not a man, who pos-

legem, non ad promissionem (= Evang.) Wittenb. V. 68 n.

([83]) De Wette II. 183. Opera... sunt fructus jam praesentis et praecedentis remissionis, et bonae conscientiae“. Wittenb. II. 293 n. (De votis mon.)

([84]) Tischr. I. c. 14. § 2. — Fatemur opera bona fidem sequi debere, imo non debere, sed sponte sequi, sicut arbor bona non *debet* bonos fructus facere, sed *sponte* facit“. Wittenb. I. 386 n. (Disp. de fide, thesis 34.) — Fides ... non manet sola i. e. otiosa, Non quod non sola in suo gradu et officio maneat, quia perpetuo sola justi-

ficat. Sed incarnatur et fit homo, hoc est, non est et manet otiosa, vel sine charitate.

Wittenb. V. 347.

([85]) Jen. II. 483.

([86]) Ibid. 174.

([87]) Döll. III. 95.

([88]) Walch XII. 519.

([89]) Mala (opera) non possunt aliunde proficisci, nisi ex arbore mala i. e. incredulitate in corde. Wittenb. V. 97. Quod si opera non sequuntur, certum est fidem hanc Christi in corde nostro non habitare, sed mortuam illam.

Wittenb. I. 386 n. (Disp. de fide thesis 30.)

sesses faith, fall into sin? The Ecclesiastes of Wittenberg
decrees: _No_. For if a man commits a sin, he must have
lost faith beforehand. This startling theory is fully explained
in the vulgar answer, which Luther gave to Henry VII,
„by the disgrace of God king of England“.([90]) „Now
look, my dear man, I will lay open before thee King
Harry's (Königs Heinzen) heart, that thou mayest see,
whether he is a Christian or a heathen. He says: Does
not adultery condemn? does not murder condemn? So
blind is his thomistical head, that he thinks faith may
coexist with sins, that one may commit adultery and
murder and yet believe .... He, who believes cannot
commit adultery or sin, as S. John says (!) I. Ep. I., for
the word of God, on which he depends, is almighty and
is God's power, which will not let him fall. But if he
commits sin, faith must have disappeared beforehand, he
is fallen away from the word. ... And where faith is
wanting, there follow of course adultery, murder, hatred
etc. Therefore, before the exterior sin is committed, the
capital sin has been committed interiorly, viz. unbelief.
Therefore it is true, that there is no sin, except unbelief,
this is sin and does sin.“ ([91])

If we consider Luther's Evangelium as a whole, that
man necessarily commits a sin by every act, that his will
is not free, that he cannot fulfil the law of God, that, to
be saved, he has only to believe, without any regard to
the law, that the best he can do, is, to put away the whole
decalogue, ([92]) we cannot be astonished at his pronounced
indifference as to sin. Nay, his *advice, to commit sin for
the sake of comfort*, though apparently too portentous to be
explained by his own doctrine, is really an organic part of
the whole system.

In a letter to Melanchthon (A. D. 1521) he says: Be
a sinner and sin away, but believe yet more firmly and
rejoice in Christ, who is the conqueror of sin and death

([90]) Walch XIX. 296.   ([92]) De Wette IV. 188.
([91]) Ibid. 342. 343.

and the world. We have to commit sin, as long as we live . . . It is sufficient that through the riches of God's glory we know the lamb, that takes away the sins of the world: no sin can part us from him, though we were to commit in one day thousands of times fornication or murder." ([93])

In a sermon preached at Erfurt, on his way to Worms, he said: „What does it matter, that we commit a fresh sin, if only we do not despair, but think: O my God, thou art still alive! Christ our Lord is the destroyer of sin! The sin will vanish immediately." ([94])

To his friend Hieronymus Weller, who was rather inclined to melancholy, he writes the following lines, to cheer him up: „Why do you think that I drink stronger wine, talk more freely and frequently enjoy a good dinner, if it were not to mock and to torment satan, who is ready to torment and to mock me? Oh! *if I could only devise an extraordinary sin*, merely to mock the devil, to make him understand, that I do not acknowledge any sin!" ([95])

([93]) Esto peccator et pecca fortiter, sed fortius fide et gaude in Christo, qui victor est peccati, mortis et mundi: peccandum est, quamdiu sic sumus ... Sufficit quod agnovimus per divitias gloriae Dei agnum, qui tollit peccatum mundi: ab hoc non avellet nos peccatum, etiamsi millies, millies uno die fornicemur aut occidamus. Putas, tam parvum esse pretium et redemtionem pro peccatis nostris factam in tanto ac tali agno? Ora fortiter: es enim fortissimus peccator.   De Wette II. 37.

([94]) Erl. XVII. 98 seqq.

([95]) Est nonnunquam largius bibendum, ludendum, nugandum, atque adeo peccatum aliquod faciendum in odium et contemptum diaboli ... Si quando dixerit diabolus, noli bibere, tu sic fac illi respondeas: atqui ob eam causam maxime bibam, quod tu prohibes atque adeo largius in nomine Jesu Christi bibam. Sic semper contraria facienda sunt eorum quae Satan vetat. Quid causae aliud esse censes, quod ego sic meracius bibam, liberius confabuler, commesser saepius, quam ut ludam diabolum et vexem, qui me vexare et ludere paraverat. Utinam possem aliquid insigne peccati designare modo ad eludendum diabolum, ut intelligeret, me nullum peccatum agnoscere ac me nullius peccati mihi esse conscium. Omnino totus decalogus amovendus est nobis ex oculis et animo; nobis, inquam, quos sic petit ac vexat diabolus. De Wette IV. 188. — Quisquis Satanicas illas cogitationes aliis cogitationibus, ut de puella pulchra, avaritia, ebrietate etc. pellere potest, aut aliquo irae affectu, huic suadeo; quamvis hoc summum est remedium, in Jesum Christum credere eumque invocare.

He told his friend that to drink, to play, to talk nonsense, to commit a sin, to think about pretty girls, to get angry and similar things are exellent remedies against melancholy — let us say, against remorse of conscience.

If Luther drew such consequences from his system on justification, we cannot be astonished that with the masses of the people „Evangelical liberty" became identical with licentiousness. A few more words of Luther may find a place here; the reader may judge, what fruit they were apt to produce. „Christians are freed from all laws by Christ, not that they should not keep them or should not be exteriorly pious; but though they do not keep the law, the law cannot condemn them."(^{96}) Good works are not only unnecessary for salvation, but they may be dangerous, in as much as they make man trust in himself. „*This a prostitute never does, for as she lives by her public infamy she has her heart always wounded by sin. She has no merits or good works to trust in. She will be much more easily saved, than a Saint,* for a Saint is, by his works, prevented from having a desire of grace."(^{97}) „The more abominable thou art, the sooner will God give thee grace."(^{98})

„*Evangelizo vobis gaudium magnum!*"

(^{96}) Tischr. II. c. 18. § 4.

(^{97}) Walch VI. 548. Cfr. Wittenb. V. 291 B.: Publicani et meretrices ne mali quidem sunt si conferas eos cum istiusmodi hypocritis san- ctis (the Catholics). Illi enim peccantes remorsum conscientiae habent nec sua impia facta justi- ficant.

(^{98}) Döll III. 130.

Chapter IX

Luther on the priesthood and on monasticism.

„It is much better to be a hangman or a
murderer, than to be a priest or a monk."
Luther. Walch XIX. 1333.

From the Wartburg Luther followed the movement started by him most attentively; partly by letters to his friends, especially Melanchthon, Spalatinus, Amsdorf and Link, partly by books and pamphlets, he did his best to further the work of the „Reform." Two of his books published during this period deserve to be specially noticed here, one against the Mass, the other against monastic vows.

The former (¹) is remarkable not only because in it Luther finally rejects the doctrine of the Church on so important a point, but also because he establishes and proclaims those principles, the natural and logical outcome of which was to plague him only too soon in the shape of ranterdom.

He dedicates this book to his brethren of the Augustinian Order at Wittenberg, whom he praises for having been the first to abolish the Mass. In the Preface he mentions the doubts and interior struggles he had experienced before he succeeded in quieting his conscience. „How much work and trouble have I had, and have

(¹) De abroganda Missa privata.   brauch der Messen. Walch XIX.
Wittenb. II. 257 seqq. — Vom Miss-   1204. seqq.

10*

hardly managed to justify my own conscience, that I
alone have dared to oppose the Pope, to consider him
as the Antichrist, the Bishops as his Apostles, the Universities as his brothels! How ofter has my heart been
trembling (wie oft hat mein Herz gezappelt!) and has
reproached me and has put before me their only and
strongest argument: Art thou alone wise? Should all
the others err and have erred for so long a time? What
if thou art in error and leadest so many people into error,
who should all be lost eternally?" (²) He continues saying
that Christ has consoled and confirmed him. But he has
not neglected freely to use also his favourite remedy against
remorses of conscience, viz. reviling the Pope.

The first argument urged by Luther against the Mass
is the universal priesthood. „Let every genuine Christian
properly know that in the New Testament there are no
exterior visible priests except those whom the devil has
made such through the lies of men." (³) „There is a spiritual priesthood common to all Christians, through which
we are all priests through Christ, i. e. we are children of
Christ, the highest priest." (⁴) Hence he thinks himself
justified in addressing the Catholic priests in the following
amiable way: „Where do you come from, you priests of
idols? why have you robbed us of the name belonging
to all of us and usurped it for yourselves? Are you
not thieves and robbers and blasphemers of the Church
of Christ? ... Do you begin to see what you have deserved, you hypocrites and robbers?" (⁵)

The texts of Holy Scripture in which man is called
upon to offer up a contrite heart, an offering of praise,
a sacrifice of justice etc. are cited as a proof to show
that *such things only* have to be offered up to God. Such
a salto mortale is nothing unusual in Luther's logic. But
of course from that assertion it would follow that the
Mass cannot be a sacrifice, but only the use of a Sacra-

(²) Walch XIX. 1305. (⁴) Ibid.
(³) Ibid. 1311. (⁵) Ibid. 1314.

ment. „All pious Christians take care not to offer anything to God in their Masses, but to use the Mass, as
God has instituted it in the Holy Scriptures." (⁶)   „The
Papists are against the Bible and the Divine commandments," therefore: „fly, o brother, and abandon the Pope's
damned priesthood." (⁷)

But Luther has some „thunderclaps of S. Paul" (⁸)
ready which will finish his adversaries completely.

It is a priest's office to preach.

Atqui *everybody* has a right to preach. Ergo.
„With irrefutable texts I will prove that the only right
and true office of preaching is, just like the priesthood
and the sacrifice, common to all Christians. S. Paul
says (II. Cor. 3. 6.): Who also hath made us fit ministers
of the New Testament, not in the letter, but in the spirit.
These words S. Paul has said to all Christians, so as to
make them all ministers of the spirit ... Of course not
all shall preach at the same time, though all have the
power ... For when S. Paul was speaking, Barnabas
held his peace. But should therefore Barnabas not have
had the power to preach?" (⁹) „Out with thee, thou
villain! all Christians have a good right to read and to
preach out of the Holy Scriptures, even if thou shouldst
burst. " (¹⁰)

What answer will Luther have to give to the numberless
sects which started on this selfsame principle? His rage
against the priesthood makes him forget that he is forg-
ing weapons which will be used against himself and which
will cut him to the quick. His feelings find vent in the
expression, that „it is much better to be a hangman or a
murderer, than to be a priest or a monk." (¹¹) We find
the some sentiment expressed by him, years afterwards,

(⁶) Ibid. 1325. [Cfr. Luther's expression on this point in his „Babyl.
Capt." supra, 89 & 90.]
   (⁷) Ibid.
   (⁸) Ibid. 1327.
   (⁹) Ibid. 1326.

(¹⁰) Ibid. 1328. The latin edition has: Ut rumpatur Behemot
cum universis squamis suis.
         Wittenb. II. 262.
(¹¹) Walch. XIX. 1333.

in a „revised edition": „I wish I had rather been a
brothelkeeper or robber than that I should have blas-
phemed Christ for fifteen years by saying Mass." ([12])

In the latter part of the book he says very little
about the Mass, it is more a general invective of the most
venomous kind against priests, bishops, and especially the
Pope „that sow of the devil, which with its snout has
fallen into the holy, splendid, joyful, gracious (universal)
priesthood, dirtying everything" etc. ([13]) There is no necessity of following „the dear man of God" into his favourite haunts. But we may mention that towards the end
he pays a compliment to his powerful protector, Frederick
of Saxony. In him the old prophecy will be fulfilled,
that through a Frederick the Holy Sepulchre will be freed!
Not the Sepulchre in which our Lord was buried — for
that God does not care more than for the cows in
Switzerland! — but that sepulchre in which the word
of God, killed by the Papists, has been buried etc. etc. ([14])

In the beginning of his sojourn on the Wartburg
Luther had already made up his mind that the celibacy
of the priests was an abomination and had to be abolished,
though on more than one occasion he found it necessary
to protest against the unsatisfactory, nay absurd arguments urged by Carlstadt for the same purpose. ([15]) When
therefore Bernhard von Feldkirchen, provost of Kemberg,
one of Luther's own disciples (the same that had defended
his master's heretical theses in a public disputation A. D.
1516) gave to the Clergy an example by taking a wife,
his late professor greatly admired him and warmly congratulated him on his courage; ([16]) at the same time he
expressed his fear that the married priest would have to
suffer on account of this step. ([17]) But the „Reformer"

([12]) Tischr. II. c. 3. § 32.
([13]) Walch XIX. 1399.
([14]) Ibid. 1435.
([15]) De Wette II. 42.
([16]) Cameracensis novus maritus mihi mirabilis, qui nihil me-
tuat atque adeo sic festinarit in
tumultu isto. De Wette II. 9.
    ([17]) Metuo ne expellatur, atque
tum duplo egeat ventre, et quotquot inde ventres processerint.
                              Ibid. 11.

had to overcome great difficulties, before he managed to persuade himself, that monks also were free from „that devilish prohibition."([18]) He tried very hard to find a reason, for, as he says, he pitied them from his very heart.([19]) He was inclined to be more lenient to the young religious, but was very doubtful about those, who had passed the greater part of their lives in the monasteries; the free vow taken by them was the greatest obstacle.([20]) As late as 6th Aug. 1521 Luther is shocked at the news that his followers at Wittenberg will allow wives to the monks, and declares that at any rate *he* will not have one,([21]) and on the 9th of the same month he answers Melanchthon's argument „that a vow which cannot be kept must be rescinded," by saying that this is not to the point. For there are the words of the Bible: „Vow ye and pay to the Lord your God" (Ps. 75, 12). He who takes a vow, voluntarily puts himself under this law, and if the vow can be dissolved on account of the impossibility of keeping it, all the precepts of God have to be given up for a similar reason. No, it is necessary to prove that the vow *in itself* is bad, „*in quo ego sudo.*"([22]) In this his hard work he thought at last he had been successful.([23]) On the 1st of November he wrote to Gerbellius that he had satisfactorily settled the matter with Melanchthon,([24]) and a few days later he

([16]) De Wette II. 35.

([19]) Vellem enim et ego monachis et monialibus succurrere, ut nihil aliud aeque. Adeo me miseret miserabilium hominum, pollutionibus et 'uredinibus vexatorum juvenum et puellarum.

Ibid. (Letter to Melanchthon.)

([20]) Sua sponte statum elegerunt et Deo obtulerunt, quamquam eos qui ante annos pubertatis vel intra sunt, et has fauces ingressi, sine scrupulo exire posse paene definiam: misi quod me adhuc remoratur sententia de iis qui jam senuerunt et diu in hoc statu morati sunt. De Wette II. 34.

([21]) Bone Deus! nostri Wittenbergenses etiam monachis dabunt uxores? At mihi non obtrudent uxorem.   Ibid. 40.

([22]) De Wette II. 45.

([23]) Wittenb. II. 294.

([24]) De votis religiosorum et sacerdotum Philippo et mihi est robusta conspiratio, tollendis et evacuandis scilicet. De Wette II. 90. — Tanta monstra mihi iste adolescentum et puellarum coelibatus miserrimus quotidie manifestat, ut nihil jam auribus meis sonet odiosius monialis, monachi, sacerdotis nomine, et paradisum arbitror conjugium vel summa in-

announced to Spalatinus that he was going to attack religious vows. ([25])

His book on monastic vows expressed his perfected
„evangelical“ views on this point. Spalatinus to whom he
entrusted the publication of it, seems to have disliked it
so much, that for some time he kept it back, together
with the other on the Mass, but a thundering letter from
the Wartburg and the threat, that in his anger Luther
would write even in a more violent style ([26]) made the
disciple obedient. The „Evangelist“ dedicated the book
to his father. The denunciation of monastic life was to
be a kind of satisfaction or compensation to the old man,
who had tried hard, but unfortunately invain, to keep his
son back from entering that state. In a letter to Spalatinus Luther says, he has heard that some monks have
thrown off the cowl, and as he is afraid that they may be
troubled in conscience, he wishes to use his authority in
order to quiet and comfort them. ([27])

From the perusal of this book it is evident, that either
during the whole time that Luther wore a monk's cowl,
he never for a moment understood the idea which under-
lies religiouš life, or that, if he ever understood it, he
wilfully distorted it. Charity would oblige us to suppose
the former and to apply here the words of the apostle
S. Jude: Quodcunque ignorant, blasphemant. Anyhow, in
this book Luther gives only a carricature of monastic
life, nay, some of his statements are such, that it seems
impossible to describe them by any other name than that
of calumny. Protestants who get their idea of monasticism only from such or simular sources, naturally have

---

opia laborans. Ibid. 91. He landed in the „paradise“ in the course
of time.

([25]) Jam et religiosorum vota
aggredi statuo et adolescentes lib-
erare *ex isto inferno*, coelibatus
uredine et fluxibus immundissimis
et damnatissimis. De Wette II. 95.

([26]) Quodsi exemplaria amissa

sunt, vel tu ea retinueris, exacer-
babitur mihi spiritus, ut multo ve-
hementiora deinceps in eam rem nihilominus moliar. De Wette II. 109.

([27]) ut et mei nominis, si qua
est, auctoritate vel apud pios et
bonos, levarentur et apud semet-
ipsos magis animarentur.
                              De Wette II. 106.

a horror of it. All the rage and hatred that an apostate is capable of nourishing, finds vent in this book — to stifle the voice of the apostate's conscience.

Luther arranges his arguments under six headings. Monastic vows are:

1) *Against the word of God.* He denies that in the New Testament there are, besides the precepts, also evangelical counsels. „This distinction only shows that those who make it, do not know what the Evangelium is." (²⁸) What the Papists call counsels, are in fact precepts, for instance, the words of Our Lord (Matth. V. 39 seqq.): If one strike thee on thy right cheek, turn to him also the other; if a man will contend with thee in judgment, and take away thy coat, let go thy cloak also unto him; whosoever will force thee one mile, go with him other two; *love your enemies; do good to them that hate you: and pray for them that persecute and calumniate you* etc. (²⁹) Luther supposes then that Catholics consider *all* the above words as containing *mere counsels,* a supposition, on the refutation of which no words need be wasted. But from this supposition he argues. This is dishonest, and his adversaries, whom he challenges with the words: „Come now, you blind moles and bats of Paris," (³⁰) may well decline controversy with such an antagonist, and may moreover leave it to him to prove that the words: „If one strike thee on thy right cheek, turn to him also the other," contain a strict *precept. If they do, Luther has never fulfilled it.* Of his Bible interpretation we find in this part a specimen in his remarks about the words of Christ: Qui potest capere, capiat! In these words, the „Reformer" tells us, Christ has not counselled virginity, but has deterred from it! (³¹)

(²⁸) Walch XIX. 1823.
(²⁹) Ibid. 1825.
(³⁰) Walch XIX. 1827.
(³¹) Christus ipse plane non consuluit, sed potius deterruit, monstravit solum et laudavit, dum memoratis eunuchis dixit: Qui potest capere etc. Et iterum: Non omnes capiunt hoc verbum. Nonne haec verba sunt potius avocantis et deterrentis? Wittenb. II. 289.

2) *Monastic vows are against faith.* Luther's argument is this:

All that is not of faith, is sin. (Rom. XIV. 23.)
Atqui monastic vows are not of faith. Ergo. ([32])
There remains the minor to be proved. Behold the proof!
Law is not of faith. (Gal. III. 12.)
But monastic vows are law. Ergo. ([33])

In the whole argumentation of Luther we meet on the one side his fundamental dogma of justification by faith alone, on the other side the *calumnious* supposition, that monks and nuns, or in fact all Catholics, expect their salvation through their own works. ([34]) Will Protestants never believe that this is calumny? Will they never believe that Catholics attribute all the meritorious value of good works to the union which exists between Christ and his members, between the vine and the branches? Is it not a calumny and a ridiculous calumny, when Luther represents Catholics as believing that, to go to heaven, it is sufficient „to be buried in a holy, lousy monk's cowl?" ([35]) If what he supposes were true, the conclusion he draws from it, would also be true, viz. that to become a monk or a nun means to apostatize from faith, to deny Christ, to turn a Jew, to enter a pact with the devil. ([36]) But let him first prove that „those accursed people" ([37]) do say what he makes them say.

3) *Monastic vows are against Christian liberty.* „Christian liberty is the liberty of conscience, whereby the conscience becomes free from works, not as if they had not

---

([32]) Walch XIX. 1848.
([33]) Ibid. 1859.
([34]) Qui remissionem, satisfactionem peccatorum, justificationem alteri quam fidei soli tribuerit, et aliunde quam per fidem quaesierit, hic Christum negavit, graciam abjecit, et Evangelium reliquit apostata .... Vota et opera votorum lex et opera sunt, non fides, nec

ex fide. Quid est enim votum, nisi lex quaedam? Wittenb. II. 293 D. — Wherever Luther mentions „lex", he is sure to get into a hopeless muddle.
([35]) Walch XIX. 1867.
([36]) Ibid. 1870.
([37]) das vermaledeyte Volk.
                                    Ibid.

to be done, but in such a way that no one trusts in them. For conscience is not a thing which does works, but a thing which judges of the works ... It has been made free by Christ from all works, for he teaches us not to trust in any work, but to trust in his mercy." (³⁸) A Christian conscience therefore is free both from good and from evil works of its own, neither trusting in the former, nor despairing on account of the latter. (³⁹) But monastic vows tie man again to his own works. Ergo. (⁴⁰)

4) *Monastic vows are against God's commandments,* and especially against the first commandment. (⁴¹) „For as soon as they become monks or nuns, they give up the name of Christians and are henceforth called Benedictines, Dominicans, Franciscans, Augustinians etc. (⁴²) (Lutherans, Calvinists, Wesleyans etc. will be pleased to take the hint.) Atqui: „no man hath ascended into heaven, but he that descended from heaven, the son of man, who is in heaven" (S. John. III. 13.) Ergo he, who does not call himself after the son of man, but calls himself a Benedictine, Franciscan, Dominican etc. cannot enter into heaven. (⁴³)

5) *Monastic vows are against charity.* The Papists allege texts like the following: (⁴⁴) „He that loveth father or mother more than me, is not worthy of me." (Matth. X. 37.) „There is no man that hath heft house, or brethren, or sisters, or father, or mother, or children, or

---

(³⁸) Walch XIX. 1884.

(³⁹) Ibid. 1885.

(⁴⁰) Vota (in the sense which Luther says they have) a Christo avellunt conscientiam piam et in opera dilaceratam dispergunt. *Docent enim justitiam et peccatorum remissionem extra Christum operari!* Wittenb. II. 299.

(⁴¹) Walch XIX. 1912.

(⁴²) Ibid. 1910. — Ilos et suos patres *prae Christo* jactant. Wittenb. II. 302 B.

(⁴³) Cum enim solus Christus ascendat in coelum, qui et descendit et est in coelis, impossibile est, ut Benedictinus, Augustinianus, Franciscanus, Dominicanus, Carthusianus et sui similes, in coelum ascendant.. Omne enim hoc hominum vulgus coelum petit lampadibus inanibus, id est, operibus propriis. Wittenb. II. 302 n. — Quod sacrum rapiunt? Iloc, quo omnia sanctificantur, sanctum nomen Dei. *Nomen enim Christianum extinguunt et suum statuunt in ejus locum, volentes in eo salvi fieri.* Ibid. 303.

(⁴⁴) Walch XIX. 1926.

lands, for my sake and for the Gospel, who shall not
receive an hundred times as much etc." (Mark X. 29. 30.)
„Hearken o daughter, and see, and incline thy ear: and
forget thy people and thy father's house." (Ps. 54, 11.)
What has Luther to answer? „O Lord God, how they
stretch the Scripture! ... I wish I could save God's
honour and avenge myself against the robbers and blasphemers, against their raving and raging lies ... On account
of this abomination alone I wish that all monasteries were
destroyed and, as they ought to be, rooted out. And
would to God (if only Lot and his daughters can escape)
that through fire from heaven, through brimstone and
pitch, like Sodom and Gomorrha, they would sink into
the deepest abyss, so that their memory should die away
like the sound of a bell. *The whole world's curses and
maledictions are here insufficient.*" ([45]) — What Luther
has to say against the selfishness, coldness and uncharit-
ableness of monks and nuns, is more than sufficiently re-
futed by the history of monasticism.

6) *Monastic vows are against reason.* If anywhere, it
is here, that Luther displays his power of sophistry. The
vow of chastity (this is always the principal thing) need
not be kept, if it appears impossible. „For instance, you
have taken a vow to make a pilgrimage to St. James (of
Compostella), you die, you get poor, or you fall ill, or
are taken prisoner; you need not scruple about the
vow." ([46]) „Therefore I conclude clearly and strongly
that vows always exclude the case of necessity. ([47]) *The*

([45]) Walch XIX. 1927. — Hic
veni in locum indignationis meae,
et ardeo me ulcisci de plus quam
sacrilegis et blasphemis istis men-
daciis et insaniis, sed desunt et
verba et cogitatus, quibus monstra haec pro dignitate aggrediar.
Propter hanc vel solam abomina-
tionem eradicata, extincta, abolita
cupio sicut et oportuit, universa
monasteria, quae et utinam, erep-
tis Lot et filiabus suis de medio

eorum, Dominus igne et sulphure
coelesti ad exemplum Sodomae et
Gomorrae demergeret in profundum, ut ne memoria eorum quidam superesset; neque enim satis
fuerit illis anathema imprecari.
Wittenb. II. 304 n. In this and in
many other places the latin edition of Luther's works is milder
than the original.
([46]) Walch XIX. 1941.
([47]) Ibid. 1942.

same impossibility, which through illness prevents a man from making a pilgrimage, excuses him also from keeping his vow of chastity. According to Luther, chastity (apart from the matrimonial state) is a *physical* impossibility; where it exists, it is a great and extraordinary miracle. ([48]) We may ask, where is the paritas between the two cases, that of a man to whom illness makes it impossible to carry out this vow of a pilgrimage, and that of another, who, after taking the vow of chastity, has to struggle against temptation? Luther shows the paritas by saying, that also the illness which prevents the pilgrimage is an *interior* impediment! ([49])   He does not take the trouble to prove that the will of man assisted by the grace of God, can avoid *illness*, just as it may resist *temptation*. But will a logician consider the argument complete without this proof? Moreover, he argues ab absurdo. If the physical impossibility of remaining chaste did not exempt me from the vow of chastity, it would follow that, having vowed, as an Augustinian Friar, obedience to certain rules, I should be guilty of the sin of breaking these rules, even where captivity or illness would prevent me from keeping them. ([50])

Is it not time to answer Luther in his own words: Non sic nugandum est in rebus ad conscientiam et salutem attinentibus? ([51])

([48]) Ibid. 1818.

([49]) Walch XIX. 1945. — Nonne et devotarius ille S. Jacobi morbo laborans, *intrinseco* impedimento impeditur? Wittenb. II. 308.

([50]) Walch XIX. 1948.

([51]) Wittenb. II. 308 b.

Chapter X

The first fruits of private judgment.

„Prophetas istos novos passus sum, et inventus est Satan sese permerdasse in sapientia sua."

Luther. De Wette II. 179.

The „Evangelium" and the „Evangelical liberty" which
Luther preached, found more and more friends; but the
„Reformer" was obliged to protest against the way in
which the latter was used and the former was established
by his followers.

We have seen that immediately after his passing
through Erfurt on the way to Worms, the mob, excited by his sermon, had attacked the Clergy; more
disgraceful scenes followed in a short time.(¹) Luther's
friend Lange did his best to keep the excitement alive;
inflamed by his sermons, a lot of ruffians, amongst
whom there were numerous students, demolished the
houses of the Erfurt Clergy and destroyed the official
records preserved in the Archiepiscopal buildings. The
„Reformer" was very much displeased with such proceedings, which were of course apt to discredit his cause,(²)
but, as he frequently did under trying circumstances, he
consoled himself with the idea, that it must have been the
work of the devil who was anxious to throw obstacles in

(¹) Kampschulte II. 166 seqq.
(²) Audio Erfurdiae in sacerdotum domus vim fieri: quod miror permitti et dissimulari a senatu,
tum taceri a Lango nostro.
De Wette II. 7.

the way of the „Evangelium".([3]) He seems to have trusted
a great deal in the effect of his fundamental article, justification through faith alone; if this article could only be
established, all the rest would come as a natural consequence in the course of time. ([4]) Hence he dissuaded his
followers from using violence, ([5]) but when his passion
upset what much or little he had of prudence, he forgot
his own advice and gave utterance to expressions which
the mob could not help considering as equivalent to an
appeal to violence.

His denunciation of monastic life had the effect, that
hundreds of monks left their houses. So far Luther was
pleased, but he disapproved of the tumultuous scenes which
usually accompanied that step. ([6]) However he thought it
might possibly be a just punishment for the sinful vows
of the monks, that what had been established in impious
harmony, should be dissolved in dissension! ([7]) The evidently unworthy motives which made many of the apostate
monks throw off their cowls, „the care of their bellies and
the love of carnal freedom" made him afraid that through
such „Evangelicals" the devil should succeed in raising „a
great stench against the Evangelium". ([8])

([3]) Erfordiae satanas suis studiis nobis insidiatus est, ut nostros mala fama inureret, sed nihil
proficiet: non sunt nostri qui hoc
faciunt. Ita cum resistere nequeat
veritati, stulto stultorum in nos
zelo cogitat infamare eam.
                  De Wette II. 31.
([4]) Cfr. letter to Count von
Stolberg, De Wette II. 189. „So
würde das äusserliche Ding von
ihm selbst wol fallen."
([5]) Ante omnia cavete, ne Er-
fordienses nostratium imitentur
tumultum in auferendis imaginibus, missis, una specie et aliis
omnibus. Verbo solo sunt aufer-
enda omnia scandala, ut sponte
sua cadant. Letter to Lange, De
Wette II. 180. — Memor (sis) quod
mitteris ad eos, qui lacte alendi

sunt et a laqueis Papae solvendi,
quod non facies, nisi solo verbo
opereris. Letter to Didymus.
                  Ibid. 184.
([6]) Non probo egressum illum
tumultuosum, cum potuissent et
pacifice et amice ab invicem separ-
ari.   De Wette II. 115.
([7]) Displicet sane mihi egressus
iste cum tumultu, quem audivi.
Oportuit enim mutuo consensu et
pace ab invicem dimitti, nisi haec
poena sit male et impie emissi
voti, ut cum dissensione dissolver-
etur, quod impia concordia fuerit
compositum. Ibid. 117.
([8]) Video monachos nostros
multos exire nulla causa alia quam
qua intraverunt, hoc est, ventris
et libertatis carnalis gratia, per
quos satanas magnum foetorem in

But far greater troubles were in store for the „Reformer" from his cherished principle of private judgment, when his own followers too claimed it for themselves. Luther saw his dictatorship threatened. Against the wish of his protector, Frederick of Saxony, he returned to Wittenberg,([9]) where during his absence „the devil had broken into his fold."([10]) Carlstadt, formerly Luther's fidus Achates, had begun to follow a new line of reforming. Assisted by another fanatic, Gabriel Didymus (Zwilling), he insisted that the people should receive the Eucharist under both kinds, also that they should take it with their own hands; he had thundered against confession and the veneration of images. Excited by his words and led by him personally, the mob had broken into the Churches and had destroyed statues and pictures, altars and crucifixes. Even the schools and University were threatened with destruction by Carlstadt, who in his fanaticism demanded that the ministry should be confided to simple and unlearned people.

Luther's growing anger about such proceedings is expressed in many of his letters. He wrote to the Wittenberg congregation, complaining that they had been far too hasty and had given scandal to those who as yet had not joined the movement.([11]) Though not a friend himself of Communion under one kind, of images etc., he told the people in a series of sermons, which he preached immediately after his return to Wittenberg, that such things were of quite inferior importance compared to the duty they had so much neglected, of faith and charity. On the duty of

nostri verbi odorem bonum excitabit, Ibid. 175.

([9]) The Elector was afraid of the consequences which this step would have for himself; hence Luther drew up a document in which he exempted him from all blame in the matter. See De Wette II. 141 seqq.

([10]) De Wette II. 156.

([11]) De Wette II. 119. — Cfr.

Walch XX. 193: When the hearts are properly instructed that we can please God only through faith, not with images, the people willingly give them up and despise them. — Ibid. 194: If the Holy Ghost were here, he would say: Yes, my dear Luther, I am well pleased that thou destroyest the images in the hearts.

charity Luther insists under the circumstances perhaps more, than his sola fide Evangelium would seem to admit. (¹²) „My dear friends, *follow me! I* have not spoiled the thing. I have been the first, whom God has sent forward. I have been the one, whom God has inspired first to preach to you his word.“ (¹³) „It will never do to abolish all bad things so suddenly and without the proper order. Wherefore, if the Mass were not such a wicked thing, I would re-introduce it, to spite those that have suppressed it in that disorderly way, for I cannot defend or maintain that you have done well in this·point. I might do so against the Papists and against stupid heads; I would say: How do you know whether it has been done in a good spirit or in a bad spirit, since the work is good in itself? But I should not know how to defend it against the devil.“ (¹⁴) „Summa summarum, I will preach and speak and write, but I will not force or urge anyone with violence, for faith must be willing and free and must be embraced without violence. *Take an example from me.*“ (¹⁵) „Would to God that all monks and nuns had the necessary understanding, to run away from the Convents, and that all Convents in the world came to an end. That would be my wish and the desire of my heart. But they have no understanding; they leave their monasteries because they hear that others do so, they marry because they hear that others marry . . . this is bad.“ (¹⁶) In a similar way Luther expresses himself about Communion under both kinds, images etc. The Pope's laws are „stupid, foolish laws,“ (¹⁷) and the followers of the „Evangelium“ are of course free from them, but they must not impose this their freedom as a law on others. Those that are still under the Pope's tyranny, have to be fed first with milk, like children. When one has gone through Luther's antipopish works, published even before his

(¹²) See Walch XX. 9—12. (¹⁵) Ibid. 23.
(¹³) Ibid. 14. (¹⁶) Ibid. 28.
(¹⁴) Ibid. 16. (¹⁷) Ibid. 42.

But far greater troubles were in store for the „Reformer" from his cherished principle of private judgment, when his own followers too claimed it for themselves. Luther saw his dictatorship threatened. Against the wish of his protector, Frederick of Saxony, he returned to Wittenberg, (⁹) where during his absence „the devil had broken into his fold." (¹⁰) Carlstadt, formerly Luther's fidus Achates, had begun to follow a new line of reforming. Assisted by another fanatic, Gabriel Didymus (Zwilling), he insisted that the people should receive the Eucharist under both kinds, also that they should take it with their own hands; he had thundered against confession and the veneration of images. Excited by his words and led by him personally, the mob had broken into the Churches and had destroyed statues and pictures, altars and crucifixes. Even the schools and University were threatened with destruction by Carlstadt, who in his fanaticism demanded that the ministry should be confided to simple and unlearned people.

Luther's growing anger about such proceedings is expressed in many of his letters. He wrote to the Wittenberg congregation, complaining that they had been far too hasty and had given scandal to those who as yet had not joined the movement. (¹¹) Though not a friend himself of Communion under one kind, of images etc., he told the people in a series of sermons, which he preached immediately after his return to Wittenberg, that such things were of quite inferior importance compared to the duty they had so much neglected, of faith and charity. On the duty of

nostri verbi odorem bonum excitabit, Ibid. 175.

(⁹) The Elector was afraid of the consequences which this step would have for himself; hence Luther drew up a document in which he exempted him from all blame in the matter. See De Wette II. 141 seqq.

(¹⁰) De Wette II. 156.

(¹¹) De Wette II. 119. — Cfr.

Walch XX. 193: When the hearts are properly instructed that we can please God only through faith, not with images, the people willingly give them up and despise them. — Ibid. 194: If the Holy Ghost were here, he would say: Yes, my dear Luther, I am well pleased that thou destroyest the images in the hearts.

charity Luther insists under the circumstances perhaps
more, than his sola fide Evangelium would seem to admit.[12] „My dear friends, *follow me! I* have not spoiled
the thing. I have been the first, whom God has sent forward. I have been the one, whom God has inspired first
to preach to you his word."[13] „It will never do to
abolish all bad things so suddenly and without the proper
order. Wherefore, if the Mass were not such a wicked
thing, I would re-introduce it, to spite those that have
suppressed it in that disorderly way, for I cannot defend
or maintain that you have done well in this·point. I might
do so against the Papists and against stupid heads; I would
say: How do you know whether it has been done in a
good spirit or in a bad spirit, since the work is good in
itself? But I should not know how to defend it against
the devil."[14] „Summa summarum, I will preach and speak
and write, but I will not force or urge anyone with violence, for faith must be willing and free and must be embraced without violence. *Take an example from me.*"[15]
„Would to God that all monks and nuns had the necessary understanding, to run away from the Convents, and
that all Convents in the world came to an end. That
would be my wish and the desire of my heart. But they
have no understanding; they leave their monasteries because they hear that others do so, they marry because
they hear that others marry ... this is bad."[16] In a
similar way Luther expresses himself about Communion
under both kinds, images etc. The Pope's laws are
„stupid, foolish laws,"[17] and the followers of the „Evangelium" are of course free from them, but they must not
impose this their freedom as a law on others. Those that
are still under the Pope's tyranny, have to be fed first
with milk, like children. When one has gone through
Luther's antipopish works, published even before his

[12] See Walch XX. 9—12.　　　　[15] Ibid. 23.
[13] Ibid. 14.　　　　　　　　　　[16] Ibid. 28.
[14] Ibid. 16.　　　　　　　　　　[17] Ibid. 42.

ined the „Prophets of Zwickau" personally. The result
of the interview is contained in a letter to Spalatinus.
He demanded that the prophets should do miracles in
proof of their doctrines, which were beyond and against
the Bible. [25] Of course they refused. On their part
they might have demanded miracles from the Prophet
of Wittenberg for *his* vocation. If he had the right to
say that their tenets were beyond and against the Scriptures, they had, according to his own principle, just as
much right to deny that such was the case. [26] Luther
had in the course of his life many occasions to say:
Scriptura habet cereum nasum. But he was in power at
Wittenberg, and Carlstadt as well as the Prophets of
Zwickau had to leave the town. [27]

[25] However Luther had also
other means to settle ranters, viz.
showing his contempt of the devil.
„One came to me from the Nether-
lands, intending to dispute with
me, though he was an unlearned
man. To him I said: Let us discuss a pot or two of beer. He
went away: for the devil, that
proud spirit, cannot stand contempt. Tischr. II. c. 14. § 2.
  [26] Prophetas istos novos passus sum, et inventus est Satan sese
permerdasse in sapientia sua: vehementer superbit et impatiens
est iste spiritus eorum, qui nec
blandas ferre potest monitiones,

sed credi vult plena auctoritate
ad primam vocem ... Jussi tandem
ut miraculis probarent suam doctrinam, qua ultra et contra Scripturas gloriarentur. Illi recusabant
miracula, minati tamen sunt, fore
ut credere tandem eis cogerer ...
Ego dimissis *interminatus sum cor-*
um Deo, ne miracula ederet invito
Deo meo: sic discessimus. DeWette
II. 179. In a letter to Lange he
adds: Indignantes recesserunt, uno
eorum plane furente, ut furentio-
rem non viderim hominem unquam.
            De Wette II. 181.
  [27] Keller 19.

Chapter XI.
Charity and tolerance.

„He who does not embrace my doctrine,
cannot be saved."

Luther. Walch XIX. 838.

From the time of his return to Wittenberg Luther may be considered as the acknowledged head of a sect, and as such he began the work of organization.

For a short time he remained faithful to his resolution to spread the „word" without resorting to force. To make to the people the change of religion less surprising he re-introduced at least the exterior forms of the ancient Catholic worship: the same ecclesiastical vestments were worn as of old, the same latin hymns were sung, even the elevation was exteriorly observed. [1] However all words referring to the Mass as to a sacrifice were carefully omitted; but this omission was not perceptible to the laypeople, so that it did not cause any scandal amongst them. Riffel properly observes: [2] „Not too hastily were the people to be robbed of their faith and to be alienated from their Church. To this end the initiated ones were to tolerate for a time a number of things and not to interfere with rites and customs, which formed part of the life of the nation, and even to join in them when there was occasion." It was much easier to draw the people away from the

[1] Köstlin I. 549.　　　　　[2] I. 355.

Pope by representing him as the Antichrist, than to make
them give up the old worship, as Melanchthon reluctantly
confesses.(³) Luther was proud of his service. Almost
twenty years later, A. D. 1541, he wrote to the chancellor
Brück: Thanks be to God, in neutral things our Churches
present such an appearance, that at the sight of our Mass,
choir, organ, bells, chasubles etc. a layman or Italian or
Spaniard, who could not understand our sermon, would
think them to be true papistical Churches.(⁴)

In the Convent Church of Wittenberg and in the parish Church, where Pomeranus was minister, all private Masses
were forbidden;(⁵) for a long time no services took place
except on Sundays and during Lent. Luther seemed for
a while to be indulgent not only to the „obstinate" priests,
who would still retain the Canon of the Mass, but also to
the scruples of his own congregation; hence the Eucharist
was given to the latter just as they wished to receive it,
either under one kind or under both, and at separate
tables.(⁶) But the priests of the Collegiate Church of All
Saints, which was under the immediate patronage of the
Elector, remained for a long time faithful to the ancient
creed and worship, and even Luther's protector Frederick
himself protested against any changes being made in the
services of that Church and against the foundations, made
by his forefathers, being interfered with. For two years
the struggle went on; but as Luther changed his policy to
invectives, some of the priests were intimidated and gave
way. At the end of his „Formula Missae" (a decree
about ceremonies issued in 1523, in which he takes upon
himself the duties of a whole Congregatio Rituum) he was
able to announce to his friend Nicolaus Hausmann that
„only three or four hogs and bellies were left in that
house of perdition and that they remained only for the

(³) Corp. Reform. I. 842.
(⁴) De Wette V. 341. — Against
Carlstadt Luther defends the use
of the latin language in his „Mass".
Walch XX. 264.

(⁵) Kirche oder Prot. 189.
(⁶) Köstlin l. c.

sake of filthy lucre. It almost seems impossible to him
to suppose any honest motive in any of his opponents.
In the same place he says that he has to keep back the
people from forcibly interfering with *All Saints, i. e. All
Devils' Church.*([7])

Luther must have had a curious idea about „feeding
our weak brethren, who are still under the Pope, with
milk and treating them with all kindness“, when, probably
towards the end of 1524, he published his pamphlet „Against
the abomination of the private Mass“.([8]) To a Catholic it
is a most painful thing, to see how here the venerable
liturgy of the Church in its most solemn and touching
part, and every word of it, is besmeared with the venom
of an apostate, in whose opinion opprobrious names have
the force of arguments. Of his vaunted tolerance towards
„massing priests“ nothing appears here, on the contrary,
he openly appeals to the secular power to stop their
„blasphemies“.([9]) The attitude of the mob, excited by
this pamphlet and by Luther's tÌreat that he would leave
the place if the Mass was not suppressed, became more
and more menacing, the symptoms of an approaching
popular rising increased.([10]) The „Reformer“ addressed
an ultimatum to the Chapter. Let the reader judge whether there was much „milk“ in it. „It has been brought

---

([7]) Denique vix tres aut quat-
uor porci et ventres sunt in ipsa
illa perditionis domo, qui pecuniam
illam colunt, caeteris omnibus,
simul et universo populo insignis
nausea et abominatio est ... In-
freno populum quotidie, alioqui
jam dudum domus illa Sanctorum,
imo domus omnium diabolorum
alio nomine ferretur in orbe.
                    Wittenb. 417.

([8]) Von dem Greuel der Still-
messe, so man den Canon nennet.
Walch XIX. :459 seqq. De abom-
inatione Missae privatae. Wittenb.
II. 419 seqq.

([9]) (Si) spectatores nos praebu-
erimus tantae abominationis et

laesionis nominis divini, pari poena
cum ipsis afficiemur ... Multis locis
legibus cautum est contra blas-
phemos. Quanto aequius est magistratum his blasphemiis occurrere, quae in Missa non minus
manifeste, quam ab improbis in
plateis rabiose evomuntur. Wittenb.
II. 424. The latin translations of
Luther's writings are as a rule
comparatively weak and tame;
they lack that peculiar lutheran
flavour, which had such an enormous success with the masses of the
people.

([10]) Kirche oder Prot. 190. Köstlin I. 564.

before me again, that in your Church the Sacrament is
given under one kind ... As therefore I find that the
great patience which we have hitherto shown towards
your devilish work and idolatry in your Church will be
useless ... I am forced, as the appointed preacher of this
congregation, to devise ways and means against it, with
the grace of God ... In case of refusal you may suppose
that I shall not gainsay if God should help me, so that
you should be obliged to do it without obliging anybody.
According to this you will know how to act. And I demand a right, straight, immediate answer, yes or no, before next Sunday." ([11]) The few priests who had remained
at the Collegiate Church gave way, without the consent
of the Elector; on Christmasday 1524 the „Evangelical"
service was held there for the first time; Wittenberg was
„reformed" — only to become a new Sodom, as the „Reformer" himself called it.

Of the many journeys which Luther made during this
period, to establish and further his work at Torgau,
Zwickau, Borna, Eilenburg and other places([12]), there is
no occasion to speak here; but it will be necessary to
notice some more of his most important writings of the
same period, not only because in general they help us to
form an exact idea of the „Reformer", of the high opinion
he had of himself, and of his way of treating his opponents, but also because they throw some light upon the
social character of the revolution started by him, and
upon his relation to the secular power.

In March 1522 he wrote a letter to Hartmuth von
Kronberg, to console him about the losses he had sus-
tained on account of his political connexion with Franz
von Sickingen. This letter appeared also in form of a
pamphlet addressed to „all who suffer persecution on account of the word of God". After complaining of the
troubles which the devil has caused him at Wittenberg

([11]) De Wette II. 565.   ([12]) Köhler 123 seqq. Köstlin
I. 557.

through Carlstadt, Luther expresses his readiness to consider them as a just punishment „for that, to please some good friends, and lest I should appear too obstinate, I kept my spirit down at Worms, and did not make my confession before the *tyrant* in a harder and severer way ... Many a time have I repented of this my humility and reverence."([13]) „The sin at Worms, where divine truth has been so childishly despised, and openly, wickedly, knowingly condemned without being heard, is a sin of the whole German nation."([14]) „God is my witness, I am afraid in my heart, that unless the last day interferes, God will take away his word and will make the German nation so blind and so obdurate, that it will be a horror to think of it. Lord heavenly Father, let us fall into all sins, if sin we must, but preserve us from obduracy."([15]) Further on we find, what the obduracy would consist in, viz. in not acknowledging Luther's special mission. „Though they have not shed my blood, they have had the full and sincere will, and still they murder me continually in their hearts. *Thou unhappy nation, must then thou before all others be the Antichrist's hangman to the Saint of God and his prophet?"*([16])

Amongst others King Henry VIII had appeared in the lists against Luther with an answer to the latter's Babylonian Captivity, in defence of the seven Sacraments.([17]) The „Reformer's" reply furnishes an additional proof, that, to say the very least, nothing could be more groundless than the supposition, that he was a gentleman. In this reply([18]) there is a perfect shower of the most opprobrious and abusive names for his antagonist. Henry VIII is a „liar," „a stupid head," „a mad brain," a „sow" etc. He helps to confirm the truth of the proverbial saying, that there are no greater fools, than kings and

---

([13]) De Wette II. 165. 166.
([14]) Ibid. 167.
([15]) Ibid. 168.
([16]) Ibid. 169.

([17]) Assertio septum Sacramentorum adversus Lutherum.
([18]) Walch XIX. 295 seqq

princes. ([19]) He has as much right to his kingdom, as the Pope to his Popedom. „Therefore the two rub each other as the mules do." ([20])

We need not go through the whole of Luther's dictionary of slang. His opinion of his own mission and of the Church from which he had apostatized, and his *tolerance* are more important. „For ever shall I maintain the things which I have taught, and shall say: He who teaches differently from what I have taught, or condemns me on that account, he condemns God and must remain a child of hell." ([21]) He thinks the king cannot have read his book on the Babylonian Captivity. „But even if he had read it, how could a liar understand it? For all the Papists put together in one heap, know less abouth faith and good works, than a goose knows about the Psalter." ([22]) His former expressions about the Pope have not been strong enough! „I ought to have said: The Papacy is the abomination of the chief of devils . . . Moreover do I say, I am sorry that at Worms before the Emperor I humbled myself so far, that I was willing to admit judges over my doctrine, and to listen if anyone were to prove my error. *I ought not to have shown such foolish humility.* For I was certain and (knew that) before the *tyrant* it would be of no use." ([23]) „The Thomists and Papists are a Church, just as a whore is a virgin." ([24]) „Against the saying of all the Fathers, against the art and word of all angels, men and devils, I set the Scripture and the Evangelium. Here I stand, here I defy, here I glory and say: God's word is to me above everything, divine majesty is on my side, therefore I do not care a fig, if a thousand Augustine's, a thousand Harry's Churches should be against me; I am sure that the right Church holds with me the word of God, and leaves Harry's Church to hold the word of man." ([25])

([19]) Ibid. 341.
([20]) Ibid. 345.
([21]) Ibid. 298.
([22]) Ibid. 300.

([23]) Ibid. 303.
([24]) Ibid. 324.
([25]) Ibid. 336.

That Luther considered his teaching to be identical with the word of God, need hardly be mentioned, but per superabundantiam we will quote a saying of his to this effect, which also shows the elasticity of his logic. He justifies the bad opinion he had conceived of Duke George of Saxony,([26]) whom, he elegantly and generously remarks, he will not give a cut across the snout, as he might do,([27]) by the following admirable series of syllogisms and enthymemata:

Duke George is an enemy of my doctrine.
Atqui my doctrine is thé word of God.
Ergo Duke George is an enemy of the word of God.
Ergo he raves against God and his Christ.
Ergo he must be possessed by the devil.
Ergo I must suppose that he intends to do the worst things. ([28])

Not only Catholics, but also those Protestants wo differ from Luther, will be interested to hear what opinion the „Evangelist" has of them. The above argument, if argument it is, with is deductions, applies not to Duke George only.([29])

As we have been speaking of Luther's reply to Henry VIII, we may at once briefly mention the principal events in the progress of the controversy between the two. A few years after the publication of his answer, the „Reformer" thought it prudent to secure more friends amongst the crowned heads of Europe. Hence he wrote

([26]) Otto von Pack, one of Duke George's counsillors, had invented a conspiracy between his master and a few other Catholic princes against the Lutherans, in the hope of obtaining money from Philip of Hessen by disclosing the pretended snare. The whole tissue of lies was soon exposed. Luther who had eagerly swallowed everything, tried to excuse himself in the way mentioned in the text. It is remarkable that Philip of Hessen had the impudence to demand compensation for the preparations he had made to repel the pretended onslaught, but much more remarkable, that the Bishops of Würzburg and Bamberg were actually compelled to pay!

([27]) Walch XIX. 623.
([28]) Ibid. 642.
([29]) Protestant historians like Ranke (Deutsche Geschichte IV. 135 seqq.) and Kolde (Friedr. der Weise 32) speak very highly of Duke George.

a most abject letter of apology to the King of England, in
which he implored the royal pardon for his former temerity,
that he, an unworthy man, nay a worm, should have dared
to write as he had done against so high a potentate and
mighty king.([30]) At the same time he made some allusions
to the supposed inclination of Henry to the „Evangelium“.

But the king's answer to this letter([31]) coming in
the shape of an exhortation to do penance for his apostasy and for the ruin he had caused and there being
a rumour that the apology had been taken for a retractation of doctrine, Luther's anger was roused to the
highest pitch. His reply shows how rage, pride, hatred
and contempt were working in him. The very mention
of retractation gives him occasion to sayings like the following: „This cannot be tolerated. This touches not my
person (which will have to be silent and to suffer) but my
doctrine (which shall cry out loud). Here may God give
me no patience, nor meekness. Here I say: No, No, No,
as long as I can move a finger, no matter how it may
displease king or emperor or princes or devils or anyone
else.“ Though sarcastically, yet with evident satisfaction
he continues: „Am I not a dear and noble man? Verily
in a thousand years there has been no nobler blood than
Luther's. How so? Look for yourself. There have now
been three Popes, so many Cardinals, Kings, princes,
bishops, priests, monks, big chaps (grosse Hansen) learned
men and the whole world, who are traitors, murderers
and executioners to Luther's blood, or at least wished to
be, likewise the devil with all his own. Really I am angry with my own blood, that I should have such glorious
and precious executioners. Such honour ought to be reserved for the Turkish Emperor, not for a poor beggar like
me. But as they wish it, I must submit to the honour, and
out of their raving and raging I must have some joy for
my heart.“ ([32]) „As truly as God lives, any king or prince,

([30]) The text ap. Walch XIX. 468.   ([32]) Walch XIX. 508.
([31]) ap. Walch XIX. 472.

who thinks that Luther will humble himself before him,
so as to repent of his doctrine, to recant and to seek
pardon, deceives himself thoroughly, he dreams a golden
dream and will find nothing but dirt, when he awakes."(³³)
„Summa, my *doctrine* is the chief thing; I depend on it
(darauf ich trotze) not only against princes and kings,
but against all devils; I have nothing else to keep up and
strengthen and gladden and embolden my heart, the longer
the more." (³⁴)   He is sorry to have written that letter of
apology; it has been like casting pearls before the swine.(³⁵)
„As it is certain that either Luther or they (his adversaries) will have to burn and roast for ever in the fire of
hell, those may be glad, who are sure that they are in
the right . . . For as sure as Cain and Judas are in hell,
it is certain, as if they were there already, that either
Luther or his enemies, whichever are wrong, must go to
hell." (³⁶) „If my doctrine had no enemies except the king
of England, Duke George and the Pope and their followers — the poor bubbles! — I would have settled the
matter long ago with a piece of the Our Father." (³⁷)

The „tolerance" of the Reformer and his revolutionary tendencies receive further illustration from a number
of letters in which he threatened even the secular powers
opposed to him and actually outlawed the Clergy that
refused allegiance to his „Evangelium". Luther expected
a popular rising, but took care to throw all the blame of
it beforehand on his antagonists. In March 1522 he wrote
to his friend Link: „We triumph over the papal tyranny,
which formerly oppressed kings and princes; how much
more shall we conquer and despise the princes themselves! ... But I am very much afraid, that if the princes
continue to listen to that stupid brain of Duke George,
there will be a rising, which will upset princes and magistrates all over Germany and will engulf the whole Clergy ...

(³³) Ibid. 509.   (³⁶) Ibid. 515.
(³⁴) Ibid. 510.   (³⁷) Ibid. 516.
(³⁵) Ibid. 513.

the masses are excited, they have eyes, they neither will nor can be oppressed. It is God who does this and who hides from the eyes of the princes these threats and the dangers that are preparing; nay through their blindness and violence he will do such things, that I think I can see Germany swimming in blood." (^{36}) „Let the princes remember that the people are not now such as they have been hitherto; let them know that the sword of civil war is hanging over their necks." (^{39}) He must have thought that such expressions would startle his friend, for he found it advisable to add at the end of the letter: „I write this sober and early in the morning." (^{40})

When the Canons Regular at Altenburg opposed the appointment of Gabriel Didymus (who, unlike Carlstadt, had done penance for his former independent reformatory tendencies) (^{41}) Luther wrote to the Mayor and towncouncil: „The Canons (Die Regelherren) have no longer authority, if they oppose the Evangelium, but like wolves they have to be shunned and abandoned. Anybody may judge of their doctrine and may recognize the wolves. *For everybody must for himself believe and know what the right faith is and what the wrong."* (^{42}) Everybody? Why then not the Canons too? About the same affair Luther wrote also to the Elector Frederick: „I have given my advice, that the same Regelherren have no power to prevent this (the appointment of Didymus), but that *God himself has abolished all authority and power which acts against the Evangelium* . . . Therefore the town council of Altenburg and your grace are obliged to oppose false preachers and either to aid or (at least) to permit that a right preacher should be appointed there. Against

(^{36}) De Wette II. 157.

(^{39}) Sciant gladium domesticum suis cervicibus certissime impend-ere.   Ibid.

(^{40}) Sobrius haec scribo et mane.
                         Ibid. 158.

(^{41}) Gabriel quidem sese agnos-

cit et in alium virum mutatus est. De Wette II. 156. — Also in another letter Luther mentions with evident satisfaction, that he has accepted Gabriel's penance and amendment. Ibid. 193.

(^{42}) De Wette II. 191.

this it is no use appealing to seals, documents, customs or any right . . . I have sufficiently shown to them, that they have the power and the right to discern and to judge between right and wrong doctrine: Matth. VII. 15. Attend-ite a falsis prophetis, so that everywhere the Canons' right, power, claim to taxes aud authority is come to an end, because they openly oppose the Evangelium." ([43]) We shall have to remember such words, when we come to the history of the revolt of the peasants.

It was natural that if the lower Clergy !were wolves, the Bishops deserved this appellation still better and should therefore have a larger share of Luther's wrath. Against them he published in 1522 a pamphlet, ([44]) that can only be compared to the book which, in the last year of his life, he wrote against the Pope, to a book of which Döllinger says that it must have been written under the excitement produced by intoxicating liquors; nay, it may be said that in many places the former is worse than the latter. The vileness of the expressions which Luther uses in that pamphlet and the revolting filth [and indecencies with which it abounds, are such, that]it will be impossible to reproduce here anything like the substance of it.

With regard to the title he gives himself in the beginning: „Dr. Martin Luther, by the grace of God Ecclesiastes at Wittenberg" he remarks: „If I call myself an Evangelist by the grace of God, I think that I can prove this sooner, than any of you will prove his episcopal title or name and I am sure that Christ calls me so and considers me as such, he who is the master of my doctrine, and who will be witness on the last day, that it is not mine, but *his* pure Evangelium." ([45]) „Therefore I give you to know, that henceforth I shall not do you the honour to submit to you or to an angel from heaven, to judge or to enquire

---

([43]) Also dass allenthalben der Regeler-Herren Recht, Macht, Zins und Oberkeit aus ist, weil sie öffent-lich dem Evangelio entgegen sind. De Wette II. 192.

([44]) Wider den falsch genannten geistlichen Stand des Papstes und der Bishöffe. Walch XIX. 836 seqq.

([45]) Ibid. 837.

about my doctrine. There has been enough of foolish humility." ([46]) „Since I am sure of it (of my doctrine) I shall be, through it, your judge and the judge of Angels, as S. Paul says, Gal. I. 8. so that *he who does not embrace my doctrine, cannot be saved.* For it is God's doctrine and not my own, therefore the judgment too is God's and not mine." ([47]) „A Bishop who does not teach God's word, (lege: Luther's word) has to be shunned as carefully as the devil himself. For where there is not the word of God, there is certainly nothing but devilish doctrine and murder of souls, since without God's word the soul cannot live nor be snatched from the devil. But they say, it is to be feared that there will be a rising against spiritual authority. Answer: Should therefore God's word be neglected and all the world be ruined? Is it just that all souls should be murdered for ever, only that the temporal pomp of those larvae may not be interfered with? It would be better that all Bishops were murdered, that all Collegiate Churches and Convents were destroyed, than that one soul should be lost, let alone that *all* souls should be ruined on account of those useless idols. What are they good for, except to live in luxury on the sweat and labour of others and to hinder the word of God? ... If they will not hear God's word (lege: Luther's word), if they rave and rage with excommunicating, burning, murdering and all sorts of evil, what is more just, than that a strong rebellion should sweep them from the face of the earth?" ([48]) „To come out with it plainly: Let everybody know that the Bishops who are now in power, are not Christian Bishops, nor through divine ordination, but through devilish ordination and human wickedness, and they are the devil's messengers and lieutenants." ([49]) Luther also adds what he himself calls a Bull of his own. „All who cooperate and risk even their lives, possessions and honour in the destruction of the

---

([46]) Ibid. 838.
([47]) Ibid. 838. 839.

([48]) Walch XIX. 844.
([49]) Ibid. 877.

Bishoprics and of the power of the Bishops, they are dear children of God and the right sort of Christians." ([50]) „Since it is manifest that the Bishops are not only larvae and idols, but a tribe cursed by God . . . every Christian ought to help . . . that their tyranny should be despised and come to an end and ought to do gladly whatever is against them, just as if it was against the devil himself." ([51]) „It is certain that all Collegiate Churches and monasteries, containing people who think that their state will make them pious and save them, are worse than brothels, and dens of murderers. This shall be mine, Dr. Luther's bulla, which gives God's grace as a reward to all that observe and follow it. Amen." ([52]) We need not follow „the dear man of God" any farther through this book. The effect which such language must have had upon the mob, can be imagined. The smoking ruins of Monasteries and Churches and the corpses of murdered monks and priests soon bore witness to it.

And yet, Luther is said not to be in the least answerable for the horrors of the rebellion, which made a desert of the fairest part of Germany!

([50]) Ibid. 879.
([51]) Ibid. 885.
([52]) Ibid. 892. — Luther says about the style of his book: Libellum meum Episcopos larvales invadentem ex proposito volui tam acrem esse, sed et in Regem Angliae nihil ero blandior. Video frustra me humiliari, cedere, obsecrare et omnia pacifica tentare (!) ideo cum furiosis et cornua quotidie magis erigentibus durior ero: et mea in ipsos exercebo cornua, irritaturus satanam, donec effusis viribus et conatibus corruat in se ipso. Tu ergo noli timere, nec speres me illis parciturum. Letter to Spalat. De Wette II. 235.

Chapter XII

Luther on the mandatum of Nürnberg.

„That miserable mortal sack of maggots,
the Emperor.“

Luther. Walch XV. 2737.

Towards the end of 1521 Leo X had died, and Hadrian VI, a German by birth, formerly professor and Vice-
chancellor at the University of Louvain, afterwards tutor
to Charles V and Bishop of Tortosa, had ascended the see
of S. Peter. Unlike his predecessor he had an aversion for
all exterior pomp and one of his first acts was to introduce into the papal court as much simplicity, as was compatible with its dignity.(¹) Blameless in his life, distinguished by his sincere piety and his vast erudition,(²) capable of doing an enormous amount of work, deeply conscious of the necessity of a true Reform, he seemed to
possess all those qualities, which would give greater power
to his voice to make itself heard in the tumult of religious parties. Unfortunately his Pontificate was too short,
to give to his endeavours a chance of success. — The
state of Germany naturally received his greatest attention.

During the absence of Charles V in Spain, a Diet
was opened at Nürnberg in 1522, which showed once
more only too clearly how thoroughly miserable the state
of the Empire had become. Whilst Germany was in the

(¹) Reumont III. 2. p. 149 seqq.
(²) Vettori and others. quoted
by Reumont l. c. Vianesio, quoted
by Janssen II. 267, speaks of „la
sua santissima vita che certo in.
questo mondo non ha pari.

utmost danger from the Turks who every day were gaining ground in its eastern part and were ravaging the
country with fire and sword, the princes assembled at
Nürnberg could not make up their minds to make any
real sacrifice against the common enemy; almost everyone
of them seemed to be wrapped up in his own private
interests. With regard to the religious affairs, which formed a subject of long debates, there appeared a similar
want of decision, energy and straightforwardness. The
edict of Worms, on the observance of which the Emperor
strongly insisted, was simply ignored; to such an extent,
that in Nürnberg itself, during the diet, the booksellers
did a lucrative trade in Luther's writings and that the
Elector Frederick's representative defended the protection
granted by his master to the „Reformer" with the assertion, that the latter taught no heresy. (³) Hadrian addressed
to the princes a Breve, in which he exhorted them to do
their duty with regard to the suppression of the new
heresy and warned them, that those who despised the
authority of the Church, would not show greater respect
to the authority and the laws of the Empire. (⁴) The
events which soon followed proved the justice of his
words.

With a frankness which does him the greatest honour,
the Pope acknowledged through his legate, Francesco
Chieregati, that a thorough Reform of the Church in capite et membris was absolutely necessary, and that great
abuses would have to be suppressed also in the Roman
Curia. (⁵) „It is no wonder that from the head the ill-

(³) Janssen II. 266.
(⁴) An putatis alio tendere istos
iniquitatis filios, quam ut libertatis
nomine obedientia omnium sublata,
quid cuique libuerit faciendi licentiam inducant? An ullius pensi
jussa et leges vestras habituros
creditis, qui sacros Canones et
Patrum decreta necnon sacrosancta
concilia ... non solum vilipendunt,

sed etiam diabolica rabie lacerare
et comburere non verentur? — An
speratis contenturos sacrilegas manus laicorum bonis et non omnia
potius sibi quae poterunt vendicat-
uros, qui res Deo dicatas quotidie
vobis praesentibus ferunt aguntque.
                          Wittenb. II. 381.
(⁵) Hergenröther II. 264.

ness has extended to the members, from the Popes to other prelates. We have all declined from the way of justice, we must all therefore give honour to God alone and humble ourselves before him. As far as we are concerned, we shall do our best, that the Roman Curia, from which perhaps all these evils have taken their origin, be reformed." (⁶) Considering the great danger from the Turks, he earnestly warned against interior strife and dissension; he demanded that according to the laws of the Empire the edict of Worms should be carried out and promised the speedy convocation of a general Council.

The character of Hadrian VI was sufficiently well known to prevent his words from being taken for mere diplomatic phrases. His openness and honesty of purpose deserved a better reward than that which it met with. The fact that he acknowledged the existence of evils, was, wrongly enough, considered by the Lutheran party as a justification of their complaints. (⁷) They had now fresh pretexts for an evasive policy. With many protestations of fidelity towards the Apostolic See and the Emperor the Diet declared that it would not be wise to carry out the edict of Worms, for such a step would be considered by the people as implying the upholding of ecclesiastical abuses! With regard to the promised Council it was first demanded that in it the secular princes should have a vote just like the Bishops, but this point was given up afterwards.

A hundred grievances (gravamina) of the German nation were drawn up, which were to be forwarded to the Pope, some of them most unjust ones. If the members of the Diet complained of the annates which were paid to Rome, they ought to have remembered that far greater sums were paid by the Popes to Germany as subsidies for the wars against the Turks. (⁸) The decision that „the pure Evangelium" should be preached according to the doctrine

---

(⁶) Pallav. l. II. § 27 seqq.
(⁷) Pallav. l. II. § 33: Una sì fatta istruzione ... appresso molti fece desiderare in lui maggior prudenza e circuspezione.
(⁸) Hergenröther II. 265.

and interpretation of the books approved of by the
Christian Church, was a measure, the vagueness of which
was not calculated to put an end to religious controversy,
and the promise that nothing should be printed against
the existing authorities proved a mere mockery. The
legate, seing that a straightforward line of action would
not be followed, left Nürnberg before the end of the
deliberations.

As was to be expected, Luther put his own interpretation on the mandatum of the Diet, ([9]) which did not
hinder him for a moment from sending out pamphlet
after pamphlet against the Pope and the Catholic Church.
When in May 1523 Hadrian VI canonized S. Benno,
Bishop of Meissen, Luther reviled him to his heart's content in the little book entitled „Against the new idol and
old devil that is to be set up at Meissen.“ ([10]) „I will
only write against the living Satan, who now, that through
God's grace the Evangelium has reappeared, shedding
a great light, knows no other way of avenging himself
than spiting God and dishonouring God's word by such
tomfoolery, causing himself to be set up and adored under
the name of Benno.“ ([11]) „It is not Benno, but the devil
under the name of Benno.“ Apart from Luther's general
protest against the veneration of Saints, apart from his
aversion against canonization as *implying a new article
of faith* ([12]) and against spending in their honour money
which only serves to feed „the lazy gluttons and idle
fattening hogs“ in the Churches and monasteries, ([13]) the
„Reformer“ has a special reason for protesting against
this particular Saint, because he had been on the side of
Gregory VII in the latter's struggle with the Emperor
Henry IV. „He has confirmed the Pope in his villainy“ ([14])
— which villainy of Gregory consists, according to Luther,
in great part in the fact that, contrary to the Evangelium,

([9]) De Wette II. 367 seqq.   ([12]) Ibid. 2788.
([10]) Walch XV. 2772 seqq.   ([13]) Ibid. 2773.
([11]) Ibid.   ([14]) Ibid. 2775.

he resisted evil. ([15]) Perhaps, he thinks, this cooperation
of Benno has only been invented to please the Pope —
for the Popes like to have their ears scratched in that
way ([16]) — but „in case it is true, I say: If Benno has
died in that conscience, without having repented of his
misdeed, he is surely gone to the devil." ([17]) At the end
he sums up his opinion in the words: „This tomfoolery at
Meissen about Benno is nothing but lies and tricks of
the devil." ([18])

Whilst the above mentioned mandatum of the Diet of
Nürnberg decreed that priests who attempted to marry
and religious who left their monasteries, should, according
to Canon Law, lose their benefices and privileges, Luther
wrote about the same time that famous letter to the Lords
of the Teutonic Order, in which he exhorted them to
give a consoling example by breaking their vows, by
marrying and dividing amongst themselves the property
of their Order. „Behold now is the acceptable time,
behold now is the time of salvation. The word of God
illumines and calls you. You have plenty of reasons to
follow it, *also on account of temporal goods.* ([19]) We
shall have to mention more of the almost incredible contents
of this letter in the explanation of Luther's views on
matrimony.

The climax of hatred and at the same time of absurdity seems to be reached in the pamphlets of Luther and
his friend Philip Melanchthon („the man of a tender
Christian mind") on two pretended monsters, in the existence and form of which they find a divine condemnation
of Popery and monasticism, and a prediction of either great
wars or the last day. ([20]) Melanchthon explains the Pap-

([15]) Ibid. 2776.
([16]) Ibid. 2777.
([17]) Ibid.
([18]) Ibid. 2792. With evident
satisfaction Seckendorf (lib. III. p.
221) relates how, fifteen years afterwards, at the command of the

Evangelical Visitatores the shrine
of S. Benno was destroyed.
([19]) Walch XIX. 2157.
([20]) significant certo rerum pu-
blicarum mutationem per bella potissimum. Quod et mihi non est
dubium Germaniae portendi vel

asellus", the „Pope-ass,ʽ (²¹) Luther puts an appendix to it
under the title of „Amen" (²²) and adds his interpretation
of the „Monacho-vitulus," the „Monk-calf." (²³) Engravings
representing the two monsters accompanied the pamphlet for
clearness' sake, they are also reproduced in the Wittenberg
edition. The „Papasellus" is said to be a monster found dead
in the Tiber A. D. 1496. In variety of composition from
different beings it certainly beats the classical chimaera, but
each grotesque part has according to Melanchthon a deep
meaning and conveys a solemn divine warning to the world.

The donkey's head signifies the Pope, who is just
as fitting a head to the Church, as a donkey's head
would fit a human body; whose donkey's brain moreover understands nothing about the word of God or
the Holy Scripture, nor even about the law of nature
and the light of reason! The right hand, similar to an
elephant's foot signifies the spiritual power of the Pope
which crushes the conscience of man, the left hand, to
all appearances a human one, the secular power of the
same; the right foot, resembling that of an ox, the popish
doctors, preachers, confessors etc.; the left foot similar
to the fangs of a griffin the Canonists. The female
breasts represent Cardinals, Bishops, monks etc. „the
impure and well fed hogs of Epicure's herd" (²⁴) etc. etc.
For the rest we refer the reader to the subjoined note;
the text contained in it throws further light upon Melanchthon's „tenderness of mind." (²⁵) The absurdity of such

summam belli calamitatem vel ex-
tremum diem. De Wette II. 301.
Of Luther's belief in signs and
omens many proofs are extant in
his letters. He writes to Rühel
(De Wette II. 667) that the birth
of a headless child at Wittenberg
was the sign of the Elector Frederick's death. Tó Link he writes
(De Wette IV. 290) that a comet
has appeared and adds: Nihil boni
significat.

(²¹) Wittenb. II. 424 B. seqq.

(²²) Ibid. 428.

(²³) Ibid. 429 seqq.

(²⁴) id genus lenones et bene
saginatos Epicuri de grege porcos.
Wittenb. II. 426.

(²⁵) Draco ex podice papaselli
prospectans, apertisque faucibus
flammeum torrentem minitans, significat minaces, virulentas horri-
bilesque Bullas atque maledicta
scripta quae Pontifex cum satelliti-
bus suis in totum orbem evomit.
Ibid. 427.

an invention and of its interpretation might almost make
one forget the bitterness which inspired it. The whole
would appear as a bad and utterly tasteless joke, if the
Ecclesiastes of Wittenberg did not solemnly assure us
that, God's sacred Majesty having made and shown this
monstrous form, man has to tremble at it and to learn
from it God's thoughts and designs! (²⁶) His own interpretation of the second monster, the „Monacho-vitulus,“
the „Monk-calf“ is a worthy pendant to the foregoing
dissertation, only this monster is a divine protest against
monasticism. He winds up with an exhortation addressed
to monks and nuns to throw off their religious habits and
to look out for wives and husbands. „I have done my
duty and have warned you!“

It was about this time that Luther lost one of his
greatest friends and protectors, Franz von Sickingen.
This nobleman, who had long been the terror of every
peaceloving and industrious person and town along the
Rhine, thought that the time had arrived to carry out his
far-reaching ambitious plans. The lower nobility that were
smarting under real or imaginary grievances, and many
of whom had fallen into such abject poverty that they
had nothing to lose, willingly put their swords at his
disposal in the hope of plunder. The Emperor not having
followed the advice of Hartmuth von Kronberg, to use
the ecclesiastical property for the suppression of Popery, (²⁷) others were found who were ready to act upon

---

(²⁶) Quia sacratissima majestas
Divina condidit nobisque simul-
acrum tale proposuit, oportuit
omnes homines, quoties in mentem
venit, expavescere et trepidare,
velut unde non obscure capi con-
jectura possit cogitationum, con-
silii voluntatisque Dei. Ibid. 428.
— At the end of his „Amen“ Luther adds: Audire cogor quod verbum Dei, confessa et agnita veritas,
vocatur haeresis et velut infra
mortuos amandatur. Tales viperae

merito capite draconis insigniuntur
qui ex papaselli podice prospectans, luculentam cloacam evomit.
Verum Dei gratia (papatus) *cadaver
est tamquam ipse papasellus nec
unquam vitam viresque reparabunt.*
                              Ibid. 428 B.
(²⁷) si refragetur Pontifex, Cae-
sari jus esse ut eum cogat, et media
ex ipsis bonis quae ecclesiastica vo-
cantur, corroget.
            ap. Seckend. lib. I. 225.

it. Sickingen's first blow was aimed at Richard von
Greiffenklau, the Elector-Archbishop of Treves, against
whom he nourished deep feelings of enmity on account
of the warnings given by this prelate against him to the
princes of Germany.

Religion and the love of the „Evangelium" was used
as a pretext for this brutal war, which was begun apparently
„to open a door to the word of God," which the Elector
had hitherto excluded from his dominions. ([28]) The fanatical preachers who accompanied the band of robbers under
Sickingen's command, did their best to make him appear
as the illustrious and disinterested hero of the Evangelium. ([29]) But the siege of Treves, where the Elector,
showing great courage and prudence, commanded in person, proved unsuccessful, and Sickingen had to return with
no other honour, than having laid waste the country and
having burned Churches and monasteries on principle ([30])
and in imitation of Ziska, the great Bohemian leader.

At last Treves, Hessen and the Palatinate formed an
alliance to rid Germany of this continual source of trouble
and danger; in May 1523 Sickingen's stronghold, the castle
of Landstuhl, fell into their hands; he himself, mortally
wounded, expired soon after. „I have heard," writes Luther
to Spalatinus „the true and pitiful history of Franz von
Sickingen. God is a just, but a wonderful judge."([31]) Hutten
found himself obliged to look after his own safety. Erasmus coldly refused him his assistance. The bitter controversy which in consequence of this began between the two
humanists and which filled Melanchthon with fear for the
cause of the„ Evangelium," would probably have assumed
greater proportions, if death had not put an end to it. ([32])

([25]) Ibid. 226.
([29]) Janssen II. 235.
([50]) Strauss, Ulr. v. Hutten II.
237.
([31]) De Wette II. 340.
([32]) Before this refusal of Erasmus, Luther had already complained of the duplicity of the

same. Erasmus prodit tandem
hostis Lutheri et doctrinae ejus
ex animo. sed fucis et astu verborum mentitur sese amicum . . .
Hunc tergiversantem et subdolum
tum amicum, tum hostem detestor.
					De Wette 196.

In the month of August in the same year Hutten died,
at the age of 36, of the consequences of his licentiousness,
not caring to wear to the end that mask of religion which
he had put on for political purposes. ([33])

The new Diet of Nürnberg (A. D. 1524) produced
just as little effect for the religious pacification of Germany as the preceding one. Clement VII, who had
followed Hadrian VI, sent as his legate Cardinal Campeggio,
who bitterly complained that he did not find the same
country which he had known before. Without entering
into the discussions which took place, we will mention
the mandatum in which the decision of the Diet was contained, a document which was not suited to satisfy either
party, and plainly contradicted itself. ([34]) For whilst it decreed in the first part, that every member of the Diet, within
his own territory, was to carry out the edict of Worms
as far as possible, the authority thus acknowledged was
practically denied in another part, according to which
Luther's books were to be examined by learned men.
If the condemnation of these books was not yet sufficient,
the edict of Worms became simply nonsense. This mandatum filled the Emperor with indignation. From Burgos
he threatened with the greatest punishment those who
would refuse to accept the condemnation of Luther's heresy as a final decision and insisted once more on the
strict execution of the edict of Worms. But as the mandatum of Nürnberg had been published under the Imperial
name, Luther made the best of the evident contradictions,
to discredit the authority of the Emperor. He published
the two decrees with a prologue, an epilogue and a
commentary consisting of short sarcastic notes. ([35]) „Out
of pity for us poor Germans,“ he says, „I have caused
these two edicts to be printed, thinking that perhaps God

([33]) Strauss. l. c. II. 314.
([34]) Hergenr. II. 266.
([35]) Zwei kaiserliche uneinige
und widerwärtige Gebote. Walch
XV. 2712 seqq. Some of the notes

are: „Where is this written? Up
in the chimney!“ „O Lord, how
blind the people are!“, „the Church
of God means here the Antichrist“
etc.

in his great mercy will move a few princes and others to
feel — for it is not a question of seeing, sows and asses
can see it — how blind and obstinate they are I
am condemned, and at the same time I am spared for
future judgment. The Germans will have to consider me
as a condemned man and to persecute me as such, and
yet they have to wait, whether I shall be condemned or
not. *Must these not be drunk and mad princes?"* ([36]) „In
the end I beg of all dear Christians, to help to pray to
God for *such miserable, blinded princes, with whom God
has plagued us in his wrath;* we ought not to follow them
against the Turks, nor contribute (towards the war), for the
Turk is ten times more prudent and more pious, than
our princes are. How could *such fools* have any success
against the Turks, since they tempt and blaspheme God
to such an extent? Here you see, how *that miserable
mortal sack of maggots, the Emperor,* who is not sure
of his life for a moment, *impudently* boast that he is the
true and supreme protector of Christian faith." ([37]) „How
mad has the world become! Thus also the king of
England boasts that he is a defender of the Christian
Church and faith, nay, the Hungarians boast that they
are God's protectors, for in the litany they sing: That
Thou wouldst vouchsafe to hear us, Thy protectors (Ut
nos defensores tuos exaudire digneris.) Would that a
king or a prince would undertake the protection of Christ,
and then another the protection of the Holy Ghost; I
suppose the Blessed Trinity and Christ and the faith
would then be in proper keeping. These things I lament
from the bottom of my heart before all pious Christians,
that, with me, they may have pity *on such mad, foolish
senseless, raving, frantic lunatics . . . May God deliver
us from them, and in his mercy give us other rulers,*
Amen. ([38])

For the last twelve years the Catholics of Prussia

([36]) Walch XV. 2712.   ([38]) Ibid. 2739.
([37]) Ibid. 2737.

have been deprived of their religious liberty. To make this possible, even the Constitution of the kingdom, which guaranteed their liberty, has been changed. Not only have the religious orders been driven into exile, but, where the gracious permission of the Government is withheld, even the celebration of Mass and the administration of the last Sacraments to the dying has become a crime, for which hundreds of priests have been sent to prison. If Prussian Catholics were to use expressions like those we have quoted above, what would be thought of them and what would become of them? But let the reader remember that not many months ago Emperor and kings and princes have feasted the memory of the man who *did* use such language — and from his heart too — against a Catholic Emperor and against the princes of the Empire. But then he was Dr. Martin Luther, the „dear man of God,“ „the Ecclesiastes of Wittenberg!“

Chapter XIII.
De servo arbitrio.

Humana voluntas in medio est posita ceu
jumentum.
Wittenb. 46S.

For some years the friendship between Luther and Erasmus had considerably cooled down and bitter and sarcastic remarks had frequently been exchanged. The open and final rupture took place when Erasmus wrote his Diatribe, to prove against the „Reformer" the freedom of the human will. Luther answered him in the book „De servo arbitrio" which appeared in 1525. A short analysis of this remarkable production may not be out of place here. We shall not of course be able to give the outlines of everyone of his numerous works, but just for this reason it may be advisable to give the reader an idea of the value of Luther as a theological writer, by going over a book, of which he himself was not a little proud, and in which he treats of the very basis of his whole system. In his answer to the king of England's „accursed book", the real author of which he suspected in Erasmus, he says that neither the king, nor Erasmus, nor the devil himself will ever refute his book de servo arbitrio.(¹) Though disgusted with Erasmus' book,(²) he thanks him

(¹) Provoco regem, provoco Erasmum et ipsum denique Satanam, exerant hic suas vires omnes, omnes huc conferant facultates et copias, ut solidis Scripturae argu- mentis librum meum de servo ar- bitrio refutent. Wittenb. II. 534B.
(²) tuus libellus mihi viluit ac sorduit. Ibid. 457.

for having given him an opportunity fully to discuss the
matter and for not having bothered him with trifling questions such as the Papacy, purgatory, indulgences etc., but
having come straight to *the* point. (³)

The first part of the book is an answer to the arguments
of Erasmus — whether taken from reason or from Scripture — and a vindication of the arguments which Luther
had formerly used and which had been impugned by his
antagonist: in the second and shorter part the author
produces all the Bibletexts which in his opinion prove that
the human will is not free. The quintessence of the whole
work we find in the words, that „the will of man is like
a beast of burden: if God mounts it, it goes where God
directs it, if the devil, it goes where the devil directs it.
It cannot chose its rider, but the riders quarrel between
themselves, which will get into the saddle." (⁴)

The exordium is chiefly directed against the remarks
of Erasmus, that, with regard to the question in hand, Luther ought not to presume to say that there is no difficulty in Holy Scripture. This provokes Luther's anger.
He maintains that, with the exception of some unimport-
ant words, the meaning of which is not yet quite understood, the Bible is absolutely clear about all the mysteries
of faith. (⁵) To say that there are obscurities in it, is a
pestilent, impudent and blasphemous assertion of the Sophists i. e. Catholics. (⁶) Let them produce only one text

---

(³) Hoc in te vehementer laudo
et praedico, quod solus prae omnibus rem ipsam es aggressus, hoc
est, summam causae, nec me fati-
garis alienis illis causis de papatu,
purgatorio, indulgentiis ac similibus nugis potius quam causis . . .
Unus tu et solus cardinem rei
vidisti et ipsum jugulum petiisti,
pro quo ex animo tibi gratias ago.
                           Ibid. 525 n.
(⁴) Humana voluntas in medio
posita est ceu jumentum; si insederit Deus, vult et vadit quo
vult Deus, ut Psalmus dicit: Factus

sum sicut jumentum et ego semper
tecum. Si insederit satan, vult et
vadit quo vult satan, nec est in
ejus arbitrio ad utrum sessorem
currere, aut eum quaerere, sed
ipsi sessores certant ob ipsum ob-
tinendum et possidendum. Ibid. 468.
(⁵) Hoc sane fateor esse multa
loca in Scripturis obscura et abs-
trusa, non ob majestatem rerum,
sed ob ignorantiam vocabulorum
et grammaticae, sed quae nihil
impediant scientiam omnium rerum in scripturis. Ibid. 459 n.
(⁶) Pestilens illud sophistarum

to prove their insane opinion! It is the suggestion of the devil, who wishes to deter people from reading the Bible.([7]) Through God's word all doubt and uncertainty has been taken away.([8])

The chief arguments of Erasmus taken from reason, to which Luther has to answer, may be briefly expressed in these words:

If the will of man in not free,

1) Who will try to lead a good life? Will not everybody find a ready excuse for all sins and vices by saying: I could not help it? The devil was riding me?

2) the whole legislation of God becomes a farce and a mockery. What is the use of laws, if the people for whom they are made, have it not in their power to obey?

3) how can God punish or reward those who cannot be answerable for their good or evil deeds?

In a general way the Reformer begins his answer by inveighing against the supposition that reason has anything to do with faith, or should ever be listened to in questions touching the mysteries of Religion.

But with the greatest submission to Divine revelation, and without the slightest wish to penetrate the inscrutable, we cannot help remembering that both reason and revelation are granted by the same God, that both flow from the same fountain of truth, that therefore the two can never be at variance. Nor can we find fault with a theological argument, merely because it condemns a theological proposition on account of its evident opposition to the evident truth as apprehended by reason. On the other hand we know that the highest mysteries of faith, though high *above* reason, can never be *against* reason. But on a hundred different occasions Luther protests against such a way of reasoning.

---

verbum. Scripturas esse obscuras et ambiguas. Ibid. 473 n. Impudens et blasphema illa vox. 474 n.

([7]) Talibus larvis satanas absterruit a legendis libris sacris. 459 n.

([8]) Nihil prorsus relictum est obscurum aut ambiguum, sed omnia sunt per verbum in lucem producta · certissimam, et declarata toti orbi, quaecunque sunt in Scripturis. Ibid. 460.

Reason, he says, has to be absolutely excluded from theology; it most impertinently tries to put its nose into everything. (⁹) Reason is, as he calls it in another place (¹⁰) „the
devil's bride and archwhore,‟ that „has to be throttled like
a beast, before we can arrive at faith. (¹¹)

God has given his law to man, to a reasonable being,
may it not therefore be supposed that he has spoken in
such a way as to make himself intelligible to man? may
not man apply the natural faculties given to him by his
Creator, to understand the law? According to Luther
decidedly not! It would be an insult to God! it would
be like measuring the infinite with our finite understanding. (¹³)

Let us come to the answers in particular.

1) If the will of man is not free, who will care to lead
a good life? With the greatest coolness Luther answers:
Nobody! We state a principle and we must take the consequences. It is not in the power of man to lead a good
life, since God works in him and through him. Whether
a man is good and consequently goes to heaven, or bad
and consequently goes to hell, this depends entirely on
the other question, whether he is an elect or not. If apparently through this doctrine the doors are opened to impiety, we console ourselves whith the thought, that on
the other side the gates of heaven are open to the elect. (¹³)

(⁹) Est nasuta et dicax. Ibid.
487 n. — Cfr. Wittenb. V. 304:
Nihil fortius adversatur fidei quam
lex et ratio.

(¹⁰) Wider die himmlischen Pro-
pheten. Walch XX. 309.

(¹¹) Cfr. Wittenb. V. 335: Fides
rationem mactat, et occidit illam
bestiam. Cfr. Ibid. 336.

(¹⁴) Respondeo haec sunt argu-
menta rationis humanae ... Dices:
sic videtur natura verborum et
usus loquendi exigere inter homines. Ergo divinas res et verba
metitur ex usu et rebus hominum.
Quo quid perversius, cum illa sint

coelestia, haec terrena? Ibid. 480 B.
— Quae (ratio) cum in omnibus
verbis et operibus Dei caeca, surda,
stulta, impia et sacrilega est. hoc
loco adducitur judex verborum et
operum Dei. Ibid. 494.

(¹³) Quis, inquis, studebit cor-
rigere vitam suam? Respondeo
nullus hominum, neque etiam ullus
poterit ... Corriguntur autem electi
et pii per Spiritum Sanctum. Caet-
eri incorrecti peribunt. Quod vero
his dogmatibus fenestra aperitur
ad impietatem. Esto: illi pertineant
ad lepram superius dictam: toler-
andi mali. Nihilominus simul iis-

You need not come with arguments from reason, for where there is reason, there can be no faith. ([14]) — We shall have to speak afterwards of Luther's views on pre-destination.

2) If the will of man is not free, what can be the meaning of God's law? Why should God give command-ments, and in such a solemn way as he has done, if he knows that man has no choice, but acts under absolute necessity? Does not divine legislation become a farce?

Not at all, says Luther, though it is perfectly true that God does not expect us to keep his commandments, for he knows that this is an impossibility to us. You, so the „Reformer“ tells his antagonist, argue wrongly, when you say: God cannot give a law, which cannot be kept. Ergo, from the very existence of a Divine law, necessarily it follows that man can observe it; the truth is: A praecepto ad posse *non* valet illatio, the existence of a law does *not* prove the possibility of keeping it. ([15]) The law of God has been given to us — according to Luther — for no other purpose but this, *to convince us of the absolute impossibility of conforming to it*, to thoroughly humble us, to destroy that pride, which makes man think that he can do something. The whole virtue of the law is in the knowledge it gives us of our nothingness. ([16])

dem (dogmatibus) aperitur porta ad justitiam et introitus ad coelum. Ibid. 467.

([14]) Ut fidei locus sit, opus est ut omnia quae creduntur, abscond-antur ... Si possem ulla ratione comprehendere quomodo is Deus sit misericors et justus, qui tantam iram et iniquitatem ostendit (in puniendo) non esset opus fide. Ibid. 467 B. — If this is true, Lu-ther must either deny that man, with his natural faculties, can come to the knowledge of God's exist-ence, or if he grants this, he must deny that man can *believe* God's existence. Non datur tertium.

([15]) When applied to a *human*

precept the principle may be true, but L. states it absolutely.

([16]) Haec est causa legislationis divinae, ut Paulus (!) docet. Caeca est enim humana natura, nonvericat sui ipsius vires seu morbos potius. Deinde superba videtur sibi nosse et posse omnia. Cui superbiae et ignorantiae nullo Deus remedio praesentiori mederi potest, quam proposita lege sua. Ibid. 481. — Tota ratio et virtus legis est in sola cognitione, eaque nonnisi peccati, praestanda, non autem in virtute aliqua ostendenda aut conferenda. Ibid. 482. — Congere igitur omnia verba imperativa in unum cahos... mox dicam, semper illis significari

3) If the will of man is not free, how can God punish or reward? This question only shows, so Luther replies, that his opponent knows nothing about the matter. It can only be put by one, who thinks that between the action of man and the punishment or reward, there exists a real connection as between cause and effect, which is a great mistake. The fact is, that if a man does good, *though he cannot help it*, he is given something; if he does evil, *though he cannot help it*, he is punished. The one merely *follows* the other, but does not proceed from it.([17]) There is the simple fact, that the kingdom of heaven is ready for the just and that hell is ready for the wicked.([18])

But if the salvation or damnation of man does not depend on his own choice, on his own works — aided by grace or despising grace — but entirely on the fact, that he is either amongst the elect or not, how can this be reconciled with God's solemn protestation that he wishes not the death of the sinner?

Here Luther answers with his horrid distinction between the will of God as it is manifested to us and as it is hidden from us.([19]) Practically this means that God

quid debeant. non quid possint aut faciant homines. Ibid. 482 B. — Verba ... sunt imperativa et nihil probant, nihil statuunt de viribus humanis ... Per legem fit cognitio peccati et admonitio impotentiae nostrae, ex qua non infertur quod nos aliquid possimus. Ibid. 489 B. — With regard to Eccl. XV. 16. „If thou wilt keep the commandments etc., Luther says: Non est admittenda illa sequela: Si volueris, ergo poteris. Ibid. 481 B.

([17]) Necessitas neque meritum neque mercedem habet ... Iis qui volenter faciunt bonum vel malum, *etiamsi hanc voluntatem suis viribus mutare non posssunt*, sequitur naturaliter et necessario praemium vel poena. Ibid. 489.

([18]) Ita manet pios regnum, *etiamsi id ipsi neque quaerant nec cogitent*, ut quod illis a Patre suo paratum est ... Quomodo merentur id, quod jam ipsorum est et ipsis paratum, antequam fiant? Ibid. — Si sequelam spectes, nihil est sive bonum sive malum, quod non suam mercedem habeat. Ibid. — Nihil aliud probatur, quam *sequela* mercedis. Ibid. 490.

([19]) Aliter de Deo vel voluntate Dei nobis praedicata, revelata, oblata. culta, et aliter de Deo non praedicato, non revelato, non oblato, non culto disputandum est.
Ibid. 485 B.

tells us one thing and does another. „God does many
things which he does not show us in his word. He
wills many things, which, in his word he does not show
that he wills. In this way he wishes not the death
of the sinner — viz. in his revealed word. But he wills
it by his inscrutable will. We have to do with the word
and must leave his inscrutable will aside. (^{20})

Let us see what, according to Luther, becomes in this
way of Christ himself. Erasmus reminds the „Reformer" of
the fact mentioned by S. Matthew, that Our Lord shed tears
at the sight of Jerusalem. „If everything happens through
necessity, might not Jerusalem have justly answered to Our
Lord: Why doest thou torment thyself with useless tears?
If it was not thy will that we should hear the Prophets,
why didst thou send them? Why should we suffer for
what happened through thy own will and our compulsion?
The answer is worthy of Luther. *As man*, he says,
Christ, who had come to redeem the world, had of course
to shed tears over the eternal perdition of the wicked,
but this does not exclude that at the same time *as God*
he should *purposely* leave them to perdition. (^{21})

We come now to the discussion of the texts from
Holy Scripture. Luther thinks, curiously enough, that the
onus probandi lies entirely with Erasmus, (^{22}) when it
would rather seem, to be *his* duty to prove a doctrine
which, as he himself admits, is quite new in the Church. (^{23})
But Erasmus produces a number of texts which prima

(^{20}) Illudit sese Diatribe ignor-
antia sua, dum nihil distinguit inter Deum praedicatum et abscon-
ditum, hoc est inter verbum Dei
et Deum ipsum. Multa facit Deus.
quae verbo suo non ostendit nobis.
Multa quoque vult quae verbo suo
non ostendit sese velle. Sic non
vult mortem peccatoris, verbo scilicet. Vult autem illam voluntate
illa imperscrutabili. Nunc autem
nobis spectandum est verbum, re-
linquendaque illa voluntas imper-
scrutabilis. Ibid. 487.

(^{21}) Hujus Dei *incarnati* est flere,
deplorare. gemere super perditione
impiorum, cum *voluntas majestatis
ex proposito* aliquos relinquat et
reprobet, ut pereant. Ibid. 487 B.

(^{22}) Nos. cum in negativa stemus,
exiginus a vobis locum produci,
qui claris verbis contineat quid
sit et quid possit liberum arbitrium.
Hoc facietis forte ad Calendas
Graecas.   Ibid. 478.

(^{23}) Non est hoc mirum in
rebus divinis. quod tot saeculis
viri excellentes ingenio caecutiunt.

13*

facie show the freedom of will, and which had always
been understood to prove the same. For instance Eccl.
XV. 14—18; „God made man from the beginning and
left him in the hand of his own counsel. He added his
commandments and precepts. If thou wilt keep the commandments and perform acceptable fidelity for ever, they
shall preserve thee. *He hath set water and fire before
thee, stretch forth thy hand to which thou wilt.* Before
man is life and death, good and evil, that which he shall
choose, shall be given him." Luther gets over this text
in a wonderful way. He says, that, to enable us to gather
from it the freedom of will, it ought to be plainly: Man
has a free will. But nothing can be gathered from the
expression „if thou wilt," for this is only conditional, it
affirms nothing! For instance: „*If* a donkey flies, he
must have wings.(²⁴) Could we conclude from this that
he *has* wings? — If this is not a masterpiece of sophistry,
what can be called by that name?

We could certainly not arrive at that conclusion, but
where is the paritas? Luther forgets that it is God, who
speaks and as a lawgiver, that *he* speaks who thoroughly
knows the nature of man; that it would be unworthy of
God to scoff at the weakness of his creatures. What else
but scoffing would it be, if he were to speak as he does
through the inspired writers, giving man his choice, yet
knowing that man has no choice? Luther reminds us
ad nauseam that even in the text from Eccl. nothing
appears, but the impossibility of doing any good.(²⁵) Qui
potest capere, capiat.

It would tire the reader if we were to drag him
through a discussion of all the Bibletexts quoted in Luther's
book, pro and contra; let it be sufficient to say that the

Ibid. 475 ᴮ. — Nonne et ipsi (Patres) omnes pariter caecutierunt?
Ibid. 519.

(²⁴) Non video quomodo istis
verbis liberum arbitrium probetur.
Est enim verbum conjunctivi modi,

quod nihil asserit ... ut: Si asinus
volat, asinus habet alas.
                                        Ibid. 480 ᴮ.

(²⁵) eo verbo et similibus mo-
neri hominem suae impotentiae.
                                        Ibid. 481 ᴮ.

Bible has to be understood, as the Ecclesiastes of Wittenberg says it has to be. But we must cast a glance at the
last part of the book, where a few more surprising assertions meet our eyes.

According to Luther, God's prescience of a future
event will cause that event to happen. If so, the liberty
of the human will becomes of course chimerical. The
explanation, that the event does not take place *because*
God has seen it from all eternity, but that the infinite
knowledge of God finds as an object the event which will
in time be owing to the free decision of man, this is, to
him, sophistry. ([26]) He will admit such a principle only
with regard to human knowledge. „An eclipse does not
come, *because* it was known to be coming." ([27]) But the
prescience of God takes away the liberty of man. „If
God foresaw that Judas was to be a traitor, Judas necessarily became a traitor, nor was it in the power of Judas
or of any other creature to act differently or to change
his will." ([28]) Hence „the omnipotence and prescience of
God thoroughly destroys the liberty of the will." ([29])

But if man is a mere tool, or a beast of burden, to
be ridden without any choice of its own either by God
or by the devil, is this not enough to make him lose all
sense of dignity? Well, Luther tells us, that more than
once he has been nigh despair on this account, so as to

([26]) Est itaque et hoc imprimis
necessarium et salutare Christiano,
nosse, quod Deus nihil praescit
contingenter, sed quod omnia in-
commutabili et aeterna infallibili-
que voluntate et praevidet et pro-
ponit et facit. Hoc fulmine ster-
nitur et conteritur penitus liberum
arbitrium. Ibid. 461 B.
    ([27]) Ibid. 497 B.
    ([28]) Si praescivit Deus, Judam
fore proditorem, necessario fiebat
Judas proditor, nec erat in manu
Judae aut ullius creaturae aliter
facere aut voluntatem mutare.
    Ibid. 497.

([29]) Pugnat itaque ex diametro
praescientia et omnipotentia Dei
cum nostro libero arbitrio. Aut
enim Deus falletur praesciendo,
errabit et agendo (quod est impossibile); aut nos agemus et agemur
secundum ipsius praescientiam et
actionem ... Res est plana et fa-
cilis, etiam communi sensu judicio naturali probata, ut nihil faciat quantavis series saeculorum,
temporum, personarum aliter scrib-
entium et docentium." Ibid. 498 B.

wish he had never been born, until he found out how
salutary this despair is.([30]) Yet, a few lines afterwards
he says: „it is written in the hearts of all men, that there
is no freedom of will!" ([31])

How does he explain the existence of moral evil, if
after all man has no will of his own, if God acts in him?
Nothing easier! The instrument is thoroughly bad, if
therefore the effect is bad, it is the fault of the instrument,
not of him who uses it. There is the devil and man,
whose very nature necessarily makes them act in a sinful
way.([32]) God acts in them according to their state, as he
finds them.([33]) If a man drives a lot of horses, some of
which are lame, the halting of the latter is not owing
to the driving, but to their lameness. In hardening the
heart of a sinner God must not be supposed to *create*
moral evil, he does not act like a man, who pours poison
into a clean receptacle.([34]) If a workman has bad tools,
if a carpenter has to use a bad hatchet, the defective
quality of the work is the fault of the tool, not the fault
of the carpenter.([35]) Hence though the hardening of
Pharaoh's heart was intended by God and effected by

([30]) Ego ipse non semel offensus
sum usque ad profundum et abyssum desperationis, ut optarem nunquam esse me creatum hominem.
antequam scirem quam salutaris
esset illa desperatio et quam gratiae propinqua. Ibid.

([31]) In omnium cordibus script-
um invenitur, liberum arbitrium
nihil esse! Ibid. 499.

([32]) Jam satan et homo lapsi
et deserti a Deo, non possunt velle
bonum. Ibid. 495.

([33]) agit in illis taliter quales
illi sunt et quales invenit. Ibid.

([34]) Ibid. 495 B. — (Intelligen-
dum) in nobis i. e. per nos Deum
operari mala, non culpa Dei, sed
vitio nostro, qui cum simus natura
mali, Deus vero bonus, nos actione
sua pro natura omnipotentiae suae
rapiens, aliter facere non possit,
quam quod ipse bonus malo instru-
mento malum faciat. licet hoc malo
pro sua sapientia utatur bene ad
gloriam suam et salutem nostram.
Sic satanae voluntatem malam in-
veniens, non autem creans, sed
deserente Deo et peccante Satana
malam factam, arripit operando et
movet quorsum vult; licet illa voluntas mala esse non desinat hoc
ipso motu Dei. Ibid.

([35]) Vitium ergo est in instru-
mentis, quae otiosa esse Deus non
sinit, quod mala fiunt movente ipso
Deo. Non aliter quam si faber securi serrata et dentata male se-
caret. Hinc fit quod impius *non*
possit *non* semper errare et pec-
care, quod raptu divinae potentiae
motus ociari non sinitur, sed velit,
cupiat, faciat taliter qualis ipse est.
Ibid. 495.

him, God cannot be blamed for it; it was Pharaoh's nature, to be hardhearted. ([36])

We have said enough to give the reader a sufficient idea of Luther's book. After a patient perusal of it, we think we can express its general character in these few words: A medley of flimsy arguments — if arguments they can be called at all, of astonishing statements which we are expected to accept on the word of Luther, of expressions of utter contempt for the Fathers, of arbitrary and violent explanations of the Bible by the man who in this very book complains of the arbitrary explanations of others, ([37]) the whole spiced occasionally with invectives against Pope, Councils and Sophists, every page strongly flavoured with the „ipse dixit“ — this is Luther's famous book De servo arbitrio, which he defies Erasmus and the devil to refute. Ex uno disce omnes.

([36]) Sic indurat (Deus) Pharaonem, cum impiae et malae ejus voluntati offert verbum et opus quod illa odit. Ibid. 495 B. — Certissimus erat et certissime pronuntiabat Deus, Pharaonem esse indurandum, ut qui certissimus erat, Pharaonis voluntatem nec motui omnipotentiae resistere, nec malitiam suam deponere, nec oblatum adversarium Mosen admittere *posse*, sed manente voluntate ejus mala, necessario pejorem, duriorem et superbiorem fieri. Ibid. 496.

([37]) Neque enim nostri arbitrii est, ut Diatribe sibi persuadet, verba Dei fingere et refingere pro libidine nostra. Ibid. 492. Frequently one is tempted to answer Luther in his own words: Nos non contenti dicto, probatum quaerimus.
Ibid. 492 B.

Chapter XIV

Luther on Matrimony.

Famosus sum amator.
Luther. De Wette II. 655.
Maledicta et incesta illa castitas!
Luther. De Wette II. 319.

Whilst Germany was plunged into an abyss of misery by the wild prophets and followers of the „Evangelium", an event took place, which deserves special notice; Luther, the apostate monk, married an apostate nun. In connexion with this event, we may turn here our attention to Luther's views on matrimony. His most important writings on this subject were published before he himself took a wife, and the views expressed in them throw a light on this step.

In a popular instruction, given in 1518,([1]) Luther still calls matrimony a Sacrament. Though the definition, which he gives in the same place of Sacraments in general([2]), is in itself not a full and correct one as the words he uses do not express the grace given through the opus operatum, it appears nevertheless, that he did not as yet exclude this grace, for he compares the effect of matrimony on the soul to the effect of the Sacrament of baptism. He comes to the conclusion, that „matrimony is called a Sacrament, because it is the type of a most holy and noble thing viz.

([1]) De Matrimonio.   signum est, spirituale quippiam
    Wittenb. I. 90 n. seqq.   significans. coeleste et aeternum.
([2]) Sacramentum rei sacrae   Ibid. 91.

of the union of the human and divine natures in Christ." ([3])

In the „Babylonian Captivity" however (A. D. 1521) he denies the sacramental character of matrimony. Not only is matrimony considered as a Sacrament without any scriptural authority, but the very traditions which have been adduced to prove it to be such, have made a mockery of it. ([4]) His reason for so saying is, that „a Divine promise is attached to every sacrament," but „nowhere do we read, that he who takes a wife, will receive any grace from God." ([5]) He even denies in the same place, that is it a Sacrament in the wider meaning of the word, for „we do not read anywhere, that it has been instituted by God to signify anything; like many other things it may be taken for an allegory of things invisible, but not for anything else. ([6])

He especially inveighs in this book against the ecclesiastical laws concerning marriage, against impediments and dispensations from the same. Those are „impious human laws" ([7]); the fact that a marriage is forbidden by the Church, does not invalidate it, and if the Pope declares such a marriage to be null and void, he is the Antichrist.([8]) We shall see afterwards whether any Pope claimed as much power over matrimony as Luther himself claimed.

The Ecclesiastical impediments, he says, have been condemned beforehand by S. Paul, who warns against future heretics „forbidding to marry" (I. Tim. IV. 3). Therefore all the „nonsense" ([9]) of spiritual relationship has to

---

([3]) Ibidem.

([4]) Wittenb. II. 86. (Walch XIX. 113.)

([5]) Ibidem. Nusquam legitur, aliquid gratiae Dei accepturum, quisquis uxorem duxerit.

([6]) Nec enim uspiam legitur a Deo institutum ut aliquid significaret, licet omnia, quae visibiliter geruntur, possint intelligi figurae et allegoriae rerum invisibilium. At figura aut allegoria non sunt Sacramenta, ut nos de Sacramentis loquimur. Ibid.

([7]) Ibid.

([8]) Papa vel Episcopus vel officialis si dissolverit aliquod matrimonium contra legem papalem contractum, Antichristus est et violator naturae et reus laesae majestatis divinae. Ibid. 87 n.

([9]) Walch XIX. 122 has „Lügen" (lies).

be done away with.([10]) For are we not all brothers and
sisters through baptism? Dispensations are not necessary,
for, where the Pope can grant them, there may also a
brother grant them to his brother, or a man may dispense
himself. ([11]) On the question of divorce the „Reformer"
is not yet prepared to pronounce an opinion. ([12])

The Wittenberg and Jena editions, as also that of
Walch, omit a most important passage, in which Luther
appears for the first time in his quality of lawgiver on
matrimonial affairs. With regard to the impedimentum
impotentiae he says, that if the wife does not wish to
have the marriage dissolved publicly, if she does not feel
inclined to go through the juridical process required by
the law in such cases, she may, with the consent of her
putative husband, contract a new and secret marriage,
either with his brother or with another man. If her (putative) husband should not consent, she may run away and
marry somewhere else where she is not known. We give
this important text in a note, and shall return to this
question later on. ([13])

In the sermon on matrimony, which Luther preached
at Wittenberg in 1522 we meet with far more startling

([10]) Itaque debent istae nugae
compaternitatum, commaternita-
tum, confraternitatum, consororie-
tatum et confilictatum prorsus ex-
stingui. Wittenb. II. 87ᵇ.

([11]) Si urgeat ... necessitas,
propter quam dispensat Papa, dis-
penset etiam quilibet frater cum
fratre, aut ipse cum seipso, rapta
per hoc consilium uxore de manu
tyrannicarum legum utcunque poterit. Utquid mea libertas tol-
litur aliena superstitione et ignor-
antia? Ibid. SS.

([12]) Ego quidem detestor divortium, sed an liceat, ipse non audeo
definire. (Wittenb. II. 88.) The opp.
lat. (Frankf. 1865—68, vol. V. 100)
give this same passage in the following form: Ego quidem detestor

divortium, *ut digamiam malim quam
divortium*, sed etc.

([13]) Videamus itaque de impotentia. Quaero casum ejusmodi, si
mulier, impotenti nupta viro, nec
possit nec velit forte tot testimoniis
et strepitibus. quot jura exigunt,
judicialiter impotentiam viri prob-
are, velit tamen prolem habere,
aut non possit continere, et ego
consuluissem, ut divortium a viro
impetret ad nubendum alteri, con-
tenta, quod ipsius et mariti conscientia et experientia abunde testes
sunt impotentiae illius, vir autem
nolit, tum ego ultra consulam, ut
cum consensu viri (cum jam non
sit maritus, sed simplex et solutus
cohabitator) *misceatur alteri, vel
fratri mariti*, occulto tamen matrimonio, et proles imputetur pu-

things.([14]) Throughout this sermon, as also in his sub-
sequent books and in his tabletalk, Luther supposes that
the Pope, and the Catholic Church with him condemn
matrimony! We can hardly believe our eyes, when we
read words like the following: „The source of all fornication and impurity in Popery is this, that they condemn
the most holy state of matrimony."([15]) It is still more
incredible, that educated men of our own time should repeat
such things, that for instance the Archbishop of York should
publicly launch against the Catholic Church the charge:
„She disregarded some true principles — that marriage is
an honourable state," that the same prelate of the Church
of England should say of Luther: „He restored to its
proper place in public esteem marriage and wedded purity
and the home."([16]) Does the Most Reverend Dr. Thomson
not know, that the Catholic Church has always considered
matrimony as a *Sacrament?* Does he really think that
Luther's views on divorce, and the dispensation he gave
to the licentious Landgraf of Hessen have contributed
towards raising wedded purity in public esteem?

In the above mentioned sermon Luther advances for
the first time and in the crudest possible manner his conviction, that matrimony is obligatory on every individual.
„As it is not in my power, not to be a man, so I have
not the right, to be without a woman. And again, as it
is not in thy power, not to be a woman, so it is not in
thy power, to be without a man."([17]) The words of God,

tativo (ut dicunt) patri. Opp. lat.
p. 9S. Ulterius, si vir nollet con-
sentire, nec dividi vellet, antequam
permitterem eam uri aut adulter-
ari, consulerem, ut, contracto cum
alio matrimonio, anfugeret in locum ignotum et remotum.
            Ibid. 100.
([14]) Wittenb. V. 119 seqq.
([15]) Tischr. II. c. 20. § 138.
([16]) In the sermon at S. Michael-
le-Belfrey. York. on the occasion
of the Luther festival. See York-
shire Herald Nov. 15. 1883.

([17]) Ut non est in meis viribus
situm, ut vir non sim, tam non
est etiam mei juris, ut absque
muliere sim. Rursum. ut in tua
manu non est, ut foemina non
sis. sic nec in te est. ut absque
viro degas. Nec enim libera est
electio aut consilium, ut res natura necessaria, ut marem foeminae,
foeminam mari sociari oportet.
          Wittenb. V. 119.

„Increase and multiply" (Gen. I. 28) are not simply a precept, but much more than a precept; they enjoin a divine
work, which is just as necessary, as eating, drinking etc. ([18])
After alluding to the words of Christ (Matth. XIX. 12.)
„There are eunuchs etc," Luther continues: He that does
not find himself in any of these classes, ought to think
of matrimony at once . . . If not, you cannot possibly
remain chaste . . . you cannot withdraw yourself from
that word of God (Increase and multiply), if you will
not necessarily and continually perpetrate the most horrid
crimes." ([19])

This same opinion, that chastity is not possible except
in the married state — an opinion, which contains an
awful charge against a large part of mankind — the
„Reformer" frequently repeats. „As little as we can do
without eating and drinking, just as impossible is it, to
abstain from women . . . The reason is, that we have
been conceived and nourished in a woman's womb, that
of woman we are born and begotten, hence our own flesh
is for the most part woman's flesh, and it is impossible
to keep away from it." ([20]) „Chastity is not in our power,
as little as all other miracles and graces of God . . . He
who resolves to remain single, let him give up the name
of human being, let him prove, that he is an angel or
spirit . . . Why do you hesitate and trouble yourself a

([18]) Verbum hoc, quo Deus ait,
Crescite et multiplicamini, non est
praeceptum, sed plus quam praeceptum, divinum puta opus, quod
non est nostrarum virium, vel ut
impediatur vel omittatur, sed tam
est necessarium, quam ut masculus
sis, *magisque necessarium*, *quam
edere*, *bibere*, *purgare*, *mucum
emungere* . . . Quare ut Deus ne-
mini in mandatis dat, ut sit mas
aut foemina, sic nec ut sese multi-
plicent, praecipit, sed homines ita
condit, ut mas aut foemina sint,
utque generationi studeant. Ibid.
. . . *est enim haec naturae necessitas,
non arbitrii libertas.* Ibid. 119 B.

([19]) Qui sese in hoc generum
uno non reperit, is matrimonium
omnino maturare cogitet . . . Neque
enim possibile est, ut castus per-
maneas . . . nec hinc te surripere
potes, ni horrenda perpetrare crimina necessario sine intermissione
velis. Ibid. 119 B. Cfr. Walch XIX.
2191 (n. 99 and 100). In Luther's
book „Adversus falso nominatum
ordinem Episcoporum" the following occurs: „Si non fluit semen
in carnem, fluit in vestes." Wittenb. II. 352. — Walch XIX. 905.

([20]) Tischr. II. c. 20. § 27.

great deal with serious thoughts? It *must* and *shall* and *will* be thus, and not differently. Put such thoughts away and proceed courageously (to marriage). *Your body demands it and wants it; God wills it and forces you.* How will you get over this? ... Every day we see, how difficult it is, to observe conjugal chastity in matrimony, and should we, outside matrimony, resolve on chastity, as if we were not human beings, as if we had neither flesh nor blood?" ([21])

„To avoid sin, we cannot do without women, we *must* have them." ([22]) „If a girl has not a great and extraordinary grace, she cannot do without a man, just as little as she can do without eating or drinking or sleeping. Likewise a man cannot do without a woman. And the reason is this: To beget children is just as deeply rooted in nature, as eating and drinking. ([23]) These few quotations will be sufficient, though ten times as many could be given.

The conclusions, which Luther draws from his axiom, are ([1]) the assertion that the vow of chastity is an abomination, and ([2]) an appeal to the religious, to enter matrimony. „If priests, monks and nuns find themselves fit for generation, they must abandon their vows; if they do not, nothing remains for them, but inevitable impurity and fornication." ([24]) Hence those parents, who advise their children to enter the religious state, offer them to the devil." ([25]) The vow of chastity is an *impossible*

([21]) Letter to Reissenbusch. De Wette II. 637 seqq.

([22]) Tischr. II. c. 20. § 134. In another place he goes so far, as to explain this necessity with the following comparison: „Wer seinen Mist oder Harn halten müsste, so er es doch nicht kann, was soll aus dem werden?" De Wette II. 372. Some of Luther's sayings on this point are so cynical, that we cannot reproduce them.

See v. gr. Lauterb. 101.

([23]) Walch XIX. 904. (Wider den falsch genannten etc.)

([24]) Ut adeo sacrifici, monachi et monachae vota sua relinquere debeant necessario, ubi creaturam Dei ad generandum et multiplicandum in sese efficacem depre-henderint. Persuasum tibi sit, illos haudquaquam permanere puros.

Wittenb. V. 119 B.

([25]) Satanae hoc modo filios suos dicantes. Ibid. 124.

vow: (^{26}) „We are all created to do, as our parents did, to beget children and to bring them up.“ (^{27}) To say that virginity is better than matrimony, means „to send Almighty God to school, or to stroke the Holy Ghost's feathers.“ (^{28}) The word of St. Jerome, that virginity fills heaven, is the most impious, sacrilegious and blasphemous word. (^{29}) The vow of chastity is worse than adultery! (^{30}) The smallest sin is theft, after that comes adultery, then murder, last and worst celibacy in the clergy! (^{31}) Monks and nuns are therefore not worthy, to rock even a bastard to sleep or to give him a spoonful of gruel. (^{32})

In his sermon „De Matrimonio“ Luther finds it necessary to protest against a false interpretation of the advice he had formerly given, as if in the case we have mentioned, (^{33}) he had allowed fornication or adultery. He therefore repeats his advice, the text of which will be found in the subjoined note. (^{34}) He then makes a fresh

---

(^{26}) Walch XIX. 2172.

(^{27}) Ibid. He adds: Noch wollen uns die Verstockten zwingen, ein Mann solle nicht fühlen seinen männlichen Leib, noch ein Weib ihren weiblichen Leib.

(^{28}) Walch XIX. 2164.

(^{29}) Quid magis impium, sacrilegum et blasphemum dici potest, quam id quod Hieronymus solet: „Virginitas coelum, conjugium terram replet?“ De servo arb. Wittenb. II. 472.

(^{30}) Walch XIX. 2161.

(^{31}) Ibid. 2174.

(^{32}) Tum monachos, tum nonnas, fidei expertes, quique de suo coelibatu et ordine gloriantur, indignos esse adfirmo, ut baptisatum infantem in somnum collocent, aut pulmentum ei conficiant, etiamsi nothus sit .. nec gloriari possunt, quod sua opera Deo grata sint, *ut mulier, etiamsi nothum in utero ferat.* Wittenb. V. 125.

(^{33}) page 202.

(^{34}) Itaque in hunc modum consului. Si mulieri ad rem aptae

contingat maritus impotens, nec ipsa publice alii nubere posset, ipsaque invita publico usui contraveniret, honoremque suum et famam obscurari nollet, cum hic multos testes et rationes nequicquam requirat Papa, ita maritum eam compellere debere: Ecce, mi marite, debitam mihi benevolentiam praestare non potes, meque et juvenile corpus decepisti; praeterae in famae et salutis meae periculum me adduxisti, neque coram Deo inter nos matrimonium est. Fave, quaeso, ut cum fratre tuo, aut proxime tibi sanguine juncto occultum matrimonium paciscar, sic ut tu nomen habeas, ne res tuae in alienos haeredes perveniant; ac permitte, ut sponte tua a me decipiare, quemadmodum et tu praeter voluntatem meam imposuisti mihi. Perrexi porro, maritum debere in ea re assentiri uxori ... Quod si renuat, ipsa clandestina fuga saluti sua consulat, et in aliam profecta terram, alii etiam nubat. Wittenb. V. 120.

onslaught on Ecclesiastical impediments. We will notice at least a few of his decisions. That he should say that such impediments have been established by the Church merely in order to get money for the dispensation from the same, is exactly what must be expected from him.

With regard to consanguinity, Luther ascending his cathedra, allows marriage to cousins, likewise marriage between a man and his stepmother's sister, or his father's or mother's halfsister, (quae ei ex noverca fuit), or his niece. ([35])

With regard to affinity, we will notice, that in this place Luther allows marriage with a deceased wife's sister and with a deceased brother's widow. ([36]) On other occasions he forbids it, ([37]) but it would be difficult, to find many points, on which Luther has *not* contradicted himself.

The impedimentum criminis, which makes matrimony impossible between persons, of whom one at least has been married before, and who, with a view to matrimony have committed adultery, or murder of the other married party, or both crimes, displeases Luther to such an extent, that he exclaims: „Here *it rains* fools!" According to him such criminal parties must have the right to marry. ([38]) The legislation of the Church on this point has for its object, to make adultery or murder of a married person less possible or less enticing, by forbidding the marriage of the guilty parties. What the natural consequences of the Wittenberg Reformer's Jus Canonicum would be, nobody can fail to see. It is the same with the legislation on divorce. The Prussian Consistorium has more

---

([35]) Ibid. 120 B. — Ap. De Wette III. 83. Luther comforts a man, who had married his niece. „You have done it with my advice and permission, i. e. with God's advice and permission, which I have taken from Divine Scripture.

([36]) This follows from his enumeration of the *forbidden* degrees, amongst which he puts: uxoris meae sororem, *uxore mea vivente.*

Wittenb. V. 120 B. Quod, ut jam non est praeceptum. sic nec vetitum. He confirms this in another decision ap. De Wette II. 277.

([37]) Tischr. II. c. 20. § 111.

([38]) Hic supra quam dici potest, stultos pluit . . . Crimina et peccata sane punienda sunt, alia tamen mulcta, quam conjugii vetatione.

Wittenb. V. 121.

·than once bitterly complained, that nowadays adultery is frequently committed *in order* to obtain a divorce.'

: Of the impediment arising from holy Orders Luther will say no more; he thinks he has shown clearly enough, how ridiculous it is. (^{39})

We come to the question of divorce. The Wittenberg Reformer does not like divorce at all, (^{40}) but there are three causes, he says, which make it lawful.

1) Impotentia. We have heard him about this point before.

2) Adultery. This part he tries to prove with the words of Christ, Matth. XIX. 9. (^{41})

3) The persistent refusal of the debitum conjugale. It is here, that we hear Luther utter the well known words: „If the wife refuses, let the servantmaid come." He distinctly says that, if after repeated admonition before others, the wife does not amend, her husband may repudiate her and take another wife. By right, he continues, *the wife ought to be put to death* by the authorities, but if they neglect this duty, the husband may consider her as dead

---

(³⁹) Undecima ratio est sacer ordo. ut *rasura et carum oleum* tam forte sit. ut et matrimonium excedat et absumat. et ex viro non-virum faciat ... Stultitia eorum satis in lucem edita est.
                              Ibid. 121 B.

(⁴⁰) mihi omnino nihil in deliciis esse matrimonii dissipationem aut divortium. Ibid. 120.

(⁴¹) These words of Our Lord really prove anything but the right of divorce in the case of adultery. It is evident. that in this verse either one expression or the other cannot be taken in the strict sense. It is impossible to take both γυνή and πορνεια in that sense. If the woman is really γυνη, uxor, her crime is not simply πορνεια, but μοιχεια: but if the crime is really πορνεια, she cannot have been

γυνη, uxor. but only a concubine. At the very least therefore these words would be doubtful, and can *just as well* mean, that a man may not divorce a woman, except if she were his wife only apparently. In cases of doubt we accept the word of God as understood not by private judgment, but by the authority of the Church. We will not omit to notice, that many interpreters explain the words of Christ: παρεκτος λογου πορνειας, as meaning, that Our Lord did not then wish to enter into this particular question, considering the circumstances and the hardheartedness of his hearers, who would probably have gone away. as others had done on another occasion. saying: Durus est his sermo. See Patrizi. De Interpr. Bibl. p. 161.

and proceed to a new marriage. In the subjoined note we give this important text in full. ([42])

Such teachings have caused a great deal of controversy. Protestants indignantly deny, that Luther ever allowed incest or adultery. In our Wittenberg edition we find on the margin of fol. 123 vol. V, written by the hand of is former proprietor, the remark: „Haec male intellecta Papistas male offendent." We will try to understand the words rightly and not to be more offended, than Luther's teaching gives us a right to be.

Has the Ecclesiastes of Wittenberg ever approved of incest and adultery? As to adultery, he has undoubtedly sanctioned it, not only in the case of Landgraf Philip of Hessen, *but in the case of all princes.* He calls their concubinage a „true marriage before God, though not celebrated with pomp and festivities, though the children, begotten in such unions, have no right to wear the father's arms." He compares this concubinage with that of the Patriarchs! ([43]) But about this particular point we shall

---

([42]) Tertia ratio (divortii) est, ubi alter alteri sese subduxerit, ut debitam benevolentiam persolvere nolit, aut habitare cum renuerit. Reperiuntur enim interdum adeo pertinaces uxores, quae; etiamsi decies in libidinem prolaberetur maritus, pro sua duritia non curarent. Ilic opportunum est, ut maritus dicat: *Si tu nolueris, alia volet, si domina nolit, adveniat ancilla,* ita tamen ut antea iterum et tertio uxorem admoneat maritus, et coram aliis ejus etiam pertinaciam detegat, ut publice et ante conspectum Ecclesiae duritia ejus et agnoscatur et reprehendatur. Si tum renuat, repudia eam, et in vicem Vasti Ester surroga. Assueri regis exemplo. Porro hic tu divi Pauli I. Cor. VII. innitaris verbis: Maritus proprii corporis potestatem non habet, sed uxor. Et uxor sui corporis jus non habet, sed maritus. Ne fraudetis vos mutuo. nisi uter-que consenserit. Ecce, mutuam hic fraudem vetat Apostolus ... Ubi ergo alter debitum obsequium negat, tum alteri corpus suum deditum spoliat et vi aufert. quod proprie conjugii repugnat juri, *immo et conjugium dissipat.* Igitur hanc uxorem cohibere Magistratus est, *atque interimere.* Hoc si intermittat Magistratus, imaginandum est marito, suam sibi uxorem a latronibus raptam et interfectam esse, considerandumque ut aliam ducat. Wittenb. V. 123.

([43]) Tischr. II. c. 20. § 63. — Cfr. Lauterb. 120 (24 Aug.) Postea dixerunt vonn der fursten heimlichen ehe, quae *vera essent conjugia,* sed tamen non principali pompa confirmata. Das dieselbigen kinder auch nicht helm vnnd schilt hetten. Et videtur quaedam similitudo concubinatus Patriarcharum [qui etiam cum aliis uxoribus] liberos generabant. sed non haeredes.

have occasion so speak later on. Meanwhile we beg the
reader to give his attention to the following:

1) From our own standpoint as Catholics, keeping
before our eyes the principles maintained by the Church,
which represents Christ's power on earth, we say without hesitation, that what Luther allows in the above mentioned case (de impotentia) *is incest*. For though, propter
impotentiam, the marriage in question should not have
been valid, there would have been an impedimentum
dirimens between the woman and her husband's brother,
viz. the impedimentum publicae honestatis, arising from
the first sponsalia. It cannot even be urged, that the
very sponsalia might possibly have been invalid; for before
the Council of Trent (see Sessio XXIV. c. III. De Re-
formatione Matrimonii) also invalid sponsalia induced the
impedimentum publicae honestatis.

2) What Luther allows in the case of adultery or of
persistent refusal of the debitum conjugale, *he* may call
divorce, *we* call it adultery. To mention only the latter
case, where is there a *proof*, that through the criminal
and obstinate refusal on the part of the wife marriage is
annulled, as Luther expressly says it is? He appeals to
the Bible. But everybody knows, what a genius Luther
is in finding his doctrine in the Holy Scriptures, or
rather in carrying it into the same; everybody knows that
„Hic liber est, in quo quaerit sua dogmata quisque,
Invenit et pariter dogmata quisque sua.“

3) It will be urged, that, at least, the „Reformer“ did
not consider his words as allowing incest and adultery;
he based his decision on the supposed fact, that the
parties are not really married, or in the last case, on the
supposed fact, that the marriage was annulled. Therefore,
at any rate, he must have been in good faith and cannot
be blamed. We are ready to grant, that he was as much
in good faith, as any other heresiarch or apostate from
the Church. But supposing he had been in perfectly
good faith, are we therefore deprived of the right of

criticizing his actions? If so, we shall make a rhyme to this prohibition. We shall say: The Mormons are probably in good faith, when they teach and practise polygamy, *therefore* let nobody blame them on that account. Perhaps this juxtaposition of Luther and the Mormons may be offensive to some of his friends. But we shall have occasion to prove that Mormonism may confidently look up to Luther as a patron.

4) The objectionable character of the „Reformer's" Jus Canonicum on matrimony appears also from the fact, that, whilst the Catholic Church, in her great respect for the sanctity of this Sacrament, uses all possible precautions to prevent its profanation, he leaves the decision even in the most important cases entirely to private judgment and to the private action of the interested parties. Whether in the case we have mentioned above, ([14]) it is honest or not, that the children should be pretended to be of the first husband and should be heirs to his property, the reader may judge for himself.

5) Whence has Luther his pretended right, to oppose *his* laws on matrimony to those of the whole Church? We are sure, Protestants, who will agree with him when he decrees a divorce on account of adultery, will not approve of his decision in the other case. ([45])

At the end of the second part of the famous sermon on matrimony Luther has some words of comfort for those, whose husbands or wives are ill. He will not allow such illness to be considered as a legitimate cause of divorce. „Blessed art thou, if thou acknowledgest such a grace, and servest thy sick partner willingly in the name of God. If thou sayest, thou canst not contain thyself, I answer: thou liest."([46]) But alas! Words! Words!

([14]) See note 34.

([45]) Luther invariably allows a new marriage, where one party has left the other. Some of his decisions will be found Tischr. II. c. 20. § 82. 93. 100. 117. 120.

([46]) Quid vero, si alter conjugatorum morbo degravatus sit, adeo, ut ejus ad rem nullus possit usus esse, num aliam is matrimonii lege copulare sibi potest? *Nullo pacto*, ni salutis tuae nullam rationem

We are used to see the „Reformer" change his opinion and contradict himself. In 1527 a case is brought before him, of a certain Hans Behem, whose wife is suffering from leprosy. Luther decides, that, if the wife consents, the husband may consider her as dead and proceed to a new marriage. Car tel est notre plaisir. ([47])

Matrimonial affairs belong, according to him, exclusively to the *secular* forum. „Dr. Martin Luther said to the preachers: *Matrimonial affairs have nothing to do with the conscience* but have to be sent to the secular authorities. Therefore none of you shall meddle with them, except when the authorities command it." ([48]) „Marriage has nothing to do with the Church, it is outside the Church; it is a temporal and secular thing, therefore it belongs to the (secular) authority." ([49]) In another place however he puts a restriction on this, when he says: „Matrimony, with all its circumstances, is a worldly thing, is has nothing to do with the Church, except so far, as the conscience is concerned." ([50]) But *how far* the conscience may be concerned, he does not tell us. Anyhow the secular authorities have *full* power over matrimony. It is written, what God has joined together, no man shall put asunder. Know then, whenever the Emperor or the authority by their laws and ordinances

habere velis. Caeterum hic Deo in aegroto illo inservias, ejusque curam gerens cogita Deum per hunc aedibus tuis sancta immisisse, quibus coelum tibi comparandum sit. (By the way, does this not sound „papistical"? Merits acknowledged by Luther!) Perbeatus es et iterum perbeatus, si tale donum et tantam graciam agnoscens, aegro Dei nomine libenter obsequaris. Si vero te continere non posse improperes, te plane mentiri respondebo. Ubi enim ex animo aegro tuo conjugato inservieris, tibique a Deo id afflictionis ad rogatum agnoveris, cum gratiarum actione. tum illi relinque curam. nam haud

dubie tibi robur impertiet, ut quam vires tuae possint, non plüs toleres. Fidelior est Deus, quam ut tuo conjugii te compare per aegritudinem privet, nec rursum carnis tuae lasciviam eripiat. si modo fidam operam languenti praestiteris. Wittenb. V. 123 B.

([47]) De Wette III. 194. This decision will also be found Tischr. II. c. 20. § 108.

([48]) Tischr. l. c. § 52.

([49]) Ibid. § 97.

([50]) Ibid. § 83.

annull a marriage, it is not man, that does it, but God." (⁵¹)

If we return once more to the principle laid down by Luther, that outside the married state man cannot possibly remain chaste, except where, in one case out of a thousand, God does a special miracle, (⁵²) it is surprising that towards the end of his sermon on matrimony he should say that he only means to protest against those (but who are they?) who *vilify* the married state, by praising virginity as a better one. For the rest he will not reject celibacy and virginity, nor persuade any one to enter marriage. (⁵³) We refer the reader to the quotations which we have given from the same sermon in notes 17 and 18. It really seems as if the Ecclesiastes did not know his own mind. Only on the preceding page he had quoted and praised the proverb:

„Früe aufstehen und frü freien

Das sol niemand gerewen,"

i e. Early rising and early woeing you will never repent, and on the same page he had said: *„Verum profecto est, eum lenonem esse oportere, qui matrimonium fugiat, et qui aliter eveniret?"*

Nobody will be astonished, that spite against the Pope should be to Luther an additional motive for declaring and maintaining the necessity of marriage. „Though one may have the gift, to live chastely without a wife, *yet one ought to marry to spite the Pope,* who insists on celibacy and forbids the Clergy to marry." (⁵⁴) A worthy motive in a „Reformer"! But his spitefulness

---

(⁵¹) Ibid. § 107.

(⁵²) Rari admodum sunt, ut inter mille vix unus reperiatur; *sunt enim Dei praecipua miracula.*

Wittenb. V. 120.

(⁵³) Nec ideo coelibatum aut virginitatem reprobare mihi animus est, nec inde quemquam ad jugale vinculum invitare.

Ibid. 126 B.

(⁵⁴) Tischr. II. c. 20. § 3. In the same place he says that he had fully made up his mind, in case of serious illness, to marry even on his deathbed, on principle, to honour the state of matrimony.

and hatred made him say far worse things, In his letter
to the Lords of the Teutonic Order (March 28. 1523) we find
the following passage: „If it should happen, that one, two, a
hundred, a thousand and more Councils were to decree, that
priests might marry . . . I would rather, trusting in God's
grace, close an eye in favour of a man, who kept one or
two or three whores all his lifetime, than justify the man,
who, merely in virtue of such a Council's decree, were to
take a legitimate wife . . . And I would, in God's place, command and advise all, not to take a wife in virtue of such
a decree, *under penalty of losing the salvation of their
souls*, but that they should live chastely, and *if this should
be impossible*, that they should not despair in their weakness and sin, but invoke the help of God.“ ([55]) On the
following page he repeats that he who keeps a whore,
commits less sin and is nearer to God's grace, than a
man, who would take a wife by permission of a Council. ([56])
The disgusting sophistry with which he tries to prove his
assertion, need not find a place here. The reader will
be able to judge, whether such a thing *can* be proved.

Luther speaks frequently of the temptations he suffered, when he was a monk and also after his apostasy. ([57])
With this fact in itself nobody could reproach him, though
it is curious to hear him say, that, the more he did to
mortify himself, the more he „was on fire“. ([58]) If we
believe Wolfgang Agricola, the Dean of Spalt, Spalatinus'
birth place ([59]), Luther must have felt at the time, when he

([55]) Walch XIX. 2165.

([56]) We refer the reader to Luther's remarks about prostitutes:
at the end of the Chapter on the
„Evangelium“. p. 146.

([57]) Carnis meae indomitae uror
magnis ignibus . . . . ferveo carne.
libidine. De Wette II. 22.

([58]) Tischr. II. c. 20. § 3.

([59]) The real name of Spalatinus was George Burkhart: he was
the son of a tanner at Spalt. One
of Luther's most intimate and
active friends, he fell into mad-

ness towards the end of his life,
and died in that state. Some years
before his death he visited his native place and opened to the then
Dean Ludel his heart, which was
harassed by despair and remorse.
„We have intoned the Allelujah
at too high a pitch“ he said. But
he had not the courage to retract,
though he gave to the Church at
Spalt a statue of Our Lady which
is there to the present day. Eich-
stätter Pastoralblatt 1880. n. 27.
Germanus 284.

was a monk, that absolute necessity of marrying, on which later on he insisted so much. The report of Agricola, who had the information from Spalatinus, if not directly, at least through his predecessor Ludel, contains nothing improbable in itself, but is in perfect keeping with Luther's character and tenets. Protestants, wo agree with the „Reformer" in his views on matrimony, can all the less be scandalized by it, as they will see how early his views were developed. Wolfgang Agricola says([60]): Whilst Luther was studying at Erfurt, he used to get leave from the superior of the monastery, to visit Spalatinus, who lived in the town, apparently to study with him, but „the widow (who was his friend's landlady) had a pretty daughter, whom he liked so much that she had to sit near him and he taught her lacemaking (Portenwürken) — which he had learned at home — and when he looked at the girl, he sighed and frequently said to Spalatinus: O Spalatine, Spalatine, thou canst not believe, how I have this pretty girl in my heart, I will not die, until I manage to woe a pretty girl." ([61]) To which Spalatinus answered: Brother Martin, this will never do; remember thou art a monk! But Luther said: What does it matter to me? When at last there was too much of the lacemaking business, the mother forbade the house to the monk."

It is rather surprising, that Luther should have waited as long as 1525 before he took a wife, and should even shortly before he took this step declare his unwillingness to take it. ([62]) Whilst he unhesitatingly tried to persuade others of the necessity of marrying and expressed his joy

([60]) Bibliotheca Eystettensis, num. 258.

([61]) Du kannst nicht glauben, wie mir dies schöne Megdiken in dem Hertzen lieget, ich wil nicht ersterben, bis ich so vil anricht, dass ich auch ein schön Megdiken freyen darf.

([62]) Quod Argula de uxore mihi ducenda scribit, gratias ago, nec miror talia de me garriri, cum garriantur et multa alia .... Hoc tamen corde, quo hactenus fui et modo sum, not fiet uxorem ut ducam, non quod carnem meam aut sexum non sentiam, cum neque lignum, neque lapis sim: sed animus alienus est a conjugio, cum expectem quotidie mortem et meritum haeretici supplicium. Letter to Spalat. De Wette II. 57.

at the marriage of priests, ([63]) it seems that he could not
easily persuade his conscience, to follow his own advice.
A number of his letters are exstant, in which he encourages
and urges his friends, especially Bugenhagen (Dr. Pomeranus) Link, Reissenbusch ([64]) and Spalatinus, to enter the
matrimonial state. ([65]) Nor was he too bashful, to write
the following lines to a number of *nuns:* „Though the
womenfolk are ashamed to confess it, yet it is proved by
Scripture and experience, that there is not one amongst
many thousands, to whom God gives grace, to keep pure
chastity; but a woman has no power over herself. God
has created her body, that she should be with a man and
bear children, as it clearly appears from I. Moses I. 28,
and as the members of the body created by God prove.
As eating, drinking, sleeping and waking is ordained by
God, so he also wills, through the order of nature, that
man and woman should be united in marriage." ([66])

The pity he felt for the unfortunate religious, who
in their Convents were unable to follow their „natural
vocation", caused him to enter into a scheme for the
liberation of some of them. ([67]) Nine nuns of the Con-

([63]) Mirifice placent nuptiae
sacerdotum et monachorum et
monialium apud vos. Letter to
Capito.   De Wette II. 522.

([64]) See note 21.

([65]) Et quare tu non procedis
ad conjugium? cum tot ego argumentis alios urgeam, ut ipse paene
movear, cum non cessent hostes
hoc genus vitae damnare, et nostri sapientuli quotidie idem ridere."
De Wette II. 643. Spalatinus married a little later than Luther, but
in the same year. The „dear man
of God" congratulated his friend
in the following words: „Saluta
tuam conjugem suavissime, verum
ut id tum facias, cum in thoro
suavissimis amplexibus et osculis
Catharinam tenueris, ac sic cogita-
veris: En hunc hominem, opti-
mam creaturulam Dei mei, donavit

mihi Christus meus, sit illi laus
et gloria. Salutat te et costam
tuam mea costa in Christo. De
Wette III. 53. When, on account
of his marriage Spalatinus met
with great difficulties, Luther exhorted him to assert, that he had
taken a wife to protest against
„sceleratum, impurum, impium et
diabolicae Ecclesiae coelibatum
sive potius Sodomam igni et sul-
phuri coelesti devotam et propediem
devorandam. De Wette III. 54.

([66]) De Wette II. 535.

([67]) He acknowledged that he
had had part in it. Köstlin I. 595.
Of another abduction of nuns Luther writes to Stiefel: Hac nocte
tredecim moniales ex ditione ducis
Georgii afferri curavi, et rapui
tyranno furenti hoc spolium Christi.
De Wette III. 32.

vent of Nimtzsch (near Grimma) left their house secretly
during the night from Good Friday to Holy Saturday.
They were received by some of Luther's friends under
the leadership of Leonard Koppe, a town councillor of
Torgau, and were secretly (it is supposed, in empty
barrels) conveyed to Wittenberg. ([68]) For his cooperation
in this transaction Koppe received the greatest compliments
from Luther. If they call you a robber, the „Reformer"
says, „you are indeed a blessed robber just as Christ was
a robber in this world . . . You have freed those poor
souls out of the dungeon of human tyranny, just about
the right time of Easter." ([69]) The reason of the secrecy
was, that according to Germanic law the abduction of nuns
was a capital crime, and that Duke George of Saxony, the
staunch supporter of the old faith, through whose territory
the deserters had to pass, would certainly have interfered,
had he known anything about it. In a letter to Spalatinus([70])
Luther announces to his friend the arrival of the waggon-
load of escaped nuns. He calls them „vulgus miserabile",
„a pitiful lot", and of course, improves the occasion by
uttering some compliments about monastic life in general([71]),
and by inveighing against the Pope. „Who can sufficiently
curse thee, o Pope, and you, o Bishops?" ([72]) No occasion
of using such elegant language is ever passed over by the
„man of God".

But now we find the same „man of God" in the
fresh quality of lover. Amongst the nine escaped nuns
there was also Catharina von Bora, who afterwards became
Luther's partner. At first the Reformer fell in love with
another, Eva von Schönfeld, as he told his friends in later
years.([73]) Why he did not chose her, we do not know.

([68]) Seckend. I. 57. § 153; II.
5. § 5.
([69]) De Wette II. 321.
([70]) Seckend. I. 57. § 153.
([71]) quae (moniales) ubique in
tanto numero pereunt *maledicta
et incesta illa castitate.* Ibidem.

([72]) Te, o Papa, et vos, Episcopi, quis digne maledicat?
                                    Ibidem.

([73]) Tischr. II. c. 20. § 2:.

Catharina von Bora was the last of the „vulgus miserabile“ to enter matrimony. Luther had destined her for his friend Dr. Glaz; but Kate strongly objected. She went to Amsdorf, and told him plainly that she was ready to marry either him or Luther, but not Glaz, and Mrs. Luther she became. ([74])

On the 9. October 1524 Luther at last flung away his monk's cowl. Why he should have worn it so long after he had finally left the Church, after he had poured out in the largest measure all his hatred and anger on monastic life, this would be difficult to understand. A few days later, on the 12th of the same month, he wrote to Hieronymus Baumgärtner, another flame of Bora: „If you wish to keep your Katie, you must be quick, before some one else gets her.“([75]) Perhaps the „someone else“ was himself. Anyhow, not many months elapsed, before he called her *his* .Katie. On the 16th April 1525 he writes to Spalatinus: „Don't be astonished, that I, who am such a famous lover, do not yet take a wife. It is rather a matter of wonder, that I, who write so often about matrimony, and am so much with women, have not become a woman myself long ago, not to mention, that I have not yet married one. But if you wish to have my example, here it is, the very strongest. I have had three wives at once, and have loved them so ardently, that I have lost

<hr>

([74]) Ecce autem, dum Lutherus de Catharina a Bora, virgine Vestali (sic!), Doctori Glacio, Pastori Orlamundico, collocanda deliberat, venit Catharina ad Nicholaum Amsdorffium, conqueriturque, se de consilio Lutheri D. Glacio contra voluntatem suam nuptiis locandam: Scire se, Lutherum familiarissime uti Amsdorffio: itaque rogare, ad quaevis alia consilia Lutherum vocet. Vellet Lutherus, vellet Amsdorffius, se paratam, cum alterutro honestum inire matrimonium: cum D. Glacio nullo modo. Hoc ubi Lutherus intellexit, audissetque ex D. Hieronymi Schurfii ore: Si Mo-

nachus iste uxorem duceret. risuros mundum universum et diabolum ipsum, facturumque ipsum irritas actiones suas universas, ut aegre faceret mundo et diabolo, ut parenti etiam hoc suadenti gratificaretur, Catharinam sibi uxorem ducendam censuit.

Seckend. II· 5. § 5.

([75]) Caeterum si vis Ketham tuam de Bora tenere, matura factum, antequam alteri tradatur, qui prae manibus est. Necdum vicit amorem tui. De Wette II. 553. Kate, the „Virgo Vestalis“, seems to have been a great flirt!

two of them, who are going to take other husbands. The third I hardly keep with my left arm; she too may perhaps be taken away from under my nose. But thou, lazy lover, hast not the courage, to become the husband of *one*." ([76]) On the 4th of May he writes to Rühel: „If I can, I will, before I die, marry my Kate, to spite the devil. ([77]) On the 3d of June he tells the same friend, that if the Cardinal Elector of Mainz should perhaps be waiting for a good example, he, Luther, is willing to give it. ([78])

„To spite the devil" then, we presume, or to give a good example ([79]) or to save his soul, or to aggravate the Pope, or to fulfil his natural vocation and to give Kate the same chance, or to fully renounce Popery ([80]), or to please his father ([81]), or to reerect the „Evangelium" which was suffering from the revolt of the peasants ([82]), or to stop the mouths of the slanderers ([83]), or perhaps for all these reasons together, Luther married Catharina von Bora, in a very quiet way, on the 13th of June 1525. ([84]) On the

([76]) Caeterum, quod de meo conjugio scribis, nolo hoc mireris, me non ducere. qui sic famosus sum amator. Hoc magis mirum, quod qui toties de conjugio scribo et misceor feminis, quod non jam dudum femina factus sum; ut taceam, quod non duxerim aliquam. Quamquam si exemplum meum petis, habes ecce potentissimum. Nam tres simul uxores habui, et tam fortiter amavi, ut duas amiserim, quae alios sponsos accepturae sunt. Tertiam vix sinistro brachio teneo. et ipsam forte mox mihi praeripiendam. Tu vero, segnis ille amator, ne unius quidem audes maritus fieri. De Wette II. 655.

([77]) De Wette II. 655.

([78]) De Wette II. 678. Seckend. II. Sect V. § 5.

([79]) Non duxi uxorem. ut diu viverem, sed ... ut meam doctrinam forte mox post meam mortem conculcandam iterum proprio exemplo relinquerem confirmatam pro infirmis. De Wette III. 32.

([80]) ut nihil ex priori mea vita papistica retineam. Seckend. l. c. De Wette III. 1.

([81]) De Wette III. 13.

([82]) Münzer et rustici sic apud nos Evangelium oppresserunt. sic animos Papistarum erexerunt. ut videatur de novo esse prorsus erigendum. Qua causa et ego jam non verbo solum, sed et opere testatus evangelium, nonna ducta uxore in despectum triumphantium et clamantium Jo! Jo! hostium, ne videar cessisse, quamvis senex et ineptus, facturus et alia si potero, quae illos doleant et verbum confiteantur. De Wette III. 21.

([83]) Os obstruxi infamantibus me cum Catharina Borana. De Wette III. 2.

([84]) Köstlin (I. 766) seems to think it important to prove, against the „Catholic adversaries of Luther", that the wedding took place in the proper legal form and with ecclesiastical ceremonies. This is of no importance whatever. If

27th of the same month another more public festivity took place. Between the two dates the „Reformer" announces to his friends the rather sudden event. His correspondence of this period is of a very mixed character. To Leonard Koppe (who had fetched „Mrs. Luther" out of the Convent) he writes: „I have been tied up in my girl's plaits" ([85]), to Link: „The Lord has thrown me suddenly into the state of matrimony" ([86]), of Stiefel he begs a prayer, that God would bless his new state of life ([87]), of Spalatinus he begs some game for the wedding dinner ([88]), likewise of Dolzig ([89]).

He tells Amsdorf, that the regard for his father has been one of the motives, likewise the necessity of proving by his own example, that he himself is convinced of what he has taught others. ([90]) It sounds strange indeed, that not only whilst preparing for his wedding Luther should urge again and again the severest measures against the rebellious peasants and warn the Councillor of the Count of Mansfeld against clemency being shown to them, ([91]) but that in the very same letters in which he announces his wedding to some friends, he should with satisfaction tell them the news of the wholesale slaughter of the rebels. In the above mentioned letter to Amsdorf he informs him, that in Franconia 11,000, in Würtemberg

---

the „Reformer" and his „wife" had gone through the most scrupulously observed forms a hundred times, their union would be no marriage in the eyes of Catholics, on account of the transgression of their vows.

Justus Jonas says in a letter to Spalatinus, that at the sight of the new couple's thalamus he was unable to repress tears of the deepest emotion. We make no comment to this.

([85]) Ihr wisset auch, was mir geschehen ist, dass ich meiner Metzen in die Zöpfe geflochten bin. De Wette III. 9.

([86]) Dominus me subito, alia-que cogitantem, conjecit mire in conjugium cum Catharina Borensi. De Wette III. 10.

([87]) De Wette III. 9.

([88]) Te non modo adesse oportebit, verum etiam cooperari, si quid ferinae necessarium fuerit. De Wette III. 3. Ne ergo ferina tardius veniat. De Wette III. 14.

([89]) De Wette III. 11.

([90]) Hoc novissimum obsequium parenti meo postulanti nolui denegare spe prolis, simul ut confirmem facto, quae docui. Tam multos invenio pusillanimes in tanta luce Evangelii.
De Wette III. 13.

([91]) De Wette II. 653. 666.

6000, in Suabia 10,000, in Alsace 20,000 have been killed.
Altogether the corpses of 100,000 men, who had carried
out the principle of „evangelical liberty,“ were rotting on
the battlefields, when the „Reformer“ was joined to his
Kate. But this circumstance does not seem to have
greatly disturbed his matrimonial happiness or to have
spoiled his appetite for the game.

Catholics were scandalized by what they necessarily
considered as a sacrilegious attempt to contract matrimony; Luther consoled himself with the thought, that a
work of God has always this effect. If the world were
not scandalized, then he would be afraid that this his work
were not divine.([92]) But even Luther's most intimate
friend Philip Melanchthon was anything but edified by
the marriage.([93]) Though he did not object to it on
principle, he thought it would have been better to avoid
this step; however he expressed his hope, that by it
Luther would be cured of his scurrility. Melanchthon
also mentions that the „Reformer“ was rather sad and
disturbed on account of the change of life. ([94]) Should
the voice of conscience have had something to do with
this sadness? Luthers friends will say *No*, we beg to
be allowed to think *Yes*. We do not expect to agree.([95])

([92]) Si meum conjugium est
opus Dei, quid mirum, si in illo
caro offendatur, offenditur etiam
in carne ipsius divinitatis et cre-
atoris, quam ipse pro salute mundi
in pretium et cibum dedit. Si non
offenderetur mundus in nobis, ego
offenderer in mundo, metuens, ne
non esset divinum, quod gerimus.
De Wette III. 32.
([93]) Köstlin I. 769.
([94]) Ipsum Lutherum quodam-
modo tristiorem esse cerno et per-
turbatum ob vitae mutationem.
ap. Seckend. L. II. Sect. V. § 5.
([95]) This letter of Melanchthon
proves, how „history“ used to be
made. It is written in Greek and
addressed to Camerarius, who in
1569 edited Melanchthon's letters.

Germanus (p. 285) justly remarks,
that the words on the titlepage
„accuratâ consideratione“ have a
deep meaning. · The original of
this letter has been found, some
years ago, in the Chigi library
(Accounts of the Bavar. Acad. of
Science 1876 fasc. 4 & 5). Not
only ¡does it not agree 'with the
letter as published by Camerarius,
but there appear in the margin
his notes: „Omittantur“. „non de-
scribantur“. Camerarius makes
Melanchthon say, that in Luther's
marriage there has been „something mysterious and divine“.
(χρύφιον καὶ θειότερον τι). There
is nothing of the sort in the original. On the contrary Mel. thinks,
that the intercourse with so many

Anyhow Luther was landed in „paradise." In time he
got over his surprise to see, when awaking, two plaits
lying by his side on the pillow ([96]) and became even
accustomed to the „howling and yelling" of children, ([97])
and when Kate had a little Johnny, she was proud of
that blessing, „of which the Pope was not worthy." ([98])
On many occasions, ([99]) also in his last will and testament ([100]) Luther praises his Kate as a faithful, pious
and careful wife, whom he would not give up for all
France and Venice: ([101]) but on his part he thought he
was able to assure her: „Kate, thou hast a pious husband,
that loves thee." ([102]) But this did not prevent him from
speaking about his „cerva," as he frequently called her, ([103])
and about women in general in a very indelicate, nay indecent way, nor did he abstain from downright filthy
puns and jokes. ([104]) He generally gives her most endear-
ing names, he calls her even „Most holy M. Doctor." ([105])
When he speaks of her as" Catena mea" ([106]) „Domina et
hera mea Ketha" ([107]) „Dear *Master* Keth," ([108]) „*Meus
Ketha*" ([109]) and calls her even his *Moses* ([110]) (i. e. she

escaped nuns must have done harm
even to a noble and magnanimous
person like his friend. *(γενναιον
ὄντα και μεγαλοψυχον.)* In this
way Luther seems to have been
circumvented *(τοιτον τροπον εἰσ-
πεσειν δοχει).* Camerarius entirely
omits the further words, in which
Mel. expresses his hope, that L.
will be cured from that scurrility,
with which he has been so often reproached. *Προς τοιτο και ἐλπιζω
ὁτι ὁ βιος οἱτωσι σεμνοτιρον αὐτον
ποιησει ... ὠστε και ἀποβαλειν την
β..λ..ιαν, ἡς πολλακις ἐμεμψαμεσθα.*
Some writers have thought it necessary to fill up the word β..λ..ιαν
with „*ἡμολογιαν*". but considering the number of blanks left by
Melanchthon, *βδελυριαν* will answer
much better.

([96]) Tischr. II. c. 20. § 11.

([97]) Ibid. § 17.

([98]) Keta quoque tibi omnia
optima imprecatur, maxime Spalat-
inulum, qui te doceat, quod se
doctam jactat a suo Johannello,
hoc est, fructum et gaudium conjugii, quibus indignus erat Papa
cum suo mundo. Letter to Spalatinus. De Wette III. 148.

([99]) v. gr. Tischr. l. c. § 28.
([100]) Seckend. lib. III. § 135.
([101]) Köstlin II. 479.
([102]) Tischr. l. c. § 7.
([103]) De Wette III. 119, IV.
237 etc.
([104]) De Wette III. 18. Tischr.
II. c. 20. § 75.
([105]) De Wette V. 789.
([106]) Ibid. III. 35. 92. 128 etc.
([107]) Ibid. 145.
([108]) Ibid. 512.
([109]) Ibid II. 629.
([110]) Köstlin II. 495.

laid down the *law* for him), the reason is, that Kate had
a will of her own, which she also knew at times, how to
maintain against that of the Ecclesiastes. The suspicion,
which Luther had had of her before the wedding, that she
was inclined to pride and imperiousness, seems not to have
been unfounded. The lodgers they usually had in the
house, complained of this, as also of her economizing
ways, some left in consequence of it.([111]) Luther writes
to his friend Agricola, that he means to send him a little
goblet as a present, but he has to put in a postscript,
saying that meantime Kate, who did not wish to part with
it, had snatched it away.([112]) If before his marriage
Luther had had to complain many times of his scanty
means, ([113]) he was in the course of times freed from such
cares. The Elector assigned to him a fixed salary, and
presents flowed in from many parts. ([114]) The monastery
buildings, where he had formerly lived as a monk, had
been given to him as a present by the Elector, to whom
in 1524 he had offered the same as a bonum derelictum.

Those buildings, which had been put up with the
alms of the „Papistical" faithful, now harboured the „Reformer" and his „wife." The very walls, which had seen
Luther strive, to serve God in chastity and mortification
and prepare for the most beautiful day in a priest's life,
that of his first Mass, now saw him put his pen to the
paper, to outdo himself — and that says a great deal —
in reviling the Church and the Mass and monasticism,
they saw him, the new Pope under petticoat-government,

([111]) Köstlin II.496. Cfr. Seckend,
l. c. „Observavi ex litteris Pontani,
quod uxor Lutheri animum paulo
elatiorem et imperiosum habuisse
visa sit, atque tenax in victu domestico fuerit. — After Luther's
death his widow and children were
quite neglected by his friends. In
1550 Bora begged some assistance
from the king of Denmark, but
without any result. When in 1552

she „a poor widow, abandoned by
everybody" renewed her request,
she received a small donation. She
died in misery at Torgau towards
the end of the same year.

([112]) De Wette III. 111.

([113]) Ibid. II. 473. 506. 584.

([114]) Köstlin II. 489.

issue his decrees, his „sic volo, sic jubeo," they saw the
Ecclesiastes sitting over his beerpots, and again, walking
about „accompanied by the devil," they heard him, at
the dinnertable, crack his filthy jokes and tell his dirty
tales. —

Quantum mutatus ab illo!

Chapter XV.

Luther and the peasants.

Hoc exemplum (Pauli) et nos imitari debemus, ut erga miseros et seductos discipulos
sic affecti simus, ut parentes erga liberos.

Luther. Wittenb. V. 284.

Let everyone than can, strike, slay, stab,
publicly or secretly .... It is just like killing
a mad dog.

Idem. Walch XVI. 93.

The year 1525 witnessed a terrible conflagration,
which brought ruin and desolation upon a large part of
Germany and caused endless misery also to the coming generation. We shall not of course attempt here to give
a full history of the revolt of the peasants; its incidents
are here of interest only as far as Luther is connected
with them and as far as they throw a light upon the
character and teaching of the „Reformer." The question,
whether and how far he is answerable for this revolt and
the almost incredible horrors which accompanied it, has
been frequently and eagerly discussed; most of his friends
and admirers have given and give now an indignant denial to it. Nobody would say that Luther directly intended
those horrors or even the revolt. But if a man standing on
one of the snowcapped giants of the Alps were to roll
down a little stone, knowing what the consequences
would be, he would be answerable for the desolation
caused by the avalanche in the valley below. Luther put
into motion not one little stone, he hurled down rock

15

after rock. He must have been very shortsighted indeed,
or his blind hatred must have made him such, if he was
unable to estimate beforehand what effect his flaming
appeals to the masses of the people and his wild denun-
ciations of the Catholic Church would have. It has been
stated over and over again that the rebels misunderstood
Luther's words. Perhaps so. But in that case it was a
misunderstanding which, considering Luther's style and the
incapacity of the mob of making nice and subtle distinct-
ions, was absolutely inevitable. However we mean to
record here *facts*, which will enable the reader to judge
for himself, whether or not Luther can be absolved from
the charge of being an accomplice to that national calamity.

· Before anyone dreamt of Luther's „Reformation,“
there had been revolts of peasants. The revolutionary
ideas of the Hussites had infected part of the lower
classes of Germany, and the real grievances, under which
they were smarting([1]) had helped to cause outbreaks in
Franconia (1476), in Alsace (1493), the „Bundschuh“ of
1502([2]) and the „arme Conrad“ of 1514.([3]) If Luther
had never appeared, there would in all probability have
been further outbreaks, but that the outbreak of 1525
assumed such large proportions, that it found such an
enormous number of fanatical adherents, that it was
accompanied by horrors which will for ever be one of
the darkest blots on the history of the German nation,
this is the fault of Luther's Evangelium. This is a serious
charge which will have to be proved. We beg the reader
to consider the following points.

([1]) See introductory chapter. —
We shall however hear from Luther that *he* considered those grievances as unfounded.

([2]) The word „Bundschuh“ originally means a particular sort of
shoe which was worn by the peasants, something like the „cioccia“
worn now by many of the Abbruz-

zesi; it was fastened with straps
round the calf of the leg. It was
adopted by the rebels as their arms
and appeared on their banners. In
the course of time the conspiracy
itself received the name of „Bundschuh“.

([3]) For a full account of these
revolts see Janssen II. 391 seqq.

1) Everywhere, without a single exception, did the
rebels of 1525 appear under the banner and with the
watchword of the „Evangelium." Their social grievances
formed avowedly an object of secondary importance. The
principal end for which they took up arms and for which
they murdered, plundered and burned, was: to establish
and to protect „the word of God." The whole revolt
was characterized by that most dangerous element, religious fanaticism. Hence:

2) The rebellion arose and prospered only in those
parts of Germany, where Luther's Evangelium had been
preached and had been embraced by the people. Riffel
justly observes([4]) that the true and genuine Evangelium
would not have fanned the flames, but would have shown
its divine power by calming the discontented masses and
by preventing revolt and bloodshed.

3) Not only had the preachers of the new Evangelium
overrun the country, denouncing the Catholic Church and
prelates, priests and monks in the most violent words and
in the vilest manner as tyrants, idolaters and priest of Baal
— just as their master, Dr. Martin Luther, was wont to
do — but every band of the rebellious peasants was
accompanied by such fanatics. Nay, in many cases they
were the leaders and they had personally an active part
in the destruction of Churches, monasteries, altars, crucifixes, libraries etc. and in the illtreatment of the Clergy.
True that many of them were not friends or adherents
of Luther's person; true, that many of them acknowledged
Thomas Münzer as their head and therefore nourished
even feelings of personal enmity against the „Reformer"
of Wittenberg. But also in these cases the principles
underlying their preaching were Luther's principles. If
in the application of these principles they went farther
than he was inclined to go, they were still able to appeal
to that freedom of thought and of interpretation, which

([4]) I. 513.

he considered as the most glorious acquisition and which he had *distinctly* granted to every Christian.

4) That the principles of the rebels were identical with those of Luther appears from a comparison between the writings of the latter and the demands of the former. The rebels used sometimes Luther's own words.([5]) They demanded the right to appoint and to dismiss their ministers as they liked and to be the supreme judges of the ministers' teaching — this right the Ecclesiastes had granted already to every Christian Congregation. They demanded that the „pure Evangelium" should be preached everywhere, without any human additions — the very same vague phrases which allowed plenty of room for the wildest fancies of every individual head, had been used by Luther hundreds of times. They interpreted the Bible according to their own ideas and had continually Bible texts on their lips — again they were able to appeal to Luther's permission and example. They demanded „Christian liberty" — the liberty which Luther granted had not only regard to the law of Moses, but, in the case of the believing Christian, to all laws and all authorities. ([6]) A Christian, he had said, needs for himself neither law nor right, since a good tree naturally and necessarily bear good fruit without being commanded to bear it, and if he is subject to law, his reason can only be this, to give a good example to those who are not yet good Christians. Luther could not deny (and when he did, he did so against his own principles) that the rebels were believers.

5) If the principles of the bands of rebels were those of Luther, their actions only realized some of the dearest wishes of his Christian heart. For years he had sent out one incendiary pamphlet after another, in which in

---

([5]) Alzog 725. — Erasmus said to Luther: you do not acknowledge the rebels, but they acknowledge you.

([6]) See chapter on the Evang. page 143.

unmeasured terms, in terms the invention of which astonishes the reader, he had denounced the spiritual „tyrants" and had held them up to popular execration. If, according to him, monasteries were „worse than brothels and dens of murderers" (⁷), bishoprics only the seats of „wolves" and of the lieutenants of the devil", Churches, were Mass was celebrated, the „houses of abomination", what was more natural, than that the sincere friends of his Evangelium should resolve to rid their country of such nuisances? If it was better, that all Bishops should be murdered and all Collegiate Churches and Convents should be destroyed, than that one soul should be lost, why should not those who did not wish to see one soul lost through the snares of Popery, willingly do that which was better? If nothing could be more just than that a strong rebellion should sweep them (the Bishop) from the face of the earth, why should not the Evangelical rebels practically prove their love of Justice? If Luther had complainingly exclaimed: „Why do we not wash our hands in their blood?" why should his adherents not do that which had been omitted? It will be said that Luther never meant justice to be entrusted to the hands of the mob, but that he wished to see it carried out by the secular authorities only. Perhaps so. But why did he in that case not adress his demands exclusively to the same authorities? Why did he publish his incendiary pamphlets printed in *German* and in a style which could only prove tasteful to the very dregs of the mob? Why did he not at least say at the same time that private persons ought to abstain from taking upon themselves the office of carrying out such justice? No such restriction appears in the very wildest of his appeals to the fury of the populace. We reproduce here once more his, Dr. Luther's, „Bulla." *„All who cooperate and risk even their lives, possessions and honour in the destruction of the Bishoprics and of the power of the*

(⁷) For these quotations we refer the reader to chapter XI.

*Bishops, they are dear children of God and the right sort
of Christians.* But all that uphold the Bishops' power and
are subject to them in willing obedience, they are the
devil's own servants and are opposed to God." „Since it
is manifest, that the Bishops are not only larvae and idols,
but a tribe cursed by God, . . . every Christian ought to
help with his body and his goods, that their tyranny should
be despised and should come to an end, and ought to do
gladly whatever in against them, just as if it was against
the devil himself. This shall be mine, Dr. Luther's, Bulla,
which gives God's grace as a reward to all who observe
and follow it. Amen." A man who uses such language,
who distinctly approves of that work of destruction also
in case it was done iniquitously (ob es auch Jemand aus
Frevel thäte) should not be answerable for it? Why should
not his followers be naturally desirous of becoming „dear
children of God and the right sort of Christians?"

6) Luther had done his best, to discredit not only
spiritual but also temporal authority. When he publicly
called the Emperor a tyrant and„ a sack of maggots", and
the princes „mad, foolish, senseless, raving, frantic, lunatics",
and when he prayed that God might deliver the German
nation from them([8]), it will hardly be supposed that such
expressions were apt to foster in the people respect for
their rulers and willingness to obey them. Nor can it be
supposed, that his „Exhortation adressed to all Christians
to abstain from rebellion" ([9]) would produce much effect,
since in it he allowed that the common people had plenty
of reasons to use flails and cudgels; nor would his activity
in the pulpit contribute much towards pacifying the minds,
since in a sermon, which he preached in 1522 we find the
following words: „Reason thinks, the Evangelium might
be preached in a simple and plain way, without a rebellion
of the world . . . *The devil has said that.*"([10]) If the secular
rulers of the period had been as bad as Luther paints

([8]) See chapter XII.   ([10]) Erl. 12. 245.
([9]) Walch X. 406 seqq.

them, still, it would seem strange that an „Evangelist"
should make it his business to flatter and to excite the
mob by exposing the faults of their masters in the most
glaring colours. „They know of nothing but flaying and
squeezing and putting one tax upon the other, one rate
upon the other; here they send out a bear and there a
wolf; no justice, no fidelity, no truth is to be found in
them; they act in such a manner, that it would be too
much for robbers and knaves ... there are few princes,
who are not considered fools and knaves ... People
will not and cannot stand in the long run your tyranny
and your arbitrary proceedings. ... the world is not now
what it used to be, when you drove and hunted the
people like beasts". ([11]) We have seen above how Luther
denied all rights, all power, all authority to those who
opposed the word of God i. e. his own doctrine.

The rebellious peasants, whose numbers were swelling
to an enormous extent, drew up their demands and grievances under twelve headings; the document containing
them was scattered all over Germany. The introduction
to it shows how much they had learned from Luther, since
with him they knew how to exonerate the „Evangelium"
from all blame and how to throw the blame on the
adversaries of it. To facilitate the comparison, we will
give Luther words and the rebels' words in juxtaposition.

Luther:	The rebels:
God so disturbs the minds (of the princes) that they act foolishly and try to domineer over the souls, just as the others (the Bishops) endea-vour to have temporal power, that they may burden them-selves with the sins of others, with the hatred of God and	The Evangelium is not a cause of risings and rebelli-ons, for it is the word of Christ, the promised Messias, which word and life teaches nothing but charity, peace, patience and unity (!) ... how then can the antichrist-ian people call the Evar-

([11]) Von weltlicher Oberkeit, wie weit etc.

man, until they go to pieces, with bishops, priests and monks, the whole lot of knaves together. And after that they blame the Evangelium, and instead of confessing their guilt, they blaspheme God, saying that *our* preaching has done the mischief ... Behold, here you have the design of God with regard to these big chaps (grosse Hansen). But they shall not believe it, lest they should repent and thus prevent God's plan being carried out. ([12])

gelium the cause of rising and rebellion? ... The peasants who in their articles demand the said Evangelium for their rule of faith and life, must not be called disobedient or rebellious. ...Who will blame the will of God? who will interfere with his judgment? who will resist his majesty? If he has heard the children of Israel when they cried out to him and has freed them out of the hands of Pharao, may he not deliver his own even today? Yea, he will deliver them, and in a short time. ([13])

Of the twelve articles the most important is the first, which we have mentioned already, and which treats of the „pure Evangelium" and the rights of the congregations over their ministers; the other articles demand the suppression of tithes, servitudes, heriots etc. The article, which pleased Luther more than any other, was the twelfth, in which the peasants declared their readiness to be taught better, if their demands should not be found to be in harmony with the Bible. But at the same time they reserved their right to make further demands, if they should find any more in the same source.

Several of the leaders of the rebellion added projects for a general political and social reform of Germany, they demanded, for instance, suppression of the Roman Law and exclusion of the lawyers from the courts of justice, likewise suppression of the trading companies, destruction

([12]) Riffel I. 526.
([13]) Walch XVI. 24; where also the twelve articles of the peasants are to be found.

of all fortifications, introduction of general equality among
men, abolition of the nobility etc. Their appeals to violence are sometimes such as would do honour to the
wildest Sansculotte of the French Revolution. „Only throw
these Moab, Agab, Achap, Phalaris and Nero from their
thrones, this is a thing most pleasing to God. The Scripture calls them not servants of God, but serpents, dragons
and wolves. Perhaps the ears of the Lord of Sabaoth
have heard the pitiful cries of the reapers and labourers
and he has mercifully granted that the day may come for
butchering the fattened beasts, that have fed in luxury
on the work of the poor man; James, Chapter the fifth." ([14])
Münzer wrote to the Mansfeld miners: „Strike the iron
whilst it is hot; let not your swords get cold with the
blood." ([15]) Advice of this sort was faithfully followed
by the rebels: it was truly a time of cruel coldblooded
butchering, a fearful illustration to the „charity and peace"
which was pretended to be the object. The scenes that
were enacted at Weinsberg make one shudder. As afterwards in the French Revolution, so it happened there also,
that women were worse than men in their insatiable hatred.
An old hag which accompanied the bands of murderers
and promised to protect them against swords and bullets
with her incantations, plunged her dagger into the dead
body of the Count of Helfenstein who had been pierced
with numberless halberds and greased her shoes with his
fat and blood.

The rebels sent their articles to Wittenberg asking
Luther's opinion about them. His answer came in the
shape of a pamphlet, entitled „An exhortation to peace,
with regard to the twelve articles of the peasantry in
Suabia." ([16]) We have said before that Luther cannot
be supposed to have directly intended the revolt, we
must also acknowledge that he sincerely wished to

([14]) „dass der Schlachttag soll   ([15]) Walch XVI. 152.
angen über das gemest Vieh" ap.   ([16]) Walch XVI. 58 seqq.
Janssen II. 452.

see an end put to it. Even if he had not detested
those enormous crimes and the *manner* of realizing
his wish for the destruction of monasticism etc., motives
of prudence would have made him anxious to remove
the scandal which was falling upon the „Evangelium."
But whether this „Exhortation to peace" was in the least
apt to further the cause of peace, this is a different question. The reader will be able to form a judgment from
the following extracts. The pamphlet consists of two
parts, one addressed to the princes, the other to the
peasants.

In the first part we hear Luther throw once more
the blame upon the princes. „Noone on earth have we
to thank for this mess and rebellion, than you, princes
and lords, especially you, blind Bishops and mad priests
and monks, who, even now obstinate, do not cease your
raving and raging against the holy Evangelium, though
knowing that it is true, though unable to refute it. In
your secular rule you do nothing more than squeeze and
flay the people to satisfy your pomp and pride, until
the poor man can stand it no longer. The sword is on
your neck, you still think you are firm in the saddle and
cannot be lifted out of it, but such security and obstinate
presumption will break your necks. Many a time have
I told you to beware of the words Psalm 107. 40.
„Effundit contemptum super principes. You seem to
intend it, you *will* have a knock on the head, all
warning and exhortation is invain. As you then are the
cause of this wrath of God, it will no doubt come
upon you, if you do not amend in time." ([17]) „For know
this, dear Lords, it is God's work, that your tyranny
cannot and will not and shall not be suffered much longer.
You must change and must give way to the word of God.
If you do not do so in a friendly and willing way, it will
come about in a violent and deplorable way. If these peas-

([17]) Walch XVI. 60.

ants do not accomplish it, others will. If you kill them all,
they are still unconquered; God will raise others. For he
means to strike you and he will strike you. Those, who oppose you, dear Lords, are not peasants, no, it is God himself,
who comes to visit you on account of your tyranny." ([18])
„If God intends to punish you and to allow the devil
through his false prophets (the followers of Münzer) to
excite the mad populace against you, and if perhaps he
wills not that I should or could hinder it, what can I do?
and what can my Evangelium do?   And if I were so inclined to have my revenge of you, I might laugh in my
sleeve and might remain a looker on or might even go
over to them and help them to make matters worse. But
from that may God protect me, as hitherto he has done.
Therefore, my dear Lords, whether you be friends or
foes, I humbly beg of you, do not despise my sincerity,
though I am poor man.   And do not, I beg of you,
despise this rebellion.   Not that I think or fear that they
will be too powerful for you, nor do I wish that you
should be afraid of them.   But fear God and consider
his wrath.   If *he* means to punish you, as you deserve, —
and I am afraid he does mean is — he will chastise you,
if there was only the hundredth part of the number of
peasants; he can raise peasants out of stones and through
one peasant he can slay an hundred of you." ([19])

Let the reader remember that this is not a private admonition, but that Luther is lecturing to the
princes in a pamphlet, which is likewise destined for the
hands of their bitterest foes.   This is indeed a curious
way of pacifying two parties which are at daggers drawn
or which have already come to blows! After having
pronounced *in favour* of the twelve articles, ([20]) Luther
begins to adress the peasants.   His words are most interesting, not only because from the incredible contradictions
they contain it appears how little clearness he possessed on

([18]) Ibid. 61.   ([20]) he calls them fair and just
([19]) Ibid. 62.   (billig und recht) Ibid. 64.

the important points, on which he gave advice, but also
on account of the whole tone of them, which is so different
from that of another production, which was to follow
almost immediately. „Until now, my dear friends“, he
adresses the peasants, „you have only heard me confess
that unfortunately it is only too true and certain, that the
princes and lords, who prevent the Evangelium from being
preached, and who put such intolerable burdens on the
people, are worthy and fully deserve that God should
throw them from their thrones; for they grievously sin
against God and man, nor have they any excuse. Nevertheless you will have to be careful, to act with a good
conscience and right. For if you have a good conscience,
you have the consolation and advantage, that God will
assist you. And though you were conquered for a time
or suffered death, you would be sure to win in the end
and your souls would be saved eternally with all the Saints.
But if you are not right, if you have not a good conscience, you will be conquered, and though you were to
triumph for a time and to slay all princes, you would in
the end be lost eternally, both body and soul.“ ([21]) It
ought to be remembered here that, according to Luther,
man wants no other guide for his conscience, but „the
word of God“, in the interpretation of which man does
not depend on any one except the Spirit. This principle
the „Reformer“ had also applied to the question which in
the preceding year had been put to him about polygamy.
His answer had been, that if a man could form a conscience from the word of God as to its being lawful, he
certainly might have two wives at the same time.([22]) That
the rebels had formed a „conscience“ as to the lawfulness
of their proceedings would appear from their continual
recourse to the Bible. He continues: Therefore, *my dear
masters and brethren*, I beg of you kindly and as a brother,

([21]) Ibid. 64.

([22]) Oportere ipsum maritum
sua propria conscientia esse firmum
ac certum per verbum Dei, sibi
haec licere. De Wette II. 459.

consider carefully what you do, and do not believe all
sorts of spirits and preachers, now that that wicked Satan
has raised so many wild spirits under the name of the
Evangelium". He seems to overlook that the power of
and the right to a discretio spirituum, which he had granted
to everybody, had evidently been made use of already by
the rebels. But now Luther tells his „dear masters and
brethren", that, no matter how much they are oppressed,
no matter how much the Evangelium is oppressed, they
have no right to be judges in their own cause or to act
as they act, (²³) except they „can show a fresh and distinct
command from God, and prove it by signs and wonders." (²⁴)
He tells them it is the duty of a Christian „not to resist
injury, not to take the sword, not to seek revenge, but to
give up body and possessions; let rob who choses to rob.
Our Lord is enough for us; according to his promise he
will not abandon us. Suffering, suffering, cross, cross, this ·
and nothing else is a Christian's right."(²⁵) From this it
would follow that if the princes wished to be Christians,
they too would have to suffer patiently and would do
wrong in resisting the rebels, who tried to deprive them
of everything. Which party then is right after all, and
which is wrong? Luther decides that neither party has a
right to the name of Christian, that they are *all* going to
hell. „Christians do not fight with the sword, nor with
the rifle, but only with cross and suffering." (²⁶) „You,
Lords, are not fighting against Christians, for Christians
would not do anything to you, they would suffer everything; you are fighting against public robbers, against
blasphemers of the Christian name; *those amongst them
that fall, are damned eternally.* Again, you peasants are
not fighting against Christians either, but against tyrants
and persecutors of God and men, against the murderers
of the Saints of Christ, and *those amongst them, that fall,
are likewise damned eternally.* There you have, both

(²³) Walch XVI. 67.   (²⁵) Ibid. 72.
(²⁴) Ibid. 68.   (²⁶) Ibid. 77.

parties, your certain judgment from God." ([27]) Is this pacification? In his anger about the „stench" raised by the devil against his Evangelium, Luther tells his „dear masters and brethren", that they are only instruments of the devil. „I see it clearly, the devil, who has been unable to murder me through the Pope, is trying to destroy and to devour me through the bloodthirsty prophets and spirits that are amongst you. Well, let him devour me, his belly will get narrow enough then, I know." ([28])

In the first part of this pamphlet, when adressing the princes, *Luther had approved of the twelve articles* of the peasants and had pronounced them to be fair and just; in the second part of the *same* pamphlet, when adressing the peasants, he partly restricts, partly rejects and condemns the very *same* articles, calling them robbery, anti-evangelical etc. ([29]) He says they have nothing to do with Christians, for a Christian is a martyr on earth and must suffer to be robbed, oppressed, flayed, devoured etc.

What fruit could be expected from such a singular „Exhortation to peace? The rebellious peasants went on murdering, plundering and burning, worse than before. In Thüringen alone 70 monasteries became a prey to the flames([30]), in Franconia 293 Castles. Brutal excesses, corpses of noblemen and priests and monks and smoking ruins marked the route of those new Vandals. When at last the judgment overtook them, it proved to be of unparallelled severity. It was mere butchery, but *it was what Luther had wished it to be.* When it became evident that his exhortation to peace was fruitless, as well it might be, he, the „dear man of God", worked himself up to a degree of rage which makes one shudder. Not a word of intercession, of charity, of mercy is to be found in his new pamphlet, „Against the robbing and murdering peas-

---

([27]) Ibid. 90.
([28]) Ibid. 78.
([29]) eitel Raub und öffentliche Strauchdieberei. Ibid. 80, 81.

([30]) See the list ap. Janssen II. 524.

ants". (³¹) "Everybody that can kill them, does right and
well, for over a rebel every man is both judge and
executioner . . . *Let everybody who can, strike, slay and
stab*, secretly or publicly, let everybody remember that
there is nothing more venomous, nothing more pernicious,
nothing more diabolical, than a rebel. It is just like killing
a mad dog; if you do not kill him, he will kill you and
a whole country with you." (³²) "I believe there are no
devils in hell now, they have all gone into the peasants." (³³)
"A Prince or Lord has to consider that he is God's representative and the minister of his wrath, that to him the
sword has been entrusted against such knaves, that if he
does not fulfil his duty, he sins before God just as grievously as a man that comits murder . . . . Don't talk here
of patience or mercy, it is the time of the sword and of
wrath, not the time of grace. Let therefore the authorities
proceed confidently and strike with a good conscience as
long as they can move a finger. For here is the advantage,
that the peasants have a bad conscience (how does
Luther know this?) and are in the wrong, and what peasant soever is killed, he is lost, body and soul, and *is the
devil's in all eternity*. But the authorities have a good
conscience and are in the right". (³⁴) "Hence it may happen
that he who is killed on their side, may be a true martyr
before God . . . but whosoever falls on the side of the
peasants, is a brand of hell for eternity, because he is a
member of the devil . . . It is such a wonderful time
now, that a prince may gain heaven by bloodshed, better
than others can by prayer". (³⁵) After mentioning those
who against their will had been forced to join the ranks
of the rebels, he continues: "Therefore, dear Lords, loose
them, save them, help them, have pity on those poor people.
Let every one, who can, stab, strike, kill. If thou fallest
in this work, blessed art thou, a happier death thou couldst

(³¹) Walch XVI. 91 seqq.
(³²) Ibid. 93.
(³³) Ibid. 94.
(³⁴) Ibid. 96.
(³⁵) Ibid. 97.

not have, for thou diest in obedience to the word and command of God and in the service of charity, endeavouring to save thy neighbour from the fetters of hell and of the devil. ([30])"

We would gladly suppose this to be nothing more, than a sudden outburst of rage, did not Luther over and over again in his letters repeat such language and try to justify it. Nay many years afterwards he still boasted of it in his Tabletalk. „I, Martin Luther, have during the rebellion killed all the peasants for I have commanded that they should be killed. *All their blood is upon my head*, but I put it all on our Lord God, for he had commanded it to me." It is indeed surprising to see the „Evangelist" address a letter to Rühel, the Councillor of the Count of Mansfeld, for no other purpose but this, to beg of him repeatedly that he would dissuade his master from showing mercy and clemency to the rebellious peasants. ([37]) In another letter to the same Rühel we meet with the following reasoning: „If there are some innocent ones (amongst the rebels) God will save them and preserve them, as he has saved Lot and Jeremias. *If he does not, they are certainly not innocent.*" He adds: „The wise man says: Cibus, onus et virga asino ... they hear not the word, they have no sense, therefore they must hear virgam, the rifle, and serves them right. We must pray for them that they may obey; if they do not, mercy is out of place; let the bullets whistle amongst them ([36]), otherwise they will be a thousand times worse ... O Lord God, *it is time indeed, that the peasants were killed like mad dogs*" ([39]). In a letter to Amsdorf he says that his conscience feels quite safe about the advice given with regard to the rebels and justifies the same advice by saying, that since they have taken to the sword without the authority of God, to have

---

([30]) Ibid. 9S.

([37]) De Wette II. 653 seqq. — Cfr. Ibid. 666.

([38]) lasse nur die Büchsen unter sie sausen.

([39]) De Wette II. 669. 670.

mercy on them would be tantamount to a denial of God, or to blasphemy. ([40])

Though at first Luther had made up his mind „to stop his ears and to leave the blind ungrateful hearts, that only tried to be scandalized in him, in such scandal until they should rot" ([41]), he could not help seeing that his murderous pamphlet against the murderous peasants caused general indignation. Therefore he tried to justify it in a long letter to Müller, Chancellor of Mansfeld, which appeared in print. To this end he represents the „slanderers" of his pamphlet as very suspicious persons. „Those that blame it, ought to be warned to shut their mouths and to be careful. For surely they too are rebels in their hearts." ([42]) „A rebel is not worthy that one should answer him with reasons, he is not accessible to them, *the fist has to answer such jaws, until the blood spirts out from the nose.* The peasants would not hear, they would not be talked to, therefore it was necessary to open their ears with bullets, so as to make the heads fly in the air . . . If people say that here I am unkind and unmerciful, I answer: mercy has nothing to do here; we are speaking of the word of God, which will have the king honoured and the rebels destroyed." ([43]) Sarcastically he thanks those who teach him a lesson on mercy. „How should I know what God's mercy demands, I, who hitherto have taught and written about mercy more, than anyone else has done in a thousand years?" ([44])

With regard to Luther's dogmatical teaching it is interesting to observe that he, who in the same year 1525

([40]) Gaudeo sic satanam indignari et blasphemare, quoties a me tangitur ... Nostra conscientia tuta est, rectum esse coram Deo quod egressum est ex labiis meis ex hac parte ... Erit forte tempus ut et mihi liceat dicere: Omnes vos scandalum patiemini in ista nocte... Ego sic sentio esse melius omnes rusticos caedi, quam principes et magistratus, eo quod rustici sine auctoritate Dei gladium accipiunt... Hoc ergo justificare, horum misereri, illis favere, est Deum negare, blasphemare et de coelo velle dejicere.   De Wette II. 671.

([41]) Walch XVI. 99.
([42]) Ibid. 101.
([43]) Ibid. 102.
([44]) Ibid. 104.

published his book de servo arbitro, here protests against
the excuse urged by some, that many of the peasants had
been forced into the rebellion, to save their lives. „Who
has ever heard that a man has been forced, to do good
or evil? Who can force man's will? . . . Why do they allow
themselves to be forced? If this excuse were worth
anything, no sin or vice could be punished." (⁴⁵) To the
objection that he had contradicted himself, when promising
heaven as a *reward* for bloodshed (since he so decidedly
rejected meritorious works), he answers with the complaint,.
that not even the *common form of speech* will be allowed to
him. „Christ also says . . . Blessed are you if you suffer
persecution, for your reward is great in heaven, and yet
it remains true that works are nothing before God, but
only faith." (⁴⁶)

On the one side Luther thinks that the cruel suppression of the rebellion has been a good lesson to the
peasants, *to teach them that they had been too well off,* (wie
ihnen zu wol gewest ist) and hopes that their Lords will
be strict with them for the future; „a donkey wants blows,
and the mob has to be ruled by force. God knew this;
therefore he put a sword into the hand of the authority,
not a foxbrush." (⁴⁷) On the other side he takes great
care to give a warning to the same Lords. „If the
time and the thing demand that I should act, I mean to
attack the princes and lords as well." He especially
threatens those „who oppose the Evangelium and try to
reestablish Collegiate Churches and monasteries and to protect the Pope's crown." (⁴⁸) With regard to tyrannical
abuses of power he adds: „I was afraid that if the peasants
were masters, the devil would be abbot, but if such tyr-

(⁴⁵) Ibid. 116. 117.
(⁴⁶) Ibid. 125.
(⁴⁷) „Whilst the Catholic Church
always, at least theoretically, disapproved of tyranny on the part
of spiritual or secular princes, and
powerfully, and as a rule victori-
ously, defended the rights of the

people even against the Emperors,
the Evangelical Reformers have
sullied their names by preaching
and teaching servility and absolutism."
Bensen, Gesch. d. Bauernkr. 19.
(⁴⁸) Walch XVI. 124.

ants were to be masters, the devil's mother would be abbess." ([49])

The conclusion of the pamphlet is in the true and genuine Lutheran style. „I wish people would let me alone; they will not get the better of me. *What I teach and write, shall remain right, if the whole world were to burst.*" ([50])

([49]) Ibid. 127.　　　　　　　　　　([50]) Ibid.

Chapter XVI

Luther and the Sacramentarians.

„You pigs, hounds, ranters, you irrational asses."

Luther. Walch XX. 1015.

We have mentioned before that Carlstadt had begun to follow a new line of reforming. Luther seems to have been almost paralized at the idea that his former friend should endeavour to become independent. „If Carlstadt has no regard for *me*, for whom amongst us will he have any regard?" (¹) The principle of private judgment in religious matters, which he had so openly proclaimed and on which his own teachings and actions were entirely based, was now denied to Carlstadt, who, when he claimed the same right for himself, became in Luther's eyes a dwelling-place of a thousand devils and the perfection of pride. (²) Neither at Wittenberg, nor at Jena did Carlstadt find it possible, to have his polemical writings printed. In denouncing him to the Chancellor Brück Luther was barefaced enough to appeal to the imperial decree, accord-

(¹) Walch XX. 221.
(²) Carolstadius traditus est tandem in reprobum sensum, ut desperem ejus reditum. Semper alienus a gloria Christi fuit, eritque forte in perpetuum, huc perpulit eum insana gloria et laudis libido. Infensior mihi, imo nobis est, quam ulli hactenus fuerint inimici (a wonder he does not except here the Pope and the devil!) ut puto non uno diabolo obsessum miserabilem illum hominem. De Wette II. 55. — Carlstadius, totus daemonibus traditus, contra nos furit, editis multis libellis plenis veneni mortis et inferni. Ibid. 611. — Totus est obsessus non uno daemone. Ibid. 612

ing to which no books were to be published that had
not been examined by censors, a decree, which, he added,
he faithfully observed! ([3]) To secure freedom of action
Carlstadt went to Orlamünde, where he managed to get
himself elected by the people as pastor. This again was
strictly according to Luther's Jus Canonicum, for he had
distinctly !given the congregations the right to dismiss or
to appoint their ministers. ([4]) But in this case it became
a crime! Luther says that Carlstadt ought not to have
asked to be elected! „If he pretends, with the people of
Orlamünde, that by them he has been elected as pastor
and that thus he has been called, I answer: the fact that
afterwards they have elected him, means nothing, I am
speaking of the first entrance. Let him show letters to
prove that he people of Orlamünde have called him from
Wittenberg and that he has not run there on his own
account!" ([5])

In his new parish Carlstadt began the work of reforming in the same tumultuous way which he had formerly
observed at Wittenberg before Luther's return from the Wartburg. To establish practically, [as much as possible the
idea of the universal priesthood, he even abandoned in his
dress everything that might have distinguished him from
the rest of the people, wore, as Luther tells us, „in his
great humility a grey coat and felthat and would not be

([3]) Carlstadius Jenae typographi-
am crexit... Elector simul et Aca-
demia nostra literis et verbis con-
senserunt ac promiserunt juxta
edictum Caesareum nihil edendum
permittere, nisi per deputatos re-
cognitum et exploratum. Quod
cum princeps et nos omnes servemus, non ferendum est, ut solus
Carlstadius... non servet. DeWette
II. 458. — That Luther did not
mean to grant liberty of action to
his opponents (though whenever
his party was interfered with, he
cried out against tyranny) appears
also from a letter, in which he
begs the Elector to bring about
the suppression of Emser's New
Testament. (De Wette III. 528.)
„From an historical point of view,"
says Döllinger, „nothing can be
more unfounded, than the assertion
that the Reformation has been a
movement in favour of the liberty
of conscience. Just the contrary
is true." (Kirche u. Kirchen 68.)

([4]) In the two pamphlets: „Grund
und Ursache etc." Walch X. 1794
seqq. and „Wie man Kirchendiener
wählen und einsetzen soll." Ibid.
1808 seqq.

([5]) Walch XX. 230.

called Doctor, but neighbour Andrew; in him dwells God and the Holy Ghost, feathers and eggs and all." (⁶)

Carlstadt's greatest crime however was that he denied the real presence of Christ in the Eucharist, though it is difficult to understand why he should not have as much right to deny it, as Luther had to deny the transsubstantiation and to be satisfied with impanation. In fact, no controversy ought to exist between the advocates of Luther's fundamental principle, but everyone ought to be content with what the Spirit teaches him. The Wittenberg Reformer confessed that to him nothing would have been more welcome, than a conclusive proof of the truth of Carlstadt's teaching. „If Carlstadt or anyone else had been able to show that in the Sacrament there is nothing but bread and wine, I should have considered it as a great service. On that account I have suffered great troubles; *I have been wrestling and writhing to get out of it,* because I saw that in that way I should have been able to give Popery the greatest blow (den grössten Puff) . . . But I am a captive, I cannot get over it, the text is too powerful, no words can change its meaning." (⁷) In fact, Luther's whole system on justification would not only have been just as good, but would even have become less self-contradictory, if he could have done away with the Real Presence as Carlstadt did. The latter moreover justly observed that either such an article of faith is irreconcilable with the universal priesthood, or that every Christian must be supposed to have the power of consecrating the body of Christ. But some of Carlstadt's arguments were so very absurd, that it was not difficult to his antagonist to ridicule them. This was duly done in the book entitled: „Against the celestial prophets." For instance, Carlstadt had said that in the words of the institution of the Eucharist he word τοῦτο could not possibly refer to ἄρτος, bread, since the latter is masculini generis, that therefore it could only refer to σωμα, the body of Christ. Hence he supposed that Christ had given to his disciples only bread, saying at the same time: *This* (pointing to his own body) is my body, which will be delivered up for you. Now this argument was evidently like the other which, with regard to Christ's word: „Thou art Peter, and upon *this* rock etc." supposes that Christ pointed to himself as to the rock. Luther gets over this, by decreeing that what will hold good in one case, will not hold good in another. His arguments against Carlstadt, though not of a very dignified character, are very telling, only it seems that their force is the same in *both* cases. „How would it sound, if I were to give to a man a common coat, saying: Take it and put it on, this is my velvet furtipped cloak, pointing at the same time to the garment I wore myself? . . . Or if a man were to give to another a mouthful to drink, saying: take it and drink, for here sit I, Johnny, in a pair of red breeches (Hans mit den rothen Hosen)?" (8) The controversy went on for so long a time that, Carlstadt not showing any signs of amendment, Luther was afraid *he would have to pray against him* (9), which would of course have meant his antagonist's perdition. He thought that Carlstadt had been treated far too leniently. „Many princes would have long ago cut off his head and the heads of his mob." (10)

When Luther publicly denounced Carlstadt in the pulpit as a ranter and false prophet, the congregation of Orlamünde adressed to him a letter which was not over-polite. They had the audacity to call him simply „dear brother", omitting his title of Doctor, an offence which he particularly resented and on account of which he considered them as enemies.(11) „Thou publicly scoldest and

(8) Walch XX. 302. 303.
(9) Dolens legi monstra Carlstadii ... Et per nos jam diu Christus Carlstadio resistit, verum ille non cessat, pergitque accelerare sibi pernitiem, et metuo, dum nos cogit etiam contra se orare, merebatur (De Wette proposes: ne merentur) tandem permitti ut noceat in perditionem.
De Wette II. 488.
(10) Walch XX. 223. cfr. 232.
(11) Walch XV. 2439. When at Orlamünde, he bitterly reproached the people with this omission.

revilest us, who are members of Christ, planted by the
Father, without hearing or convicting us. This shows that
thou thyself art not a member of this true Christ and
Son of God." ([12]) In the end they asked him over to a
conference. This was too much for Luther, who thought
that the whole was only a trick of Carlstadt; he set out
immediately for Orlamünde. When passing through Jena,
at the inn called „the black bear", which since that day has
become so famous, · he had an interview with his former
friend, which only widened the rupture between the two
men. Luther gave Carlstadt a goldflorin as a pledge, that
he had full liberty to write against him and emptied his
glass as a further confirmation of this permission ([13]). When
after his arrival at Orlamünde the people who were just
busy in the fields with the harvest had |been summoned to-
gether, Luther expressed to them his great dissatisfaction
with the letter adressed to him. Carlstadt too, suddenly appeared, but was obliged to leave again, when Luther threatened to go away in case that he were allowed to stop.
There arose a discussion about images and the peasants proved from the Scripture that all images were abominations,
whether they were to be adored or not. The general character of the arguments proposed by unlearned, fanatical
men may be imagined. A shoemaker advanced an argument, which we would rather not describe here and which
filled Luther with despair ([14]). But the „Reformer" was
fairly beaten with the weapon which he himself had forged
and thrust into the hands of everybody against Popery. Practically he renounced his own principle in opposing the free
interpretation used by cobblers and tailors, and he had
only to thank himself when they took leave of him with
the words: Go in a thousand devils' name. Mayest thou
break thy neck before thou art out of the town. ([15]) At the
same time Luther thought that the devil had been rather

([12]) Ibid. 2434.
([13]) Walch XV. 2431.
([14]) Ibid. 2440.

([15]) Luther's own report. Ibid.
2450.

afraid of *him*. „I preached against this ranting nonsense as
well at I was able. The devil received me, as I had deserved of him. How he snorted and hurried and trembled,
just as if Christ had been there to drive him out!" ([16])
The upshot was, that Carlstadt had to fly the country.
He took leave of his people in two letters which were
signed: Andreas Bodenstein, driven out by Luther, not
heard and not conquered. ([17]) He first went to Strassburg — and immediately Luther warned the people there
against him, ([18]) — then into Switzerland, where he found
many friends, especially Zwingli and Oecolampadius, who
like him rejected and condemned the Wittenberg teaching
on the Eucharist. After a vain attempt to settle at Schwein-
furt he reopened his iconoclastic activity at Rotenburg. ([19])
But when he was obliged to leave also this place, in fear
of being made answerable for the revolt of the peasants,
his spirit seemed to be broken and he begged Luther's
intercession for permission to settle in the Elector's dominion. That Luther entertained this application and
even hid his late antagonist in his own house for some
time, ([20]) would say a great deal for his generosity and
magnanimity, it we did not know the enormous price
at which Carlstadt had to buy this protection. It was nothing less, than a full and complete retractation of his system,
published in the shape of a Declaration „how he wished
people to think of his teaching on the Eucharist." ([21]) In
the strongest terms he expresses his unutterable surprise,
that anyone should ever have thought he meant to advance
anything on this point as definite. All that he had written,
contained nothing but mere opinions! How should *he*

([16]) Walch XX. 232.

([17]) Walch XV. Append. 250.

([18]) Walch XV. 2443.

([19]) Carlstadius Rotenburgae ad
Tauberam furias suas exercet et
nos ubique persequitur ipse fugi-
tivus. Schweinefordiae ipse stat-
uerat nidulari, sed comes Henne-
bergensis ad senatum datis literis
prohibuit. De Wette II. 643. Rotenburgae agit ... tumultuans more
suo imaginibus. Ibid. 644.

([20]) Fuit homo miser apud me
clanculo servatus.
De Wette III. 21.

([21]) Walch XX. 409 seqq.

presume to *teach* anything, when thousands of men were
so much cleverer than himself! when so many Saints and
martyrs had held the contrary! Let people be ashamed
of themselves that they have ever believed a thing because
he, Carlstadt, had taught it! „But many stumble over their
consciences and over their feet into his books, as hungry
sows into the dirt, and as it is the wont of sows, they
bring filth with them, and the noble pearl, God's word, is
trampled upon in the dirt!" It cannot be supposed that
anyone believed in the sincerity of such an abject retractation which, if not dictated by Luther, was at least inspired by him. But he tried to be generous and in the introduction which he wrote to this declaration([22]) he apologized
for having wrongly considered Carlstadt's dogmatic utter-
ances as seriously meant and acknowledged that, if he,
Luther, had more carefully looked at their titles and pre-
faces, the lamentable misunderstanding would never have
happened!([23]) As might have been expected, this comedy
of reconciliation did not last a long time. On condition
that he would not preach, Carlstadt received, at Luther's
intercession, permission to settle at Kemberg, where the
Provost, the „Reformer's" old pupil, could have an eye on
him([24]). The ex-Reformer opened a little shop and a
public house, but soon lost everything. His misfortune only
nourished his bitterness and hastened the renewal of hostilities. If the insincerity of his former retractation had
been doubtful, all doubts were removed by his own declaration that he had recanted with his mouth, not with his
heart([25]). As after this is was no longer advisable for
him to remain in Saxony, he began again his wanderings
and found at last a resting place at Basel, where he died
A. D. 1541, without having had again a great part in the
religious controversies of the time. Luther's correspondence however still contains complaints about Carlstadt's

([22]) Walch XV. 2472 seqq.
([23]) Ibid. 2473.
([24]) This is particularly mentioned by Luther in his letter to the
Elector. De Wette III. 137.
([25]) Walch XV. 2479.

infernal letters([26]) and about the devil's work through the same. His opinion of Carlstadt's worth is expressed in the short sentence: Est, fuit, erit manebitque Carlostadius semper.([27]).

Carlstadt's protector, Ulrich Zwingli, caused further troubles to the Ecclesiastes of Wittenberg. This unfortunate priest, who had long disgraced himself and his office by a licentious life — a fact which he unblushingly acknowledged in the most cynical way ([28]), — set up as the Reformer of Switzerland. The principle on which he started, was identical with that of Luther, viz. private judgment, but it was only natural, that from this principle he should arrive at different conclusions. Every „Reformer" of that class must have a theology and an activity sui generis. It is not the place here to give a full explanation of Zwingli's system; let it be sufficient to observe that it makes all religion a mockery, since it totally destroys even the possibility of morality. For not only does it represent man's will as unfree, but it distinctly represents God as the author of moral evil. ([29]) The fact that Zwingli inclined

---

([26]) De Wette III. 549.

([27]) De Wette III. 337. — About Carlstadt's death Luther writes to Propst: Carlstadius Basileae peste interiit, pestis ipse Ecclesiae Basileensis. De Wette V. 452, and to Amsdorf: Carlstadium interiisse nosti, quem Basileenses Ecclesiastae scribunt fuisse pestem suae scholae venenosissimam. *Mortuus est autem occidente diabolo.* Scribunt enim, apparuisse ei concionanti et aliis multis virum grandis staturae, ingressum templum et in vacua sede juxta civem quendam stetisse, rursus egressum et in aedes Carlstadii intrasse, ibi filium solum inventum manibus levasset, quasi ad terram collisurus, sed illaesum dimisisse, jussisseque ut patri diceret, sese reversurum esse post triduum cumque ablaturum. Ita post triduum esse defunctum. Addunt ipsum finita concione civem illum adiisse et interrogasse quis ille vir fuerit? Civis autem se nihil vidisse dixit. Ita credo subitis terroribus correptum, nulla alia peste, quam timore mortis exstinctum. Misere enim mortem horrere solebat. De Wette V. 455.

([28]) See extracts from his letters ap. Janssen. An meine Kritiker, 136 seqq.

([29]) This enormity Zwingli tried to justify by saying that. in causing moral evil, God could not be accused of doing any moral evil himself, since he is *above* the law. Quantum enim Deus facit, non est peccatum, quia non est contra legem; illi enim non est lex posita, utpote justo, nam justis non ponitur lex. Unum igitur atque idem facimus, puta adulterium aut homicidium; quantum Dei auctoris, motoris atque impulsoris opus est, crimen

to the side of Carlstadt was in 'the eyes of Luther a
sufficient condemnation. Like Carlstadt he was an ardent
and barbarous iconoclast [30], and soon found out that the
views of the same on the Eucharist were much more in
harmony with the „reformed“ doctrine on justification,
than Luther's impanation. Only he arrived at his conclusion in a different way. Whilst Carlstadt urged that the
word τοῦτο referred not to what Christ gave to his disciples, but to his own living body, the Swiss Reformer
directed all his endeavours towards proving that the „is“
means only „signifies“. To this end he collected a great
number of Scripture texts, in which no doubt the word
to be has this meaning, [31] for instance: „the seven fat
cows *are* the seven fertile years“, „I *am* the vine“, „the
seed *is* the word of God“, but Luther had no difficulty
in showing the fallacy of such argumentation.

The appearance and the rapid spread of this new
heresy caused the Wittenberg Reformer a great deal of
anguish. [32] He could not disguise from himself the fact,
that its originators were his own children, his own Absaloms,
that raved against their father, even more than the Papists
did. [33] He had to confess to himself that, as he had
granted the interpretation of the Bible to everybody, he
had now no other weapons but his own opinion and his

non est, quantum autem hominis
est, crimen est ac scelus est.
Zwingli. De provid. c. VI. Also
Melanchthon had entertained similar views, but they were suppressed in the later editions of
his works. Nos dicimus non solum permittere Deum creaturis ut
operentur, sed ipsum omnia proprie agere, ut sicut fatentur, proprium Dei opus fuisse Pauli voca-
tionem, ita fateantur opera Dei
propria esse sive quae media vo-
cantur, ut comedere, sive quae
mala sunt. ut Davidis adulterium;
constat enim Deum omnia facere,
non permissive sed potenter, i. e. ut
sit ejus proprium opus Judae pro-

ditio, sicut Pauli vocatio. — Cfr.
Möhler, Symbolism. I. 52 seqq.
[30] Janssen III. 83.
[31] Walch XVII. 1893.
[32] In a letter to the Christians at Reutlingen (Jan. 1526) he
complains that the new sect has
already three heads (De Wette III.
81), but their number increases to
five or six. Habet Sacramentaria
secta jam ni fallor, sex capita uno
anno nata. (De Wette III. 98.)
[33] Cogor ferre filios uteri mei,
Absalones meos, qui furiosissime
mihi resistunt. Illos puto Sacra-
mentomagistas, prae quorum insania Papistas cogor mites judicare.　　De Wette III. 87.

own deductions, for which he could not expect that his adversaries would care in the least, and — Switzerland was not Saxony! Luther's personal influence over the Elector would not avail against Zwingli, as it had caused the expulsion of Carlstadt.

It seems that Luther took up arms against the Zwinglians most unwillingly and was, at times, glad of any excuse for avoiding the struggle. He wrote to his friend Hausmann that the whole affair was not worth that it should be taken up by him, it might be left to others([34]), and in a letter to Crusius he spoke of the „ridiculous spirit“ of his enemies([35]); again he pleaded his many occupations([36]) and a great dislike, caused perhaps by the devil.([37]) Yet at other times he clearly perceived the great importance of the question, he acknowledged that either Zwingli's party or his own must be the ministers of the devil,([38]) and bitterly complained of the opprobrious language used against Christ and against those that believed him to be really present in the Eucharist.([39]) „You are right, he writes to Hess, that until now there have been none but lazy devils, for until now we have been fighting about profane things, which are outside the Scriptures, such as the Pope, purgatory and similar nonsense, but now we

([34]) Invadunt nos Zwinglius et Oecolampadius, sed hoc aliis relinquatur, vel potius contemnatur.
De Wette III. 32.

([35]) Ibid. 36.

([36]) Ibid. 107.

([37]) Pestis Sacramentaria saevit et acquirit vires eundo. Ora quaeso pro me torpente et frigente. Nescio enim quo vel taedio tentor vel Satana occupor. ut non plura faciam quam facio, sive haec est ingratitudo nostra. sive alia culpa.
Ibid. 132.

([38]) Alterutros oportet esse Satanae ministros, vel ipsos vel nos: ideo hic nulli consilio aut medio locus.   De Wette III. 44.

([39]) Annon est convicium, quod illi modestissimi nos carnivoras esculentum Deum impanatumque colere ... traducunt Ibid. 43. — The German edition has: dass wir Fleischfresser einen Essgott. einen brödernen Gott ehren.
Walch XVII. 1908.

come to serious matters." (^{40}) At last he feels himself
again burning with the desire of entering the arena. (^{41})

His two most important publications against the Zwinglians are „The words of Christ *this is my body* are still
unshaken" (^{42}) and his „Great testimony on the Lord's
supper." (^{43}) They are of a very different character; one
is extremely violent, the other is comparatively calm. As
a matter of course the Zwinglian heresy is fathered upon
the devil, whose rage is awakened by the light of the
Evangelium, which Luther has made to shine in the world;(^{44})
this is sufficiently proved by the dissensions amongst the
Sacramentarians themselves, who moreover are men conspicuous by their stupidity, ignorance, arrogance etc and
who faithfully observe their master's (the devil's) custom
of introducing pert reason into the mysteries of faith; they
know exactly what God can do and what not, they must
have climbed into heaven one night, when God was firmly
asleep and have weighed his omnipotence. Luther was
aware that such compliments would not put the Zwinglians into the best humour(^{45}) and that a furious reply
might be expected.(^{46}) Perhaps this certainty of more unpleasantness to come, combined with a sudden serious
illness(^{47}) and with the trouble caused at Wittenberg by
the plague, contributed to plunge him into a most unhappy
state which brought him to the verge of despair.(^{48}) He
thought that, like Job, he had been delivered over to the

(^{40}) De Wette III. 104. He adds:
Hic jam draconem pugnantem vide-
bimus .... Hic Satanas quis sit,
quantus sit, cognosces, quem hactenus non satis vidisti, neque satis
cognovisti.

(^{41}) Ardeo meam fidem adhuc
semel profiteri. Ibid. 131.

(^{42}) Walch XX. 950 seqq.

(^{43}) Ibid. 1118 seqq.

(^{44}) This same idea occurs very
frequently in Luther's letters. v. gr.
De Wette III. 59. 61.

(^{45}) De Wette III. 174.

(^{46}) Expecto illorum furiosam
responsionem. Ibid. 172.

(^{47}) Repentina syncope ita cor-
ripiebar, ut desperans prorsus ar-
bitrarer me exstinctum iri.
Ibid. 187.

(^{48}) Plus tota hebdomada in
morte et inferno jactatus, ita ut
toto corpore laesus adhuc tremam
membris. Amisso fere toto Christo
agebar fluctibus et procellis desperationis et blasphemiae in Deum.
De Wette III. 189.

fury of Satan.([⁴⁰])   In this case it can be no ordinary devil
of the rank and file, but only the prince of all demons,
since he is so very clever in arguing from Holy Scripture;([⁵⁰])
and well may the devil try to have his revenge, considering
how much Luther has done against him! ([⁵¹])

It was after this storm had subsided that Luther wrote
the second of the above mentioned books, in which he
preserved more calmness, than his adversaries probably
expected. It is remarkable that here, as also in the disputation at Marburg ([⁵²]) Luther not only falls back upon tra-
dition, but that he also tries to soften down his „Impanation“ as much as possible. He thinks that after all the
only really important question is this, whether or not the
body and blood of Christ is really present in the Eucharist;
how he is present, *with* the substance of bread and wine,
or *without* is a secondary thing.   Though he says: „I
hold with Vigleph (Wickleff) that the bread remains, and
with the Sophists (the Catholics) that the body of Christ
is present“,([⁵³]) he says further on: „To me it matters little
whether the wine remains or not; to me it is sufficient
that Christ's blood is there; what becomes of the wine,
remains with God. But before I would have there nothing
but wine with the ranters, I would rather have nothing but
blood with the Pope.“ ([⁵⁴])

Also outside Switzerland Zwinglianism found numerous
patrons, many of the „reformed“ towns of Germany adopted
it. This caused a great deal of uneasiness to Philip of

([⁴⁹]) Ipse Satan per se cum tota
virtute sua in me furit. posuitque
me Dominus illi velut alterum Hiob,
in signum et tentat me mira infirmitate spiritus. De Wette III.
193. — Agon iste meus supra vires
est. Ibid. 190. — Satanam et an-
gelos ejus habeo infensos ultra
modum.   Ibid. 195.

([⁵⁰]) Ego sane suspicor, non
igregarium aliquem, sed principem
istum daemoniorum in me surrex-

isse, tanta est ejus potentia et
sapientia Scripturis in me armat-
issima. Ibid. 222.

([⁵¹]) Vere credo Satanam in me
furere, nam multa in ipsum feci
et dixi et scripsi. Ibid. 225.

([⁵²]) Melanchthon's report. Walch
XVII. 2364.

([⁵³]) Grosses Bekäntniss n. 337.
(Walch XX.)

([⁵⁴]) Ibid. n. 394.

Hessen, who was very anxious to unite all Protestants into
one great political league of defence.([55]) To prevent further internal strife he invited both parties to hold a friendly
colloquium at Marburg. Luther disliked the idea extremely,
for as he told the Landgraf, there was but little hope of
a satisfactory result.([56]) „I know that I shall not give way.
I cannot, because I know that they are wrong . . . If they
do not give way, we shall part without any result, we
shall meet invain and Your Grace will lose expense and
trouble." ([57]) To escape the invitation, Melanchthon resorted
to a trick Luther had used before, he begged of the Elect-
or to kindly *refuse* permission to go to Marburg,([58]) but
at last they had to give way to repeated entreaties. The
result was what Luther had anticipated, nil.([59]) The disputation which lasted three days, only showed that both
parties had come with the firm intention not to give way
a hairsbreadth; they acknowledged no authority that might
have settled the dispute; the meeting rather widened the
rupture than healed it. Luther refused to acknowledge
the Zwinglians as brethren,([60]) but both parties promised
to preserve charity towards each other „as far as conscience
would allow it." ([61]) On his return from Marburg the „Reformer" had a fresh attack of the deepest melancholy,
which, as usual, he attributed to the enmity of the devil.([62])

([55]) Riffel II. 326. Luther says
of him: Juvenis ille Hassiae in-
quietus est et cogitationibus aest-
uat.   De Wette III 491.

([56]) Walch XVII. 2352.

([57]) De Wette III. 474. Cfr.
Köhler 174, Nota.

([58]) Walch XVII. 2357.

([59]) Nos a principio valde de-
trectavimus. Sed cum juvenis ille
Macedo Hessiacus sic fatigaret
principem nostrum, coacti sumus
promittere, sed sic, ut copiose
significaremus bis aut ter nihil spei.
nihil fructus, nihil boni, sed omnia
pejora timenda esse.
          De Wette III. 501.

([60]) He wrote to his „dear master
Keth": We will hear nothing of
brothers and members.
          De Wette III. 512.

([61]) Walch XVII. 2361. — About
this promise Luther says: Quod
fecimus ne nimis mungendo san-
guinem eliceremus.
          De Wette III. 511.

([62]) Angelus Satanae. vel quisquis est diabolus noster, ita me
fatigat. Ibid. 515.

Two years later he was freed from his troublesome antagonist. Zwingli fell in the battle of Cappel, sword in hand. (11. Oct. 1531) His death was in Luther's opinion a judgment of God.([63])

([63]) Judicium Dei nunc secundo videmus, semel in Munzero, nunc in Zwinglio. Propheta fui, qui dixi: Deum non laturum diu istas rabidas et furiosas blasphemias, quibus illi pleni erant, irridentes Deum nostrum, vocantes nos carnivoras et sanguibibas et cruentos.
De Wette IV. 332.

Chapter XVII.

„Pope" Luther.

Sic volo, sic jubeo.
Luther. Walch XXI. 314.
The Scripture forbids me to believe those
that give testimony to themselves.
Idem. Walch XI. 1907.

It was not often that Luther *called* himself a Pope; he did so now and then, for instance, when he taught his disciples how to absolve i. e. how to curse the Pope „at the command of our Lord Jesus Christ and of the most Holy Father Pope Luther the First." ([1]) Though he applied the title to himself only in bitter satire, yet he claimed and exercised as much power as any Pope has ever done, nay more.

What the Popes are most bitterly reproached with, is *intolerance,* manifested in maintaining

1) that the doctrine of the Church they represent is the only true one.

2) that there is no salvation outside the Church.([2]) From Luther, the champion of religious liberty, it may be expected that he will be as far removed from such intolerance as the North is from the South. Let us see!

([1]) Wittenb. (Germ.) XII. 360. The whole quotation will be given afterwards.

([2]) That the principle „Extra Ecclesiam non est salus" is not adopted by the Church, except in the case of those who are outside the pale *through their own fault,* this is generally ignored. Those who charge the Church with intolerance on account of this principle would probably be astonished to see how widely the term „Ecclesia" is understood.

Hundreds of times had Luther promised to the people a full, an absolute, a golden liberty. *They* were to be the judges of the truth, *they* were to determine the meaning of the Bible, *they* were to be the only priests, *they* were to be the superiors of the ministers, approving or disapproving of their teaching, appointing them or dismissing them at their pleasure. Considering how naturally the „Non serviam" comes to everybody, it is no wonder that thousands followed Luther's banner. But where was their liberty, when they had finally severed their connection with the old Church? The „Reformer" soon perceived that the liberty he had promised, would in a short time undermine his own authority and put an end to his dictatorship. We have seen how in the case of Carlstadt he curtailed the power of the congregations, inventing the limitation of it to those cases, in which the minister had been called without asking to be called, but only a few years afterwards he formally and unreservedly handed over the congregations to the secular authorities. It was owing to his repeated and urgent advice([3]) that, at the command of the Elector, a visitation of the „reformed" Churches was instituted. The Visitatores may have done a great deal of good in punishing or dismissing unworthy ministers and in trying to stem the torrent of licentiousness([4]), but according to Luther's own principles they had no right to do what they did at Luther's advice, when they formed a kind of Inquisition ([5]), when they enquired into the teaching of ministers and insisted on their preaching nothing but the pure Creed of the Prophet of Wittenberg. It was here that the „Reformer's" selfcontradiction became most glaring. He who had denied to the Church the gift of infallibility, now claimed it for himself; he, who had despised the Pope's excommunication, now excommunicated

([3]) De Wette III. 51. 136.
([4]) We shall have to speak at length of the state of Protestantism at that time in a later chapter.

([5]) This very appellation occurs Walch X. 2614.

17*

those who, on the strength of *his* principle presumed to disagree from him. Of *his* Church he now said: „I believe that nobody can be saved who is not in this community, remaining in communion with it in one faith, word, sacrament, hope and charity, and that no Jew, pagan, heretic or sinner will be saved with it, except he becomes reconciled and united to it and conforms to it in all things." (⁶) Considering that the truth can be but one and that therefore all who sincerely consider their Creed to be true, are logically compelled to consider all other creeds as wrong (if religion is not to be mere guesswork or to consist in a feeble attempt at arriving at the truth) we could understand that Luther arrived at such a conclusion, if there were not the fact that, to arrive at it, he had to give up the very principle on which his rebellion against the Church was based. Is there tolerance in his demand that those who disagree must be *compelled* to listen to Lutheran sermons? „Wherever possible, no discordant (zwieträchtige) doctrine should be tolerated under the same authority. Though they do not believe, let them, for the sake of the ten commandments, be *driven* to the sermon." (⁷) Luther does not approve of heresiarchs being executed, because innocent blood might be shed, as in fact it has been shed by the Papists, (⁸) but he demands that they shall be banished. (⁹) That Carlstadt had to leave the country on account of his discordant views we have seen above; also Martin Reinhard, who had committed the enormous crime of publishing the report of Luther's visit to Orlamünde was banished, with five florins as an alms, besides the

---

(⁶) Walch X. 203.

(⁷) De Wette III. 498.

(⁸) In other words, if Luther were to approve of it, he would implicitly approve of the justice of the sentence passed on Huss, since he could not deny that this sentence was based on the imperial law, which considered heresy as a crime against the Christian state.

(⁹) Nullo modo possum admittere falsos doctores occidi: satis est eos relegari, qua poena si posteri abuti volunt, mitius tamen peccabunt et sibi tantum nocebunt. De Wette III. 348.

trifles which he had been permitted to beg from house to house. ([10])

It sounds very charitable and tolerant, when in the preface to his instruction on the Visitation Luther exhorts „all pious and peaceloving pastors who seriously love the Evangelium,“ to submit to the visitation „willingly and without force,“ when he expresses his hope that they will not ungratefully despise „our most gracious Lord's care and our own love and good intention“, but unfortunately there comes the *Quos ego* immediately afterwards in the shape of a threat that His Grace, the Elector, *as the spiritual head* will be obliged to see that no discord, no sects, no rebellion will disgrace his dominions.([11]) Luther may have had some very kind intentions when he wrote his larger Catechism and the „Postille“, to be used by the ministers in their instructions and sermons, but |he seems to have been rather touchy on hearing that some of them refused the kindness. At least he calls them gluttons and bellyservants „that had rather be sowherds or kennel-keepers, than pastors, lazy paunches and presumptuous Saints, who ought to remember that they are not yet quite such learned doctors as they fancy they are.“([12])

With the dissolution and suppression of monasteries, Collegiate Churches and similar institutions there naturally came the important question: what is to become of the property they owned? Luther was right in thinking that those who no longer performed the services prescribed by the foundations, had no right to the emoluments;([13]) it is therefore all the more surprising when he adds that he has

([10]) Orlamundae acta nequiter edidit Martinus Reinhardus Jenensis praedicator in meam ignominiam et Carlstadii gloriam ... jussus cedere, plorans valefecit in cathedra, supplicansque pro venia, quinque florenos pro responso accepit, deinde per oppidum mendicare procurans 5 grossos accepit. De Wette II. 557.

([11]) Riffel II. 58. 59.

([12]) Ibid. 63.

([13]) Cum jam nec legamus, nec boëmus, nec missemus, nec quicquam faciamus, quod fundatio instituit, otiosum videtur factum beneficium et officium et merito repetendum. De Wette II. 43.

a right to expect something from those same funds in order
to carry on the war against the Pope.([14]) The Pope's
dominion destroyed, the „Reformer" thought that naturally
his Church would come in for the inheritance.([15]) He did
not wish to see ecclesiastical property appropriated by
everybody indiscriminately, though from his own words it
is clear that a good deal of it went into the private pockets
of the princes and noblemen,([16]) a fact for which at times
he thought to have a claim on their thankfulness.([17]) By
his supreme power he decreed that the secular authority
might seize the ecclesiastical goods and spend them on the
erection of schools, endowments of parishes, relief of the
poor and other wants of the country.([18]) That most of
these purposes were directly against the intention of the
Catholic founders, was a matter of no importance. In 1524
he offered the monastery in which he still lived to the
Elector Frederick as „heir",([19]) but it was assigned to
him as his own property. Two years later he assured
once more Frederick's successor, Johannes, that all eccles-
iartical property belonged to him as the „supreme head",([20])
but reminded him of the duty of spending it in the above
mentioned way.

Luther displayed a wonderful activity as the head of
his new Church, in arranging the form of services,([21]) in

([14]) Nisi quod nos ad tempus ali possumus propter bellum adversus Papam.   Ibid. 433.

([15]) A nostris jura Papae non debent invadi, nisi prius regno Papae destructo. Ubi enim non regnat, ibi sane juribus et bonis ejus relictis utamur, non ante.   Ibid. 505.

([16]) Seria sunt valde, mi Spalatine, de rapina monasteriorum et crede, macerat me res ista vehementer.   De Wette III. 147.

([17]) . . . . Evangelium per nos ortum, quo et animae vestrae salvantur, et substantia mundi non parva ad marsupium principis redire coepit ac quotidie magis redit,

ut si ab aliis meremur invidiam, a vobis certe meliorem quam hanc gratiam mereri debueramus.
     De Wette II. 569. cfr. 592.

([18]) See letter to the Congregation at Leisnig.
     De Wette II. 383 seqq.

([19]) De Wette II. 582. cfr. III. 19.

([20]) De Wette III. 136.

([21]) But this form, he said, may be changed at any time, like a pair of shoes. (Walch X. Teutsche Messe, 267 seqq. n° 52) the services are not at all meant for those that *are* Christians — *they* worship in the spirit — but for those that have to be *made* Christians.
                              (Ibid. n° 4.)

writing those books which were to be a dogmatical guide to the ministers, in organizing the visitation, in answering questions about theological matters, in giving advice how to dispose of ecclesiactical property, in settling matrimonial cases, in issuing decrees, in excommunicating the stubborn, in preaching and lecturing.

Those who had refused allegiance to the Pope of Rome, had now a Pope at Wittenberg, Luther the First.

The world had a right to ask: Who sent you? Who gave you that power? How do you prove your calling? Whence have you the right, to sit in judgment on a Church, which for centuries had been acknowledged as God's representative on earth by all civilized nations? Luther fully expected these questions and allowed that they were fair. It may therefore be expected that he had a satisfactory answer to them. At any rate the answer he gave, greatly contributes towards a faithful portrait of the man.

He tried very hard indeed to convince not only others, but also himself of the justice of the claim he set up, and sometimes he produced in favour of it arguments, which strongly remind one of the drowning man who will grasp at a straw. To put that ugly word of „apostasy“ out of his mind, he maintained that he had been *forced* out of the Catholic Church. „The Pope thinks that we are rebels and heretics, that we have separated ourselves from the Church in which we have been baptized and instructed. But the fault is not ours, we have not separated ourselves from them, but they separate themselves from us, nay they expel us and our word from the Church. Hence we necessarily come to the conclusion, that the Holy of Israel is with us and not with the Pope.“ ([22]) The more violently he denounced the Catholic Church as the whore of Babylon the more specious, as Döllinger remarks, ([23]) did his allegation of the voice of the apocalyptic angel become.

([22]) Walch VI. 833.   ([23]) Die Reformation III. 200.

„The Pope's Church is brimful of lies, devils, hell, murder and all mischief; it is time to hear the voice of the Angel (Apoc. XVIII. 4): Go out from here my people, that you be not partakers of her sins and that you receive not of her plagues."(²⁴) This is the stereotyped excuse of all heretics, as appears also in our own days from the case of the so called Old-Catholics, who also fly to another of Luther's favourite means of confirming themselves in their belief, viz. reviling the Church and the Pope to their heart's content. How amply Luther used this never failing remedy will appear from another chapter. Still he confessed: „How often has my heart been trembling and has reproached me and has put before me their only and strongest argument: Art thou alone wise? Should all the others err and have erred for ¦so long a time?"(²⁵) He perpetually changed his idea about his vocation. After the rupture with the Church had been completed in 1521, he was still doubtful about it. „I *hope* I have begun in the name of God; but *I am not bold enough to judge of it for certain* and to proclaim that it is certain. I should not like to suffer¦ God's judgment on it; but I crawl to his grace, hoping he will allow that it has been begun in his name"(²⁵) Such *hope* was indeed a very weak foundation to build upon, when one thinks of the man's awful responsibility.

To secure for himself some sort of ¦vocation and authority, he was forced to start the idea that, though *de jure* every Christian is a priest, yet *de facto*, for the sake of order, only those can exercise their office, who are chosen to it by the congregation or by superiors. „To exercise such power is not everybody's business, but of those

(²⁴) Jen. VII. 414.
(²⁵) Walch XVIII. 1551. — Hieronymus Emser had stated that in his presence Luther had said with regard to his „Reformation": „Devil take it! this matter has not been started for the sake of God, nor shall it end for the sake of

God. Luther (l. c. 1542) replied that his words had referred to his opponents, Emser, Eck etc. But the latter proved that the tenor of the conversation did not admit of such an interpretation. See particulars ap. Janssen II. 82.

that are called by the multitude or by those who have command over the multitude."([26]) If this principle was
right, Luther was safe, for the people of Wittenberg and
the Elector of Saxony were sufficiently attached to him; in
this way their will became the infallible sign of his vocation. Just as he changed his opinion about the requisites
of vocation, — not less than fourteen times within twenty-
four years, as Döllinger proves([27]) — so he changed his idea
of the value of his degree as doctor of theology. He fully
repudiated it, when he left the Church. „Being in disgrace with the Pope and the Emperor, I am deprived of
my title; *the mark of the beast has been washed off* with
so many Bulls, that now I may not be called Doctor of
Divinity or anything like a creature of the Pope; I was
startled at that, just as a donkey is when he loses his
sack. Such larvae were my greatest ignominy before God;
in those days I too was in error, I was a liar, cheat, se-
ducer and blasphemer as you are now"([28]). Who would
believe that after this Luther should appeal to his degree,
taken under the Pope, granted by that Church which to
him was now only „the devil's arch-whore", as to a support for his pretended mission to upset the same Pope and
the same Church? „I would not for a hundred thousand
worlds have interfered with the office of any Bishop, but as
I am a Doctor in Holy Scripture, I am bound to do it,
for I have taken an oath to teach the truth."([29])

But his assertion „I have the Evangelium not from
men, but from heaven"([30]) could hardly be supposed to be
sufficiently proved by the fact of his being a Doctor created
by the Pope. Further proofs were found in his „temptations" i. e. in the struggles he had to go through, to convince himself of the truth of his teaching, struggles which,
he declared, were only reserved for the elect, and of which
the Papists had no idea, since they had only the little devils

<hr />

([26]) Walch XVIII. 1669.
([27]) III. 205.
([28]) Walch XIX. 838.

([29]) Erl. 50. 292.
([30]) Walch XV. 2379.

to attack them,([31]) likewise in the parallel which he was very fond of drawing between S. Paul and himself([32]). Here is a specimen of his *desperate* argumentation, from his Commentary in Galatas.

He who teaches not his own opinion, but what his divine master commands him to teach, teaches the right thing.

Atqui, I teach nothing but what heaven has commanded me to teach. Ergo.

Technically the syllogism is in perfect order, no logician can find the smallest fault with it; there is only this flaw, that Dr. Luther totally forgets to give us a proof for the minor. In the same place we find the following enthymema: *The Jews and Gentiles rave against me. Ergo* is my doctrine the true and pure one. This will also be perfect reasoning, as soon as Luther shows 1) that „Jews and Gentiles" is equivalent to „Catholics" and 2) that eo ipso that Catholics say a thing, this same thing must be wrong. But such minor points are beneath the great „Reformer's" notice, and he comes straight to the conclusion: *Therefore every doctrine differing from mine is false, uncertain, impious, blaspheming, cursed and devilish, and the like has to be said of those that hold it.*([33])

If only Luther could have caught hold of a prophecy speaking in his favour! This would have been a gain, it would have stopped the mouths of the slanderers! How

([31]) Tischr. II. c. 1. § 121. — Cfr. Wittenb. V. 291. „Adversarii, ut homines otiosi et nullis tentationibus probati etc." The same argument occurs ibid. 284ʙ. against the „Schwaermer."

([32]) See the chapter on Luther's Evangelium. pp. 129. 131.

([33]) This specimen of Luther's argumentation deserves to be quoted here in full: Qui ea loquitur quae Dominus et Magister suus ei mandavit, et non se, sed eum cujus Apostolus est, glorificat, is certum et divinum verbum affert et docet. At ego ea tantum quae

mihi divinitus mandata sunt, doceo, nec me ipsum, sed eum qui misit me, glorifico. Praeterea concito mihi iram et indignationem Judaeorum et Gentium. Igitur doctrina mea est vera, pura, certa et divina, neque potest esse alia, (multo minus melior), quam haec mea. Quare quaecunque alia, quae non eodem modo docet ut mea, omnes homines esse peccatores et sola fide in Christum justificari, necessario est falsa, incerta, impia, blasphema, maledicta et diabolica, talesque sunt omnes qui eam docent et accipiunt. Wittenb. V. 288ʙ.

much he would have valued an acquisiton of this kind
appears from a letter written A. D. 1529 to Myconius. A
rumour of such a prophecy had reached his ears, therefore he conjures his friend, for the love of God, to send
him all the particulars about that monk who, being imprisoned on account of heresy, had foretold that someone
else would appear and state again his own opinions. And
let Myconius be careful to send a full, even verbose account, not omitting the slightest circumstances! „for you
know how important this is to me!“ ([34]) In this case however the enquiries seem not to have been quite satisfactory; but later on, behold! a prophecy has been found!
„Saint John Huss has prophesied of me, saying: They are
going to roast a goose (for Huss means a goose) but after
a hundred years they will hear the singing of a swan.“ ([35])
This would be something like a prophecy, if only the
proofs were forthcoming 1) that it had ever been uttered,
2) that Luther was something like a swan. As to the first
point we have only Luther's own word, as to the second,
Luther's „singing“ reminds one of anything but a swan.

If the prophecies fail, we may expect other and even
more convincing proofs of the „Reformer's“ special mission
in the shape of miracles. ([36]) For he says: „If a man starts
new things (in religion) he must be called by God and
must prove his vocation by true miracles. *If he cannot*

([34]) Per Christum te oro et
obtestor, ut res istas ... quam primum expedias. Hoc est de mon-
acho illo in excommunicatione
mortuo et prophetante, fore, ut
illi ipsi qui aderant, visuri et audi-
turi essent eum qui ea doceret,
quae ipse docuisset et sensisset.
Hanc inquam historiam vide ut
plenis, multis, totis et superfluis
verbis nobis scribas et mittas, nihil
omittens; de libro sub lateribus
sepulto, et quod nomen sit ejus
sacerdotis, et ubi sit qui eum librum adeptus sit; scis enim mihi
in hac re multum esse situm.
De Wette III. 514.

([35]) Walch XVI. 2061.

([36]) Some Chronics speak of a
miracle wrought by Luther when
preaching at Erfurt. A great noise
arose in the Church, filling all
with terror. He said it was the
work of the *devil* and commanded
the same to be quiet, and the
noise ceased. „This, a Chronist
says, was the first miracle of
Luther, and his disciples came
and ministered unto him.“
See Kampschulte II. 98.

do that, let him be off, so packe er sich seiner Wege." (³⁷)
To those who, formerly with him, had left him in the
course of time, to enjoy the present he had made to them
of private judgment, he addressed the following words:
„You are boasting of the spirit, give me then a sign; for
you give testimony to yourselves, and the Scripture forbids
me to believe those who give testimony to themselves."(³⁸)
Again he writes, with regard to Münzer: „If he says that
he has been sent by God like the apostles, let him prove
it by signs and wonders, or do you forbid him the pulpit;
for wherever God does something extraordinary, he always
adds miracles. „*I,* he continues, — and now we may
surely expect an appeal to a miracle of his own — *I
have never preached, nor wished to preach, except where I
have been asked and called by men".* (³⁹) Either this must
be taken as a Lutheran miracle, which hardly anybody
would affirm, or Luther will have to say that he does not
claim a special mission to teach a new and until then
unknown doctrine. With regard to this latter point we
hear him claim such a merit most distinctly; yet, again,
we hear him state in his controversy with Erasmus that
those who maintain the ƒold doctrine of the freedom of
man's will, ought to prove it, not he his new doctrine of
its servitude. It really is such a maze, that one does not
know where to turn.

At other times he acknowledged that miracles might
be expected from him. „If it becomes necessary . . . we
should have *to go at it,* we should have to do miracles,
rather than allow the Evangelium to be reviled and
oppressed. But *I hope it will not be necessary."* (⁴⁰) Very
considerate! But after all, the Papists are not worthy to
see any miracles of his, just as little as the Jewish nation
were worthy to see signs wrought by Christ (a sign shall
not be given to it. Matth. XII. 39.)(⁴¹), nay *he, Luther,*

(³⁷) Walch IX. 1009.   (⁴⁰) Walch IX. 1295.
(³⁸) Walch XI. 1907.   (⁴¹) Walch VII. 1768.
(³⁹) Walch XVI. 8.

*has prayed to the Father, not to do a miracle through him
or for him, lest he should become proud.* ([42]) Very humble!
But somehow the thought of Mahomet and of the Mahdi
comes into our head here. At last the case of necessity
seems to have come. Not only did a misformed calf come
into this world, a monster which was *evidently* a divine
protest against monkery, and therefore, implicitly, an
approval of Luther's doctrine ([43]), but there was the actual.
and bodily proof of a miracle in the shape of *an escaped
nun*, Florentina von Oberweimar. The escape of this
16th century edition of Maria Monk and Edith O'Gorman
is actually declared a miracle by the Ecclesiastes of Wittenberg. ([44]) We therefore expect that a host of Angels came
to deliver her from a terrible dungeon, or that the fetters
and chains fell from her hands and feet, or that she walked
through a six-foot wall or something of that kind, but the
prosaic words of Florentina herself ([45]) tell us, that one day
her prisondoor was left open and — she walked out! The
quotation in the note will give every reader an opportunity
of verifying this extraordinary miracle.

But the success of the „Evangelium!" There was a
miracle indeed, most welcome to Luther and urged by
him on many occasions. Did not his „Evangelium" conquer a great part of Germany and spread over adjacent
countries in an incredibly short space of time, more rapidly
even, than Christianity had spread in the beginning of the
Church? „I know whence my doctrine comes and who
has sent me. The work itself sufficiently shows it. Though
I have not wrought any of the small signs — which, if
necessary, we might perhaps do — it has to be taken for

([42]) Walch VI. 125. — Ego neque
signis neque revelationibus peculi-
aribus doctus sum, neque unquam
Deum pro signis rogavi, imo con-
trarium potius rogavi, ne efferrem
me. (In cap. S. Isaiae) Wittenb.
IV. 142 B.
([43]) About the monacho-vitulus
see chapter XII.
([44]) Walch XIX. 2096.

([45]) Walch XIX. 2104. Aber
Gott, dem alle Dinge möglich,
schickte aus seiner göttlichen Weis-
heit, dass eines Tages nach Essens,
da ich in meine Celle gieng, die
Person die mich sollte verschlies-
sen, die Celle liess offen stehen
und ich also vermittelst göttlicher
scheinbarer (= offenbarer) Hülfe
entkommen.

a great miracle that Satan's highest head and greatest power, the Pope with his body has received through me a blow, such as neither secular nor spiritual power has ever been able to give."([46]) Let us compare for a moment the introduction of Christianity and the spread of Lutheranism.

There are the Apostles and their disciples confronting a proud heathen world, yet they succeed in making that world humbly embrace the belief in the sublimest mysteries; here is Luther flattering the pride of man by abolishing authority and constituting everybody for himself supreme judge of God's sublime truth.

There are the Apostles and their disciples not only preaching Christ crucified, but crucifying their own concupiscences; they are a pattern to their converts and in that way succeed in making virtue respected and beloved in a world which formerly was buried in vice; — here is Luther unfettering and flattering the passions of man by his attacks on good works, by his pronounced indifference to sin, by his permitting and counselling sin on more than one occasion, by his doctrine that the will of man is not free, but like a horse, ridden either by God or by the devil, and that a prostitute will be more easily saved than a Saint.

There are the Apostles and their disciples, beset by bitter enemies and persecutors in the persons of the rulers of this world, without any worldly protection whatever — here is Luther, throwing himself upon a number of German princes and petted by them, because through him they obtain possession of the Church property or even, as it happened in one case, of the singular privilege of having two wives.

That the Apostles conquered the world for Christ was, no doubt, a miracle; but it would rather have been a miracle, if Luther's Evangelium had *not* found millions of adherents, since it was so very easy and comfortable, and found such powerful allies in the passions of the hearts.

([46]) Erl. 28, 288.

For a time the success or non-success of an undertaking appeared in Luther's eyes as a sure sign of its legitimacy or illegitimacy. In the failure of Münzer's undertaking he saw a divine condemnation of Münzer's doctrine.
„He who from this evident judgment of God cannot learn
that these fanatics have been against God and that they
have taught mere lies, is willingly and knowingly seduced
and condemned . . . Though I am very sorry that the poor
people have been so miserably deceived and are now lost,
body and soul, I must nevertheless rejoice that God has
delivered his judgment . . . to make us see and confess
that the fanatics have taught falsely and that their teaching
and preaching is against God and condemned by him."(⁴⁷)
In time however Luther saw the argument, drawn from
the rapid spread of his „Evangelium" slip out of his hands.
For not only was the moral character of the bulk of his
adherents very dubious,(⁴⁸) but those who separated themselves from him and set up Churches of their own against
his, especially the Zwinglians, met with no smaller success.
Consequently Luther had either to acknowledge that their
Churches were equally approved of by God, or he had to
give up his argument founded on his success. He made
a desperate attempt at saving it. „It is clear that our
word is the word of God, since it is troubled not only by
violent measures, but also by new heresies."(⁴⁹) At last
he did give it up. „The word teaches that Christians
ought to be of one mind, and yet amongst those that call
themselves Christians there is more disharmony and dissension and strife, than there was under the Papacy. The
word teaches that Christian ought not to condemn each

(⁴⁷) Walch XVI. 149.
(⁴⁸) This fact which afterwards made Luther almost despair, seems not to have made
a great impression upon him at
first. At least he wrote to Staupitz in 1522: „Quod tu scribis me
jactari ab iis, qui lupanaria colunt,
et multa scandala ex recentioribus

scriptis meis orta, neque miror
neque metuo." De Wette II. 215.
(⁴⁹) Inde cernitur verbum nostrum esse verbum Dei, cum jam
non modo vi, sed et haeresibus
novis vexetur. De Wette II. 510.
— Cfr. his letter to the Christians of Liefland. De Wette III. 3.

other, and yet this is the rule, that those who call themselves Christians, condemn each other more than used to
be done under the Papacy. Here then *reason* concludes,
saying: This teaching must come from the devil . . . *Reason
cannot conclude differently from this:* It would be the right
doctrine if only the practice were in harmony with it; but
as the practice is just the contrary, how can it be the right
doctrine?"([50]) Considering that Luther was aware of the
identity of the principle on which he and his *protestant*
foes had started, and that therefore he was aware of the
necessity of dissension and strife, his words may be considered as containing a very valuable concession on his part.
But the conclusion he arrives at, characterizes the man.
Reason, he acknowledges, *must* condemn a doctrine, the
natural fruit of which is not religious unity, but dissension.
Therefore? „Defy reason and all the wisdom of the world
and make them jump over this scandal."([51]) Catholics are
frequently taunted with their „blind faith." The blindness
consists in this, that, acknowledging the authority of the
Church, which has the promise of the perpetual assistance
of her Divine Founder, they know they can implicitly rely
on her teaching. They would scorn such blind faith, as
the „Reformer" demands in the above words.

Luther was fully aware of the awful responsibility he
had taken upon himself in attacking the Church and in
tearing hundreds of thousands from her allegiance.([52]) His
heart trembled when the devil, or perhaps his good angel,
asked him: „What, if thou art in error and leadest so
many people into error, who should all be lost eternally?"([53])
In his own interest therefore it is to be deplored, that he
has never given a satisfactory answer to the all important
question:

„*Who has sent you to preach?*"([54])

([50]) Walch XIII. 446.   ([53]) Walch XIX. 1305.
([51]) Ibidem.•   ([54]) Tischr. II. c. 1. § 3.
([52]) See Tischr. II. c. 1. § 3.

Chapter XVIII

The Confessio Augustana.

Audio vos .... inceptasse mirificum opus,
scilicet concordandi Papae et Lutheri. Sed
Papa nolet et Lutherus deprecatur.
Luther. De Wette IV. 144.

Considering how little had been done at the different
Diets towards the religious pacification of Germany, and
how little those assemblies were fit for work of this kind.
not much was to be expected from the Diet which had
been convened to Augsburg for April 1530, though the
Emperor did his best to carry out his cherished plan and
strictly commanded all princes of the Empire to appear
personally. Still there was something to look forward to,
inasmuch as the Lutheran party were preparing a document,
in which they intended to state distinctly their tenets and
their grievances. But even this document, when at last
presented, was by its vagueness found to be anything but
satisfactory.

The Emperor arrived at Augsburg on the eve of the
festival of Corpus Christi and had at once a taste of the
unpleasantness that was awaiting him. When he invited
the Lutheran princes to join in the procession, they declined
in a most rude and offensive way, calling this ceremony,
without any regard to the Emperor's faith, „impertinence,
insolence, impiety" etc.,([1]) and on the following day, whilst

([1]) verzweifelte Bosheit, Frechheit. Leichtfertigkeit. gottlose Menschensatzungen. Walch XVI. 877.

18

assisting at High Mass, they scandalized the people by
their indecorous behaviour.([2])

The Elector John of Saxony appeared at Augsburg
accompanied by Ph. Melanchthon, Justus Jonas and Dr.
Pomeranus (Bugenhagen). Luther, who had started with
them, was left behind at Coburg, „for certain reasons",
as he says([3]), or for a reason unknown to himself, as he
says in another place([4]). But the reason was obvious
enough. The „Reformer" was still under the Imperial ban,
the Edict of Worms had never been annulled. His presence
at Augsburg therefore, quite apart from his safety, for which
there was little to fear under the circumstances, would have
been too glaring an insult to the Emperor.

His stay at Coburg was in a measure a repetition of
his sojourn on the Wartburg, hard literary work([5]) and
despondency caused by illness and by imaginary attacks
of the devil alternating([6]). In many of his letters of that
period he describes to his friends the rooks' nests he saw
from his windows; in the life and habits of those birds he
found a representation of what was going on meanwhile
at Augsburg, and as usual, improved the occasion by
making some pious reflexions on the wickedness of Po-
pery([7]).

([2]) Spalatinus relates that they
went up to the Altar „mit einem
Gelächter", Ibid. 937.

([3]) Cum principe itinere sui
dominii tantum ibo, certis de causis.   De Wette III. 568.

([4]) Ego jussus sum a principe,
ubi alii abierunt ad comitia, Co-
burgi manere, nescio qua de causa.
             De Wette IV. 1.

([5]) He translated there some
parts of the Old Testament.

([6]) Caput tinnitibus, imo toni-
truis coepit impleri et nisi subito
desiissem, statim in syncopem fuis-
sem lapsus, quam et aegre hoc
biduo evasi ... Eo die quo literae
tuae e Norimberga venerant, habuit
Satan suam legationem apud me.

Eram autem solus .... et certe
eatenus vicit, ut me expelleret
cubiculo et cogeret ad hominum
conspectum ire. Letter to Melanchthon. De Wette IV. 15.

([7]) Ego interpretor eas (monedulas) esse totum exercitum sophistarum et Cochleitarum ex toto
orbe coram me congregatorum, ut
eorum sapientiam et suavicinium
istud melius cognoscam. De Wette
IV. 4. — Hic videas magnanimos
reges, duces proceresque alios,
regni rebus et natis seria consul-
entes, et infatigabili voce decreta
et dogmata sua per aërem jactan-
tes ... Caesarem eorum nondum
vidi nec audivi. Ibid. 13. — Haec
per jocum, sed revera arbitror

In his new hermitage, as he calls it, he did not lose sight of what was going on at the Diet; he addressed to the Clergy assembled there a long epistle([8]) „to promote unity and peace,“ but he himself characterizes the style of it best, when in a confidential letter to Melanchthon he calls this production „my invective *against* the Clergy.“([9]) His proud assertion: „We want no diet, no counsel, no teaching“([10]) did nod hold out much hope of reconciliation.

The great event of the Diet of 1530 was the presenting of the „Confessio Augustana“, which became one of the symbolical books of Lutheranism. A short time before this, the Reformer himself had drawn up certain articles (known as those of Schwabach), the publication of which displeased him extremely. He did not disavow them, but „they are far too good and too precious, that I should argue about them with the Papists. What do they care for such beautiful, divine, high articles? I might just as well treat with sows about pearls or with dogs about holy things. Such Saints (as the Papists are) require articles about husks and chaff and bones. Of what use are nutmegs to a sow?“([11]) But the same Schwabach articles became the foundation of the Confession of Augsburg. Melanchthon had to draw up the latter and he did his duty in his own way, trying to smooth down a difficulty and to conceal a chasm, where the frank avowal of the existence of either would have been much more honest and straightforward.

This remarkable document was accepted by all Lutheran princes in a private meeting, where the only opposition was offered on the part of Philip of Hessen, who still entertained the hope of entering into a political alliance with the Swiss Protestants and therefore objected to those

allegoriam seu augurium esse, sic ad verbum Dei trepidare veras illas Harpyias, non monedulas, sed verso verbo Edelmannos (noblemen) jam Augustae quiritisantes et papisantes. Ibid. 39.

([8]) Walch XVI. 1120 seqq.
([9]) Ego invectivam meam contra ecclesiasticos jamdudum absolvi.   De Wette IV. 15.
([10]) Walch XVI. 1123.
([11]) Walch l. c. 779.

18*

parts which, more or less directly, went against Zwingli-anism. Luther himself had approved of the „Apologia“, as he called it, in a letter to the Elector of Saxony. „I am very much pleased with it, he said, nor should I know how to change or to improve it, nor would it be becoming, for I should not be able to proceed so softly and cautiously.“ When one remembers Luther's impetuosity, it seems aston-ishing that he should be satisfied with Melanchthon's vague document, but he had his own designs, of which we shall hear more by and by.

A full examination of the Augsburg Confession would of course be out of place here; it will be sufficient for our purpose, briefly to describe its general character. The do-cument (¹²) is divided into two parts. The first explains the Lutheran faith, the second deals with alleged abuses in the Catholic Church.

Many points of the first part treat of those articles which the socalled Reformation did not touch at all, and about which there was therefore no fear of dissension, the Blessed Trinity, the Incarnation of Christ etc. The other points seemed to make upon the Catholic princes a much ·less unfavourable impression, than they themselves hat anti-cipated; but the cause of this was one which does not do much honour to Melanchthon, for he had simply omitted those questions, with regard to which Lutheranism had gone as far as possible from the teaching of the Church and which constituted the very essence of the new heresy.

He speaks of Sacraments (¹³), without mentioning how many of them he will admit; of the administration of the Church (Kirchenregiment) he says that nobody ought to enter upon it without due vocation (¹⁴), but he does not ex-plain what sort of vocation is required. Of the Lutheran fundamental principle „nothing but the Bible“ we find nothing in Melanchthon's document, on the contrary, he bases several articles of his Creed more or less explicitly on tra-

(¹²) Walch XVI.988—1040 gives the full German text.

(¹³) Article XIII. Walch l.c. 997.
(¹⁴) Article XI. Ibid. 898.

dition and on the universal belief of the Church through all ages. Universal priesthood, predestination, the power of the Papal See, purgatory, indulgences and similar points on which the bitterest controversy had been going on for more than ten years, were not even mentioned.([15]) The Protestant theologians were of opinion, that these were „hateful and unnecessary articles, about which schools were in the habit of disputing", but which were of no importance to the people at large.([16])

Of course it was Melanchthon's interest to put forward the Confession in terms which were as elastic and as vague as possible and which might be capable of Catholic interpretation. If those terms were agreed upon, they would still bear the most uncatholic explanation; if they were rejected, he was able to pretend that his adversaries had refused the hand of reconciliation offered to them.

The conclusion of the first, dogmatic, part of the Confessio is very characteristic: „*The controversy* (die Irrung und Zank) *is principally about some traditions and abuses.*"([17])

Let this mild language be compared to the unparalled violence with which up to that time the Reformers had inveighed against the Catholic Church, which they denounced as the devil's own home on earth. Now, all at once, there is only a controversy about some traditions and abuses! If so, how were the same Reformers justified in doing what they did, in creating schism and rebellion, in setting up an altar against the altar, in dragging away hundreds of thousands from the Church, nay in endeavour-

---

([15]) When the Catholic members of the diet of Augsburg had asked why these important points had not been touched, Luther wrote to Justus Jonas: Nunc video quid voluerint istae postulationes, an plus articulorum haberetis offerendum. Scilicet Satan adhuc vivit, et bene sensit Apologiam vestram dissimulasse articulos de purgatorio, de Sanctorum cultu et maxime de Antichristo Papa. De Wette IV. 109. In this same letter Luther calls the Apologia „Leisetretterin", a word which can hardly be translated, but which very well expresses the vague and undecided character of the same document.

ing to pull the Church down altogether? Was there an excuse in the existence of those traditions and abuses? Melanchthon demands *in the same breath* patience and indulgence for the faults of his own party. Who can help thinking here of „diverse weights and diverse measures, which are abominable before God?"

We should have to go again over old ground, were we to enter into a discussion of the second part of the Augsburg Confession, which contains the enumeration of the „traditions and abuses" suppressed by the Lutherans.([17a]) Some light in thrown upon Melanchthon's honesty by what he says there about the Mass as celebrated in the Lutheran Churches. „In the public ceremonies of the Mass *no perceivable change* (keine merkliche Aenderung) has been made, except that in some places also German hymns are sung. ([18]) No *perceivable* change! There he is right, for the exterior ceremonies, the vestments etc. had all been left as before, and the *essential* change which had been made by order of Luther, the suppression of the Canon, of the words which referred to the Mass as to a sacrifice, was not perceivable to the people.([19]) It had been too dangerous, to rob the people at once of the worship to which their hearts were so strongly attached, they had to be cheated out if it.

Evidently Melanchthon agreed with his master, that there was „no harm in telling a big lie for the sake of greater good and of the Christian Church." Otherwise

([16]) Walch XVI. 1059.
([17]) Ibid 1006.
([17a]) To those who kept harping on abuses existing in the Church Government, the Lords Spiritual, present at the diet of Augsburg, most properly answered that these very abuses were in great part owing to the arbitrary and unjust way in which the secular powers interfered in ecclesiastical matters. „The *secular* noblemen frequently pick out ignorant and immoral men, even grooms, cooks, pursuivants and stewards and secure to them not only lower, but also higher ecclesiastical offices and dignities, contrary to the will of the Bishops, Archdeacons and Provosts, and with the understanding, that they themselves shall have certain emoluments and part of the income." Ap. Riffel II. 443.
([18]) Walch XVI. 1012.
([19]) See Chapt. X.
([20]) Corp. Reform. II. 168.

he could not have written to Cardinal Campeggio, the Papal Nuncio, as he did in the beginning of July: „We have no dogma different from that of the Roman Church. We have kept down many people who tried to disseminate dangerous doctrines. This can be publicly proved. We are ready to obey the Roman Church, if only in that mildness which she has always shown to all nations she will overlook a few things, which we ourselves could not now change with the best intention. Nothing causes us to be so much hated is Germany as this, that we defend the doctrines of the Roman Church with the greatest constancy. Please God, we shall preserve this our fidelity to Christ and to the Roman Church to our last breath."[20] The wildest onslaught of Luther is preferable to such hypocrisy.[21] Only a few weeks later Melanchthon called the Pope again the Antichrist![22]

Luther was of opinion that the presentation of the Apologia or Confessio to the Diet was quite sufficient and that his party ought not to wait for an answer; hence he urged his friends to leave Augsburg.[23]

Riffel very justly observes[24] that the Augsburg Confession was hardly worth answering. For it had been drawn up by Melanchthon, who was not the acknowledged head

[21] Matthes, a Protestant, whilst condemning Melanchthon's language as thoroughly dishonest, says that probably he satisfied his own conscience by thinking of the very earliest Church, as it existed in his mind, when speaking of the Roman Church. This excuse seems almost worse than the fault.

[22] Corp. Reform. II. 284.

[23] Nostra causa expedita est, nec ultra quicquam melius aut felicius efficietis. Quod Campegius jactat potestatem dispensandi, respondeo verbis Amsdorfii: I — on the legate's and his master's dispensation, we shall find plenty of dispensations. Quando herus praecipit, servi dispensationem non curate, si servus dicendus est tantus latro

et invasor regni. Home! home! De Wette IV. 97. Satis erat nos reddidisse rationem fidei et petere pacem: convertere eos ad pacem quare speramus? — Cfr. ibid. 171: Ego paene rumpor ira et indignatione. Oro autem, ut abrupta actione desinatis cum illis agere, et redeatis. Habent confessionem, habent Evangelium: si volunt admittant, si nolunt, vadant in locum suum. Wird ein Krieg draus, so werde er draus, wir haben genug gebeten und gethan. Dominus paravit eos ad victimam, ut reddat illis secundum opera eorum. Liberabit vero nos populum suum, etiam de incendio Babylonis.

[24] II. 396.

of the so called Reformation, in many points it ignored
the distinctively Lutheran creed, in some it was at variance
with the same, in others it was capable of any interpretation; it was not presented as a final expression of faith,
nor was it presented by men who could be considered as
competent judges in matters of faith, but by secular princes.
However by the desire of the Emperor and the Catholic
members of the Diet Eck, Cochlaeus, Wimpina and other
theologians were commanded to draw up an answer. This
document, written under the impression created by the
unsatisfactory character of the Confessio, turned out to
be too virulent and bitter, hence it had to be remodelled
several times, before it was publicly read on the 3d of
August.([25])

There is no necessity of speaking here of the long
but fruitless discussions which arose between the two
parties. There was no possibility of arriving at a satisfactory conclusion where one party rejected all authority
except its own private judgment.([26]) Let us rather return
to the attitude of Luther, who, as was to be expected, full
of his own importance, had nothing but contempt for the
Diet and gave the most drastic expression to the same
feeling. „How many devils, do you think — he said in
the pulpit — have been last year at the Diet of Augsburg? Each bishop has brought with him as many devils,
as a dog has fleas in the hottest part of summer (um St.
Johannistag)." ([27]) He himself was anxious to withdraw
from the discussion his „Evangelium", i. e. the point on
which everything else depended; hence in his letters to

([25]) Walch XVI. 1220—1267.
([26]) Eck fully perceived the fu-
tility of all such disputations. In
a few words he describes the tact-
ics of his antagonists: Quodsi
sancti Patres eis afferantur testes,
clamant eos quoque homines fuisse;
si citentur canones, obganniunt statim frigida esse haec decreta; si
eligendi forte sunt judices, recu-
sant subito dicentes verbum Dei

non ferre judicem; quodsi allegentur
concilia, clamitant ea saepius errasse; atque e sacris literis etiam
si afferatur aliquid, et has suo ingenio tractant, suamque tantum
expositionem ratam haberi volunt,
contradicente etiam universa Ecclesia jam inde a temporibus Apostolorum.
Ap. Raynald. ad annum 1530.
([27]) Erl. 17, 210.

his friends he kept harping on the real or imaginary abuses existing in the Church and exhorted them to urge this same matter.([28])

The same sort of argumentation, partly in the same words, he puts forward also in an insulting exegetical explanation of the second Psalm, which he dedicated to the Elector Archbishop of Mainz, Albrecht of Brandenburg.([29]) At the same time he did his best to fill his friends at Augsburg with distrust, representing the Catholic party as a mass of sly and cunning intriguers, who would try to get as many concessions as possible and interpret the same in the widest manner.([30]) From his own standpoint Luther was perfectly right, when he thought that reconcilitation was impossible, except if the Pope consented to the destruction of the Papal power.([31])

This would seem straightforward, if it did not appear from some confidential letters, that the „Reformer" cared very little how many concessions were made by his own party, as long as his „Evangelium" remained in its glorious uncertainty, open to the interpretations which he was confident to be able to put on it. „When we have escaped violence, and peace is established, we shall easily mend our tricks and our faults."([32]) On the same day on

---

([28]) Restituant tot animas impia doctrina perditas, restituant tot facultates fallacibus indulgentiis et aliis fraudibus exhaustas, restituant gloriam Dei tot blasphemiis violatam, restituant puritatem ecclesiasticam in personis et moribus tam foede conspurcatam. Et quis omnia numeret? Tum agemus et nos de possessorio. Letter to Justus Jonas.   De Wette IV. 90.

([29]) De Wette IV. 72 seqq.

([30]) Scio vos Evangelium semper excipere in istis pactis, sed metuo, ne postea perfidos et inconstantes insimulent, si non servemus quae voluerint. Ipsi enim nostras concessiones large, largius, largissime accipient, suas vero stricte, strictius, strictissime dabunt.   Ibid. 146.

([31]) Summa, mihi in totum displicet tractatus de doctrinae concordia, ut quae plane sit impossibilis, nisi Papa velit Papatum suum aboleri.   Ibid. 147.

([32]) Si vim evaserimus, pace obtenta, dolos ac lapsus nostros facile emendabimus. De Wette IV. 156. In Chytraei Histor. Conf. August. 295 the word „mendacia" is found after dolos. Walch (XVI. 1790) gives the following translation of the latin text: *Their* (the Catholics') tricks and lies and *our* faults." (Wollen wir *ihre* List und Lügen und unsre Fehl etc.) Very convenient!

which he wrote this to Melanchthon, he said in a letter
to Spalatinus: „Even if you should have allowed something
which is manifestly against the Evangelium and if thus
this eagle should have been shut up in a sack, doubt not,
Luther will come and set the same eagle free, gloriously.“(39)“

He concludes this epistle in *his* apostolic way, by
advising his friend Spalatinus to settle the matter à la
Amsdorf (ut Amsdorfice respondeas in aliquem angulum)
and to say: „The Pope and his legate may — — —.“
„Vale, mi Spalatine, et parce levitati huic.“

Rude and filthy as the expression, he uses, is, the
whole Prophet of Wittenberg is in it.

---

(39) Et esse, aliquid manifeste
(quod non facietis Christo invenae)
contra Evangelium concesseritis,
et im in saccum aliquem conclu-
seriat, veniet, ne dubita, veniet
Lutherus hanc aquilam liberaturus
magnifice.   De Wette IV. 155.

Chapter XIX.

Schmalkalden.

Deus vos impleat odio Papae'
Luther. (On an illustr. in the Altenb. Edit.)

It was the duty of Charles V as head of the Empire and chief representative of justice, to protect the vital interests of those who would not be torn away from their Church, to secure to them liberty of conscience against the tyrannical oppression of Protestant princes and to see that they were not disturbed in the possession of their lawful property. On this point however he found himself unable to abtain any concession — if the granting of a just claim may be called so — from those who, whilst continually harping on the favourite theme of Roman tyranny, had become most cruel tyrants.

The Protestant princes, instigated by their theologians, refused liberty of conscience. In conformity with Luther's opinion[1] the theologians of the Elector of Saxony would not grant to his Catholic subjects the right of celebrating Mass or assisting at it. They declared that such liberty would soon reestablish Popery in the country.[2]

---

[1] „The Mass. being the greatest abomination amongst all abominations that can be named, may not be approved or tolerated."
Walch XVI. 1562.
[2] Luther confesses that the Catholic faith was so deeply rooted in the hearts of the people, that if he had had a mind, he could easily have preached his congregation back again into Popery by two or three sermons. „Es sollten hier zu Wittenberg kaum zehn sein, die ich nicht verführen wollte."
See Erl. 43. 316.

If the „Reformers" had not had the assistance of the
small selfish potentates who reformed vi et armis, their
creed would not have conquered so large a part of Germany. (³)

The Church property had been a most welcome prey
to the Protestant princes. Catholics looked upon its confiscation as barefaced robbery and their feelings were
further hurt by seeing to what unworthy purposes this
same property was applied. George of Brandenburg-
Culmbach paid with the chalices, monstrances etc. which
he had taken from the Churches the gambling debts of
his brother to the amount of 50,000 Gulden. (⁴)

Let us see how Luther, whom so many fondly consider as the champion of religious liberty, justifies the
violent measures of his friends. „If the princes had been
uncertain or doubtful whether monastic life and the celebration of Mass is right or wrong, they would have
done wrong in suppressing monastic institutions. But as
they knew the Evangelium to be right and are sure that
the Mass and monasticism are a blasphemy against the
same, they have been obliged not to tolerate it, as far as
they have had jurisdiction and power." But then there
arises a difficulty! Luther seems to give a weapon into
the hands of his adversaries. For is not Charles V just
as sure that the new Evangelium is false and that *his* Creed
is divine? and may he not therefore follow the same logic?

The „Reformer's" answer is too marvellous, to be
omitted here. „Let that pass, let God be the judge of it.
We know that he (the Emperor) is *not* sure and that he
cannot be sure, because we know that he is in error and
goes against the Evangelium. We are not obliged to believe that he is sure, for he acts without God's word and

---

(³) It is interesting to hear
Luther acknowledge this. „Wen
fursten vnnd herrn nicht thun,
sollen wir nicht lang bleiben. Ideo
dixit Esaias: (49. 23) Reges erunt
nutritii ejus, paurn werdens nicht

thun. Sicut proh dolor hodie
experientia videmus in ingratis.
Lauterb. 131. — Oremus pro Elec-
tore nostro, ut ipse Ecclesiam et
studia conservet.   Ibid. 148.
(⁴) Janssen III. 187.

we with God's word . . . It would never do, if a murderer or adulterer were to say: I am right, you must
approve of my actions, for I am sure of them etc.; he
would have to show clearly that the word of God justifies
his actions." (⁵)

The measures — he continues — adopted by the
Princes for the suppression of Popery are no tyranny over
the minds. They do not wish to *force* anyone to believe;
they only prevent the blasphemies against the Evangelium.
„I cannot make a bad servant pious, but I can prevent
his doing evil. A prince cannot make a villain pious, but
it is his duty to punish and to hang villains." (⁶)

Liberty was the watchword of the Reformers. In the
light of their actions it reads: *Liberty for ourselves, and
for nobody else.* (⁷)

The „Reichsabschied" (⁸) proposed by the Emperor at
Augsburg, was rejected by the Protestants, though it only
demanded that, until the Convocation of a General Council,
no fresh innovations should be made and that the religion
of those who wished to remain faithful to the Catholic
Church should not be interfered with. The possibility of
a civil war seemed to increase every day.

A large party amongst the Protestants were still so
deeply imbued with the highest idea of the Empire and
of its representative, that open rebellion against both would
have been most distasteful to them. This loyalty was
shaken by some pamphlets which were published by Luther
close upon one another and which must be considered as
masterpieces of the art of stirring up the masses.(⁹) He

(⁵) De Wette IV, 94.
(⁶) Ibidem.
(⁷) Butzer, for instance, said that
the secular authority had the right
of exterminating with fire and
sword the adherents of a false religion. Not that all papistical towns
should be destroyed, for then the
greater part of the world would
have to be laid waste! But if
once the Evangelium is established,
then the sword will have to cut
off all who apostatize from it.
                    · See Janssen III, 192.
(⁸) The „recessus," the docu-
ment containing the decisions of
the Diet.
(⁹) They are a) D. Martin
Luther's Warnung an seine lieben
Deutschen. Walch XVI. 1959 seqq.
b) Glossen auf das vermeinte kay-
serliche Edict. Ibid 2016 seqq.

develops in them the wildest eloquence and appears amaz-
ingly „well skill'd in curses."

The chief object he had in view was this, to exonerate
his own party, to throw all the blame of a possible civil
war on the Catholics and to discourage his adversaries,
as being the object of God's special wrath. He plainly
promises that for the future he will have nothing but curses for the Papists. „I care not if they complain that
there is nothing but bad words and devils in my book
(the „Warning"); this shall be my honour and my glory,
and I will have it so, that they shall say of me that I am
full of bad words and reviling and cursing for the Papists.
For more than ten years I have frequently humbled myself
and have given the best words; this has only made them
worse . . . but now I will curse the villains until I am
dead; they shall never hear from me another good word.
My thundering and lightning shall be their funeral bell.
For I cannot pray without cursing." ([10])

To hide the treasonable character of his object from
the eyes of others, perhaps also from his own, „the Prophet of Germany", as now he thought he had to call him-
self([11]), protested against the supposition that he had any
evil designs against the Emperor. He even pretended that
the Imperial decree was only a forgery and that his object
was to unmask those who had shamefully abused Charles'
confidence, especially the „Hauptschalk", Pope Clement VII
and his servant Campeggio([12]). Nay, he had many words
of praise for the Emperor's mildness, justice and peace-

---

c) Wider den Meuchler zu Dresden,
zur Rettung der Warnung an seyne
lieben Deutschen abgefasset.
          Ibid. 2062 seqq.
   ([10]) Walch XVI. 2084.
   ([11]) Der Deutschen Prophet, denn
solchen hoffärtigen Namen muss
ich mir hinfort selbst zumessen,
meinen Papisten und Eseln zu Lust
und gefallen.   Ibid. 1983.
   ([12]) Ibid 2017. — Cfr. ibid. 1990:

Let nobody be astonished or fright-
ened at seeing the Emperor's name
under documents, which are against
God and justice. He cannot help
it. Be sure that this is only the
doing of the chief villain in the
world, the Pope, who through his
shavelings (Plattenhengste) and
hypocrites tries to cause a massacre
amongst us Germans and to ruin us.

fulness,(¹³) but for the Catholic members of the Diet there
was not a particle of mercy. „Oh you unfortunate people
that have been on the Pope's side at Augsburg! Your
children will have to be ashamed of you for ever! . . .
Oh, the shameful Diet! , . . To all princes and to the whole
Empire it will always remain a stain and dishonour, and it
ought to make all Germans blush before God and the whole
world. What will the Turks say of it? What will the
Tartars say of it and the Muscovites? Who in the wide
world will be afraid of us Germans or will esteem us, when
people hear that we allow that accursed Pope and his
masks to make fools of us and children, nay, blocks?"(¹⁴)

Luther maintained in the bitterest terms that his adversaries were not in good faith but acted against their conscience, that they knew perfectly well they were wrong
and his Evangelium the true word of God. „The perjured
murderers and villains act out of malice."(¹⁵) Such wickedness of course obliged him and his party, to stop their
prayers for them, those prayers, which had wrought so
many miracles at Augsburg!(¹⁶) Woe to them! „If it
comes to rebellion, my powerful God and Lord Jesus Christ
can save me and mine, as he has saved dear Lot at Sodom . . . If he does not save me, praise and thanks be to
him. I have lived long enough, I have deserved my end
and have honestly begun to avenge my Lord Jesus Christ
of mad Popery. It is after my death that they shall feel
Luther. But . . . if I should be killed, I will take with
me a lot of bishops and priests and monks, and the world
shall say:(¹⁷) *Doctor Martinus has had a large funeral procession. For he is a great Doctor, above all bishops, priests
and monks; they shall go with him to the grave (on their
backs) and the world shall talk and sing of it. Won't we
have a little pilgrimage together! they, the Papists, to the
bottom of hell, to their lying and murdering God, whom*

(¹³) Ibid. 1986, 1989, 2065.						(¹⁶) Ibid. 1961.
(¹⁴) Ibid. 1974.									(¹⁷) The italics are in Walch.
(¹⁵) Ibid. 1973.

they have so faithfully served by lying and murdering, I to my master and Saviour Jesus Christ, whom I have served in truth and peace. For he that kills Doctor Luther, will not have mercy on the priests and monks. We shall go together, they in all devils' name to hell, I in God's name to heaven . . . If they have hard heads, I shall have a harder head. If they had not only this powerful Emperor Charles, but also the Turkish Emperor and his Mahomet with them and round them, they will not frighten me, they will not unnerve me, but in the power of God I shall frighten them and shall unnerve them. My life shall be their death, and my death shall be their devil." ([18])

To inspire his party with courage in case of war, the „Prophet" foretells them, as many other Prophets have done in similar cases, that their adversaries cannot possibly be victorious, for „we know for certain that they cannot begin war in the name of God, or pray or implore God's help . . . their conscience is too much burdened with big lies, bitter imprecations, innocent blood, insidious murder and all abominations; their obstinate and impenitent hearts are full of sins against the Holy Ghost . . . I with mine will not be lazy. Confidently, constantly, incessantly we will pray to the Lord of Lords, to the powerful God of miracles, that he may give them a desponding and cowardly heart when they bear arms against us."([19])

If the Protestants (he continues) are forced to take up arms, they only act in legitimate selfdefence. „If it should come to war (which God may graciously avert!) I will not, that those who defend themselves against the murdering, bloodthirsty Papists should be called rebels."([20])

Three reasons are adduced to prove that a Christian must not obey the Emperor's summons to arms.

I) Such obedience would be rebellion against God. „In a case of this sort God has strictly forbidden to obey the Emperor, and he that obeys him must know that he

([18]) Walch l. c. 1965. 1966.   ([20]) Ibid. 1971.
([19]) Ibid. 1967. 1968.

disobeys God and will be lost, body and soul, for ever."([21])
"Thou hast vowed in baptism to keep the Evangelium of
Christ, not to persecute it. Thou knowest that in this
case the Emperor has been set on and has been cheated
by the Pope, to take up arms against the Evangelium of
Christ, for at Augsburg our doctrine has been publicly
found to be the true Evangelium founded upon Holy
Scripture. Therefore thou shalt answer the summons of
the Emperor or of thy prince in this way: "Yes, Dear
Emperor, yes, Dear Prince, if you would keep the vow
you have taken in Baptism, you should be my master and
I would take up arms at your command. But if you do
not keep your baptismal vow and christian covenant, a
villain may obey you, but not I. I am not willing for
your sake to blaspheme God and to persecute his word
and to run and jump with you into the bottom of hell."([22])

II) "Even if our doctrine should not be the right one
(but they know it is), this alone should deter thee (from
obeying the Emperor), that in this way thou wouldst take
upon thyself and shouldst become guilty before God, of all
the abominations which have been committed in Popery ...
In short it is bottomless hell itself, with all sins, that thou
wouldst become a partaker of, if thou didst obey the Emperor in this case."([23]) Here Luther gets hold of his
favourite subject and with his inexhaustible fancy draws
a fearful picture of "the abominations of Popery." We
have heard him so often on this subject, that we need not
follow him, especially as we shall be obliged to listen to
him again on another occasion. ([24])

III) He who obeys the Emperor's summons, becomes
guilty of the crime of destroying or attempting to destroy

([21]) Ibid. 1985.
([22]) Ibid. 1991.
([23]) Ibid. 1993.
([24]) After solemnly declaring:
"I lie not," he tells some of the
most atrocious falsehoods he ever
uttered, the same which also occur
in his tabletalk, about the decree

of the Lateran Council concerning
Cardinals and about the death
of Leo. We have noticed them
p. 44. 93. That he really meant
Leo X. appears also from this
place (Walch XVI. 1995), for he
says: dass auch *neulich* ein Papst
etc.

all the good that has been done already through the Evangelium and of obscuring the light it has shed over the
world.([25])

„This then shall be a warning to my beloved Germans;
and as I have done before, so I testify here again that I
do not wish to excite anyone to war or rebellion or
resistance, but I only wish for peace. But if our devils,
the Papists, will not keep peace . . . their blood be upon
their heads; I am excused; I have done my duty most
faithfully." ([26])

We will make an act of faith and believe that cursing
and swearing, as only Luther can curse and swear, is a
good means for reestablishing peace.

The Protestant princes, whose treasuries had so largely
profited by the confiscation of ecclesiastical property, were
afraid that, if the „Reichsabschied" were carried out, they
would have to disgorge their spoil.([27]) That document
decreed a restitutio in integrum and allowed those, who
had been robbed of their property by „apostolic" annex-
ation, to carry their causes before the highest tribunal of the
Empire.([28]) To avert such a calamity, they met as Schmalkalden (Hessen) and entered into a compact for mutual
protection. Though some of them, including the representatives of some free cities, objected to violence on
account of their still unconquered loyalty to the Empire,
it was carried that at least the existing dissensions should

([25]) How in this place Luther
describes the brilliancy of the light
of his Evangelium will appear from
Note 11 in the following chapter.

([26]) Walch l. c. 2016.

([27]) Aleander wrote from Ra-
tisbon: Se non fusse la avaritia
che occeca molti principi et private persone cossi catholici come
heretici, che tengono gli beni di altri,
et presertim di la povera Chiesa,
mi par che non sarria molto difficil
cosa mettervi qualche ordine cum
la assistentia di detti principi et

altri devoratori de li boni Eccle-
siastici, che pocchi vi sono hora
in questa Germania netti da questa
macchia.   Ap. Lämmer. 146.

([28]) Luther said in his criticism
of the Reichsabschied: As regards
the ecclesiastical property, revenues,
tithes and rents, ... it seems that
it would be very advisable for the
reestablishment and preservation
of peace, if the past were simply
forgotten. Walch XVI. 1862. Very
generous!

be kept as a profound secret, lest the power of the opposition should be weakened. But when the Emperor's determination that the course of justice, with regard to ecclesiastical property, should not be interfered with, became known, a formal alliance of the Protestant princes was entered into at the same place, Schmalkalden, when also particulars regarding the expenses of a probable war were fixed upon.

The Lutherans had looked with suspicion on that party, which under the leadership of Butzer was known to incline to the peculiar tenets of Zwingli regarding the Eucharist. During the Diet of Augsburg Melanchthon had ostentatiously kept aloof from them. They had not been allowed to have any part in the Confessio Augustana; they had presented a Confessio of their own, known as the „Tetrapolitana“.[29] About this same time Luther had made his friends clearly understand how unsympathetic Butzer was to him[30], but for political reasons the differences were sunk[31]; the four cities which had signed the Confessio Tetrapolitana were admitted to the Schmalkalden Confederation. However the pet scheme of Philip, Landgraf of Hessen, of admitting likewise the pronounced Zwinglians and of forming a universal protestant league[32] met with unsurmountable opposition.

For the time civil war was averted. Charles V found himself obliged to give way before the threatening attitude of the Protestant princes, who had secured a number of allies, whose combined power would have been more than sufficient the crush the already tottering fabric of the Empire.

In Germany they had found allies in the Catholic Dukes of Bavaria, whose aspirations were bitterly dis-

[29] It was presented in the name of the four cities of Strassburg, Constanz, Memmingen and Lindau.

[30] Cum his hominibus ineamus societatem? De Wette IX. 110.

[31] Feremus potius hanc discordiam minorem cum pace minore, quam ut si hanc curare studeamus, moveamus tragoedias veras majorum discordiarum ac turbarum intolerabilium. Letter to Butzer. De Wette IV. 217. Similary in the letter to Duke Ernst of Lüneburg.   Ibid. 219.

[32] See page 255.

appointed by the election of Charles' brother Ferdinand to
the dignity of German King. Outside the Fatherland (if
such a term should be used under the circumstances) they
had entered into alliances with Zapolya of Hungary, and
through him with the Turks, with King Frederick of Denmark, with Sigismund of Poland and especially with the
„most Christian" king Francis I., who owed the Emperor
a grudge for his defeat at Pavia and his captivity, and
the chief object of whose dishonest policy seemed to be
the ruin of Germany.

Surrounded on all sides by enemies, Charles V clearly
perceived that for the time the exercise of his rights had
become an impossibility. It was a minus malum, when
(23. June 1532) he quashed the decision of the Reichsabschied with regard to confiscated Church property and
suspended all litigations about it, until the Council should
meet. ([33])

He promised that he would do his best to obtain from
the Pope the convocation of a General Council within
six months, and should he be unsuccessful, to convene a
Diet after that period, for further consideration of what
was to be done for the religious pacification of Germany;
but he distinctly stated that he himself did not claim any
right for the convocation of a Council. ([34])

([33]) In his answer to this same
document Luther had strongly protest ed against „future Protestants"
not enjoying the same privilege of
toleration, which was then granted
to all who at that time were already adherents of the new religion. He said that this would
be tantamount to nailing Christ
again to the Cross. (Walch XVI.
1857.) But during the fresh negotiations, which resulted in the
above mentioned concessions being
made by the Emperor, he suddenly
and completely changed his mind
on this point and maintained that
he was not obliged to take care
of those who might join him after-

wards. See his letter to John,
Elector of Saxony ap. Walch XVI.
2216 seqq. Cfr. ibid. 2210, where
he, together with Pomeranus, exhorts his party, to be satisfied
with what is offered to them.
„Qui nimium emungit, elicit san-
guinem. Wer zu viel haben will,
der kriegt zu wenig." In this
same place he admits the principle:
Quod tibi non vis fieri, alteri non
feceris. If, he says, the Protestant
princes do not allow their Catholic
subjects the liberty of Catholic
worship, we must allow the Catholic
princes to forbid protestant service
in their own territory.   ·
([34]) Campeggio says of Joachim

The last days of Clement VII's life were devoted to the preparation of that Council, for which all parties had been loudly clamouring for many years. But when its realization seemed to approach, Luther and his party drew back under various pretexts. He did not like it, he thought it was half angel, half devil,([35]) since nobody knew whether the Pope, that „bloodhound and murderer",([36]) meant to grant real freedom at it. It would not, of course, be free, except the Pope were simply a party at it, without being a judge,([37]) but such freedom is not to be obtained from him. ([38])

Paul III lost no time after his accession to the Papal See in taking the same business in hand. But his Legate, Pietro Paolo Vergeri, soon found out that there was very little hope of reconciliation. At Wittenberg he had an interview with Luther,([39]) who declared he had no faith in the future Council, as it would only treat about foolish things,([40]) but not about serious matters of faith; and „of

of Brandenburg: „mi mandò a dire che la Maestà Cesarea gli havea detto, che non volea consentir in cosa alcuna che non fusse con satisfatione et honor di Nostro Signore et di quella Santa Sede. Ap. Lämmer, 137. — In case that the General Council is not summoned immediately, „Sua Maestà promette, subito far congregar gli Elettori et Stati et consultar alhora de ulteriore remedio, per componer le cose di Germania cercala fede, et per niente Sua Maestà ha voluto che si mette in la conclusion che essistessa habii ad intimar il Concilio, come hanno più volte tra loro concluso questi Principi et Stati. Ibid. 143.

([35]) (es) munkelt im dunkeln als ein halber Engel und halber Teufel. Walch XVI. 2273.

([36]) Ibid. 2277.

([37]) Ibid. 2275. — Melanchthon admitted that the praesidium at the Council belonged by rights to the Pope.

([38]) Weil er denn solche Bitte um ein Christlich frey Concilium abschläget und wegert, weiset uns darzu mit Spott in den Hintern, müssen wirs geschehen lassen und leiden. Ibid. 2276.

([39]) On this occasion the „Prophet" paid special attention to his toilette, and, when asked the reason by his barber, he answered that he wanted to appear young. „The Legate will think: What the devil! is this Luther still so young and has already done so much mischief! How much more is he going to do?" When entering the carriage to drive to Vergeri, he remarked: Here go the German Pope and Cardinal Pomeranus! Walch XVI. 2293.

([40]) Kappen, Platten, Essen, Trinken und dergleichen anderem Narrenwerk.

all *such* things we are sure through the Holy Ghost, hence
we are not in need of a Council." ([41])

From the members of the Schmalkalden League the
Legate received a similar, not overpolite, answer. ([42])

At the request of the Elector of Saxony Luther had
drawn up the socalled Schmalkalden Articles, which afterwards became one of the symbolical books of the Protestants.
In view of the approaching Council they were to express
once more the doctrines and demands of the „reformed"
Church. In substance they are almost identical with the
Confessio Augustana, but the style is as different as possible, since Luther alone had written them. ([43]) It is especially in the articles on the Mass and on the Pope that
this style alone would infallibly indicate the author. At
the end of the latter article he resumes all he has said by
addressing the Pope in the words of the prophet Zachary:
„The Lord rebuke thee, o Satan!" ([44])

The plan of holding a Protestant Anti-Council had to
be abandoned. Many of the Lutheran party were afraid,
that it would only help to reveal to the world the hopeless
dissension which existed in their midst. ([45]) Besides, for a
while Luther was incapacitated from work, since at Schmalkalden he suffered again cruel pain from gravel. Curses
against the Pope were resorted to as the most likely
remedy.

When starting from Schmalkalden, he took leave of
his friends with the words:

„Deus vos impleat odio Papae!" ([46])

([41]) Walch l. c. 2294.
([42]) Ibid. 2310 seqq.
([43]) Die Artikel so ich selbs
gestellet.   De Wette V. 45.
([44]) Walch XVI. 2344.
([45]) For particulars see Janssen
III. 349.

([46]) The Altenburg Edition has
an illustration of this scene. How
Luther found relief on his return
journey, is minutely described in
his letters to Melanchthon and to
his Käthe. De Wette V. 57. 58.

Chapter XX.

Fruits of the Reformation.

After the Pope's tyranny and kingdom has
come to an end, everybody despises the pure
and saving doctrine; people become simply
beasts and brutes.

Luther. Walch I. 615.

By their fruits you shall know them.

Matth. VII. 20.

The effect of the religious revolution which Luther
had started made itself felt all over Germany and in every
part of life. The intellectual life of the nation met with
a check and began to retrograde. The topic which absorb-
ed all interest and which was discussed everywhere and
by everybody, was the new heresy; it seemed as if all
intellectual activity had become concentrated on this one
point, to the exclusion of all other pursuits. As early as
1524 Erasmus complained that no books could be bought
except contraversial ones, „Lutherana ac antilutherana".([1])
The licentiousness which soon disgraced life at the Universities, caused numbers of parents to keep their sons
away from them. But the principal cause of the decadence
of the theological schools has to be sought in the prevalent
opinion about the universal priesthood, an opinion, which
Carlstadt and his adherents carried out so far, as to forbid
all study and to trust in the divine instruction imparted
to everybody individually by the Holy Ghost. Many

([1]) Opp. III. 824.

ministers preached violently against the study of philoso-
phy([2]) and in this point at least Luther heartily agreed
with them; in his deep hatred against Aristoteles he considered and denounced reason as „the devil's arch-whore."
We have seen before that he would never allow to reason
a place in theology; the endeavours of the Christian
schools to prove the harmony between faith and reason
were therefore most hateful to him. „The Universities,
the devil's schools, . . . not only boast of the natural light,
but make out that it is good and useful and necessary, in
order to see Christian truth. But it is clear that it is
the devil that has invented the Universities, to destroy and
to obscure Christian truth." ([3])

The fact that numerous totally unlearned and uncul-
tured men were frequently transferred to the pulpits from
their workshops, if they were only able to read and possessed wives,([4]) did not contribute towards making the
ministry respectable or desirable in the eyes of the better
classes of the people. To meet this difficulty, Luther not
only described in glowing terms the activity which might
be displayed by ministers, but contradicting all he had said
on this point on former occasions, represented the ministry
as a state of life willed and instituted by God.([5])

The deadening influence of the „Reformation" on the
higher studies became apparent not in the theological
faculty only. The registers of the Universities of Wittenberg, Rostock, Leipzig, Basel, Vienna etc. show an incredible falling off in the number of students.([6]) Sometimes
the number of fresh students entered in one year dwindled
down to five; in one case there were none at all; at Heidelberg there were in 1525 more professors than students.

([2]) Döll. I. 473.
([3]) Walch XI. 459.
([4]) Wicelius ap. Döll. I. 112. —
Multos novi, qui cum fuerint
sordidi opifices, urgente fame concionatores mox facti sunt.
Id. Ibid. 113.

([5]) Sermon dass man Kinder etc.
Walch X. 486 seqq.

([6]) Janssen II. 296 seqq.

Vienna which at one time had counted its students by the
thousand, now counted them by the dozen. Luther reaped
what he had sown. He had denounced the Universities in
the most violent language. In one of his pamphlets against
the Maas, after describing Moloch and applying the words
of the Psalmist „et immolaverunt filios suos et filias suas
daemoniis,"˜he had said: „Here (in Moloch) you have the
Universities, in which the best of our youth are offered
up as a holocaust." (⁷) „That they are taught false heath-
enish arts and impious human doctrine, this is the fire of
Moloch, which nobody can sufficiently deplore, and through
which at the Universities the most pious and the cleverest
youths are ruined. . . . From the beginning of the world
the devil has not been able to invent anything more efficacious than the Universities for the suppression of faith and
of the Evangelium." (⁸) „The Universities deserve to be
pulverized, *nothing more hellish or diabolical has been on
earth* since the beginning of the world." (⁹)

In 1525 we find the same Luther writing doleful letters
to the Duke of Saxony and to the Elector, imploring them
to use means to prevent the total ruin of the University
of Wittenberg! (¹⁰)

The change produced by the Lutheran „Evangelium"
in the morals of the people is even more remarkable and
deplorable. Almost from the beginning of his work Luther
was disgusted with the little fruit it produced in the lives
of his followers, and with each succeeding year he expressed
his disappointment in bitterer words. He forgot or chose
to forget that the very things of which he complained,
were the necessary and logical outcome of his own teachings. Of course he tried to find a different explanation.
The moral corruption amongst the adherents of the socalled Reformation, especially amongst the youth, was fearful. If we were to give a description of it from contemp-

(⁷) Walch XIX. 1430.

(⁹) Walch XII. 45. Cfr. Walch
XI. 123; IX. 862.; VI. 2553.

(⁸) Ibid. 1431.

(¹⁰) De Wette II. 664; III. 29.

orary Catholic writers, we might be accused of partiality; therefore the head of the Reformation, Luther himself, shall describe it. The only difficulty, with which we have to cope here, is an embarras de richesses, as his lamentations are so exceedingly frequent.

If we consider how very proud Luther was of the pretended light which through him had begun to shine, and how he used to boast that through him religion had been made accessible to man, we can understand that he felt the disappointment all the more keenly. In 1530, for instance, he wrote: „Before the „Evangelium“ (i. e. *his* Evangelium), nobody knew what Christ is, or what baptism is, or confession, or sacrament, or faith, or spirit, or flesh, or good works, or the decalogue, or prayer, or suffering, or matrimony, or parents, or children, or master, or servant, or devil, or angel, or world, or life, or death, or sin, or right, or forgiveness of sins, or God, or bishop, or parishpriest, or Church, or Christian, or cross; in short, we knew nothing of all that a Christian ought to know. It was all darkened and suppressed by the Pope-asses. For asses they are, big, rude, unlearned asses in matters of Christian religion . . . But now, thanks be to [God, man and woman, young and old know the Catechism, they know how we ought to live, to believe, to pray, to suffer and to die.“([11])

Let us see, how the „reformed“ world went on, after it had been enlightened by the Prophet of Wittenberg on all those important points. Already in 1522 we hear him complain to his friend Lange, that the power of the word is either still hidden or very weak, „for we are as bad as before, hard, insensible, impatient, reckless, drunkards, lascivious, quarrelsome.“([12]) If at that time he said: „We are as bad as before“, he soon found himself obliged to

---

([11]) Walch XVI. 2013.

([12]) Virtus verbi vel adhuc latet, vel nimis modica est in omnibus nobis, quod miror valde. Sumus enim iidem qui antea, duri, insensati, impatientes, temerarii, ebrii, lascivi, contentiosi.
De Wette II. 175.

go farther; he now had to complain that the „Evangelicals" were infinitely worse than as Papists they had ever
been. „A great plague will have to come over Germany;
I am afraid everything will come at once, pestilence, war
and famine. Nobody fears God, all are wanton; servants,
masters, peasants, artisans, all do what they like. There
is nobody that inflicts punishment, everybody lives according to his own liking and cheats the other."([13]) „Our
Evangelicals are becoming seven times worse than they
were before. For after we have learned the Evangelium,
we rob, lie, cheat, gorge and guzzle and are guilty of all
sorts of vices. For one devil that has gone out from us,
seven worse ones have entered us."([14]) Not only amongst
those who persecute the known truth of the Evangelium,
but also amongst us who receive it and boast of it, the
masses of the people are so abominably ungrateful for it,
that it is a wonder God does not punish us with thunder
and lightning, nay with all Turks and all devils from hell".([15])
We have the Evangelium, thanks be to God! . . . but what
are we doing? We talk of it and think it is enough to
know it".([16]) „We are freed from the infernal seduction
(of the Pope), but we do not thank God for it, we do not
serve him as the Evangelium teaches us, we do not care
for our neighbour, we are full of fraud and tricks."([17])
„Everywhere one hears the complaint, that a good deal
is preached and nobody acts according to it, but people
are so rude, cold and lazy that it is a shame; they do much
less than before, and yet we have so great and so bright
a light!([18]) „Except a few, who mean it sincerely, the mas-

([13]) Walch III. 2591.

([14]) Ibid. 2727. — The same expression was also used by one of
the Nürnberg Reformers, Vitus
Theodorus (Veit Dietrich), who
also said in his preface to Luther's
explanation of the second Psalm:
Quoties aspexi jam Ratisponae,
stans in ripa, flumen Danubii in-
gens et rapidum, gemens cogitavi,

non si tantum lacrymarum fundere
possem quantum undarum volvit
hoc flumen, exhauriri meus dolor
posset, quem circumfero propter
ecclesiae dissipationem. *Crescit
cyclopica feritas ubique.*

([15]) Walch XII. 1234.
([16]) Walch XI. 2171.
([17]) Walch XII. 1920.
([18]) Ibid. 1152.

ses are so ungrateful, so loose, so rude, and lead such lives,
as if God had given us his word and freed us from the
Pope's infernal prison only that we might freely do and
omit whatever we like."(¹⁹) „Unfortunately it is our daily
experience, that now under the Evangelium the people
entertain greater and bitterer hatred and envy, and are
worse with their avarice and money-grabbing than before
under the Papacy."(²⁰) The more and the longer the Evangelium is preached, the worse things are getting."(²¹) „We
are ungrateful to God and to his word; therefore the
devil that has been expelled from us, will bring seven other
devils back with him, worse than himself."(²²) „All boast
that they are Christians, all are proud of their Christian
liberty. Yet meantime they give way to concupiscence
and turn to avarice, lust, pride, envy etc. Nobody does
his duty faithfully, nobody serves his neighbour in charity: sometimes this makes me so impatient, that I often
wish those hogs that trample the pearls under foot, were
still ander the tyranny of the Pope. For it is impossible
that such Gomorrha people should be ruled in the peace
of the Evangelium."(²³) „If God had not shut my eyes,
if I had foreseen these scandals, I would never have begun
to preach the Evangelium."(²⁴) „As everybody sees, the
people are now more miserly, more merciless, more impure,
more impudent, than before under the Papacy".(²⁵) „We
have got rid of the Pope and know again, what Evangelium and baptism and Sacrament is . . . But how do
matters stand? Old and young neglect the word and rave

(¹⁹) Walch XX. 2742.
(²⁰) Walch XIII. 2195.
(²¹) Walch XII. 2120.
(²²) Walch VIII. 1012.
(²³) Wittenb. V. 413.
(²⁴) Walch VI. 920. — Cfr. Letter to Justus Jonas: Ego omnia
quae aguntur contra Turcam irrita
fore timeo. donec intra nos reges
illos Turcas feros et veros ador-
amus. avaritiam. usuram, super-
biam,licentiam scelerum horribilem,

nobilium niphlim tyrannidem, per-
fidiam, malitiam, deinde contem-
tum Verbi planc Satanicum et in-
gratitudinem et irrisionem sangui-
nis illius pro nobis fusi. De Wette
V. 408. — Ii qui evangelici esse
volunt, avaritia, rapina, ecclesiarum spoliis secure irritant iramDei,
sicut vulgus sinit nos docere, orare,
pati, ipsi interim peccatis peccata
exagerant.   De Wette V. 485.
(²⁵) Walch XIII. 19.

for quite different things: If we had bread instead!" ([26])
„Those that suffer under the tyrants, are crying out day
and night (for the „Evangelium"), and *our* hogs, which
have before them the blessed bread . . . will not even
smell at it; they upset it with their snouts, wallow in it and
trample it under their feet." ([27]) „Under the Pope people
did no end of foolish and useless things willingly, with
great devotion and at great expenses; but in our Churches the people are lazier and more indolent when anything good has to be done, than can be expressed." ([28])
I do not care so much now for the avarice of the peasants,
or fornication and impurity, *which abounds everywhere*, but
rather for the contempt of the Evangelium." ([29]) (After the
Evangelium has been preached)" *all vices, sins and infamies
have become so common, that they are no longer reputed
as such.*"([30]) „The people feel they are free from the
bonds and fetters of the Pope, but now they want to get
rid also of the Evangelium and of all the laws of God."([31])
„The youth are insolent and wild([32]) and refuse obedience,
the old people are full of avarice, usury and many other
sins that cannot even be named."([33]) „After the Pope's
tyranny and kingdom has come to an end, everybody
despises the pure and saving doctrine, *people become simply
beasts and brutes.*"([34]) „Everybody thinks that Christian
liberty and licentiousness of the flesh are one and the same
thing, as if now everybody was allowed to do what he
likes."([35]) Townsfolk and peasants, men and women,
children and servants, princes, magistrates and subjects
all are going to the devil."([36])

([26]) Ibid. 1816.
([27]) Walch V. 378.
([28]) Walch XIII. 2689.
([29]) Walch XIII. 8.
([30]) Walch XXII. 308.
([31]) Walch XIV. 195.

([32]) Cfr. Luther's words to the
Elector John Frederick: „So ist
das Maidevolk kühn worden, lau-
fen den Gesellen nach in ihre Stüb-

lin, Kammern und wo sie können,
bieten ihnen frei ihre Liebe an.
De Wette V. 615.

([33]) Walch I. 2451.
([34]) Ibid. 615.
([35]) Tischr. I. 180.

([36]) Erl. 14, 389. — Primum
cum post tenebras tantas human-
arum traditionum exoriretur lux
Evangelii, multi studebant pietati,

Another thing which frequently filled Luther's soul with the greatest bitterness, but a thing intimately connected with the growing corruption and naturally following upon his own teaching was the contempt with which the ministers of the „Evangelium" were treated by their own flocks, the want of respect shown in the Churches, the indifference with which the „word" was listened to.

„Many say: what use is there now for preachers and priests? we can read at home!" (³⁷) „Peasants and noblemen know the Evangelium *better than St. Paul and Dr. Martin Luther (!)*, they are clever and think themselves better than their pastors." (³⁸) „They say: We do not want pastors, the Spirit will teach us" (³³). (Peasants, townsfolk and noblemen) care neither for baptism nor for sermon, they honour neither pastors nor preachers, . . . they are and always will remain hogs; they believe like hogs and die like hogs." (⁴⁰) A poor villagepastor is now the most despicable man that can be found, there is no peasant now, but looks upon him as upon filth and dirt, and gives him kicks." (⁴¹) „Everywhere they send away the preachers, or oppress them with hunger and poverty and all sorts of secret tricks, only to get rid of them." (⁴²) „Nobody is willing to give a halfpenny towards the Evangelium and the ministry, nay everybody robs the Church of what she has possessed from old times." (⁴³) „It seems as if all had made up their minds to starve the ministers of the Evangelium." (⁴⁴) „In old times when people served the devil under the Papacy, everybody was kind and merciful, everybody gave with both hands to keep up a false worship;

avide audiebant conciones, honorem habebant verbi ministris. Nunc cum tam magno incremento verbi non infeliciter sit repurgata doctrina pietatis, plerique ex discipulis fiunt contemptores et inimici, qui non solum verbi studium abjiciunt, et ministros ejus negligunt, sed etiam omnes bonas literas et liberales artes oderunt, *fiuntque plane porci et ventres.* Digni certe qui *dvor̨tois* Galatis conferantur. Comm. in Gal. Wittenb. V. 285.

(³⁷) Walch XIII. 1816.
(³⁸) Walch XIV. 1360.
(³⁹) Walch IX. 2613.
(⁴⁰) Walch VIII. 1290
(⁴¹) Walch V. 577.
(⁴²) Walch XII. 1219.
(⁴³) Walch XIII. 2536.
(⁴⁴) Walch VI. 967.

now, when there ought to be in a town two or three persons to preach etc., this seems too much, though people need not give from their own property, but from what has been left from Popery." ([45]) „When Pastor Ambrosius R. exhorted his flock to listen to the word of God, they answered: Yes, dear Mr. Pastor, if you would keep a barrel of beer in the Church and invite us then, we would most willingly come." ([46]) „When the peasants in a certain village were asked, why they would not keep their pastor, as they spent money even on cowherds and pigherds, they answered: We cannot do without a herd, but we can do very well without a pastor." ([47]) „Why are pastors, preachers and ministers of the Evangelium now so poor, that part of them are nearly starving with their wives and children? The reason is, that peasants, noblemen etc. all belong to the devil." ([48]) The pastor of Holsdorf was told by his flock: We need not pray, we keep you for that, and pay you that you should pray for us. ([49])

After this, the official report of the visitation made in the neighbourhood of Wittenberg in the years 1533 and 1534 can hardly be discredited. „The sermons were interrupted by open contradictions or improper loud conversation. In Globig the full beerpots went from hand to hand during divine worship, not to mention the indecent behaviour of the young men towards the girls during service. ([50])

([45]) Walch XI. 1758. — Cfr. Comment. in Gal. Wittenb. V. 433: Ea est fortuna Evangelii quando docetur: non solum nemo dare quidquam vult pro sustentandis ministris ipsius et conservandis scholis, sed omnes incipiunt rapere, furari, circumvenire alii alios variis artibus. Summa, *homines videntur degenerare subito in immanes bestias.* Is this really the „fortuna Evangelii"? Was it so also when the Apostles preached the Evangelium? We hear nowhere that the first Christians became at once a lot of wild beasts! — Cfr. De Wette II. 567.

([46]) Tischr. I. 18.
([47]) Ibid. 22. — Cfr. De Wette IV. 275: Quae de ministorum verbi negligentia et rusticorum contemtu scribis, nimis vera sunt. — De Wette V. 586: Rustici insuper sic agunt et vivunt, ut ruralibus suis pastoribus nec fragmentum faveant panis.
([48]) Tischr. I. 398.
([49]) Ibid. 478.
([50]) Burkhardt, Geschichte der sächs. Kirchen u. Schulvisitation. Leipzig 1879. The report continues: Auch haben etliche Bauernknechte unter den göttlichen Amten und Predigten auf die Jungfrauen, Frauen, das ander Volk

We might fill some more pages with similar quotatious
from Luther's works, but those which we have given will
be sufficient to show that his prophecy „the preaching of
the Evangelium is always followed by the amendment of
impious doctrine and of life" ([51]) was not fulfilled. We have
to ask now: what was the cause of this fearful corruption?
Luthers's admirers will probably deny, with him, that his
Evangelium bore such fruits, they will look elsewhere for
an explanation. We beg the reader to cast once more
a glance at the principal articles of Luther's creed. Good
works are not necessary for salvation (Amsdorf, his disciple, went farther and said they were noxious); faith is
absolutely sufficient; man must leave himself entirely in
God's hands without any attempt on his own part to
cooperate in the work of his salvation; the will of man is
not free, but ridden either by God or by the devil; pecca
fortiter, sed fide fortius; a sin is a good means to confirm
us in the consoling conviction, that under the Evangelium
sin can do us no harm — would not the masses of the
people jump at such propositions? ([52]) and draw their own
consequences from them? and quite logically too? Supposing those teachings were true, where would be the
want of logic in conclusious like these; *I believe*, — what
then does it matter, that I commit sin? My will is not
free — therefore I am not answerable for what I do; I
could not help it; „I was ridden by the devil."

Impurity especially became the prevailing and almost
absorbing vice of the followers of Luther's Evangelium.
The descriptions given by the „Reformer's" own friends,

ihren Harn gelassen. — Many ministers were obliged to resort to
rather curious means to secure a
living. Carlstadt, when at Kemberg, kept a public house and a
small shop. See Mathesius, 6th
Serm. — Melanchthon also speaks
of the summa et intolerabilis malitia of the „reformed" peasants.
Corp. Reform. I. 982.

([51]) Walch VI. 620.

([52]) „If nowadays anyone wishes
to preach the Church empty, let
him preach about good works; if
anyone wishes to have numerous
hearers, let him revile good works."
Wicelius ap. Döll. I. 53.

by Bugenhagen (Pomeranus), Osiander, Gütel, Link, Corvin, Mathesius etc. open before our eyes an abyss that must make one shudder. „Boys that have hardly left the cradle, run already after the girls,“ „impurity and adultery are the most common things,“ „adultery is only made fun of,“ „women and girls are not safe even amongst their blood-relations,“ „impurity is the fashion, and adultery the order of the day,“ such and similar complaints are met with everywhere in their writings.([53]) The secular authorities and the Lutheran synods found it necessary to pass special laws, to stem, if possible, the torrent of impurity. The official and judicial records of Hessen, Ansbach, Saxony, Würtenberg, Prussia, Braunschweig, Hannover, Mecklenburg, Schleswig, Holstein, Denmark and Sweden reveal a degree and a universality of moral corruption which seems almost incredible.([54])

Those who have to say so much about the corruption which had formerly existed amongst Catholics, either do not know or studiously ignore the much greater corruption which disgraced Lutheranism. They either forget or chose to forget the even more important fact, that this state of things was the necessary fruit of Luther's Evangelium. This says nothing whatever against the morality of Luther's friends and admirers of the present day. For fortunately the „Reformer's“ *brutal* views about sexual matters cannot be supposed to be entertained nowadays by any of them. His own followers would be ashamed to adopt and to propose them, as in fact few of his peculiar teachings are now upheld. But let the reader imagine the effect, which such views must have had upon people, to whom every word from the „Evangelist's“ mouth was Gospeltruth, especially when it brought more freedom. They were plainly told that, outside the matrimonial state, chastity was an

([53]) For a long list of quotations from Protestants of Luther's time on this point see Döllinger, II. 432 seqq.

([54]) For extracts from those documents see Döll. l. c.

absolute impossibility, just as it would be an impossibility to live without food or drink, except in very rare cases, one in a thousand, when the gift of purity would have to be considered as a miracle.([55]) What then were the young people to do, before they were married? What was to become of the thousands and thousands in every country, in every province, nay in many towns, who for one reason or another had no chance of marrying at all? Had not everyone of them a right to excuse sexual excesses by saying: Dr. Martin Luther teaches that I cannot remain chaste, and of course I cannot expect a miracle in my own case? Not Catholics only saw the nexus between Luther's teaching and the growing immorality as between cause and effect. Sylvester Czecanovius, a Protestant, expressed the same opinion.([56])

Many eminent men, who had at first expected a great deal from Luther's energy for the suppression of really existing evils, who had praised and encouraged him, left his cause in disgust. We will name amongst them George Wizel, Ulrich Zasius, Willibald Pirkheimer and Erasmus of Rotterdam. Their writings bear witness, that nothing helped so much to open their eyes, as the natural fruits of Luther's Evangelium.([57])

([55]) We have given Luther's words on this point in the chapter on matrimony.

([56]) Döll. II. 440. The same Czecanovius has also some very cutting remarks about the married protestant ministers of the 16th century.

([57]) Hoc novum Evangelium gignit novum hominum genus, praefractos, impudentes, fucatos, maledicos, mendaces, sycophantas, inter se discordes, .. seditiosos, furiosos, rabulas. Erasmi epp. 19.

Olim Evangelium ex ferocibus reddebat mites, ex rapacibus benignos, ex turbulentis pacificos, ex maledicis benedicos: hi redduntur furiosi, rapiunt per fraudem aliena, concitant ubique tumultus, male-

dicunt etiam de benemerentibus. Novos hypocritas, novos tyrannos video, ac *ne micam quidem evangelici spiritus.* Erasmi opp. III. 819.

Vita vulgi evangelici adeo evangelica non est, ut me millies et iterum millies ejus puduerit. Eo crescunt convitia, irae, perjuria, jurgia, ut ea etiam magistratus vetare cogatur ... commessationes, crapulae, ebrietates, lasciviae, turpiloquia, eutrapelia omnem excedunt modum in turba ista, idque adeo, ut pro peccatis haec propemodum nemo ducat. Concionatores dicunt aliquando in ebrietatem, ipsi saepissime ebrii ... Avaritia incomparabilis est ... Praetereo adulteria, divortia, susurra, murmura, caeteraque tenebrarum opera

It would seem natural, that people, who enjoyed the comfortableness of Luther's Evangelium and, according to his own frequently repeated statement, had almost without exception lapsed into the greatest worldliness — not caring in the least for sin, since they believed — should feel terrorstricken at the approach of death. To his greatest grief Luther had to witness repeatedly, when the plague broke out, a panic and a consternation amongst the people, which, as he says, had been unknown in papistical times. In trying to give an explanation of this disagreeable fact, he fell of course back on the supposition, that it must be the work of the devil. In 1527 he thought that it was the devil's intention, to ruin the University of Wittenberg — on account of the importance it possessed through Luther and his friends and the pure „Evangelium", which they made shine from there over the world.([58]) „People fly from each other — he wrote in 1539, when the plague had reappeared — so that it is impossible to find a bloodletter or a nurse. I think the devil has possessed the people with a true pestilence; they are so abominably afraid, that a brother will run away from his brother, a son from his parents."([59])   „There has been here no small

quibus haec secta decorata est. Marc est vitiorum, quo secta circumfusa est: ego hujus vix pauculas guttas attigi ... Constantia nulla nisi in malo, fortitudo nulla nisi in epotandis cyathis, temperantia nulla nisi a bono. Justitiae satis habet, qui fidem habet; nihil injustum scilicet potest committere ... Auctor sectae suos istos alicubi increpans dicit, eos decies Sodomitis pejores esse; quo minus mihi vitio vertendum, quod eos suis depinxi coloribus, servata tamen aurea mediocritate. Wicelius, Retectio Lutherismi.

Omnes Evangelium in ore habere video, cum reipsa nil minus faciunt, quam quod illud exigit. Willib. Pirkheimer, ap. Döll. I. 173.

We should not have given these quotations, if the grave charges contained in them were not fully borne out by Luther's own statements.

([58]) Mirus est hominum pavor et fuga, ut tale monstrum Satanae antea non viderim; adeo terret, imo gaudet se posse sic corda pavefacere, scilicet ut dispergat et disperdat unicam istam Academiam, quam odit non frustra prae omnibus aliis. De Wette III. 191. — Pestem nostram superat suus rumor longissime, quod facit fuga ista et metus inauditus nostrorum.
                                    Ibid. 205.

([59]) De Wette V. 219. — This is also confirmed by Wicelius in his Retectio Lutherismi: Nemo nunc fere aegrotos invisit, nemo contrectare pestilentes amplius au-

hardheartedness amongst relations . . . Satan has smitten
few with the plague, but strikes down all with an incredible
fear." ([60]) In a letter to Amsdorf Luther acknowledges
that such fear and hardheartedness had been unknown
under the Pope, and in trying to account for the change,
he totally upsets his favourite theory, that Popery leaves
the conscience unsatisfied, but that his Evangelium produces
the greatest possible peace in the soul. ([61]) On this occasion
we hear from him that the Catholic faith produces a false
and deceptive calmness, whilst the light ot the Evangelium·
arouses in man a deeper feeling of his sinfulness.([62]) A
greater selfcontradiction could hardly be imagined. But
who could count Luther's selfcontradictions?

The „Reformer" was fully aware that his adversaries
would make the best use of the corruption existing amongst
the Evangelicals, to put his Evangelium to the test with
the words of Christ: By their fruits you shall known them.
„These things cause worldly-minded people to say: It it
were a holy and blessed doctrine, it would make the people
better and more pious." ([63]) „All the fault is thrown on the

---

det, nemo vel eminus videre, cepit
omnium animos pavor. See also
Döllinger I. 83.

([60]) De Wette V. 225.

([61]) See chapter on Evangelium,
page 140.

([62]) Miror quod quo copiosior
est vitae in Christo praedicatio,
hoc major est in populo pavor
mortis, sive quod antea, dum sub
Papa falsa spe vitae mortem minus
timebant, nunc vero, vera spe vitae
proposita, sentiunt quam infirma
sit natura ad credendum victori
mortis, sive quod Deus nos tentat
infirmitate et sinit in timore ita
Satanam plus audere et valere...
Sicut dum in Papatu fuimus, peccatum non solum non sensimus, sed
justitiam esse securi praesume-
bamus. Nunc securitate per cognitionem peccati sublata, timemus
plus quam oportet. De Wette V.
134. — The difficulty arising from

the frequent selfcontradictions of
Luther is easily solved by him:
His adversaries are asses, far too
stupid to understand him. He
writes to Melanchthon on this point:
Quod adversarii colligunt contradictiones ex meis libris, etiam faciunt
pro gloria suae sapientiae ostendenda. Quomodo isti asini contradictiones nostrae doctrinae judicent,
qui neutram partem contradicto-
riorum intelligunt? Quid enim
nostra doctrina aliud esse potest
in oculis impiorum, quam mera
contradictoria, cum simul exigat
et damnet opera, simul tollat et
restituat ritus, simul magistratum
colat et arguat, simul peccatum
asserat et neget? De Wette IV.
103. In his „Lutherus septiceps"
(Parisiis 1563) Cochlaeus has gathered a large number of Luther's selfcontradictions on 45 different points.

([63]) Walch XIII. 2550.

Evangelium; many begin to say: Would to God, we had
remained under the Pope! Behold, this is the fruit of the
Evangelium, that everywhere things are in such a bad
state". ([64])   Of course he would never allow that the corruption was the direct effect of his teaching on the masses.
„The Papists etc. cry out against us . . . Are the people
becoming any better? . . .   There is some appearance in
this, but if you look at it in the proper light, it is all
mere nonsense". ([65])   He protests against the conclusion:
this theologian is bad, ergo his theology is bad; this lawyer
is a villain, ergo the law itself is nothing but villainy. ([66])
Quite right too, but what, if the theologian should be bad
through the practical application of his theology? or if
the lawyer should have become a villain through a certain code?

What then was, according to Luther, the cause of
that corruption amongst his followers, which to his greatest
grief „raised such a stench" against the Evangelium?
At times he thought his simple Evangelium was so very
simple, that the people got sick and tired of hearing it
over and over again. „Now they say: If you can preach
about nothing but Christ and faith, we have had quite
enough of that, we have heard it often enough." ([67]) But
as a rule he consoled himself with his favourite idea, which
in most difficulties was his last and final refuge, viz. that
it was all „the work of the devil, who excites the hearts
against the word of God." No man has ever charged the
devil with having perpetrated more evil than Luther lays
at his door. ([68])

Let us come to the disrespect shown to the ministers
of the „reformed" Church. What man did ever more or

([64]) Walch VIII. 1012.
([65]) Walch XII. 1120.
([66]) Walch V. 114.
([67]) Walch XIII. 31. — Cfr.
Comment. in Gal. Wittenb. V.
433n: Satan privatim abducit homines etiam bonos ab Evangelio
nimia saturitate. Illa enim diligens

et quotidiana tractatio verbi nauseam et contemptum plerisque
affert.

([68]) He even complains in a
letter to his Kate, that the devil
has spoiled all the beer! De Wette
V. 788.

could do more than Luther had done, to discredit the clergy
in the eyes of the people? Not only the clergy of former
times and the then existing Catholic clergy, but clergy
simpliciter! He had told the people, that the priests had
acquired and maintained their influence only through a
shameful usurpation; he had told them that everybody had
a right to judge about truth and to explain holy Scripture
according to his own head; he had ridiculed ordination in
every possible way.

When his friend A. Lauterbach was refused a place
as chaplain because he was not ordained, he answered that
he considered himself sufficiently ordained through the
fact of his having a wife, who had been a nun. Luther
highly approved of this answer.([69]) Luther also boasted
that he had consecrated Amsdorf as Bishop of Naumburg
„without chrism, or butter, or lard, or bacon, or tar, or
grease" etc.([70]) „In the New Testament, he had said,
there are no visible priests, except those, whom the devil
has made such." ([71]) „Faith is the right sacerdotal office,
faith makes of all of us priests and priestesses." ([72])
„Whosoever has crawled out of the baptismal font, is ordained like a priest, or bishop, or pope." ([73]) „Everybody
has power to preach, it is only for the sake of maintaining
order, that out of the whole number one must be chosen
to preach, but he may be deposed at any moment."([74])
He had given to the congregations the power to judge
the minister's doctrine and to send him away, whenever
they liked. ([75]) „The teaching shall be subject to the mul-
titude([76]); the congregation shall judge and we must stand
by their judgment. This christian, divine and apostolical
order has been upset by the tyrants, by the Pope and his
followers."([77])

([69]) Tischr. II. c. 20. §. 22. Da
sprach der Doctor: Dem Bischof ist
recht und wohl geantwortet.

([70]) Hase. Kirchengesch. 432.
([71]) Vom Missbrauch der Messen.
Walch XIX. 1311.
([72]) Altenb. Edit. I. 523.

([73]) Erl. 21, 174.
([74]) Walch IX. 703.
([75]) Walch X. 1808.
([76]) „Die Lehre soll dem Haufen
unterthan sein."
([77]) Walch XI. 210.

How then can Luther blame the people, when they merely carry out his teaching in practice, when they say: We do not want preachers; we can preach ourselves and judge for ourselves; we cannot do without cowherds, but we can do very well without pastors? In this as in so many other points the „Reformer" sowed the wind and reaped the whirlwind.

As we have frequently seen, Luther likes proudly to couple his own name with that of the great S. Paul. He might !have derived some profit from reflecting on the fruits of his own work and on those of S. Paul's apostolical labours. „My dearly beloved brethren . . . my joy and my crown",([78]) and again: „You became followers of us and of the Lord . . . so that you were made a pattern to all that believe in Macedonia and in Achaja."([79])

Compare to this the words of Luther: „We profligate Germans are abominable hogs."([80]) „You pigs, hounds, ranters, you irrational asses!"([81]) „Our German nation are a wild, savage nation, half devils, half men."([82])

„My joy and my crown!"

([78]) Phil. IV. 1.
([79]) I. Thess. I. 6. 7.
([80]) Walch XX. 1014.

([81]) Ibid. 1015
([82]) Ibid. 1633

Chapter XXI.

Luther on bigamy.

John said to him: Is is not lawful for thee
to have her.

Matth. XIV. 4.

May God preserve your Highness! We
are ready to serve your Highness. Your
Highness' willing and humble servants.

M. Luther. Ph. Melanchthon etc.

De Wette V. 241.

The sanction given by the „Reformer" to the bigamy
of Philip, Landgraf of Hessen, is, according to Köstlin (¹)
„the greatest scandal" and „the darkest stain on the history
of the Reformation and on the life of Luther."

When in 1524 Carlstadt, then at Orlamünde, advocated
polygamy, Brück, the Chancellor of the Duke of Saxe-
Weimar, consulted Luther on this point. The reply was
that such a thing could [not be considered as forbidden
in the new Law. Let the prince answer: „The husband
must, by the word of God, be sure and certain in his own
conscience, that it is lawful to him. Let him enquire of
those who can make him sure through the word of God;
whether this be done by Carlstadt or by anyone else this
matters not to the prince. For if the man is uncertain,
he cannot become certain through the consent of the prince,
who in a matter of this sort cannot decide anything. It
is the duty of the priests, to answer with the word of

(¹) II. 481. 486.

God . . . *I confess that if a man wishes to marry several wives, I cannot forbid it,* nor is it in opposition to the Holy Scriptures; but I would not that such an example should be introduced amongst Christians, who ought to omit even lawful things for the sake of avoiding scandal and leading a pure life, as S. Paul demands. For it is very unbecoming to Christians, eagerly to pursue, for their own comfort, their liberty to its last consequences(²) and yet to neglect the common and necessary duties of charity. Therefore I have not in my preaching opened this window, and I hardly believe, a Christian can be so far abandoned by God, that a man who by God's action is hindered (from the use of conjugal rights) should be unable to contain himself. But let things go where they go. Perhaps they will even introduce circumcision at Orlamünde and will become Jews entirely."(³)

Philip of Hessen, a most licentious man, must have heard rumours of Luther's free views about matrimony at a very early date. For even before he was married he said to him, when he met him at Worms: „I hear, Doctor, you teach, that when a man gets old and becomes unfit for the marriage debt, the wife may take another husband." „And he laughed, says Luther in his own report of this interview, for the counsillors had put that into his head. I too laughed and said: O no, Your Grace, you ought

(²) Let the reader remember how much Luther on all occasions inveighs against the socalled evangelical counsels. Yet in this place he himself distinguishes between that which is good and that which is better, between that which is lawful and that which is advisable.

(³) Viro qui secundam uxorem consilio Carlstadii petit, sic respondeat Princeps: Oportere ipsum maritum sua propria conscientia esse firmum ac certum per verbum Dei, sibi haec licere. Eos ergo requirat, qui verbo Dei eum tutum reddant: si is Carlstadius vel alius fuerit, nihil ad Principem ... Ego sane fateor, me non posse prohibere, si quis plures uxores velit ducere, nec repugnat sacris literis. Verumtamen apud Christianos id exempli nollem primo introduci ... Vehementer enim dedecet Christianos summa et novissima libertatis tam anxie pro suis commodis sectari, et tamen vulgaria illa et necessaria charitatis negligere. Ideo in sermone meo nolui hanc fenestram aperire, et vix credo, sic desertum a Deo Christianum, ut non queat continere conjux (conjuge?) divinitus impedita.

De Wette II. 459.

not to speak thus."(⁴)   In 1523 Philip married a daughter
of Duke George of Saxony, but he did not feel contented
with only one wife. Three years after his marriage he asked
the „Reformer" whether or not it would be lawful for
him to take another.

Luther strongly *advised* him not to take such a step,
not only on account of the scandal which would certainly
follow, but also because no divine word existed to justify
it. But he does not say: It is unlawful, on the contrary,
his words clearly express his opinion that bigamy may be
lawful. „I should not know how to counsel it, but must
advise the contrary, especially to Christians, except if there
should be great necessity, as in the case where the wife
suffers from leprosy or is forcibly taken away." (⁵)

This answer of Luther checked for some time the
aspirations of the Landgraf, but his licentiousness continued. According to his own confession he had not remained faithful to his wife for three weeks;(⁶) at last he was
afflicted with a shameful disease. He must have conceived
fresh hopes of seeing his desire of having two wives realized
from a sermon which Luther preached in the following
year 1527, and in which „the difficult biblical question"
(as Köstlin calls it) „Monogamy or polygamy?" was settled
without further hesitation. In this sermon Luther calls
Abraham „a true, nay perfect Christian", who has lived
in the most evangelical way, in the spirit of God and in
faith. He says further that Abraham's life is an *example*.
„But the question arises, as it is forbidden to have more
than one wife, how can we justify him and say that he
has remained a Christian? First one might simply say, that
this (privilege) has been abolished by the Evangelium, when
Christ said: From the beginning it was not so; likewise
S. Paul to the Corinthians: Let every man have his wife

(⁴) Walch XV. 2247.   De Wette III. 139. But there it
(⁵) De Wette-Seidemann VI. £o.   is difficult to get at his real
— Of the same year 1526 there   meaning.
is another answer of Luther to   (⁶) Janssen III. 55.
the same question about polygamy.

and let every woman have her husband. Hence we might
say that in Abraham we find some exterior works, which
are now abolished. But this cannot be sufficient, for we
must endeavour to show that he is finally justified. For
in truth, everything that we find done exteriorly by the
Fathers in the old Testament, must be free, not forbidden.
Thus circumcision is abolished, but not in such a manner
that if a man were to observe it, he would commit a sin;
it is free, it is neither a sin, nor a good deed." In the
same manner Luther judges about the paschal lamb and
the rites connected with the eating of it, then he continues:
„Thus amongst other examples of the Fathers this too must
pass, that they have taken many wives, this too must have
been free . . . *It is not forbidden that a man should have
more than one wife. I could not forbid it today*. But I
would not advise it." (⁷) This was said in a public sermon
which was printed and scattered in a number of editions.
The only retractation that Luther ever made is contained
in his *latin* Commentary on Genesis, as we shall see later on.

In 1539 Philip of Hessen fell in love with a certain
Margaretha von Sala, a lady of honour to his sister, the
dowager Duchess of Rochlitz.(⁸) She consented to become
his second wife, during the lifetime of the first, with whom
she was willing to share the affection of the common husband. Her mother too approved of this singular match,
on condition that the approval of the Fathers of the Reformation should be obtained and that the wedding should
take place before competent witnesses of high standing.
Butzer, who had been working at Strassburg for a long time,
became the Landgraf's confidential agent and was despatched
to Wittenberg to lay the matter before Luther. The reasons
he had to urge in favour of Philip's application were contained partly in a written document, partly were they to be
communicated by word of mouth. Of the latter reasons

(⁷) Erl. 33. 322 seqq.
(⁸) Seckend. l. III. Sect. 21.
§ 79. add. III. where a curious

defence of the proceedings may
be seen.

Seckendorf wishes his readers to suppose that they must have been even more weighty than the former,([9]) but as they are not extant, we have to be satisfied with the written document, which is dated Melsungen, Sunday after S. Catherine's 1539 and signed by Philipp himself. In this application the landgraf stated that he lived cortinually in adultery and that he was afraid he might suddenly be called away from this world in his unhappy sinful state, for instance, if he should have to go to war on account of the cause of the Evangelium. He stated moreover that with only one wife (of whom he had already seven children and who was again pregnant when he wrote) *he neither could nor would abstain from impurity.* He applied for permission to take an additional wife, merely „to escape from the snares of the devil." The reasons on which he based his application were such that the „Reformers" found themselves unable to resist them. They are partly taken from the Bible (which of course he had a perfect right to interpret, as the „spirit" moved him), partly did they touch the interest of the „Evangelium." Neither in the Old nor in the New Testament, he said, neither by the Prophets nor by the Apostles had bigamy been forbidden. S. Paul speaks of many who shall not enter the kingdom of heaven, but *those that have two wives, do not appear amongst that number!* S. Paul moreover says clearly that a Bishop shall be the husband of only one wife, likewise the ministers, but he does not say the same of anyone else. If it had been necessary that everybody should be satisfied with only one wife, he would have said so and would have forbidden to have more than one, without any restriction! Philip also reminded the Fathers of the Reformation that he was aware of the advice given by Melanchthon to Henry VIII, king of England, when the latter contemplated

---

([9]) Fortassis tamen rationes quas allegavit, ejus non erant ponderis ut Lutherum et Melanchthonem movissent, nisi alias et graviores Bucero oretenus referendas commisisset, aut ipse in se recepisset, conscientiae testimonio Deo probandas.

Ibid. p. 278.

a divorce from Catherine of Arragon in order to marry
Anne Boleyn. The advice had been, that it would be far
better to take an additional wife, as polygamy was not
forbidden by Divine law. ([10])

If Luther had been approached by any private man
with such reasons, he would not only have rejected the
application, but considering his character, he would in all
probability have poured out a flood of invectives over
the unlucky applicant. But here the case was different.
It was the question of the „tender conscience" of a prince
of the Empire, of a friend of the „Evangelium", who
moreover gave some broad hints as to what he meant to
do, according as the decision would be given for him or
against him. Also Köstlin remarks: ([11]) „Would it not
have been much more difficult to a private person, to obtain such confidential advice? Have there not been motives
at work, which must appear strange to us, especially in
Luther, the witness of truth, always inflexible and sharp
towards high and low?"

Philip begged to be heard, that he might be able to
live and to die with a peaceful concience and *to carry out
the evangelical business all the more freely* and in a Christian manner." „May, what I ask, be granted to me in the
name of God, that I may be able to live and to die more
joyfully for the cause of the Evangelium. On my part
I will do everything in my power that is christian and
right, *whether they demand monastic property or similar
things."* The Landgraf thinks that, should the „Reformers"
refuse to grant his request, he might perhaps obtain it
from the Emperor, by bribing some of the Imperial

([10]) Si vult rex successioni pro-
spicere quanto satius est, id facere
sine infamia prioris conjugii. Ac
potest id fieri sine ullo periculo
conscientiae cujuscumque aut in-
famiae per polygamiam. Etsi enim
non velim concedere polygamiam
vulgo, dixi enim supra nos non
ferre leges, tamen in hoc casu
propter magnam utilitatem regni,
fortassis etiam propter conscientiam regis sic pronuntio: tutis-
simum esse regi si ducat secundam
uxorem, priori non abjecta, quia
certum est, polygamiam non esse
prohibitam jure Divino.

Corp. Reform. II. 526.

([11]) II. 486.

Counsillors. Not that he means to abandon the Evangelium! By no means! But he might perhaps be drawn
into other business, which would not be so profitable to
the cause of the Reformation!([12]) If the Reformers could
not publicly give countenance to a double marriage, they
might at least give a written approval of the step, for the
sake of the Landgraf's conscience.([13])

This really disgusting mixture of licentiousness, hypocrisy, threats and promises sorely perplexed the theologians
of Wittenberg, but after a few days they despatched the
permission as requested, *on condition that the matter should
be kept secret.* They first congratulate His Highuess on his
recovery — we know from what illness —" for the Church
is poor and miserable, small and desolate, and is indeed
in want of *righteous rulers!*" ([14]) — they deplore his troubles of conscience and strongly exhort him, with many
Scripture texts, to abstain from adultery for the future. As
to his request, it would not be advisable to establish
a general law allowing polygamy to everybody, on account of the scandal and difficulties which would arise.
„But in certain cases a dispensation may be granted."([15])
(They are the same cases as those mentioned by Luther
in his reply to Philip A. D. 1526). After an enumeration
of the reasons against the dispensation, the Reformers
have the courage to tell the Landgraf that in all probability even two wives will not be sufficient for him. But

---

([12]) That Luther and Melanchthon understood this hint, is
evident from a letter of the latter
to Veit Dietrich d. d. 1 Sept. 1540
„He threatened us with secession,
if we did not advise him."
     Corp. Reform. III. 1081.
   ([13]) Rive, Die Ehe, 184 seqq.
Janssen II. 404 seqq. Riffel II. 533.
   ([14]) Nam prout Celsitudo Vestra
videt, paupercula et misera Ecclesia est, exigua et derelicta, indigens
probis dominis regentibus.
     De Wette V. 237.
   ([15]) Nunc suadere non possumus

ut introducatur publice et velut
lege sanciatur permissio, plures
quam unam uxorem ducendi ...
Certis tamen casibus locus est
dispensationi. Si quis apud exteras
nationes captivus, ad curam corporis et sanitatem sibi alteram
uxorem superduceret, vel si quis
haberet leprosam, his casibus alteram ducere cum consilio sui
pastoris, non intentione novam
legem inducendi, sed suae neces-
sitati consulendi, hunc nescimus
qua ratione damnare liceret.
     De Wette V. 238.

if His Highness does not abstain from an impure life,
which according to his own statement is impossible, it is
better that he should provide for the peace and security
of his conscience by an additional marriage." For what
has been allowed about matrimony in the law of Moses,
has not been revoked or forbidden by the Evangelium."([16])
We see that *here* Moses is welcome, but when he urges
a law, he is „worse than the Pope and the devil," and deserves to be stoned to death. However the marriage
must be a secret one, known only to the parties and to a
few reliable persons, who must have knowledge of it under
the seal of confession. Before the eyes of the world it
will pass as concubinage; this does not matter at all, for
it is nothing unusual that princes keep concubines.([17]) It
will be better that apparently the Landgraf should follow
this custom, whilst in point of fact his conscience will be
easy with the knowledge thas he lives in lawful matrimony. The matter had better not be brought before the
Emperor, for (mark the kind and tender solicitude and
the devoted loyalty of the Fathers of the Reformation!)
it is greatly to be feared that he, full of Papistical, Car-
dinalitial, Italian, Spanish and Saracenic faith, would give

([16]) Si Vestra Cels. ab impudica
vita non abstineat, quod dicit, sibi
impossibile, optaremus, Cels. Vestram in meliori statu esse coram
Deo, et secura conscientia vivere,
ad propriae animae salutem et di-
tionum ac subditorum emolumen-
tum. Quodsi denique Vestra Cels.
omnino concluserit adhuc unam
conjugem ducere, juramus id secreto faciendum uti superius de
dispensatione dictum, nempe ut
tantum Vestrae Cels., illi personae
ac paucis personis fidelibus constet
Cels. Vestrae animus et conscientia sub sigillo confessionis. Hinc
non sequuntur alicujus momenti
contradictiones aut scandala· nihil
enim est inusitati. Principes con-
cubinas alere: et quamvis non omnibus e plebe constaret ratio, tamen prudentiores intelligerent, et
magis placeret haec modesta (!)
vivendi ratio, quam adulterium
et alii belluini et impudici actus:
nec curandi aliorum sermones, si
recte cum conscientia agatur,‽sic
et in tantum hoc approbamus.
Nam quod circa matrimonium in
lege Mosis fuit permissum, Evangelium non revocat aut vetat, quod
externum regimen non immutat,
sed adfert aeternam justitiam ad
aeternam vitam, et orditur veram
obedientiam erga Deum et conatur
corruptam naturam reparare.
                 De Wette l. c.
([17]) We have proved in the
chapter on matrimony that Luther
absolutely allows concubines to
princes.

no attention to your Highness' demand!([18]) It is better to
be considered by the Emperor as an adulterer, and His
Highness had better keep away altogether from „that faithless and deceitful man." „It is to be wished that Christian
princes had nothing to do with his faithless practices."
„May God preserve Your Highness! We are ready to serve
Your Highness! Your Highness' willingand humble servants,
Martinus Lutherus, Philippus Melanchthon, Martinus Bucerus, Antonius Corvinus etc."

It might seem as if the endeavours of Philip of Hessen,
to obtain the approbation of Luther before he took the
shameful step he meditated, really bore witness to the tenderness of his conscience. But it must not be forgotten
that bigamy was a crime punishable with death, according
to the German law. In taking that step which in less
turbulent times might have brought the most serious consequences on his head, it was the Landgraf's interest, not
to appear without the support of an authority. Hence he
broke the matter also to the Elector of Saxony, to secure
whose approbation he made great promises, even with
regard to a future election to the Imperial throne. The
Elector, before whom Bucer appeared as agent, seemed
shocked at the idea of a double marriage and strongly

([18]) Quod attinet ad consilium
hanc rem apud Caesarem tractandi,
existimamus, illum adulterium inter minora peccata numerare: nam
magnopere verendum, illum Papistica, Cardinalitia, Italica, Hispani-
ca, Saracenica imbutum fide, non
curaturum Vestrae Celsitudinis
postulatum et in proprium emolu-
mentum vanis verbis sustentatu-
rum, sicut intelligimus perfidum ac
fallacem virum esse, morisque Germanici oblitum. Videt Cels. Vestra
ipsa, quod nullis necessitatibus
christianis sincere consulit. Turcam sinit imperturbatum, excitat
tantum rebelliones in Germania
ut potentiam Burgundicam etferat.
Quare optandum ut nulli Christiani principes illius infidis machin-
ationibus se immisceant. De Wette
l.c. — Köstlin (II. 485) says: „It must
not be forgotten that at that time
in the Catholic Church a dispensation from the law of monogamy,
if it were given by the Pope, was
not considered as absolutely impossible." It would be interesting
to know on what grounds Mr. Köstlin bases his startling assertion.
Perhaps on the old fable about
the Count of Gleichen and his two
wives? We are glad to be able
to call his attention to the words
of the Reformers, according to
whom the Papistical Emperor
would reject an application for
the same dispensation.

dissuaded it, but concluded just like the Wittenberg Reformers: If it must be done, let it be done, only let it be kept quiet and let the second wife be considered by the world merely as a concubine. Better this apparent ignominy than the scandal of an open, though lawful, double marriage!([19]) Philips own wife, the daughter of George of Saxony, gave a written consent to the shameful arrangement, after „he had clearly proved to her that is was not against God.“ But she received the promise that she was to remain the chief wife, and only *her* children were to have a right to the honours and political privileges of the father. ([20])

On the 13th of February 1540 Christina gave birth to a daughter; three weeks later, on the 4th of March, after the new bride's scruples had been allayed by the scriptural examples of Esther and Abigail, Philip married at Rotenburg his second wife; who was to share his affections with the mother of his eight children. Melanchthon and Bucer were present at the ceremony. The officiating minister was Dionysius Melander, whose name is also under the letter which granted the dispensation. No doubt he was the right man in the right place, *since he had three wives living*. With greater unction therefore was he able „according to the grace given to him“, to dwell in the wedding sermon on the peace of conscience with which this matrimonial alliance might be entered into, and to inveigh

---

([19]) Si vero nullo modo desistere vellet (Landgravius), secretum esse necessarium ostendit (Elector), et ut conjugium illud apud alios pro mero contubernio, concubinatu et pellicatu venditetur: satius esse ut hanc ignominiam subeat(but according to Luther there was no ignominy in it!) quam cum multis magnatibus communem habiturus esset, quam ut pro digamo haberetur. Seckend. l. c. p. 278. A thing is lawful before God and safe in conscience, yet it must be carefully hidden under the appearance of adultery! This is more than one can understand!

([20]) Produxit Bucerus Christinae Saxonicae, uxoris Landgravii, diploma, quod totum sua manu d. 11. Decembris in arce Spangenbergensi exaraverat, tum subscriptione et sigillo firmaverat, per quod in nuptias illas secundarias consensit, salvis tamen pactis suis dotalibus et juribus liberorum, quos ex landgravio susceperat.

Seckend. Ibid.

against the Papal tyranny which had for so long a time oppressed the freedom of Christians." (²¹)

In his congratulating letter (10. April) Luther begged once more that the matter should be kept strictly secret. We do not say that the hogshead of Rhenish wine, for which he had to thank His Highness of Hessen a little later, was a douceur, but it was an expression of gratitude towards the man who had successfully freed Philip's tender conscience from „the snares of the devil".

But the Rotenburg scandal did not remain secret. The wedding itself had had too much of a public character, and the officiating minister, Dionysius Melander, began to preach openly from the pulpit, that digamy was a lawful and praiseworthy institution. In a very short time the transaction had become a public secret. This was a great sore to Luther, who tried many means to prevent the blame being attached to his own name. For some time he pretended even in the letters to his most intimate friends that he knew absolutely nothing about the whole affair. On the 2. of June he wrote to Lauterbach that he had heard of Margarethe von Sala giving birth to a child, but that he had no certain knowledge about the pretended double marriage of which people were talking. (²²) Again, a fortnight later, he thought that the future would show whether there was any truth in this monstrous rumour. (²³)

In a letter to the Elector of Saxony he bitterly complains that the Landgraf has not kept the matter secret,

(²¹) Heppe, quoted by Janssen III. 408.

(²²) De novis nuptiis Landgravii, quod petis, nihil possum scribere. Hoc quidem audivi, esse natum puerulum ex virginalibus de Sala. An sit verum nescio. Et si verum esset, et ipse agnosceret, se esse patrem, et matrem et prolem aleret, jure videretur facere. Si hinc natus est rumor, non sine causa est rumor. Tantum scio, et publica testimonia nuptiarum non sunt mihi ostensa... Sine igitur latrare qui latrant, donec res ipsa doceat, quid hoc monstri sit. De Principibus et principum negotiis non est temere pronuntiandum re incomperta.

De Wette V. 290.

(²³) Nihil hic, nisi hoc monstrum Landgravii, quod aliqui incipiunt mollire, aliqui negare, aliqui aliud agere ... Quidquid sit, dies declarabit propediem.   Ibid. 292.

contrary to the express injunction he had received, and repeats once more that the second wife ought to have been treated in public only as a concubine. And „had I known that the Landgraf might have satisfied his necessity with another person, as I hear now that he has with the Eschweg (this seems to have been the name of another of Philip's victims), no angel from heaven would have moved me to such advice."([24]) Where is here a vestige of consistency? First Luther gives his dispensation, to rescue Philip from adultery, and afterwards he regrets and deplores his own decision, because he finds that the occasion of adultery would not have been wanting to the prince!

To Melanchthon the disclosure of the secret was such a blow that he fell seriously ill and Luther had to console him in an exceedingly unctious letter in which he reminded his friend that Christ who had conquered Satan, would also conquer this scandal! In his own part in the matter the „dear man of God" found nothing scandalous, the scandal consisted merely in the publicity of the fact. „My Kate too bids you to be brave and joyful . . . Those words will remain: I have conquered the world and: You shall live because I live."([25])

([24]) Hette ich aber gewust, das der Landtgraff solche notturfft nhulengster wol gebüszet vnd buszen konte an andern, alsz ich nhu erst erfare an der zu Eszhweg, sollte mich freilich kein engel zu solchem rath gebracht haben. Seidemann, Lauterbach's Tagebuch, Append. 196.

([25]) De Macedonico negotio (on several occasions Luther calls Philip of Hessen „the young Macedonian") velim ne affligeres te nimium, postquam eo res venit, ut nec moerore nec gaudio possit illi consuli. Quare ergo frustra nos occidimus, aut tristitia impedimus cognitionem victoris illius omnium mortium et tristitiarum? Qui enim vicit diabolum et judicavit principem hujus mundi, nonne et cum eo judicavit et vicit hoc scandalum? Nam si etiam praesens hoc scandalum desinat, dabit (a Germanism, „es wird geben," there will be) deinde alias et forte majores turbas scandalorum, quas, si vivemus, in eodem tamen victore vincemus, et ridebimus quoque. Nihil est malorum vel inferni, de quo ille non dixerit et voluerit sese intelligi: Ego vici mundum, confidite ... Valeat Satan, propter ipsum nec moereamus nec tristemur: in Christo autem Domino laetemur et exultemus, ipse deducet in nihilum omnes inimicos nostros. Nondum sumus in Davidis exemplo,

Amongst the members of the Lutheran Church and
especially amongst the ministers and theologians who were
at that time assembled at Hagenau great anxiety prevailed
on account of Philip's double marriage. Butzer, the chief
agent in the matter, was afraid of evil consequences
„because so very few judge according to the word of
God"; together with other theologians he urged the Landgraf to deny the truth of the rumour. For such a step
he adduced the examples of the patriarchs, judges and
kings of the Old Testament, nay of God himself. „In
like manner we too must not only keep back from our
enemies such truth as they might make use of to our
detriment, but by contrary false representation (durch
widerwärtigen Wahn) we must mislead them." He even
asked Philip to get his second wife to sign, before a
public notary, a document, in which she was to acknowledge herself only as a concubine, „such as God has allowed to his dear friends." „The world has frequently to be
kept from the knowledge of truth through Angels or Saints.
Of such things the Bible is full."([26])

If a Catholic, especially a Jesuit, had ever used such
language, what an outcry there would be! But it is only
Butzer that speaks, one of the dii minorum gentium of
the Reformation. The Landgraf himself was indignant
at the proposal made to him. As the thing had been
declared lawful before God and founded on Holy Scripture,
he did not care in the least, how it was judged by others.
„If it is right in conscience before the almighty, eternal,
immortal God, what do I care for the cursed, sodomitical,
usurious, drunken world?" Nay, he threatened Luther, in
case that the latter should try to withdraw his countenance.
In that case „you will have to remember that we should

cujus causa longe desperatior fuit,
nec tamen cecidit, nec ista causa
cadet. Cur ergo te maceras, cum
finalis causa stet certe, id est, vic-
toria Christi, etsi formalis et media nonnihil deformetur isto scan-

dalo. Mea quoque Ketha jubet
te fortem ac laetum esse.
            De Wette V. 294.
    ([26]) Lenz, quoted by Janssen,
III. 430.

be forced to put before the accusers your written memorial and your signature, so as to show what has been allowed to us." Luther's own advice was in harmony with that of Butzer, that the rumour should be met with a flat contradiction. For „a secret *yes* must remain a public *no* and viceversa." ([27]) He went so far as to say: „What would it matter, if for the sake of greater good and of the Christian Church one were to tell a big lie? (eine gute starke Lüge)." ([28]) At the meeting at Eisenach he declared: „It is impossible to defend this cause publicly ... Before I defend this cause publicly, I shall either deny that such an answer has been given by me and Melanchthon (for it is a secret, and if it becomes public, it becomes nothing) or.... I will rather confess that I have made a foolish mistake and will ask pardon; the scandal is too intolerable." ([29])

But how was he to get over his own words in that sermon preached A. D. 1528, from which we have quoted above, when the Landgraf expressly appealed to them? „Before and afterwards I have taught on several occasions that the law of Moses must not be introduced again, though secretly in a case of necessity or also publicy, with the consent of the secular authorities (si magistratus jubeat) it would be lawful to use it as an exemple. Therefore though I would to an afflicted conscience give secret advice on account of necessity, to act according to the law or the example of Moses, I would not openly establish a law or an example. You cannot conclude: What another does through necessity, I do by right. In the case of starvation theft is committed with impunity, likewise manslaughter in the case of legitimate selfdefence. But these things

([27]) De Wette — Seidemann VI. 263.

([28]) See Janssen III. 432.

([29]) Impossibile est ut causa haec publice defendi queat ... Aut negabo responsum illud a me et Melanchthone datum esse (se-

cretum enim fuit et si publicetur nullum fiet) aut si haec inficiatio non subsistat ... errasse et desipuisse me fatebor potius et veniam petam; scandalum enim nimium est intolerabile.

Seckend. l. c. p. 280.

must not be alleged as examples, nor do they create a right. Necessity breaks the law, but does not make the law." ([30]) Indeed a wonderful paritas!

Invain do we look in the great „Reformer's" letters or in the letter of the Elector of Saxony ([31]) who also tried to over get the difficulty caused by the former words of Luther on this subject, or in Seckendorf for a solid and satisfactory answer to the following questions: If digamy is lawful, as it has been declared to be, why must it be kept secret? If it is part of the glorious evangelical liberty, to have with a good conscience two or more wives, why does not Luther grant to all his followers the liberty which his Evangelium has restored to the Christian Church? Is it lawful only to one and not to another? What necessity is required to make it lawful? Who judges of this necessity? And who has given Dr. Martin Luther the right to judge of it?

After all the best explanation will be, that the head of the Reformation was heartily ashamed of that decision, which he had given only through human respect and to prevent the loss of a powerful ally who was one of the columns of the new Church.

The Landgraf's threat to use eventually the document which granted him the dispensation roused Luther's anger. „I have this advantage, he answered, that Your Grace and even all devils have to bear witness and to confess: first, that it was a secret advice, secondly, that with all solicitude I have begged to prevent its becoming public, thirdly, that

---

([30]) Ap. Seckend. l. c.

([31]) The Elector wrote Landgravio concionem illam Lutheri acriter urgenti: Aliud est scribere et docere, quid in hoc vel illo casu Deo et scripturae non adversetur; aliud vero factum contra jura publica et morem universalem palam audere et defendere. In doctrina et confessione conscientia instruitur, quatenus ex necessitate excusari possit, et Canonistae quaedam scripserunt et concesserunt, quae utique in foro civili defendere nollent. Cum Lutherus scribit, se bigamiam non suadere, eo ipso indicat se nolle ut publice introducatur, et scopus concionis ejus is potissimum tunc fuit, ut Patriarchas a variis interpretum censuris defenderet, non vero ut Christianos ad licentiam provocaret. Ibid.

if it comes to the point, I am sure that not through me
it has been made public. As long as I have these three
things, *I would not advise the devil himself to start my
pen* . . . I am not so much afraid for myself, for when
it is a question of writing *I know how to wriggle out of
the matter* (mich herauszudrehen) and to leave Your Grace
in it, a thing which I do not mean to do if I can help
it."([32])

In his answer the Landgraf did not spare soft soap
to allay the wrath of the lion,([33]) but whilst he lavished
the most flattering compliments on him, he secretly did
his best to persuade the people at large that polygamy
was the proper thing. At his command one of his theologians, under the Pseudonym of Huldricus Neobulus, published to that effect a dialogue which cut Luther to the
quick.([34]) „Listen, he wrote, if you wish to hear my opinion of this book. Thus speaks D. Martin Luther about
this book Nebuli: He who follows this villain and his book
and, on the strength of it, takes more than one wife, thinking this to be a right, may the devil prepare for him a
bath at the bottom of hell! Amen! . . . If for a whole
year it did nothing but snow Nebulos, Hulderics and devils,
they should never make a right of it."([35])

For the rest he, „a rough Saxon," as he called himself,
soon got over the matter, much unlike Melanchthon.
Already in July he wrote to his Kate: „Your Grace must
know that, thank God, we are in perfect health; we

([32]) De Wette-Seidemann VI.
273 seqq.
([33]) Ego te absque adulatione
inter omnes homines pro primario
aestimo theologo ... virum te esse
agnosco, qui Deum respiciat.
    Seckend, l. c.
([34]) Illo viso vehementer exarsit
Lutherus. Seckend. l. c. 281. It
is more than probable that Butzer
was the author of this little book.
Some of his arguments presented,
as Döllinger (Die Ref. II 43) re-

marks, rather insuperable difficulties
to the Evangelicals. For instance
he said that to some people two
wives were necessary or that it
was at least advisable for them to
have more than one; nor could
it be said that if a man prayed,
God would give him grace to remain chaste whilst having only
one wife, for the same argument
would hold good with regard to
the chastity of the Catholic priests.
    ([35]) Seckend l. c.

gorge like Bohemians (but not much) and guzzle like Ger-
ans (but not much); but we are jolly. For His Grace of
Magdeburg, Bishop Amsdorf (whóm *hc* had consecrated
Bishop „without lard or bacon or grease") is our table-
companion. . . . Your Sweetheart (Dein Liebchen) Martin
L." (³⁶)

All the time that Philip's digamy was the subject of
universal talk, Luther maintained its validity before God, (³⁷)
nor has he ever, as far as we know, *publicly* retracted
the scandalous opinion which he had *publicly* stated in his
sermons. But towards the end of his life he made a retractation in his Commentary on the Book of Genesis, (³⁸)
where, after mentioning the history of Abraham and Agar,
he says: (³⁹) „From this fact we must not establish an
example, as if the same thing were lawful to us. The
circumstances will have to be considered. To us no promise of posterity is made, as it was made to Abraham."

With the introduction of the „Reformation" into
Philip's territory, public morality in Hessen had fallen tre-
mendously. The people had become so wild, a chronist

(³⁶) De Wette V. 298.

(³⁷) At Eisenach he declared:
Coram Deo defendi a se posse causam lantgravii ex secreto confessionis et necessitate, sed coram mundo
et jure ut loquitur, nunc regente
sive usitato, nec posse se, nec
velle cam defendere.
        Ap. Seckend. 1. c. 280.
(³⁸) In primum librum Mose
enarrationes. Norimbergae 1550.
The preface is dated Christmas
1544.
(³⁹) Ex hoc facto non est con-
stituendum exemplum, quasi nobis
eadem licet facere. Circumstantiae
enim considerandae sunt. Nobis
non est facta promissio seminis,
sicut Abrahae, et ut maxime habeas sterile conjugium, nihil inde
periculi est, etiamsi tota tua pro-
genies, ita volente Deo occidat...
Igitur singulare hoc conjugum

factum neutiquam in exemplum est
trahendum, praesertim in Novo
Testamento. Comment. in Gen.
tom. II f. 63в. — Melanchthon too
found it opportune to recant, when
the shameful proceedings of the
Anabaptists at Münster scandalized the whole world. „The Lord
Christ will have the married state,
as first it has been ordained by
God . . . he will not have it except between *two* persons. (Etliche
propositiones wider die Lehre der
Wiedertäufer, Walch XX. 2103.
prop. 20.) In the 21ˢᵗ proposition
he goes so far as to say, that polygamy, though allowed by God
to the Israelites in the Old Testament, is *against the law of nature.*
But perhaps he did not mean „the
law of nature" in the strictest sense
of the word.

of the period says [40], that it seemed „as if God had
given us his dear word and had freed us from the numberless abominations of Popery and its palpable idolatry only
that we should freely do and omit what we like". The
„reformed" Clergy threw the fault in great part upon the
noblemen, these retaliated by saying that numbers of the
ministers scandalized the people by drinking, gambling
and impurity.

The example of the Landgraf, especially when he
took an additional wife, was little apt to improve this state
of things.

Luther's decision in this case has not been forgotten. On
the strength of it Frederick William II. of Prussia received
from his Court theologians the permission to imitate Philip
of Hessen.

[40] Wigand Lanze, ap. Janssen III 411.

Chapter XXII

Luther's last years.

„I am free from avarice, the afflictions of
my body protect me from lust; only anger is
left.“
Luther. ap. Seckend. l. III. 643.

„They must be stupid fools, who say we
ought not to revile the Pope. Go on reviling
him, *especially when the devil troubles you about
justification.*“
Luther. Tischr. II. c. 3. § 53.

The evening of Luther's life was anything but calm
and peaceful. As far as his work was destructive, he had,
no doubt, been successful to a great extent. Favoured
by the corruption existing amongst the Clergy, by the dissatisfaction of the people, by the help of infidel allies, by
the protection of selfish princes, aided by great natural gifts,
which singled him out as a leader for a revolution, he had
succeeded, not in destroying the Papacy altogether, as
at one time he had devoutly hoped, but in extirpating its
power in a large part of Germany. But the sight of ruins is
hardly a sufficient recompense for a life's work, and that
which Luther had built up, was not of a nature to make him
feel satisfied. The letters of his closing years give us an
idea of the bitterness which filled his soul and of his outbursts of anger, when from every side the accounts of
the growing corruption amongst the people and of the
dissensions amongst the ministers kept pouring in. Numberless times he predicted that the last day was drawing

near (¹) and expressed his wish that it would come soon (²), or that he himself should soon be called away. (³) He was getting more and more morose and made himself objectionable to his friends by his bitterness. The friendship with Melanchthon had long been on the wane. Magister Philippus complained as early as 1538 in a letter to Veit Dietrich of the intolerable slavery which he was made to feel (⁴), and in 1544 he wrote again to Bucer that he would willingly leave Wittenberg, where he could not feel free (⁵). Melanchthon's tendency to soften down some of Luther's most objectionable teachings caused much dissension and aversion between the two chief „Reformers." Amsdorf warned his master against „the serpent he nourished in his bosom." (⁶)

The more Luther advanced in years, the more his thirst for hatred seemed to grow. He describes his own state in the words „I am free from avarice, from lust the afflictions of my body protect me, only anger in left to me", and no doubt, plenty of it was left; even that incredible

---

(¹) v. gr. Tischr. II. c. 28. § 3. 4.

(²) v. gr. in a letter to Propst: Minatur mundus ruinam: hoc est certum: ita furit Satan, ita brutescit mundus. Nisi quod unum illud solatium restat, diem illum brevi instare ... satur est verbi Dei idque coepit mire fastidire mundus.   De Wette V. 451.

(³) Ora pro me, ut hora bona migrem. Satur sum hujus vitae seu verius mortis acerbissimae. Ibid. 452. — Vale et ora pro me. ut Dominus mihi horam bonam concedat. Satis vixi et taedet diabolum vitae meae. et me odii diaboli. Ibid 467. — Ich habe lange genug gelebt, Gott beschere mir ein selig Stundlein, darin der faule unnütze Madensack unter die Erden komme zu seinem Volk, und den Wurmen zu Theil werde. Ibid. 638. — Ich halte dass keiner in hundred Jahren gelebt habe,

dem die Welt so feind gewesen sey als mir. Ich bin der Welt auch feind, und weiss nichts in tota vita, da ich Lust zu hätte und bin gar müde zu leben. Unser Herr Gott komme nur bald und nehme mich flugs hin. und sonderlich komme er mit seinem jüngsten Tage, ich will ihm gerne den Hals herstrecken, dass er ihn mit einem Donner dahinschlage, dass ich liege.
      Tischr. II. Append. §. 15.

(⁴) Qualis fueris, cum adesses, δοτλοτης meministi. Et tamen hunc scito nunc esse factum duriorem. Corp. Ref. III. 594 Luther's Kate also seems to have had her part in producing this dissatisfaction in Melanchthon. „Cum alia multa, tum maxime obstat η γυναικοτυραννις."
                                    Ibid. 398.

(⁵) Ibid. V. 474.
(⁶) Ibid. III. 503.

measure of it which he poured out over the Jews, the lawyers and the Pope, did not exhaust the stock, as he himself
tells us.

In our days, when the „semitic question“ attracts such
universal attention and produces so much strife in Germany, it is most interesting to see what Luther thought
about it. In his virulent book „About the Jews and their
lies“ (⁷) he not only plainly tells us his opinion, but at the
same time enables us to form a calm judgment as to his
charity and tolerance. He calls the Jews the worst plague
of Germany (⁸), he wishes they would as soon as possible
set out, bag and baggage, for their own country (⁹); he
bitterly complains that they feed on the sweat of the
nation (¹⁰). As we have seen before (¹¹), Luther found
many to join him in this complaint. But supposing the
evil had assumed the largest possible proportions, would
the seven remedies suggested by the Prophet of Wittenberg
be approved of by any sensible man? To say the least,

(⁷) „De Judaeis et eorum men-
daciis.“ Wittenberg edition vol.
VII. This latin translation is made
by Justus Jonas.

(⁸) Sunt vera pestilentia et lues
nocentissima in nostris terris.
                    Wittenb. VII. 203ʙ.

(⁹) Abeant in Syriam aut Assy-
riam, eant, equitent, currant, na-
vigent, volitent si alae dantur, in
suam terram.   Ibid. 209ʙ.

(¹⁰) Ipsi nos Christianos in nostra
propria terra captivos tenent, patiuntur nos laborare in sudore vultus
nostri. Interim sedent otiosi, fulti
pulvino, suaviter molliterque se
curant, indulgent voluptatibus,
circumfluunt deliciis, helluantur de
partis et quaesitis nostro sudore.
Ibid. As lately we have heard so
much about the Tisza-Eszlar affair,
it may be interesting to see how
Luther shared the common belief
that the Jews used the blood of
Christian victims for their rites.

„Sanguinarii canes et homicidae
sunt totius Christianitatis, summa
et plenissima voluntate ... et libenter essent re ipsa. Quemadmodum multi ex eis accusati et
combusti sunt, quod conati sint
flumina et fontes interficere, quod
infantulos furati stilis et lanceolis
sauciarint, ut ita suam sanguinariam
Caynicam sitim exaturarent. Ibid.
203. — Audio quod in ipsa Turcia
... ex Christianorum sanguine animi
impotentiam ulciscantur ... Quod
quidem incredibile non est. Ibid. 210.
— Considering how Luther raved
against the Jews it is almost amusing to see how on the occasion of
the late celebration, some Jewish
newspapers of Berlin spoke of
him as „our Luther“ — Further
specimens of the „Reformer's“ charitable views on the Jews will be
found in the Tischr. II. c. 51.
§. 1—38.

(¹¹) page 20.

most of them with be found rather drastic. But let the reader judge for himself.

1) Let the synagogues be burned and levelled to the ground, so that neither brick nor tile will be visible. This must be done for the honour of Our Lord. ([12])

2) Let the private houses of the Jews be demolished, for they do in their houses exactly the same they do in the synagogues They might be tolerated in stables and sheds like the gipsies.

3) All their prayerbooks and talmuds must be taken away.

4) The rabbis must be forbidden to teach, under pain of death.

5) The Jews must be denied safe-conduct.

6) Whatever they have, they possess by theft and robbery; therefore all their cash, their gold and silver, has to be confiscated.

7) Every ablebodied Jew and Jewess must be set to work. Let them earn their bread in the sweat of their brows.

([12]) Primum utile esset, ad tollendam blasphemam doctrinam ut omnes eorum synagogae inflammarentur et si quid reliquum fieret ex incendio, obrueretur arena et luto, ne quis ullam tegulam aut lapidem de his videre amplius possit. Et hoc debemus facere in honorem Domini nostri Jesu Christi et Sanctae Ecclesiae, ut videat Deus nos esse Christianos. Wittenb. VII. 204.

Secundo, ut eorum privatae domus etiam destruantur et vastentur. Nam idem faciunt in aedibus quod in synagogis. Interim possis eos cum uxoribus et liberis in stabulis et tuguriis ferre, ut errones illos, quos Germani Zigeuner vocant. (204n.)

Tertio, ut auferantur ab eis omnia orationalia et omnes Talmudistae. (Ibid.)

Quarto, ut Rabbinis sub poena capitis interdicatur munus docendi. (Ibid.)

Quinto, ut Judaeis publica fides et commeatus denegetur in omnibus provinciis et ducatibus. (Ibid.)

Sexto, eripiatur eis omnis prompta pecunia, omne aurum, argentum etc.... quidquid enim habent, hoc furati et praedati sunt a nobis per suam usuram. (205.)

Septimo, ut robustis, aetate florentibus Judaeis, viris et mulieribus labor praecipiatur, ut in sudore vultus quaerant panem... Non enim convenit, quod velint nos maledictos Gojim videre in labore continuo sudantes, ipsi in molli ocio. — Of such advice Köstlin (II. 601) has only to say that Luther speaks with „an awful earnestness,“ (mit furchtbarem Ernste.)

We fancy that some admirer of Luther will be inclined to excuse such enormities by saying that probably
this was not meant so seriously, that it was more the effect
of a momentary irritability. But we would refer him to
fol. 209 of the same volume, where the „Reformer“ repeats the same advice in stronger language than before.
There, for instance, he exhorts the people to bring pitch
and brimstone, and, *if possible, fire from hell*, to burn the
synagogues of the Jews.([13]) Or we would refer to fol.
211, where Luther thinks it advisable to recapitulate his
advice a second time in a few lines, the quintessence of
which appears in the words: They (the Jews) have to be
treated with hardness, without mercy.([14]) He goes so far
in his intolerance that he forbids Christians all intercourse
with Jews. Could a Christian, he says, take meat or drink
with a Jew? with a man, about whose lips there may still
be the foam, gathered there by his execrations against
Christ?([15]) „Vipers they are and cubs of the devil.“([16])
If all this does no good, they must be driven out of the
country like mad dogs.([17]) Another publication from Luther's
pen against the Jews, „Shemhamphoras“, followed allmost
immediately. Bullinger, one of the Swiss Reformers, calls

([13]) Primum, ut inflammatis
eorum synagogis, redigamus has
officinas blasphemiae in cinerem,
et qui oleum in ignem, qui sulphure ac pice ibi potest augere in-
cendium, imo qui infernalem ignem
addere, ibi strenue annitendum est,
ut Deus videat nos serio affici.
                              Ibid. 209.
([14]) Agatur cum eis duriter
immisericorditerque.
([15]) Quando vides Judaeum,
tunc apud te ipsum cogita: Ecce
hic obtueor os illud blasphemum
et impudens... Forsan vix ante
horam hodie vigesies contra nomen
Jesu, more suo, expuit in terram,
forsan reliquiae virulentissimi sputi,
spumae et salivae, viperinae ad-
haerent linguae et ori ejus, si locus
esset plus expuendi. Sic, inquam,

loquere tacite apud temetipsum:
Egone ergo apud hoc os diabolicum,
apud hoc guttur diabolici sputi
sumerem cibum ac potum? ex
eodem poculo biberem? in eandem
patinam attingerem? Absit hoc.
Possent enim in me intrare omnes
diaboli.   Ibid. 206.
([16]) Ibid. 207.
([17]) Si ne hoc quidem profuerit,
tunc cogimur eos tanquam rabie
corruptos canes abigere, ne blasphemiae participes efficiamur. Ibid.
211. — Naturally he who befriends
the Jews, finds no mercy before
Luther's eyes. Such a man „aper-
iat os et dentes oppedentibus et
cacantibus Judaeis, aut lingateorum
nates adoretque haec sancta, deinde
glorietur se fuisse misericordem.
                              Ibid. 207.

its style „houndish and lewd.“ Luthers admirers will say that only his zeal for the honour of Christ, which he vindicated against rabbinical fables and calumnies, made him write as he did. That may be, but the honour of Christ does not want a filthy shield.

Another source of trouble and a cause of great anger to Luther were his perpetual differences with the „Juristen“, the doctors in law, differences which had begun as early as 1530. Luther strongly insisted that secret engagements or engagements made without the consent of parents should not be considered as valid, except where the consummatio matrimonii could be proved. On the other side Hieronymus Schurf, professor of jurisprudence at Wittenberg defended their validity according to the Canon Law which was in force before the Council of Trent. The estrangement between the two men increased, when the latter, on the strength of I Tim III. 2., rejected the successive digamy of ministers; this was, according to Luther, tantamount to laying a snare for consciences; it also implied a wrong understanding of the words of S. Paul, which, he said, merely forbade a married minister to have criminal intercourse with a third person. Schurf seemed to be bent on introducing again Papal law, hence Luther most violently denounced him from the pulpit, saying that those who wished, might eat the Pope-ass's „Dreckheten“ ([18]), but he would not, and protesting againt religious matters being interfered with by lawyers, who were not able to interpret a single commandment of God. ([19]) The „Reformer's“ bitterness increased, when even protestant lawyers publicly taught that the marriage of a priest could not be considered as valid nor his children as legitimate. His Kate too greatly resented this. ([20])“ The lawyers — so Luther wrote to the Count

---

[18]) i. e. filth; of this ingenious jeu de mots on „Decreta“ Luther is exceedingly fond: it occurs in numberless passages.

[19]) Köstlin II. 478.

[20]) Cruciger wrote to Veit

Dietrich: Nunc totus ardet (Lutherus) contra nostros *voμιχους*, et scis illum habere ad multa quae eum inflamment *facem domesticam.* Ap. Janssen III. 185.

of Mansfeld — who always oppose our opinion, have made
me so tired, that I have flung away all matrimonial affairs,
and I have written to some that in all devils' name they
may do what they like. Let the dead bury their dead
. . . So far I have not a single lawyer who in such and
similar cases will hold with me and stand by me; they
are not willing to let my honour and my paltry goods
(meine Bettelstucke) pass to my children."(²¹)

Years afterwards the same controversy began again
and helped to make Luther's last days miserable. He solemnly, in the pulpit, sent secret engagements to the bottom
of hell, together with the Pope and the devil(²²). Up to
his last day we hear from him the bitterest remarks about
the „Juristen", the infatuated, vile and mercenary pettifoggers
who do not care for peace or religion(²³), the sycophants,
sophists and pest of mankind(²⁴), who moreover were most
ungrateful, for „before me no lawyer knew what was right
before God. What they have, they have from me."(²⁵)
He was told that a young man was going to take his
degree in law. He answered: „They are going to make a
new adder against theologians."(²⁶) The lawyers, he said,
at least the greater part of them, are servants of him, who
after the devil is the worst being in existence, viz. the
Pope; hence they are damned(²⁷), for they stick to the
Pope's law, wie dem Teufel im Hintern. (this was said in
the pulpit!) It would be no wonder, if God were to destroy the world on account of the villainous lawyers, „those

---

(²¹) De Wette V. 25. 26. He
mentions this same grievance in
a letter to the Elector John Frederick. Ibid. 715.

(²²) Köstlin II. 580.
(²³) Infatuat Juristas scientiola
juris, cujus usum mihi prorsus
omnes ignorare videntur, veluti
turpes et mercenarii rabulae, quibus nulla cura de pace, republica,
religione. De Wette V. 783.

(²⁴) Haec gratia debetur juristis
quod docuerunt et docent orbem

tot aequivocationes, cancellationes,
calumnias, ut certe loquela multo
sit confusior omni Babylone. Illic
enim nullus alterum *potuit* intelligere, hic nullus alterum *vult* intelligere. O sycophantas o soph-
istas, pestes generis humani. Ira-
tus scribo, nescio si sobrius rectius
sim dicturus. Ibid. 785.

(²⁵) Tischr. II. c. 43. § 1.
(²⁶) Ibid. § 3.
(²⁷) Ibid. § 7.

proud fools and pettifoggers ought to have their tongues torn out!" ([28])

But what was all the wickedness of all the lawyers in the world compared to that of the Pope? In the beginning of 1545 Luther gave once more vent to his feelings with regard to this subject in that astounding production: „Against Popery founded by Satan", a book of which Döllinger has said that it must have been written under the influence of intoxicating drinks or of fury of mind, bordering on madness. The immediate occasion of this book was a Papal Brief concerning the Council, addressed to the Emperor, which through a breach of confidence had fallen into the hands of the Protestants. All the rage and fury that Luther was capable of nourishing, seems to be concentrated in this one book. Of an attempt at arguments there is very little, but a whole dictionary of the filthiest slang is here poured out; the vilest Billingsgate that has ever disgraced the pen of the Ecclesiastes of Wittenberg or of any other man, is here paraded „in honour of Christ."

Lest this should seem an exaggeration, we are compelled to give here, though most reluctantly, a few specimens of the language of this „dear man of God." Other specimens wich are not fit to be printed except under the decent veil of a learned tongue will be found in the accompanying note. ([29])

([28]) Ibid. § 20, where part of Luther's sermon is printed. Should the Presbyterians of Newcastle on Tyne, who protested against Dr. Bewick's „pulpit Billingsgate" wish for some more pulpit flowers of the Prophet of Wittenberg, we would beg of them, to get the following translated: „Ich weiss besser was Jus Canonicum ist, denn ihr allzumal lernen und erfahren werdet. Eselsfürze sind es, wollt ihr's gern, ich will sie euch wol zu fressen geben. Thut mir die Eselsfürze aus der Kirche, das will ich euch gesagt haben: wo nicht, so müsst ihr. Ist doch im ganzen päpstlichen vermaledeiten gottlosen Recht (ich sollte sagen: Unrecht) nichts anderes denn Eselsfürze." Elegant, is it not? „Robust Christianity!"

([29]) I quote from the VII. vol. of the Wittenberg Edition. The Pope is sceleratus et execrabilis haereticus (458) Satanissimus Pater (468), abominatio ista Romana, quae se Papam vocat (447b), propudiosus nebulo (448), Satanas Romanus (452b) maledictus ille

The Pope is the Roman abomination, the Roman Satan, the accursed Antichrist, the Roman sycophant, the great ass, a desperate villain, a fraudulent rascal, an apostle of the devil, an execrable heretic, the stench of the devil;

Antichristus (450 B), desperatissimus sycophanta (451 B), ipsius satanae indubitatum domicilium (ibid.), desperatus nebulo bipedum nequissimus (453), Sodomitarum Papa (454 B), Hermaphroditarum et Pediconum Episcopus et Papa i. e. diaboli Apostolus (ibid.), oletum de culo omnium diabolorum ex inferno in Ecclesiam egestum (458) Asinus ille crepitibus suffarcinatus (468), devastator Turcâ duplo pestilentior (469), crepituum deflator (468 B), scelestissimus, coelestissimus inquam Pater (447 B); (this joke seems to Luther so excellent that he repeats it scores of times; in German: höllischster, heiligster.) The Pope and his followers are infernalis colluvies (448), scelerati nebulones (452 B), impii desperatique nebulones et rudes asini (ibid.), stabulum plenum magnis rudibus, stupidis et sceleratis asinis (475). Verus et naturalis asinus qui molendinarios saccos portat et carduos suos lactucas vocat, Romanam Curiam judicare potest. (ibid.) The Pope „boat, furit et prae insania expuit, more ejus qui a multis millibus daemoniorum possidetur". (457 B). Excrementosus ille asinus Romae ex sui ipsius stupido capite decernit et ex rancido suo ventre pedit (456). The Pope will never be able to prove his claim from the Bible, hence nimia anxietate tibialia foede concacabit. (459 B.) Luther makes the Pope say: Cum ego asininum meum clamorem Chika Chika magno stridore rudo, aut instar asini pedo, omnes homines pro articulis fidei habere et credere debebunt (458), and again: Qui non ventris mei crepitus adorat, peccatum mortale committit; qui non nates mihi lambit (si ita

ligare velim) mortaliter peccat. (468.) Facinus eis jus concacandi femoralia et a collo suspendendi, et haec esset bulla amaricini et osculum pacis pro id genus delicatis sanctulis (452 B). Ut te Deus perdat — he addresses the Pope — tu os impudens, os mendaciloquium, os blasphemum, os diabolicum (471 B), in abyssum inferni ad tuos antecessores praecipitaberis (454 B). Tu Papasine rudis es asinus et asinus permanebis (452). Pleni sunt Pontifices daemonibus omnium pessimis qui apud inferos agunt; pleni, pleni inquam, sunt et tam pleni ut nil nisi meros daemones expuere cacare, et emungere possint (451 B). Therefore: omnis Christiani est, ubicunque Papae insignia viderit, ea conspuere, excrementis foedare ... et hoc in gloriam Dei (459 B). Papa, Cardinales et quicquid hujus idololatriae et papisticae sanctitatis familiae est, supplicio afficiantur, tractis eorum linguis (quae poena blasphemantium impiorum est) per cervicem, quae deinde clavis transfixae, a patibulo quemadmodum eorum sigilla a bullis per ordinem dependeant .... postea permittatur eis concilii cogendi libertas ubicunque locorum velint, sive in patibulo, sive apud inferos inter omnes diabolos (460). But all this is not said strongly enough. Multis nominibus sum imbecillior quam qui Papam irridere valeam (450 B). Quidquid hic vel in aliis locis liberius vel etiam contumeliosius ... de illo pestilenti, execrabili, horrendo, ingenti monstro loquor, si quis pectoris mei cogitatus perscrutari posset, ille volens nolens dicet, me multo, multo inquam parcius et civilius quam oportuit agere. (466). He should like to

the Pope and his counsellors are the infernal Roman sink,
a holy band of villains, the desperate sons of the devil,
a stable full of great stupid asses. A donkey that carries
sacks to the mill and eats thistles like lettuce can judge
them. „Who would not wish to see the Pope destroyed
by lightning, pestilence, —, leprosy etc.?" „May God
destroy thee — so Luther exclaims — thou blaspheming
and diabolical mouth! Come, thou Pope-ass and prick
up thy long donkey's ears!" „Let every Christian consider
it his duty to throw filth on the Papal insignia." „The
Pope, his Cardinals and followers deserve that their tongues
should be torn out and nailed to the gallows; even this
would not be a sufficient punishment for them. Let them
hold their Council in hell with the devils.

In this way the muddy torrent of Luther's eloquence
rushes on, through more than sixty folio-pages, each page
more disgusting than the other, each page filthier than the
other. To wade through a mile of sewer would be a less
odious task than to go through this book. Yet the „Evangelist" excuses himself, that he speaks *far !too politely!*

use still stronger words, but non
bene decet praedicatorem maledi-
cere, qui ad benedicendum voca-
tus est!

In opening the book at random,
to give a quotation in contextu,
we happen to find in the first
paragraph wich meets our eyes:

Hoc insigne capitis gestamen
(the tiara) proponebat Christo Domino nostro diabolus, cum illum in
montem excelsum assumeretet com-
mons traret ei omnia regnammundi
et gloriam illorum, et diceret: Haec
omnia dabo tibi, si prostratus ador-
averis me. Tunx dixit illi Jesus:
Abi a me, Satan. Sed quomodo
respondet Papa? Veni ad me,
satan, et si plures quam hunc
mundos haberes, omnes acciperem
et te non adorarem modo, verum
etiam osculis et linctu podicem
tibi detergere paratus essem. Haec
sunt verba eius decretorum et de-

cretalium, ubi nihil de fide agitur,
sed omnia de ejus Celsitudine,
majestate, potestate, et dominatu
supra Ecclesias, supra Concilia,
supra Imperatores, supra Reges et
supra mundum, imo et supra coelum, ibi docentur, sed omnia illa
diplomata diaboli excrementis ob-
signantur et Papasini ventris crepitibus scribuntur. 467 B.

Claudite jam rivos, pueri! These
are only a *few* amenities, picked
out at random from Luther's book.
Open it at any page or at any
alinea, and you will find filth,
hatred, curses, imprecations. Yet
Köstlin (II. 588) calls it Luther's „last
grand testimony against Rome."!
Habeat sibi! To one of thy words,
o Luther, we will gladly subscribe,
though not in thy sense. Thou
art certainly multis nominibus imbecillior, quam qui Papam irridere
valeas.

He says he should like to use stronger expressions „but
it is not becoming that a preacher, who is called to bless,
should curse!" This book against the Pope was adorned with the
vilest and filthiest engravings, to which Luther himself
wrote the explanatory text in ribald verses.([30]) Naturally
it widened the breach between the two parties. Yet the
rage of the „dear man of God" was not satisfied([31]), but
his infirmity prevented him from carrying out further
plans. He found however some consolation in expressing
the wish, that his sufferings might he transferred to the
Pope and the Cardinals([32]).

([30]) Köstlin maintains that Luther himself disapproved of the filthy illustrations drawn by Lucas Cranach, specially of the one entitled: The birth of the Pope from Satan, and quotes to that end two letters of Luther to his friend Amsdorf. „Nepos tuus Georgius ostendit mihi picturam Papae, sed Meister Lucas ist ein grober Maler. Poterat sexui foemineo parcere propter creaturam Dei et matres nostras. Alias formas Papa dignas pingere poterat, nempe magis diabolicas, sed tu judicabis. „De Wette V. 742. Agam diligenter, si superstes fuero, ut Lucas pictor foedam hanc picturam mutet honestiore. Ibid. 743. But this protest cannot possibly have been meant against „the birth of the Pope." For

1) Luther himself had written the explanatory verses to it:
Hier wird geboren der Widerchrist
Megara seine Säugamm ist
Alecto sein Kindermeidlin,
Tisiphone die gangelt ihn.

2) Luther had, a month before the date of the above mentioned letters, explained the picture to friend Amsdorf. De furiis tribus nihil habebam in animo, cum eas Papae appingerem, nisi ut atrocitatem abominationis Papalis atrocissimis verbis in lingua latina exprimerem ... Megaera dicitur ab

invidia et odio. Haec est diabolica malitia, quae invidet humano generi salutem aeternam et temporalem etc.   De Wette V. 740.

3) The book against the Pope with its accompanying illustrations had been published already for some time, when Luther was shown by Amsdorf's nephew the drawing to which he objected.

There remains therefore no other conclusion but this, that the drawing in question was too filthy even to Luther, for which reason it was probably suppressed. — See Janssen, Zweites Wort p. 98 seqq. Janssen was obliged in selfdefence, to describe some of those abominable illustrations (of which Flacius said that they originated in divine wisdom!) and to expose the profane way, in which Luther uses words of holy Scripture in the explanation.

([31]) At the end of the book he says: Si Deo visum fuerit, in altero libello rem exactius tractabo.
Wittenb. VII. 479B,

([32]) Ego jam institueram secundam partem contra Papam ... et ecce irruit calculus meus, utinam non meus, sed etiam Papae et Gomorraeorum Cardinalium.
De Wette V. 743.

He was deeply depressed at the sight of the chaotic state of the Church which he had founded. The arbitrary proceedings of the princes in ecclesiastical matters, the immorality amongst the laity, the perpetual squabbles amongst the protestant theologians, the ever increasing number of new „views“, which grew up like mushrooms on the rich soil of private judgment, the disrespect with which the ministers were treated by their own flocks, all this embittered Luther's heart to such an extent, that he left Wittenberg in disgust. To his Kate he wrote: „Away from this Sodom! I will wander about and beg my bread from door to door rather than torment my miserable old days with that disorderly state of things.“([33]) At the urgent desire of the Elector he returned, for a short time at least, but only to be irritated again by his surrounding friends and to seek invain for night repose. We cannot help thinking that, as his end was drawing nearer, his conscience spoke to him more and more impressively. Of course his friends will either think that his mental troubles were the effect of his bodily weakness, or they will accept his own explanation, that they were temptations of the devil. It is well known that through this supposition he frequently found (or tried or imagined to find) a harbour of refuge.

On the day on which he preached for the last time at Wittenberg([34]) — warning his hearers once more against reason, „the devil's bride“ — he wrote to a friend, complaining that he was old, decrepit, indolent, tired, cold and halfblind.([35]) But one more journey he had to make, on some business which called him to his native county of Mansfeld. On his way he passed through Halle, where, old and decrepit as he was, the apostate monk's rage was

([33]) Nur weg und aus dieser Sodoma ... Will also umbher-schweifen und ehe das Bettelbrod essen, ehe ich mein arm alte letzte Tage mit dem unordigen Wesen martern und verunrugigen will. De Wette V. 753.

([34]) 17. Jan. 1546.

([35]) Senex, decrepitus, piger, fessus, frigidus ac jam monoculus scribo.   De Wette V. 778.

roused once more at the sight of some religious in their habits. He could not abstain from saying publicly in the pulpit at Halle that he wondered why „those shabby, lousy monks“ had not yet been expelled from the town and exhorted the magistrates to pluck up courage for such a pious act.(^{36}) As fate would have it, he was also exasperated by the presence of the Jews whom he happened to meet in several places. In Eisleben alone — he writes to his Kate — there are fifty of them. A cold wind, which almost made „his brain freeze“, he is inclined to attribute to their tricks; but the beer is good and this is a consolation.(^{37}) At the same time he tells his wife that he will do his best, to have all the Jews out of the country. „When the principal business is settled, I must attend to the expulsion of the Jews. Count Albrecht hates them and has given them up, but nobody touches them as yet. Please God, I will assist Count Albrecht in the pulpit.“(^{38}) A few days later he repeats the same, only that meantime he has ascertained the number of Jews to be about 400, a fact, which makes the cause of his headache more probable.(^{39}) The business on which he had come, proved very disagreeable. „I think that hell and the whole world must be free from devils now, they all seem to have come here on my account.“(^{40}) „We have enough to gorge and to guzzle (zu fressen und zu saufen) and should have some jolly days, were it not for that unpleasant business.“ (^{41}) „The Naumburg beer is good — he writes to Kate a week before his death — only I think it makes my chest bad with the pitch; the devil has spoiled the beer in the whole world with the pitch.“ (^{42}) The thought of the Council of Trent also troubled his mind at times. He said to his friends repeatedly: Pray for our Lord God, that the affairs of his Church may be satisfactorily settled, for the Council of Trent is very angry.(^{43})

(^{36}) Erl. 16, 126.

(^{37}) De Wette V. 784.

(^{38}) Ibid.

(^{39}) Ibid. 787.

(^{40}) Ibid.

(^{41}) Ibid. 786.

(^{42}) Ibid. 788.

(^{43}) Seckend. I. III. § 133.

He seemed to have a presentiment that at Eisleben, where he was born, he would also die; he said so to his friend Justus Jonas.([44]) He was troubled once more with an apparition of the devil, as his physician Ratzeberger tells us.([45]) Whilst Doctor Luther was towards evening standing at the open window, saying his prayers, he saw the devil sitting in the street, who — well, let us say, who insulted him in a peculiar manner. The night before his end — the same authority continues — he, Jonas and Caelius had been merry amongst themselves, and when after supper he was about to go to bed, he wrote with chalk on the wall: „Living I was thy plague, o Pope, dead I shall be thy death." ([46])

That same night (18. Febr. 1546) he was suddenly taken worse, all the attention of his friends could give him no relief. He once more expressed his firm belief in Christ and in the revelation of truth made to himself and expired after a short agony.

On the following day a funeral service was held at Eisleben, at which many of the deceased's friends, including

([44]) Ibid.

([45]) Man saget, Da Doctor Lutherus zu Eissleben seiner gewonheit nach abendt, ehe er sich niedergelegt, sein gebet zu Gott In aufgethanem fenster gesprochen und vorrichtet, habe er den Sathanam uff dem Rohrbrunnen, welcher für seiner Herberge gestanden, geschen, Der Ihm die posterioria gezeiget und sein gespottet, Als das er nichts ausrichten wurde, Solches soll Herr Lutherus D. Jonae und Herrn Michaeli Caelio erzelet haben. Ratzeberger 133.

([46]) Den abent zuvor vor seinen Ende zu Eissleben war er mit Doctore Jona und Michaele Caelio seinen hausgenossen heimlich guter Dinge, und da er sich nach gehaltenem Abendmal hatte wollen zu ruhe legen, hatt er folgenden Vers mit Kreiden an die wandt geschrieben:

Pestis eram vivens, moriens ero
mors tua, Papa.
Ratzeberger 137.

This same verse is found also at the end of a letter to Melanchthon. De Wette V. 58. What did Luther mean with the latter part of it? Some light is thrown upon it by a remark preserved in the Tischreden. (II. c. 24. § 15.) He speaks of having been at death's door at Thambach, when he suffered excruciating pains from gravel. (When recovering, he wrote there on the wall: Thambach est mea Phanuel,ibi apparuit mihiDominus.) „If I had died there, *it would probably have been all over with the Papists.* For when I am dead, they will see, whom they have had in me; other preachers will not be able to keep within bounds and *to preserve moderation as* I *have done!"*

many noblemen. were present. Justus Jonas and Michael
Coelius preached on that occasion.([47]) The body which
was watched during the night by ten citizens was then
taken to Wittenberg for interment. It was buried in the
Schlosskirche, not far from the pulpit.([48]) After Bugenhagen had said a few words in commemoration of Luther([49]),
Philip Melanchthon delivered a longer oration in which
he praised his friend as the last of the long line of divine-
ly sent Patriarchs, Prophets, Apostles and ·Preachers,
and thanked God for the work done through him.([50])

Luther was extolled by his adherents in pamphlets
pictures and medals as a second Samuel, a third Elias, a
thaumaturgus, a prophet etc. etc.([51])

May he have found a merciful judge!

([47]) Abstracts of their sermons
ap. Seckend. III. 647. Jonas said
on this occasion: „The Pope, the
Bishops and Cardinals call us
Germans fools, because we preach
and believe that we shall rise in
our bodies on the last day and
shall see God" (!) and exhorted his
hearers to shun the Papists as
they would the devil himself, „for
an obdurate obstinate Papist *is*
the devil himself."

([48]) Atque ita in arce Witten-
bergensi jacet terrae mandatum
corpus Reverendi Patris Martini
Lutheri, praestantissimum Spiritus
Sancti organon. Jacet autem prope
suggestum, in quo tot praeclaras
et sanctas conciones .. habuerat.
Apud Seckend. III. 645. In the
same place Seckendorf himself says:
Licet tertii decimi Apostoli locum
aut nomen vir optimus non affec-
taverit, nec nos adulatione invi-
diosa ei assignemus, apostolicae
tamen doctrinae studio et imita-
tione plerosque ante se superavit,
et vix parem sibi reliquit; titulo
Apostoli Germaniae longe dignior,
quam vel Bonifacius ille Mogun-

tinus praesul, superstitionum potius
quam purae religionis praeco.

([49]) Ita occupatus fuit dolore,
et lacrymis impeditus, ut et brevi
sermone defunctus sit et ad tex-
tum quem tractandum sumpserat
I. Thess. IV. 13. 14 fere nihil dixerit.   Seckend. III. 648.

([50]) Annumerandus est igitur
illi pulcherrimo agmini summorum
virorum, quos Deus ad colligendam
et instaurandam Ecclesiam misit,
quos quidem praecipuum florem
esse generis humani intelligamus
. . . Cum magna pars doctrinae
supra humanum conspectum po-
situm sit, ut doctrina de remissione
peccatorum et fide, necesse est fateri a Deo eruditum esse (Lutherum), ac multi ex nobis viderunt
ejus luctas, in quibus didicit fide
standum esse et recipi et audiri
a Deo ... Gratias tibi agimus omni-
potens Deus ... quod servas Evangelii ministerium et nunc quoque
per Lutherum instaurasti. Seckend.
III. 649. 650. This author gives
the whole text of Melanchthon's
oration.

([51]) See Janssen III. 538. Nota.

Chapter XXIII.

Luther's Character.

„Wo is Luther?"

L. ap. Köstlin II. 638.

We have accompanied Luther through the most important events of his life, we have seen him act and heard him speak : we may now be able to form a just estimate of his character. We are far from making a sweeping assertion, condemning everything in him; there are many bright traits in him, though on the whole, to put it in the mildest possible way, a less lovable character than his it would be difficult to find.

He certainly was a great genius, nor can anyone deny that he possessed an extraordinary strength of will, which carried him through the greatest obstacles, but his firmness only too frequently degenerated into the most deplorable stubbornness. He was a perfect master of the language ([1]), no one knew better, than he did, how to handle it for his own purpose. In his books destined for the masses and in his sermons he never speaks above the heads of the people, but he speaks in their own way, making himself intelligible to the very dullest, especially by his coarse invectives. In the invention of similes, images and telling words he is

---

([1]) Though Luther has great merits with regard to the German language, the prevailing opinion, that he almost formed it, is quite erroneous. A glance at the literary monuments of the 15th century is sufficient to show how groundless this opinion is.

simply inexhaustible. Few knew so well as he did, how to appeal to the masses, and how to fill them at least for the moment, with the wildest enthusiasm. These are splendid gifts, but do they alone make *a great man?* In these points many heroes of the French revolution have equalled the prophet of Wittenberg.

The more attentively Luther's theological books are studied, the less does he appear a theologian. Of the vast erudition, the clear perception, the logical deduction, the calm discussion, which distinguish men like S. Thomas, Bellarmin, Suarez and De Lugo, there is not a vestige in him. Frequently we have had occasion to call the reader's attention to the extraordinary performances of his logic — if logic it can be called — to his astonishing coolness in establishing principles, which he expects to be admitted merely on the authority of his word, to the clearly false and calumnious suppositions, from which he starts, to his utter contempt for reason in theological matters, to his sic volo, sic jubeo in the interpretation of the Bible, to his changing about from one opinion to another. These are not the marks of a theologial genius. The secret of his success lies elsewhere.([1a])

Whenever Luther put aside strife and controversy, he was able to be the contrary of ferocious. He doted on his own children; a letter written to his little boy in 1530 shows a marvellous gift of speaking to little ones according to their own ideas and capacities; he was very fond of children in general, their innocent looks and ways had always a great attraction for him, though even in matters of this sort he cannot help becoming, to say the least, very un-aesthetic, as the Tabletalk abundantly shows.

Nobody could say that money was the object he had in view in any part of his revolutionary work. His disinter-

---

- ([1a]) In 1536 Luther expressed his opinion of himself and other theologians thus: Res et verba Philippus (Melanchthon); Verba sine re Erasmus; Res sine verbis Lutherus; nec rem nec verba Carlo-stadius. Tischr. II. c. 50. § 11.
([2]) De Wette IV. 41.

estedness was so great, that he even refused all payment
offered to him by publishers for his books (³). He frequently
recommended charity (⁴), and just as frequently practised
it, expecially towards those ministers of the new religion,
who were in distress through the coldness and indifference
of their „reformed" flocks. His letters also bear witness
that he frequently made use of the influence he had at
different Courts, to intercede for poor people or for de-
linquents, who in his opinion were punished too severely.
He was a diligent observer and great admirer of God's
greatness in creation and very often took occasion from
trifling circumstances to speak of what God in his wisdom
and goodness has done for us in our own nature and
in our surroundings. The Tabletalk abounds with such
remarks. (⁵)

But whenever Luther descended into the arena —
and we may say that he spent the greater part of his
public life in it — the whole ferocity of his nature stood
revealed. Most strikingly appears that fault, which is the
parent of all his other faults, his unbounded pride. Köstlin (⁶) may remind us at the end of his book of Luther's own
words: „Who is Luther? — I cannot be, nor do I wish to be
anybody's master." Such expressions of humility occasionally
occur, (⁷) but they appear as mere oratorical tricks, when
we hear him thunder out his „sic volo, sic jubeo, sit pro
ratione voluntas", and when we see him follow *this* principle on almost every page of his writings. What are
humble words like these, which he addressed to Erasmus
in the exordium of his book de servo arbitrio: „In elo-

(³) Nam pecunia et ipsi pauperes
sumus valde, sed jure quodam, licet
modico, utor in typographos, ut
cum nihil ab eis pro vario labore
meo accipiam, aliquando, cum
libet, exemplar tollam. De Wette.

(⁴) Tischr. I. 460. 462.

(⁵) V. gr. „Cum videret Lutherus in campo incedere vaccas etc.
dixit: Do gehen unnsre prediger,

die Milchtreger, puttertreger, die
Kesträger, qui nobis in dies prae-
dicant fidem ergo Deum patrem.
Lauterb. 128. Cfr. Tischr. II. appendix §. 9.

(⁶) II. 638.

(⁷) v. gr. „I alone cannot say
anything against all others in this
matter (divorce)" Wittenb. II. 88n.
(De Capt. Bab.)

quence and genius thou art far my better, all say so,
quanto magis ego barbarus, in barbarie semper versatus?"([8])
Duellants, who are savagely longing to have each other's
blood, still make a polite stiff bow, before they take up
the deadly arms.

„Who is Luther?" He has given us his own opinion
of himself in the most unmistakable terms. „Sum Ecclesiastes Ecclesiae Vitebergensis,"([9]) „I am the Ecclesiastes
by the grace of God,"([10]) „Doctor Martinus Luther is a
great doctor above all bishops and priests and monks."([11])
„I will not have my doctrine judged by anybody, not even
by Angels, he who refuses to accept my doctrine, cannot
be saved,"([12]) „He, who teaches differently from what I
have taught, condemns God and must remain a child of
hell."([13]) „Though they have not shed my blood ... they
murder me continually in their hearts. O thou unhappy
nation! must thou be the Antichrist's hangman and executioner to God's Saint and Prophet?"([14]) „I must confess
that I am one of the most eminent teachers of this time."([15])
„I am known in heaven, on earth and in hell. My authority is such that you may trust to it more than to a Notary ... People can say: This is written by Dr. Martin
Luther, the notary of God, the witness of his Evangelium."([16]) „Through God's particular grace I am better
versed in the Scriptures than the Pope and all his asses."([17])
In the Fathers of the Church he has found greater confusion, than in Tartarus; he adds emphatically: „May God
destroy me, if I lie."([18]) „Ambrosius has written six books
on Genesis. How stupid they are!"([19])

([8]) Wittenb. II. 457.
([9]) Wittenb. VII. 472.
([10]) Walch XIX. 837.
([11]) Wittenb. VII. 466.
([12]) Erl. 28, 144.
([13]) Ibid. 346.
([14]) De Wette II. 165.
([15]) Walch XVII. 1645.
([16]) De Wette V. 422. (Luther's last will and testament.)
([17]) Erl. 26, 138.

([18]) Perdat me Deus, si mentior. De Wette I. 128.
([19]) Lauterb. 123. — „Hierony-mus may be read for the sake of the histories, but of faith and of the true religion there is not a word in his writings. Origenes has been excommunicated by me already. Chrysostom is nothing in my eyes, he is only a vain talker (ein Wä-scher). Basilius is worth nothing,

The immediate consequence of Luther's high opinion of himself is inexpressible contempt for all who dare to oppose him or to disagree from him; this contempt manifests itself in words, by which as the Protestant C. A. Menzel says, no pen or printingpress should be defiled. Many of the „Reformer's" own friends bitterly complained of it. Bullinger calls his eloquence „houndish and lewd",([20]) and considers Shemhamphoras to be „a piggish book, that might have been written by a pigherd, but not by a renowned pastor of souls." Though we have given many specimens of Luther's style, in different chapters of this book, we beg leave to give here a few more. The style is the man. „For the most faithful Apostles of the Pope, the Cardinals, Archbishops, Bishops and Abbots, the Rhine would hardly be sufficient, to drown all the villains in."([21]) The most opprobrious names for his adversaries are hardly sufficient to satisfy Luther's rage. Cochlaeus is dismissed with „Rotzlöffel," ([22]) Erasmus is a serpent,([23]) a viper;([24]) whosoever kills Erasmus, kills a bug, dead it stinks more than alive([25]), Eck is a hog,([26]) Witzel a perjured Mame-

---

he is a monk, I would not give a fig for him. Tischr. II. c. 34. § ?. — Since through God's grace I learned to understand Paul, I have no respect for any doctor, they are all insignificant. Ibid. c. 35. §. 6. His contempt of his adversaries makes him frequently underrate them: Cur non feremus modicum hoc mali, quod immundae muscae nos rostro suo polluant aut concacent parumper, cum hoc cogantur ab ipsis naturalibus muscis pati summae et formosissimae reginae in media facie sua. Quid vero sunt isti furiosi, quam muscae susurrantes, alisque suis nostris capitibus obstrepentes? Postquam vero valde iracundae strepuerunt, edunt stercus, quod acu tangi vixi potest.
De Wette IV. 101.

([20]) In Hess, Leben Bullinger's

I. 404. „hündisch and schmutziglüstern." Walch too disapproves of it (XIX. Introd. 15), and Seckendorf (lib. I. 187) says: Excessisse modum visus est Lutherus.

([21]) Erl. 24. 166.

([22]) Tischr. II. c. 4. §. 139. It almost seems as if the frequent use of this and similar names was owing to a false apprehension of the meaning of „Cochlaeus." This name has nothing to do with cochlear. John Dobneck adopted it from the name of his native place Wendelstein; a winding stone staircase used to be called a cochlea.
See Otto p. 1.

([23]) Ibid c. 14. § 113.

([24]) De Wette III. 98.

([25]) Tischr. II. c. 14. § 112.

([26]) Tischr. II. c. 5. § 8. Cfr. „Dr. Porcus Eckius."
Wittenb. VII. 456.

luck, ([27]) the Papists are real devils,([28]) and especially the Pope is „a real devil in disguise."([29])

In 1541 Luther sent out a pamphlet, entitled Hans-worst",([30]) which in vileness of language and bitterness of hatred has hardly an equal.([31]) It was directed against Henry Duke of Braunschweig-Lüneburg, who towards the end of the preceding year had had the courage to attack him. ([32])

If any of Luther's blindest admirers were to read the „Hans Worst", without knowing by whom it was written, they would pronounce it to be the production of a raving madman.

Let the reader not be scandalized at finding here some quotations from it, we shall take care not to reproduce the worst. It is absolutely impossible to get a true idea of this „dear man of God", without hearing him use that sort of language, which seems to form an integral part of his whole nature. Our purpose has been and is, to show to the reader the *real* Luther, and if the real Luther is disgusting, it is not our fault.

In his „Hans Worst" Luther makes an attempt at representing *his* Church as the only true one, the Catholic Church as the apostate, in fact, as „the devil's arch-whore." There is no necessity for going here through the „theological" arguments, with which he means to establish this thesis. What arguments can be expected in this mad production? As to the Scripture-texts which are freely used, it fills one with pity and with indignation, to see the sacred Word of God mixed up with Luther's revolting filth.([33])

([27]) Ibid. §. 18.
([24]) Erl. 25, 39.
([20]) Tischr. II. c. 4. § 3.
([30]) Of the meaning of the word Seckendorf (lib. III. 377) gives the following explanation. „Vocabulis his aut lurcones et qui dici solent ventres aut scurrae inepti designantur." The nearest approach to it in English would be Clown.

([31]) Even Seckendorf (l. c.) says: Bilem, si unquam, certe in isthoc scripto acriter et copiose effudisse Lutherum satis apparet.
([32]) Walch XVII 1548 seqq. gives the Duke's text.
([33]) As usual, Luther is guilty of deliberate untruth in misrepresenting the doctrine of the Church. „Who has commanded you, to

Amongst other names he gives to his adversary the following: ([34]) „Dirty fellow" [1645], „the devil of Wolfenbüttel" [1652], „a damned liar and villain" [1654], „the donkey of donkeys" [1680], „that damned Harry" [1690], „devil Harry and Harry devil" [1712], „whose name stinks like the devil's dirt" [1716], an arch-assassin and bloodhound, whom God has sentenced to the fire of hell and at the mention of whose name every Christian ought to spit out [1724]. He addresses him in the words: „Thou beautiful image of thy hellish father" [1714]. Harry, he thinks „is well up in the Bible and very nimble about it just as a cow would be in the branches of a walnuttree, or a sow at the harp [1689] How could such a blockhead presume to write a book, and against Luther too? „Thou shouldst not write a book, until thou hast heard a — of an old

establish this new idolatry, that you should introduce the worship of Saints, that you should canonize them?... to honour them just as if they were God himself so as to make people trust more in *their* merits, than in Christ himself?"
Walch XVII. 1669.

([34]) For these quotations from Hans Worst we give the number of the column (from Walch XVII.) in brackets in the text. Of this book of Luther the Protestant historian F. Chr. Schlosser says: Diese Schrift ist das gröbste und ungezogenste aller deutschen Bücher des sechszehnten Jahrhunderts, das doch an groben Büchern sehr reich ist. (Weltgeschichte für das deutsche Volk. Vol. X. p. 103.) He also says that decency forbids to reproduce its worst parts. The full title of the first edition of Hansworst (Wittenberg 1541) is as follows: „Des Durchlauchtigsten, Hochgeborenen Fürsten und Herrn, Herrn Johannes Friedrichen Herzogs zu Sachsen, des h. römischen Reichs Erzmarschallen und Kurfürsten Wahrhaftige, bestendige, ergründete, Christenliche und aufrichtige Verantwortung Wider des

erstockten, gottlosen, vermaladeiten, verfluchten ehrenschenders, bösthetigen Barrabas, auch hurensüchtigen Holefernes von Braunschweig, so sich Herzog Heinrich den Jüngern nennet, unverschempt, Calphurnich schand- und lügenbuch, so er abermals mit Datum Wolfenbüttel auf Dienstag nach Omnium Sanctorum anno 1540 nechst wider vorgemeldten Kurfürsten u. s. w. will vollbracht haben und in einen Druck ausgesprengt hat." — We may quote here Melanchthon's words in the funeral sermon of Luther: Aliqui, non mali tamen, questi sunt asperiorem fuisse Lutherum, quam debuerit. Nihil disputo in alterutram partem; sed respondeo id quod Erasmus saepe dixit: Deus dedit huic postremae aetati propter morborum magnitudinem acrem medicum ... Si quis talis est ut veteres de Hercule, Cimone et aliis dixerunt, ἀκομψος μεν, ἀλλα τα μεγιστα ἀγαθος, vir bonus et laude dignus est. Seckend. III. 649. Catholics cannot persuade themselves that God would provide a physician so *very* „ἀκομψος."

sow. Then thou mayest open thy mouth and say: Thanks
to you, my beautiful nightingale; here is a text which is
meant for me" [1726]. To give a faithful translation of
Luther's slangdictionary is impossible. It would require
an English Luther, to enrich the language with the noble
inventions of a fertile brain.

No wonder that the Pope, „the devil's head", [1669]
with his „damned Cardinals" [1713] and the whole band of
„damned blasphemers" [1699] should have an ample share
in the Evangelist's wrath. But the very thought of the
Church, from which he had apostatized seems to inflame
his rage to an appalling extent. To him she is „the devil's
Church" [1656] „a whore-Church of the devil" [1664] „an
arch-whore of the devil, an infernal school and a stenchden
of the devil" [1666], „an infernal whore and the devil's
last and most abominable bride," [1671] „the devil's brothel"
[1676] etc. etc. etc. in infinitum. *Damned, devil* and *whore*,
these are the keynotes of the whole book. In variations
the Ecclesiastes is inexhaustible. On one page [col. 1674
und 1675] the last of those three words is thrown at the
Church's head not less than twenty-seven times. And we
should not say: Nam et lingua tua notum te facit? ([35])

It seems that a sort of „furia tedesca" was required,

([35]) Vileness of language seems
to have been the distinctive mark
of a true and genuine 16th century Protestant Reformer. Calvin
and Luther rivalled in it. In the
former's „Christianae Religionis
institutio" his theological opponents receive the following names·
Blaterones, nebulones, nugatores,
phrenetici, insulso cavillo ludentes,
ore rabido latrantes, rabulae, sacri-
legi, nebulones prodigiosi, helle-
boro magis quam argumentis digni,
canes impuri, angues, porci etc. etc.
Calvin thus addresses Westphal, a
Lutheran theologian: „Your school
is nothing but a brothel. Do you
understand me, you hound? Do you
understand me, you madman? Do

you unterstand me, you big stupid
brute?" (Opuscules de Calvin, p.
799.) „Le beau style de Calvin
est souillé de toutes ces ordures
à chaque page." (Bossuet, hist. d.
var. IX. c. 81.) Melanchthon, „the
man of a tender Christian mind",
had no hesitation to call, in 1558,
his *Lutheran* adversaries „idolatrous and sophistical bloodhounds".
(Döll. I. 417.) The same Melanchthon says in his „Causae" against
the Council of Trent, (an official
document written at the command
of the Elector), that no good can
be expected from the Bishops assembled there, since they understand of Christian religion just as
much as the donkeys they ride.

to inspire Luther. I cannot write poetry or prose, I cannot pray or preach, if I am not angry."([36]) When I pray: hallowed be thy name, I curse Erasmus and all heretics." ([37]) „I cannot pray without cursing. If I have to say: hallowed be thy name, I must add: cursed, damned and dishonoured be the name of the Papists and of all that blaspheme thy name. If I have to say: thy kingdom come, I must add: cursed, damned and destroyed be the Papacy. If I have to say: thy will be done, I must add: cursed, damned, dishonoured and destroyed be all thoughts and plots of the Papists . . . Verily, thus I pray every day with my lips and with my heart without ceasing"([38]). Luther is not in the least ashamed of using such language. „I am very glad, (mirifice gaudeo) that in the cause of God I bear such a character."([39]) „This shall be my glory and honour and the world shall say of me that I am full of bitter words and curses for the Papists".([40]) Here is the form of absolution, which his disciples were to give to the Pope: „May God Almighty be thy enemy, may he never forgive thee thy sins, may he plunge thee into the abyss of eternal fire. And I at the command of our Lord Jesus Christ and of the most holy Father Pope Luther the First, refuse to thee God's grace and everlasting life, and throw thee into hell, which has been prepared for thee and for thy king from the beginning of the world."([41]) In the last year of his life Luther wrote to a friend, that he was free from avarice and lust, „only anger in left."([42])

If we look upon those frequent outbursts of rage and at the same time at the incredible filthiness of his speech,([43]) what is there that can be advanced to excuse it? None of his admirers approve of it nowadays, but

---

([36]) Tischr. I. p. 464.
([37]) Ibid. p. 486.
([38]) Walch XVI. 2085.
([39]) Wittenb. II. 513.
([40]) Erl. 25, 508. cfr. Tischr. II. c. 3. § 53. „Ich bekenne frei, dass des Papstes Greuel, nach Christo, mein grösster Trost is."

([41]) Wittenb. (Germ.) XII. 360.
([42]) Ego liber sum ab avaritia, a libidine vindicat me afflictum corpus, sola ira adhuc est reliqua. Seckend. lib. III. 643.
([43]) V. gr. „Dysenteria Lutheri in merdipoëtam Lemchen."
Lauterb. 139.

many try to justify it by saying, that such was the general custom of the time. We might deny this, and it would be easy to produce a long list of writers of that period, who never defiled their pages with such indecencies. But esto! Suppose it had been the general custom of the period. If Luther was, what he claimed to be, a special messenger of heaven sent to reform the Church of God, may we not justly expect to see him rise *above* indecent and unchristian customs? If he is an apostle and has to fight the battles of God, why should he invariably choose a dunghill to stand on? It is not only in his polemical writings, but also in his confidential letters and in his familiar talk that Luther is disgustingly dirty.([44])

Was Luther sincere? No doubt, he was, in his intention to pull down the Catholic Church. But to say of him, that truth was invariably the object he had in view, is impossible, in spite of the solemn protestation, which he makes in his controversy with Erasmus,([45]) and to which his admirers will eagerly cling. This is a grave charge, and we shall have to make it good.

The „Reformer" demanded, that Holy Communion should be given to the laity under both kinds. Some people thought, that perhaps, for the sake of peace, the Pope or a Council would grant it. What does Luther say to this?

([44]) Here are some specimens of Luther's familiar epistolary style: Gratia et Pax. Non de cloaca papyrum sumo, quemadmodum Jonas noster, qui te nihil pluris aestimat, quam ut dignus sis, qui schedas natales, hoc est, de natibus purgatis legas. Letter to Amsdorf. De Wette II. 625. — Salutabis tuum Dictative multis basiis, vice mea et Johanelli mei, qui hodie didicit flexis poplitibus solus in omnem angulum cacare, imo cacavit vere in omnem angulum miro negotio. Alioqui plura ad te mandasset, si otium illi fuisset, mox enim balneatus dormitum abivit. Mirari desines quod de cacando scribo; alias de aliis scribam. De Wette III. 213. If further proofs should be wanted, they will be found in De Wette III. 18. 256; IV. 97. Tischr. II. c. 3. § 52; c. 4. § 52; c. 38. § 9; c. 57. § 12 etc. etc.

([45]) Testor Deum in animam meam, perseverassem (in the old faith), nisi urgente conscientia et evidentia rerum me in diversum cogeret. Wittenb. II. 469 B. We may here also quote his own words about heretics: „All heretics think, and would be ready to die for it, that they have the right truth."
Tischr. II. c. 4. § 54.

„If a Council were to allow the reception of the Eucharist under both kinds, then *out of spite*, we would receive it only under one, or not at all."(⁴⁶) Is this a sincere endeavour to arrive at the truth about the Eucharist?

Again, as we have seen before, Luther denounced the celibacy of the Clergy as a must abominable institution. Some people were in hopes, that for the sake of peace a Council would allow priests to marry.(⁴⁷) What does Luther say? „If one or two or a hundred or a thousand Councils were to decree, that priests might marry, we would rather allow the priests one or two or three whores, than that they should take wives in virtue of a Council's decree."(⁴⁸) Is this sincerity?

Catholics and especially Jesuits are charged with teaching the abominable principle, that the end sanctifies the means. What do Luther's admirers say to his words, that in order to cheat and to destroy Papacy, everything is allowed?(⁴⁹) How can they excuse his words in the correspondence with the Hessian Councillors: „What would it matter, if for the sake of greater good and of the Christian Church one were to tell a big lie?"(⁵⁰)

Who will say that Luther himself believed the absurd stories, with which he tried to discredit religious life, such as the story about the 6000 children's skulls, fished out of a Convent's pond?(⁵¹) He may say, that under the Pope

---

(⁴⁶) Wittenb. (Germ.) VII. 367 B.

(⁴⁷) Elector dixit: Papa frigidas aliquas externas caerimonias relinquet, de aqua benedicta, sale, palmesel, quadragesima, item coelibatum suum non adeo defendet.
Lauterb. 24.

(⁴⁸) Walch XIX. 2165.

(⁴⁹) Nos hic persuasi sumus, papatum esse veri illius et germani antichristi sedem, in cujus deceptionem et nequitiam ob salutem animarum nobis omnia licere arbitramur. De Wette I. 478. Köstlin (I. 357) says that the words deceptio and nequitia are to be

taken in this passage as attributes of the Papacy, so that the meaning would be: „against whose cheating and wickedness etc." But even in this case there remain the words: *Omnia* nobis licere etc. in their full force. The word deceptio receives additional light from Luther's expression in a letter to Melanchthon: Si vim evaserimus, pace obtenta, *dolos* ac lapsus nostros facile emendabimus. De Wette IV. 156.

(⁵⁰) Lenz, 372—377.

(⁵¹) See chapt. II. p. 44.

no Council has ever treated about any matters concerning religion, but that they have all been occupied with money-matters only ([52]), who will believe that Luther himself was foolish enough to believe it? He may say, that under the Pope the Bible was unknown to the people, ([53]) — but if this is not unaccountable ignorance, is it a deliberate false-hood. Who can suppose that he himself believed, that „under the Pope neither the ten commandments, nor the Creed, nor the Our Father were taught, nor was it con-sidered necessary to know them"? ([54])

When a real Apostle comes to teach a benighted world, we may expect, that he himself will believe, what he teaches others. Thousands of times Luther states his fundamental dogma of „Justification through faith alone". Did he believe it himself? „I wonder, that I cannot learn it yet myself, whilst my pupils say they have it at their finger's ends." ([55]) „I used to believe the Pope and the monks everything, but what now Christ says, I cannot believe." ([56]) „When Magister Antonius Musa, then min-ister at Rochlitz, bitterly complained to Doctor Martin, that he himself could not believe what he preached to others, Luther answered: Praise and thanks be to God, that other people have the same experience; I thought that this was exclusively my own case." ([57])

Luther was not free from a common evil of his time, superstition, nay he excelled in it, especially in the strong belief in the influence, on temporal things, of the devil and the devil's associates, the witches. We should not be surprised to hear that this too was owing to the effect of Catholic doctrine; but it is not now our object, to vin-dicate the Church against this charge. ([58]) In Luther's

---

([52]) Wittenb. II. 472 B.

([53]) Tischr. I. 26. & II. 172 cfr. II. 187: „For some hundreds of years no Pope or Cardinal has ever read to Bible."

([54]) Lauterb. 151. Cfr. Ibid. 66: „Nova et insolita praedicatio est Catechismus."

([55]) Rebenstock, Colloq. medit. etc. II. 125.

([56]) Tischr. I. 440.

([57]) Mathesius 139.

([58]) The decrees of the Synods of Paderborn (A. D. 785) and of Treves (1310), and of Innocent VIII (1484) not against witches, but

time and even during the following century Catholics as
well as Protestants were imbued with such belief. But if
„the spirit of the time" is adduced as an excuse for Luther, we say that a grand „man of God", as he is said
to have been, ought to have risen above such a spirit.([59])
Even his most devoted admirers will probably shake their
heads at the monstrous absurdities, which he believed and
about which he speaks continually. In his opinion the
devil is at the bottom of *all* evil. „I think that the devil
sends every plague and sickness, for he is the prince of
death ... but he uses natural instruments and means." ([60])
„No illness comes from God, for he is good and sends
good to everybody, but it is sent by the devil, who causes
all misfortunes." ([61]) „In illness the doctors look only at
the natural causes ... but they do not remember, that the
devil moves the natural causes ... who changes hot into
cold and good into evil." ([62]) His boy being a little un-
well, Luther trembled at the thought, that the devil, having so great a grudge against him, might cause the child
to die.([63]) Sadness is owing to the same cause. „All sad-

against the common belief in
witches may be seen ap. Diel, Fr.
von Spee, Freib. 1872 p. 26 seqq.
   ([59]) If at Geneva, under Calvin,
in three months of one year (1545)
thirty-four criminals were burnt as
witches, if towards the end of the
same century in Protestant Braunschweig sometimes ten executions
of witches took place in one day,
the Catholic towns of Würzburg
and Bamberg saw no smaller number of similar atrocities. But it
was neither Luther, nor any other
Protestant Reformer, but a Catholic priest, moreover a Jesuit, who
first effectually combated such
scandalous proceedings. Friedrich
von Spee S. J. fearlessly raised his
voice to intercede for the victims
of the superstitious fury of the
people. He had had many opportunities of convincing himself of the
absurdity of the charges of witch-

craft. His sacerdotal office brought
him continually into contact with
those, who were sent to the pile
on such charges. His appeal to
common sense and justice (Cautio
criminalis, seu de processibus contra sagas liber) was so effectual,
that from the time of its publication the „Hexenprocesse" began to
disappear.
   ([60]) Tischr. II. c. 1. § 9.
   ([61]) Ibid. § 37.
   ([62]) Ibid. § 72. Cfr. Lauterb.
102: Illo die satis debilis erat Lutherus in calculo arthetica in poplitibus; dixit: Satan me undequa-
que vexat, non simpliciter, sed
composite, multis morbis.
   ([63]) Ora vero, ut mihi servet
Christus prolem contra Satanam,
quem scio nihil omissurum, quo
me laedat in filio, si Deus permi-
serit. Nam et jam non nihil vex-
atur infans, nescio quibus morbel-

ness, illness and melancholy comes from the devil ... I am
certain, it is the devil's work." ([64]) Luther believes in the
effect of philtres or love-potions, ([65]) he tells no end of
stories about people, who have been fetched, body and
soul, by the devil; ([66]) of succubi and incubi and of their
offspring, ([67]) of fallacious appearances, caused by the devil
to deceive people, in the mines, ([68]) or in the hunting-
field; ([69]) he thinks the devil dwells in monkeys; ([70]) he
relates his own experience, how the devil disturbed him
at Wittenberg, ([71]) and upset his nuts on the Wartburg, ([72])
how his own mother was bewitched; ([73]) he knows the effect
of witchcraft on eggs, milk and butter ([74]) etc. etc. „Witches"
he said, „ought not to be shown mercy, I would burn
them myself". ([75]) At another remedy against witchcraft
we can only hint in a note. ([76]) And all this is meant
seriously, for Luther frequently adds: I am quite sure of
it, it is quite certain, I heard it from Amsdorf, etc. In
short, Luther's superstition is prodigious.

It is curiously mixed up with the fearful interior struggles he suffered all his life, and of which he gave a minute
description to his disciples. It fills one with pity to see
a mind like his perpetually harassed by the most excruciating thoughts. Catholics claim the right, to call him a
heretic and his doctrine heresy, therefore they cannot help
considering his interior sufferings as remorse of his conscience, which reproached him with his apostasy; his

lis, vel potius lactis insoliti (ut
putant) cruditate. qua puerperae
primo coguntur nutrire. DeWette
III. 117.

([64]) Tischr. II. c. 1. § 26; cfr.
c. 3. § 3.
([65]) Lauterb. 101.
([66]) Tischr. II. c. 1. § 42. 73.
22. 79 etc.
([67]) Ibid. § 77. 94. 96 etc.
([68]) Ibid. § 24.
([69]) Lauterb. 142.
([70]) Mentio fiebat von affenn
vnnd meerkatzen ... Rt. Lutherus:
unt monstrosa animalia, in quibus

Sathan latet, neque cum illis ludendum. Lauterb. 110.
([71]) Tischr. II. c. 1. § 134.
([72]) Ibid. § 43.
([73]) Ibid. c. II. § 1.
([74]) Ibid. § 5.
([75]) Ibid.
([76]) Luther thinks that the
means resorted to by Dr. Pomeranus (Bugenhagen). when his cows
had been bewitched, was most excellent and efficacious. „Denn Dr.
Pommer — — — — und rührte
es um und sagte: Nun frett, Tüffel."
Ibid.

friends will look upon them as mere trials, meant to confirm him in faith. Luther attributes them always and everywhere to the action of the devil. As those struggles are
so intimately connected with his tenets, we must hear
a little about them from his own mouth.

„The devil comes frequently and reproaches me, that
great scandal and much evil has come through my doctrine.
Verily sometimes he troubles me much and fills me with
fear and terror. Though I answer, that also a great deal
of good has come from it, he knows, how to distort this
most cleverly.“ (⁷⁷) „He sleeps much nearer to me and
much more frequently with me, than my own Katie does,
i. e. he causes me more restlessness, than she gives me
joy.“ (⁷⁸) Bodily pain and temporal loss, Luther says,
are not so much after all, „but when the spiritual troubles
come, so that one is tempted to say: Cursed be the day,
on which I was born, then it is hard.“ (⁷⁹) „This is, what
the devil particulary intends, to tear out from our hearts
that article about the forgiveness of sins (through faith
alone), which is a firm rock against all his attacks, especially when he asks us: Who has commanded you, to
preach the Evangelium? Who has called you, to preach
in a way, which through many centuries no Bishop, no
Saint has dared to adopt? What, if God should not be
pleased with it? What, if you should be answerable for
all the souls that have been seduced by you?“ (⁸⁰) Luther
speaks of the great troubles of S. Jerome and others,
when they where tempted to impurity, but such troubles,
he says, are childish, when compared to his own. (⁸¹) „The
devil would have given me much more trouble, if I had
ont been a doctor. It is not an easy thing, to change all
religion and the doctrine of the Papacy. How difficult it
has been to me, will be seen on that (the last) day, at
present nobody believes it.“ (⁸²)

(⁷⁷) Tischr. II. c. 3. § 1. (⁸⁰) Ibid. c. 1. § 3.
(⁷⁸) Ibid. (⁸¹) Ibid. c. 3. § 46.
(⁷⁹) Ibid. § 47. (⁸²) Ibid. c. 1. § 3.

More than anything else it was the article about justification by faith alone, which roused perpetual doubts and
struggles in him. But why should Luther always consider
them as the effect of the action of the devil? Of course
we do not expect, that Protestants will agree, when we
say, that probably Luther tried to derive some consolation
from reasoning like this: The thought, which is harassing
me, comes from the devil, who is a father of lies; therefore I must get rid of the thought. As it was important
to him to confirm himself in his fundamental article, the
easiest remedy against all doubts was, to father them on
the father of lies. But let us hear him again. The reader
will remember the distinction, according to the Reformer,
between *Law* and *Evangelium*. „Up to the present day,
I cannot order or drive off Satan from me, as I should
like to do. Nor can I apprehend Christ, as the Scripture
represents him to me; the devil always tries, to put a different
Christ before me“. ([83]) We have seen before, that no idea
could be more distasteful to Luther, than that of Christ
insisting on the observance of the law and threatening
the sinner with punishment. „The devil's greatest arti-
fice and trick is this, to change the Evangelium into Law.
If I could only well distinguish between the two, Law
and Evangelium, I would tell him at all hours, that he
might — — —“. ([84]) „Without grace, i. e. according to
the Law, we are wicked. The devil always troubles us
with this, especially at the last hour, or when we are in
danger of death.“ [85])

However Luther had many weapons, to fight the
devil with, and some of them will be found very rough.
The first and principal was the „word of God“, of course
in the sense, which he tried to persuade himself, it had.
„Many a time has the devil had me by the head, but he
has been obliged to let me go again... Frequently he
has tormented me so much, that I did not know, whether

([83]) Ibid. § 49.   ([85]) Ibid. § 102.
([84]) Ibid. § 15.

I was dead or alive. He has even made me despair, so
that I did not know, whether there was a God ... but
with the word of God I have always repelled him." ([86])
„When I am unoccupied, ... the devil creeps up to me,
and before I can look round, he makes me sweat, but
when I hold out the halberd of the Divine word, he runs
away".([87]) It was another of Luther's favourite attempts
at getting relief in his struggles, to suppose that S. Paul
had exactly the same troubles. Hence he invariably explained the apostle's words: „Datus est mihi stimulus carnis
meae" as signifying temptations which S. Paul suffered
with regard to *faith*. „This temptation against faith was
to S. Paul a σκολοψ, a great spit and stake, which went
through his mind and his flesh, through his body and his
soul. It has not been a temptation to carnal impurity, as
the Papists dream, who have never felt any temptation,
but such. *They* have never gone through the greater
struggles, *they* have no experience of them; therefore they
talk and write about them, as a blind man does about
colours." ([88]) This is in harmony with another saying of
Luther: „ *We* have the great devils to attack us, *those devils,
that are doctors in theology;* the Turks and Papists have
only the smaller and meaner devils (to attack them), that
are not theological, but juridical devils".([89]) Of course,
as the Turks and Papists belong already to the devil, no
great efforts are needed to make sure of them.

Sometimes the „Reformer" had to use rougher means
to get rid of his Satanic majesty. „If during the night
the devil comes to torment me, I answer him: Devil, I must
sleep now; for this is the order established by God, work
during the day and sleep during the night. Again if he
will not go, if he puts my sins before me, I say: Dear
Devil, I have heard the list, but I have committed another
sin, which is not in the list; thou hadst better put it down
too. I have — — —, put that round your neck and wipe

([86]) Ibid. § 47.   ([88]) Ibid. c. 3. § 40.
([87]) Ibid. § 44.   ([89]) Ibid. c. 1. § 121.

your mouth on it".(⁹⁰) „When we are plagued by the
devil in our conscience, on account of our sins, we ought
to say: Holy Devil, pray for us! We have not sinned
against *you*, gracious Mr. Devil. *You* have not created
us, *you* have not given us life. Why do you then accuse
us so hard before God, as if you were so very holy, and
the supreme judge over God's real saints? Take thy staff
and walk to Rome, to thy servant, whose idol thou art."(⁹¹)
„Every night, when I awake, the devil is there and wants
to begin a dispute with me. My experience is this; If
you can do no good with the argument, that a Christian
is not *under* the law, but *above* the law, then send the
devil away with a —".(⁹²) The more the devil (perhaps
conscience?) urges the law, the more the law has to be
despised. Hence, „when a man is in trouble, or with
others who are in trouble, let him beat Moses to death and
throw stones upon him, but when he is well again and
free from trouble, let the law be preached to him again."(⁹³)
The thought of the Pope, the „heltrach" i. e. infernal dra-
gon(⁹⁴) against whom nobody can have sufficient enmity",
proved also a great help to Luther in his fights with the
evil one. „*They must be stupid fools, who say, that we
ought not to revile the Pope. Go on reviling him, especially,
when the devil troubles you about justification.*" (⁹⁵) „Sometimes I remind him (the devil) of the Pope, saying: What
is thy Pope and why doest thou trouble thyself so much,
that I should honour him. Behold the abomination he has
caused, it is not yet ended even now. I put before myself
Christ and the forgiveness of sins, but I put the abomination of the Pope before the devil's nose, and this abomination is so great, that I become quite courageuos.(⁹⁶)

But in spite of all these ingenious means, in spite of
remaining as much as possible in the company of friends(⁹⁷),

(⁹⁰) Ibid. c. 3. § 23.
(⁹¹) Ibid. § 41.
(⁹²) Ibid. c. 1. § 5. § 44.
(⁹³) Ibid. c. 3. § 27.
(⁹⁴) Lauterb. 64.

(⁹⁵) Tischr. II. c. 3. § 53.
(⁹⁶) Ibid.
(⁹⁷) Luther recommends this frequently (Tischr. II. c. 3. §. 71. So.
82.); he thinks it is better to go

in spite of eating and drinking([98]), the „Reformer“, up to his death imagined that the devil was after him everywhere.“ When Dr. Martin Luther was old .... as he himself confessed, the devil went with him about the dormitory of the monastery and plagued and attacked him. „For, he said, he had one or two devils, that were waiting for him assiduously.“([99])

Everybody that undertakes the tedious and at times hateful task of going through Luther's voluminous works, frequently meets with facts and sayings of so strange a nature, that the question: „Was this man at all times in his right mind?“ cannot possibly be ignored. We must leave it to others, to come to anything like a conclusive answer, but we beg the reader to give his attention to the following points.

1) In his earlier years, before he apostatized from the Catholic Church, Luther was suffering from a kind of religious mania, which was in great part owing te the false and thoroughly uncatholic idea he had formed of sanctity. Being under the impression, that he had to please God exclusively with his own good works, he made, as we have seen, almost suicidal efforts, to accomplish that task; efforts which were unable to calm a soul, that looked upon God as an enemy. He was sincerely devoted to the Church, until he found out that the Church could not approve of the system which he had gradually built up, but even this devotion was far from being of a sound nature. When he said that he would have been ready to kill anyone that

the pigstye for company, than to be alone. See Lauterb. 50: Ich gehe ehr zu meynem seuhirten Johannes, auch zu den schweynen, antequam solus essem.

([98]) Tischr. II. c. 3. § 51. 53.
([99]) Ibid. c. 1. § 137.

attacked the Pope([100]) or that, when in Rome, he almost
wished his parents to be dead, that he might have been
able to say Mass for them in the holy places([101]) we are
quite willing to make allowance for exaggeration. But
even phrases, that cannot be taken literally, may be considered as indicating the disposition of the mind. That
his ideas in later years were as different as possible, is so
far from weakening the importance of this fanatical disposition, as rather to increas it.

2) Hundreds of passages in his works show, what an
extraordinary opinion Luther had of himself. His conceit
alone would be sufficient to make one doubtful about the
state of his mind. Before him, we have heard him say, the
world had known absolutely nothing about Christianity([102]),
the Fathers had been ignorant even of the essential part of the
Evangelium([103]), S. Augustine and S. Ambrose are nothing
compared to him([104]), he is God's Notary([105]), an Evangelist, an Ecclesiastes, before whose preaching the devil
trembles, as if Christ himself were there([106]), he is one of
the principal doctors([107]); whose enemies will, by God's
judgment, perish like Arius([108]); whose prayer and prophecy
never faileth. ([109]) He is not only fond of putting himself
on a par with S. Paul (of which propensity we have given
many proofs) but he does not shrink from comparing himself to our Divine Lord. „Yes, we are like to Christ on
the cross. Before the cross there stand Annas and Caiphas
with the priests and blaspheme the Lord, whom they have
already crucified, just as the Pope, Cardinals and monks
curse us, after having condemned and murdered us and
after having shed our blood. There are the soldiers, i. e.
the secular powers, partly at least, cursing us; amongst

([100]) Wenn 'einer damals gelehrt
hätte, was ich jetzt durch Gottes
Gnade glaube und lehre, ich würde
ihn mit den Zähnen zerrissen haben.
                Ap. Jürgens. I. 583.
([101]) Ibid. II. 304.
([102]) Walch XVI. 2013.

([103]) Wittenb. V. 35Sb.
([104]) Wittenb. (Germ.) XII. 243.
([105]) De Wette V. 422.
([106]) Walch XX. 232.
([107]) Walch XVII. 1645.
([108]) Ibid. 1650.
([109]) Wittenb. (Germ.) IX. 179.

them that impenitent thief (der linke Schächer) Harry of
Wolfenbüttel etc."([110])   The reader will remember that in
his conceit Luther claimed for himself that infallibility,
which he refused to the Church, that he insisted on having
received his doctrine directly from heaven and that he
denied the possibility of salvation to all, who would not
adhere to him.([111])   A very significant fact is also this,
that according to his own confession, he considered all
who opposed him, as madmen, *because* they opposed him.([112])

3) This enormous selfesteem produced a sort of mania,
in which Luther looked upon himself as the object of
bitter persecution.   The feeling of his importance made it
credible to him, that his adversaries left no means untried to
get rid of him and that his escapes were nothing short of
miraculous.   „I shall die willingly, but they shall not do
it until my hour has come and my God calls me, though
they may rave and rage.   For he, that has preserved my
life now for three years against their will and against my
own hope is able to preserve it also for the| future."([113])
„In spite of the Pope and of all tyrants God has preserved my life, a thing, which many justly consider as a
miracle, as I myself too must confess."([114])   Not a great
miracle though, when we remember that Luther had been
in safety on the Wartburg and at Wittenberg.   But he
believes and relates even the most ridiculous things, to represent himself as a victim, whose life is eagerly sought
after.   In 1520 he communicates to Spalatinus the intelli-
gence, which has just reached him, that a physician who
has the power of making himself invisible, has been sent
out to kill him.([115])   On another occasion he relates, that
the pulpit in which he was to have preached, had been
poisoned by the Papists.   In 1525 he had a Polish Doctor,

([110]) Walch XVII. 1661.
([111]) Supra p. 176. Cfr. Wittenb.
V. 288ᴮ. Sic nos cum Paulo se-
curissime et certissime pronuntia-
mus, omnem doctrinam esse male-
dictam quae cum nostra dissidet.

([112]) Ich halte sie stracks für
Narren.   Walch XXII. 922-
([113]) Walch XV. 2713.
([114]) Walch XVI. 75.
([115]) Walch XV. app. 32.

a Jew, arrested, who, he thought, intended to poison him.([116]) Also in his book „de servo arbitrio“ he dwells with a manifest pleasure on his „pericula vitae.“ ([117])

Naturally Luther supposes that his apostolic activity must have greatly exasperated the devil and that therefore he has to suffer persecution also from that quarter. „I see it clearly that he devil, who has not been able to kill me through the Pope, now tries to destroy me through the bloodthirsty prophets and fanatics.“([118]) He is inclined to think that all the mischief in the world is owing to the devil's well founded rage against *him*. „I see the devil is angry, that hitherto he has not been able to do anything, neither by tricks, nor by force, he thinks to get rid of me, even if he should have to upset the whole world. I almost think, it is on my account, that the devil does these things in the world.“ ([119])

4) Köstlin tries to make out that Luther was a very temperate man, and that his daily expense for drink was not more than a halfpenny. ([120]) If so, wine must have been enormously cheap in those days, considering that for that amount Luther was able to get more than did him good, though he was able „to guzzle like a German“. ([121]) As he liked a good dinner, (he said he meant to give to the worms a fat doctor to eat), ([122]) so he liked a good drink; the beer plays an important part in his letters to Kate. Here is a specimen: „Dear Master Käthe . . . Yesterday I took an evil drink (hatt ich ein bosen Trunk gefasset), I had to sing . . . I thought, what good beer and wine I have at home, likewise a handsome wife, or — should I say — master. You would do well, to send me the whole cellar-full of my wine, and a bottle

---

([116]) Est hic apud nos Judaeus Polonus, missus sub pretio 2000 aureorum, ut me veneno perdat. De Wette III. 616.

([117]) Wittenb. II. 464B.

([118]) Walch XVI. 77.

([119]) Letter to Rühel. De Wette II. 654. Cfr. letter to Link. Ibid. III. 224.

([120]) Köstlin II. 507.

([121]) De Wette V. 298.

([122]) Wittenb. VI. 401.

of your beer, as often as you can." (^{123}) On one occasion
Luther excused himself by saying, that, as he was getting
old, he had to seek his bolster and pillow in the can; (^{124})
again he said: „If God can forgive me, that for almost
twenty years I have crucified and martyred him by saying
Mass, he can also forgive me, if now and then I take a
good drink in his honour; let the world think of it, what
it likes." (^{125}) If there had been no excess, there would
hardly be matter for forgiveness. It sounds rather strange,
to hear the Ecclesiastes of Wittenberg say that he means
to prepare himself for a lecture on the drunkenness of
Noah, by drinking freely, so as to be able to speak about
a bad thing from experience. (^{126}) In a letter to Gabriel
Didymus Luther speaks of the splendid living at Coburg,
but complains of „a thunder in his head", which has lasted
for almost a month; he is doubtful, whether it is caused
by the wine, or by the devil! (^{127}) A short time afterwards
he complains also to Melanchthon of the weakness of his
head (^{128}) and again he writes to the same about a bad
throat, caused either by the wine or by the devil. (^{129})

(^{123}) De Wette IV. Cfr. II. 310:
E Principali cella bibimus vinum
bonum et purum, et futuri essemus
pulchri evangelici, si sic Evangelion
nos saginaret ... Excusa nos apud
Principem, quod tantum vini Corn-
bergici linxerimus. — Cfr. a letter
to C. Müller (first published by
Evers I.) „Das Bier ist gut, die
magd schön und die Gesellen innig."
This letter is signed:
　　　　Doctor Martinus
　　　　Doctor Luther
　　　　Doctor Plenus.
(^{124}) Mathesius 151.
(^{125}) Walch XVII. 133.
(^{126}) „Cras debeo legere de
ebrietate Noah, ergo hac vespere
satis bibam, ut deinde expertus de
re mala loqui possim." Seidemann
in the Arch. für Lit. Gesch. IX. 1,
quoted by Germanus 295. In connection with this, let us give here
one more proof, what extraordinary

advice Luther could give in his
blind hatred against the Pope. In
the Kirchenpostille, a popular instruction, he inveighs against the
old law of fasting. „It was so
blasphemous and so abominable in
God's eyes, that no gluttony or
drunkenness could have been worse;
it would be better to be deaddrunk
day and night, than to observe
those laws." Walch XI. 730.
(^{127}) Valemus quidem et splen-
dide vivimus, nisi quod jam paene
mensem passus sum tonitruum capitis, non tinnitum, sive culpa et
causa sit vini, sive Satan sic me
ludificetur. De Wette IV. 44.
(^{128}) Non potui prolixe scribere,
sic me capitis imbecillitas captivum
tenet, ut neque tuto legere literas
possim, neque lucem ferre ... Satanae angelus est, qui sic me co-
laphisat. De Wette. IV. 120.
(^{129}) Mihi in gutture corrosio

Lemnius, who had been in Wittenberg for a number of years, stated that Luther's intemperance was notorious.([130])

5) A very important symptom for a diagnosis of the state of the „Reformer's" mind is to be found in his hallucinations. Luther did not merely think, that the devil was near him, but his excited imagination made him actually see the archenemy under various forms. On one occasion he saw him in the form of a dog,([131]) on another as a black pig, or as a bull.([132]) „The devil," he says, „appears at times under larvae, as I have seen myself, like a sow or like a burning wisp of straw."([133]) We have heard above from Ratzeberger([134]) that shortly before his death Luther saw the devil sitting in the street and was insulted by him in a peculiar way. Those perpetual struggles with the devil, which „made him sweat",([135]) throw further light on the state of his mind.

6) Noone that will take the trouble to read Luther's book against the Bishops, or his „Hansworst", or his „Shemhamphoras", or his last shameful pamphlet against the Pope, (productions, from which we have given some quotations), will consider it too hard, if we say, that at times he suffered from real paroxysms of rage. On those occasions he not only forgot all logic, but revelled in the filthiest and most indecent expressions and images; he developed what Bullinger called „a lewd and houndish eloquence". To say that this is a sign of a sound mind, would probably not meet with the approval of medical men. Schön, whose experience is very large, says: „For nineteen years I have had the cure of souls in one of the largest asylums of the present time (Vienna), but never

quaedam nova accessit, ut suspicer vel vini violentia salsum phlegma augeri, vel antiquas reliquias post tot annos sanitatis redire, aut esse Satanae colaphum.
        Ap. Döll. III. 241.
([130]) Lutheri vita ita omnibus est perspecta, ut pauci sint qui eam laudibus dignentur. Dum Episcopum se jactat Evangelicum, qui fit ut ille parum sobrie vivat?
                Ibid. 243.
([131]) Myconius, Hist. Reform. 42.
([132]) Mathesius 184.
([133]) See Janssen II. 177.
([134]) page 343.
([135]) Tischr. II. c. 1. § 44; c. 3. § 1.

have I heard such mad language, as that of Luther, whom his admirers call „the dear man of God." ([136]) Friends and foes speak of Luther's eyes as being remarkable through a particular lustre. Melanchthon calls them the eyes of a lion, that is ready for battle, other friends admire the genius expressed in them ([137]), Aleander calls them demoniacal. ([138]) The Polish ambassador Johannes Dantiscus gives the following account of Luther, with whom he had had a long interview: „I found the man to be witty, eloquent, learned, but he had only invectives, arrogance and bitterness against the Pope, the Emperor and a few other princes. His face is just like his books, his eyes are sharp and have an unpleasant lustre, as is sometimes the case with possessed people. His speech is violent, full of mockery and bantering .... his pride and vainglory become at once manifest." ([139])

7) We may here also mention that, from Luther's crude, nay, brutal views about sexual matters, — views which he would not have uttered, had he not come to a general conclusion from his own personal naturel — Schön comes to the conclusion, that Luther's nervous system was deeply disordered. ([140])

In putting these points before the reader and in frankly giving expression to our own opinion, that Luther was at times not compos sui, we wish to state at the same time, that by so doing we throw no further blame upon him; on the contrary, we help to extenuate a little the atrocity of many of his words and acts.

([136]) Schön, Luther auf d. Standp. der Psychiatrie, Wien 1874. p. 19. Cfr. the words of Pirkheimer: Lutherus ipse nequaquam linguae petulantia et procacitate abscondit quid habeat in corde, adeo ut plene insanire, vel a malo daemonio agitari videatur. Döll. I. 587.

([137]) Köstlin II. 527.
([138]) Esso Luther in descensu currus, versis huc et illuc daemoniacis oculis, disse: Deus erit pro me.   Balan 170.
([139]) Hipler, Kopernikus und Luther, Braunsberg 1868. p. 54. 56.
([140]) Schön. l. c. 39.

The great question about Luther is this: Has this man been a messenger of Heaven? Has he had all those qualities, which we *must* expect in an Apostle?

If any of those, who know the real Luther not from loving traditions, but from his own works, can find another S. Paul in this cursing, swearing, tippling boor, we must take for once the liberty to use his own principle of private judgment and to think, that at least one of the „Reformer's" prophecies has been fulfilled, though the question, whether this fulfilment will prove his divine vocation, remains open: *„Adorabunt stercora nostra, et pro balsamo habebunt."* ([141])

In the old imperial city of Worms, not far from the majestic and venerable Minster of S. Peter, the Prince of the Apostles, there stands the grand bronze monument, which the Protestants of Germany have erected in honour of their spiritual father, of the work he inaugurated and of his helpers in the same.

As far as it is a work of art, we have here nothing to do with it; but inasmuch as it represents history or pretends to do so, it is important enough to make a few words about it in this place allowable.

We will however omit a discussion of the minor parts of the monument; of the six basreliefs which represent remarkable scenes from the „Reformer's" life([142]), because the same events have been sufficiently noticed in the preceding chapters; also of the smaller portrait medallions, though amongst them the two of the ruffianly robber Franz

---

([141]) Walch XXII. 1906.

([142]) These scenes are: Luther affixing his theses to the Church-door at Wittenberg, Luther preaching, Luther before the Diet of Worms, Luther translating the Bible, Luther administering the Eucharist, Luther's marriage.

von Sickingen and of the debauchee Ulrich von Hutten ([143])
would in themselves be sufficient to make one address to
Luther the words of the poet:

> Du thust mir in der Seele weh,
>
> Wenn ich dich in der Gesellschaft seh,

and finally of the three allegorical figures of the cities of
Speyer, Augsburg and Magdeburg, the latter of which
especially bids defiance to historical truth, perpetuating in
bronze the old lies about stout Tilly's wickedness.

Let us restrict our attention to the principal figures,
Towering above all there is of course Luther.

Hase says of the Wittenberg Reformer: „With a strong
sensuality Luther was rooted to the earth, but his head
reaches to the sky. ([144])“. We are ready to subscribe to
first part, and think that the numerous quotations which
we have given will probably produce a similar willingness
in the reader.

It would almost seem as if the artist, who modelled
the Luther statue, had had those words of Hase before his
eyes. Of spirituality there certainly appears nothing in it,
but the rough, obstinate, selfwilled, spiteful, ferocious nature
of the „Reformer“ is admirably expressed. There he stands
in a defying attitude, his head thrown back, the Bible in
one hand and smiting it with the other, as if he was challenging the Pope and the whole world and forsooth the devil
too, as if he was just saying: „Come now, you blind moles
and bats“ ([145]), I, Dr. Martin Luther, know how to interpret, I will teach you, or, if you will not be taught, I will
annihilate you. This defying attitude, as the author of
„Kirche oder Protestantismus“ observes([146]), is almost apt
to make one smile, when one thinks of the prophecies of

([143]) It was first contemplated
to assign to Hutten a statue in
the monument at Worms, but fortunately the sculptor, Rietschel,
strongly objected to the idea, as
he had not sufficient sympathy
with that character. See Berl.
National-Zeitung 31. May, 1868.

([144]) Mit kräftiger Sinnlichkeit
stand Luther festgewurzelt in die
Erde, aber sein Haupt reicht in
den Himmel.
    Kirchengeschichte p. 384.
([145]) See Page 153.
([146]) p. 8.

speedy destruction so often pronounced by Luther against Popery, and when one compares the indestructible vitality of the Catholic Church with the ghost of Lutheranism that exists in our days.

And who can, at the sight ot the Bible in Luther's hand, forget how this sacred book, which he tore from the protecting hand of the Church to deliver it over to the fancies and whims of every individual, has been pulled to pieces by his own children?

The two secular protectors of Luther have found their places in the front corners of the monument. At his left stands the Elector Frederick of Saxony, at his right Philip, Landgraf of Hessen.

The former, to whom protestant historians have given the surname „the Wise“, has never given any startling proofs of wisdom in his life. He was an indolent, sensual man, who cared very little for religion of any kind. When he protected Luther against the edictum of Worms, he did so partly from political motives, partly in the interest of his own University of Wittenberg. But in the „Reformer“ himself he took so very little interest, that he never even made his personal acquaintance, though nothing could have been easier or would seem more likely. Nor did he ever formally profess the „reformed“ religion, except that on his deathbed he allowed Communion to be administered according to the lutheran rite.

Of Philip von Hessen we need not say much. It will always remain a puzzle to Catholics, why the friends of the Reformation, instead of being heartily ashamed of him, should parade this notorious adulterer and bigamist as one of their fathers and heroes or should spend money in erecting a monument to such a despicable character.

Two Theologians stand at the other corners of the monument, Reuchlin and Melanchthon, uncle and nephew.

The former's presence in this place shows, at the very least, a remarkable want of correctness. His bitter controversy with the converted Jew Pfefferkorn and with the

Dominicans of Cologne has nothing whatever to do with Lutheranism. Nothing could have been farther removed from him than the wish to leave the Church. He lived and died a Catholic and shortly before his death (A.D. 1522.) he gave unmistakably expression to his detestation of the new heresy by revoking the grant which he had made of his extensive and valuable library to his nephew Philip. „Yes", Hutten wrote to him, „go to Rome, the object of all thy desires, go and kiss Pope Leo's toe. Thou doest not like Luther's cause, thou disapprovest of it and wishest to see it annihilated." ([147]) Why then should he appear as a supporter of Lutheranism?

Melanchthon's peculiarities are faithfully expressed in his statue. His features betray that slyness and want of straightforwardness which characterize his dealings. During Luther's life he was obliged, not without bitter murmuring, to yield to the domineering and even tyrannical ways of his friend ([148]), but as soon as the latter had disappeared from the scene and his restraining power was no longer felt, Melanchthon declared open war to the distinctively lutheran tenets, and the war was carried on in just as determined and bitter a manner as that against Popery. The *lutheran* theologians became in the eyes of the „man of a tender conscience" „idolatrous and sophistical bloodhounds."

But at Worms Luther and Melanchthon appear as fast friends. Bronze is patient.

At the four corners of the pedestal of Luther's statue there are seen four sitting figures of men who are reckoned as the principal precursors of the Reformation.

Wickleff and Huss, the two fanatics, are there in their proper place. Their teachings and their actions have certainly prepared the way of the Ecclesiastes of Wittenberg. The seditions and rebellions in England and Bohemia, for

---

([147]) See L. Geiger, Johann Reuchlin, sein Leben und seine Werke. Leipzig 1871. p. 147 seqq.

([148]) See chapt. 22.

which they are answerable, furnish an additional proof of the fitness of their being near the man, whose agitation did so much to cause the horrors of the revolt of the German peasants.

The author of „Kirche oder Protestantismus([149]) asks with a very pardonable sarcasm: If the precursors of the Reformation are admitted to figure on the monument at Worms, would it not be fair to immortalize in the same place those men, who, following in Luther's footsteps and carrying out his cherished principle of private judgment, have „perfected" his work? Would not Socinus, Schleiermacher, Baur and Strauss look well there, and would not their statues greatly contribute towards the beauty and comprehensiveness of the tout ensemble?

But there are two more „precursors of the Reformation," Waldus and Savonarola.

It would have been an act of charity on the part of the originators of the Luther monument, if, for the benefit of minds not sufficiently well versed in history, they had stated their reasons for putting those men there.

Whatever the few Waldensians of the present day may believe, it is certain, that the only error of their founder Waldus was this, that he considered poverty not as an evangelical counsel, but as a strict duty of every individual Christian, an error as unlutheran as it possibly could be. The whole merit of Waldus, which has procured him the honour of a place at the monument, seems therefore to consist in this, that, no matter how, he opposed the teaching, of the Catholic Church. If this is the case, Arius, Marcion Eutyches and Nestorius might also have been admitted, or perhaps it might have been advisable to erect a pantheon in honour of all heresiarchs indiscriminately.

And Savonarola! When looking at him, we have thought again of the words of Göthe we have quoted before, but in a different sense. No greater injustice could

([149]) p. 25.

be done to the great Dominican monk than to drag him into such company. True, that he did his best to bring about a Reformation, but a *Catholic* Reformation. No matter how much he may have been mistaken in the means he resorted to, no matter how far he allowed himself to be carried away in his blind zeal, nobody can say that he ever intended to separate himself from the unity of the Catholic Church or to found a sect in opposition to her. Though misled, he remained her sincere son, and living and dying he showed his fidelity to her and to the religious order in which he had taken his solemn vows. His last words were a protestation to that effect. Yet „he, who all his life had been sitting at the feet of the eminently Catholic Doctor Angelicus, appears now, in defiance of history, at the feet of the eminently anticatholic and heretical Doctor vere non angelicus Martin Luther." ([150])

Salvo meliori judicio, we think that the Luther monument at Worms is a decided failure. There is a great deal in it, which is not compatible with historical truth, and that which is true, does not greatly contribute towards the „Reformer's" honour.

Has he a better and worthier monument in his work? Let us direct our attention to this question in the concluding chapter.

([150]) Kirche oder Protest. p. 88. The author of this valuable book draws a masterly comparison between Luther and Savonarola, 80 seqq.

Chapter XXIV

Luther's work at the present time.

Erit maxima confusio.
Luther ap. Lauterb. 91.

Every kingdom divided against itself shall
be brought to desolation and house upon
house shall fall.
Luke XI. 17.

To arrive at a just estimate of the value of Luther's
work, many ways are open. In the preceding chapters
we have endeavoured to give, from his own works, a faithful portrait of the man, we have pointed out the leading
features of his character and the most salient points of his
teaching, and we hope to have enabled the reader to answer
for himself the question, whether or not this man possessed those qualities which may be justly expected in an
Apostle, whether or not he presented to the world those
credentials, without wich an extraordinary messenger of
God cannot hope to be received.

Another equally conclusive way is a serious reflexion
on the manner in which Lutheranism was established. If
Lutheranism has been God's work, it must have been established by means, which are worthy of God. But he who
puts aside the trite old phrases about the spiritual yoke
of Rome and the rising of the Teutonic races against the
tyranny of the Pope, and calmly looks at the facts, which
history has preserved, will find that the spread of Luther-

anism was chiefly owing to licentiousness and avarice(¹), and that, where the people were unwilling to give up the religion of their fathers and to exchange a universal Church, embracing the whole world, for a little territorial Church under the spiritual authority of a secular prince, brutal force, bigoted intolerance, and the meanest of tricks accomplished the work. We are ready to prove this at any time.

A third way will be found in the examination of the fate of Lutheranism after the death of its founder. God's work must be lasting and solid: but nobody would consider Luther's work as possessing those qualities.

His system may be said to have gone through two chief phases: the first diagonally opposed to the spirit of the Reformation, the second as hateful to Luther himself at it would be to all lovers of Christianity.

In the first phase we meet with the most rigid hyperorthodoxy, which degenerated into a worse spiritual slavery than that which Non-Catholics so frequently fancy exists in the Church of Rome. Private judgment and absolute liberty of investigation had been the basis of Luther's work; but woe to the Protestant who would have denied the authority of the symbolical Lutheran books or deviated a hair's breadth from them. The authority of a Church which had existed 1500 years before Luther, was despised as tyrannical: yet those who raved against „Menschensatzungen", had „to swear by the word of the master" and to renounce the very principle on which their Church was founded. It will be said that they founded their Creed on the Bible. Very well, but contrary to their principle they had to interpret the Bible as Luther had done; and even to know and to prove the supernatural character and value of this book was an absolute impossibility, except

---

(¹) Also Frederick II of Prussia attributes to selfishness the greatest part of the success of the Reformation in Germany. Si l'on veut réduire les causes des progrès de la réforme à des principes simples, on verra qu'en Allemagne ce fut l'ouvrage de l'intérêt. Oeuvres I. 18.

by going back to the authority of that Church, whom the
Ecclesiastes of Wittenberg used to call the arch-whore
of the devil.

The second phase, though as different as possible from
the first, was yet caused by it. The hyper-orthodoxy
which was not founded upon an authority that could call
itself divine, naturally became distasteful and produced a
reaction. People began to remember the dear old principle
of the „Reformers“, private judgment, they claimed it once
more as an inheritance which most unjustly had been withheld from them, they followed it even beyond the line
which Luther most arbitrarily had drawn. Rationalism and
infidelity — in many cases a decent infidelity veiled under
a few christian-sounding phrases — was the consequence.
Formerly reason had been, not with the Catholics, but
with the Lutherans, „the devil's arch-bride“ and „a beast
that had to be throttled“; it was now set on the throne
as the only legitimate Sovereign, with full power to judge
of all Divine mysteries, or rather to declare that things
which would be mysterious could not be admitted by an
enlightened religion.

It would lead us too far away from the subject of
these pages, if we were to follow Lutheranism at its every
step through its development or rather its decadence. But
we may be allowed to put Luther's work to the test with
the question: *What state is it in at the present day? How
much of it is left?*

Three centuries and a half have passed, since its appearance startled the world; this time must be considered sufficient to have brought out its value and its vitality. Luther
himself has appealed to the words of Gamaliel: „If this
design or work be of men, it will fall to nothing, but if
it be of God, you are not able to destroy it.“ There is
therefore nothing unfair in the question.

The centenary of Luther's birth, kept in November
1883 was no doubt a grand demonstration which, apparently
at least, would speak volumes in favour of the continuity

of Luther's work. But let us not go by appearances. If Luther had been able to descend from his pedestal at Worms, and to get amongst the crowd that were feasting him and singing his praises, it is greatly to be feared that in the genuine Lutheran i. e. not over-elegant style he would have said some startling things, that he would have loaded a great part of his admirers with genuine Lutheran curses and given them „a cut across the snout", as formerly he had done to the prophets of Zwickau.

Nothing would have been more hateful to the Father of the Reformation, than that admirable „comprehensiveness" which now seems to form the greatest glory of Protestantism; though nobody would say that in such detestation Luther would have been very logical.

No matter how arbitrarily he dealt with the Creed of the Church from which he had apostatized, no matter how often he changed his opinions in other things — the Blessed Trinity, the Incarnation of the Son of God, the fact of redemption, the inspiration of Holy Scripture, these were truths, which not only he would have been horrified to doubt, but in the defence of which he would gladly have laid down his life. And now behold the irony of fate! Luther is praised to the skies by those, to whom the Blessed Trinity is „a remnant of heathenish-jewish philosophy," the fall of man „an old legend," the Incarnation „a sacred fable", by those who have criticized away one part of the Bible after another, until nothing but the binding is left. Not that we mean to say that *all* German Protestants have gone so far. It is a matter of congratulation that, as Möhler observes, a happy want of consequence has prevented large numbers of them from fully carrying out their fundamental principle. But it is notorious that the number of absolutely infidel German Protestants, of men, whose whole religion consists in protesting against all supernatural belief, is legion; and they all put forward their claim through the mouth of one of their principal leaders, the late Professor Bluntschli, so famous through his intense hatred of the Catholic Church: „We are legitimate children of the Reformation."

But before we come to the infidels, let us turn our attention to those who have to be called believing Protestants. Inasmuch as they hold the above mentioned mysteries, nobody would say that they hold anything distinctively Lutheran; those are the truths, which the „Ecclesiastes" took with him, when he left the Catholic Church. But how do matters stand, when we come to the distinctively Lutheran teachings?

Of course one point is too sacred to be touched, it has to be kept up at any price, viz. the hatred of Rome; but what about the want of freedom in the human will? and justification by faith alone? and Sacraments? and the absolute power of the congregations over their own pastors? and the sufficiency of Holy Scripture? One or another Lutheran preacher who has resisted the memorable forcible „Union" of the year 1817, or an antiquated minister in an out of the way corner of Mecklenburg may still stick to these things, but nobody else does. His most devoted admirers manage to keep a backdoor open to escape from his dictatorial sayings([2]), but whilst using their private judgment, many of them have unconsciously drifted back to the things, which the master detested as papistical abominations and was wont to send to the bottom of hell.

„The Bible and nothing but the Bible," this was the watchword of the Reformation of the 16th. century. Lessing in his famous controversy with Goeze([3]) was the first Protestant, who showed the insufficiency of the principle. Kahnis, Münscher, La Coste, Delbrück, Perthes and other celebrated protestant theologians of modern times have followed in his steps.([4]) The words of the last mentioned are very significant. „Scripture requires a protec-

---

([2]) „We remember his own words: ... I am not nor do I wish to be anybody's master." Köstlin II. 638. Cfr. Köhler 325. 326.

([3]) Lessing's ausgewählteWerke. Leipzig 1867. X. 101 seqq.
([4]) For particulars see Kirche oder Protestantismus 318 seqq.

tion against the arbitariness of men, and man wants an inter-
preter of Scripture. The institution which has to serve
this double purpose, is the Church, but where is it? Who
possesses it? . . . If it were not for the feeling of shame,
in the presence of the Catholic Church, how loudly and
how desperately would orthodox Protestants cry out for
the help and the authority of the Church!" ([5]) It is also
interesting to notice from the confession of Protestants, that
the Bible is so little used, „that it is hardly read in one
house out of a hundred." ([6]) „In the dark ages, when the
Bible cost as many hundreds of dollars as it now costs
pence . . . the ignorance of the Bible and the difficulty
of answering a christian question was not so great, as it
is among the present generation." ([7])

Justification by faith alone has been declared by Luther,
hundreds of times, to be the very foundation of his whole
system. With it, he said, Christianity would stand or fall.
Who believes in it now? Out of a long list of leading theologians, embracing also the non-united Protestants, who
as a rule are more faithful to Luther's dogmatic system
than the others, we will only mention here the names of
De Wette, Neander, Ebrard, Martensen, Köstlin, Beyschlag,
Hengstenberg, Harless, Kahnis, Billroth, who have all renounced it, who have all come back to maintaining the
freedom of the human will, the necessity of man's cooperation with Divine grace and the interior regeneration of
the human heart in justification. Nay, here is again the
irony of fate, that, whereas the necessity and meritorious-
ness of good works was one of those points, the mention
of which used to drive Luther into rage, now with many
of his „orthodox" disciples righteousness has become the
very substance of religion, whilst articles of faith occupy
a less than secondary position.

([5]) Fr. Perthes' Leben etc. Gotha
1861. III. 202.
([6]) Tholuck's Literarischer An-
zeiger, quoted in Kirche oder Prot.
320.

([7]) Evangelische Kirchenzeitung
1861. quoted ibid.

In the Lutheran „Evangelium" Sacraments found nowhere a place, since all justification was exclusively owing
to faith. Luther was quite logical, when he denied the
necessity of baptism and when he endeavoured, though to
his greatest regret invain, to convert himself to Carlstadt's
and Zwingli's views about the Sacrament of the Eucharist.
At the present time a large number of orthodox Protestants
do their best to reinstate Sacraments in their proper place
in the theological system and in the esteem of the people.
The acknowledged leaders of this movement — which however has not spread so far as Puseyism in England —
were Vilmar([8]), Harless and Löhe, all lately dead. Transsubstantiation, the sacrificial character of the Eucharist,
confirmation, private absolution, holy orders etc. — there
is not one amongst these and similar „papistical abominations", to which many orthodox Protestants have not been
led back by the study of the Bible and of the earliest
Church history. What would Luther say, if he saw his
pet dogma of the universal priesthood so universally rejected?

We repeat, of distinctively Lutheran doctrine there
is (with the exception of the hatred against Rome and the
Pope) only an infinitesimal part left amongst his believing
followers of the present day ([8a]). The other part of German Protestants have not only renounced their leader's
peculiar teachings, but on the strength of that freedom
from authority which they owe to him, they have thrown
over board all Christianity and it is rather a puzzle to
know why they should call themselves Christians, since to
them Christ is only an improved edition of Solon or Con-
fucius. To this party we must now direct our attention.

In the eyes of the more advanced rationalists the vague

([8]) See Jörg I. 26 seqq. 379 seqq.
([8a]) „In Germany the lutheran
Church exists only in the aspirations and longings of a few theologians, pastors and canonists, not
as a reality, not as a concrete ecclesiastical institution." Döllinger,
Kirche und Kirchen p. 403. Cfr.

ibid. 413. — It is sufficiently well
known that, at the time of the
forced „Union" under Frederick
William III, those who refused to
give up their distinctly *lutheran*
principles, were considered and
treated as „dangerous sectarians".

pantheistic pietism of Schleiermacher seemed to preserve still too much if not of the substance of Christianity, at least of Christian appearances and to attribute too much authority to the Bible. To do away with this authority became the object towards which all the efforts of the Tübingen school of theologians under F. Chr. Baur were directed. One book of the Holy Scriptures after another was criticized away; of the New Testament only four of the Epistles of S. Paul and the Apocalypse were admitted as authentic. (⁹) To characterize this school, it is sufficient to mention that Strauss, the author of the famous „Life of Jesus" and of „Old and new faith", was one of its most prominent members. H. Paulus, Professor at Würzburg and afterwards at Heidelberg, found ways and means, to explain everything miraculous, that occurs in de Bible, in a natural way. That things, which cannot be comprehended by reason, have eo ipso to be considered as untrue, this was the principle from which those men started and which necessarily led them to conclusions that are not consistent with Christianity.

Hase, the author of the well known manual of protestant polemical theology, the „Nestor" of Protestant theologians, is also the representative of this rationalism. His „dogmatic" in indeed interesting. He denies the Blessed Trinity. „We must pluck up courage to consider this dogma not as being *above*, but as being *against* all reason"; (¹⁰) the fall of man is to him „an old legend . . . not the remembrance of a fact, but a symbol of that, which takes place in the individual". (¹¹) Of the Incarnation he tells us: „The real meaning of this sacred legend is this, that Jesus was born with all the dispositions to be a perfect man; pious love has to take the place of adoration." (¹²) The work of theologians like Hase was continued by philosophers like Feuerbach and Hartmann.

(⁹) See Hergenröther, Kirchengeschichte II. 946.
(¹⁰) Evang. protest. Dogmatik p. 199.

(¹¹) Ibid. 82.
(¹²) Ibid. 220.

How far infidelity is already a recognized part of German Protestantism will appear from facts like the following. Schenkel, the author of a work on Christ (Characterbild Jesu) which was written in the spirit of Rénan, was not disturbed in his position by the supreme ecclesiastical authorities of the Grandduchy of Baden, though they were asked to interfere. ([13]) When last year the Editor of the „Hamburger Reform" was summoned for blasphemy uttered against Christ, and when his counsel quoted a number of prominent protestant theologians to prove that the Divinity of Christ was no Lutheran dogma, the bench disregarded the plea altogether. ([14])

These proceedings of a secular court appear narrow-minded, when compared to the tame reprimand administered by the Consistorium of Hamburg to Dr. Hanne, who flatly denies the Mystery of the Blessed Trinity. This minister was reprimanded, „for that he had gone close to the boundary line of that liberty of teaching, which is acknowledged by the territorial Church". ([15]) We wonder where Dr. Hanne would be, if he crossed that line. But we will make a note of the fact that, though he may have acted imprudently in stating his views — as the Consistorium remarks — he was and still is a member and a minister of the territorial Lutheran Church of the free City of Hamburg. When another minister, Sydow, openly denied the Divinity of Christ, the Consistorium of Brandenburg dismissed him from the ministry, but this decision caused so many protests, that it had to be rescinded by the superior ecclesiastical court and a reprimand was substituted.

It must not be thought that cases of utter infidelity in Protestant ministers as well as leading laymen are rare. These men have thought it advisable to seek for greater strength in union; hence the famous „Protestanten Verein" came into existence in 1865, founded by Bluntschli, Zittel, Schenkel and others. Its object is to oppose a phalanx

([13]) Hergenröther l. c. 958.   ([15]) Ibid. 82.
([14]) Westermayer p. 83.

to Protestant orthodoxy and to any dogma, to advocate and promote absolute liberty of religious thought and „Entfesselung des freien christlichen Gewissens“, i. e. the unfettering of the free Christian conscience. :

In the „theology“ of the members of this Union we meet with phrases that would seem to imply orthodoxy; they still speak occasionally of the Son of God, of miracles, of resurrection and ascension etc., but when one hears them explain the meaning of these phrases, one cannot help thinking that it would be more honest if they were to renounce the use of them altogether. Nothing is more hateful to the Protestanten Verein, than the name of dogma. At its sixth general meeting at Osnabrück (A. D. 1872), Mr. Bluntschli in the chair, resolutions were passed to the effect, that all ecclesiastical forms of Creeds were based on purely human authority, that to insist on the reception of a certain creed as a condition of membership would mean to renounce the principles of the Reformation, to attack the Constitution of the Protestant Church and to injure Christian piety and theological science. ([16])

Let us hear some prominent members of the Protestanten Verein. „Away with dogmas which belong to the Roman Catholic Church and which exist in our Church only through misunderstanding and halfmeasures ... Away with all hierarchical aspirations and with all 'great' and small priests!“ ([17]) Thus speaks Dr. Hanne, whom we have mentioned before. It is the Blessed Trinity and the Divinity of Christ, which, according to him, are believed by Protestants only through misunderstanding.

„We mean to put aside old and antiquated forms of faith, which are of no value for our time ... because they cannot subsist in the light of calm and scientific investigation.“ ([18]) Pastor Höpffner, who saluted with the above

---

([16]) Hergenröther II. 958.   ([18]) Ap. Westermayer p. 106.
([17]) Der römische Katholicismus. A series of lectures p. 52.

words the brethren assembled at Neustadt, glories in the success which has attended their labours in the Palatinate. „A new Catechism has been introduced and has been used now for twelve years, which passes over in silence those doctrines which orthodoxy values above all others, the Trinity, the Divinity of Christ, original sin and justification through a substitute ... A new Agenda has been decreed, which endeavours to do justice to all parties and which contains also such formulas of baptism as do not bind to the Apostles' Creed." Hönig gets quite enthusiastic in describing the beauties of the Religion of the Protestanten Verein: „We know a God and a Divine order established in this world. We know redemption too. We do not know a supernatural magical apparatus for the work of redemption, or the incarnation of an infinite God, or that mysterious juridical process, where the guiltless takes upon himself the punishment due to the guilty, or a series of miraculous events composing the work of redemption. But we know of a real redemption, of a regeneration of the human heart through the strong consciousness of God and a purified conscience. We also know the Redeemer, who has accomplished this not through the magical effect of his death, but through the power of his mind, which has taken hold of hearts and minds with the convincing force of truth, with an overwhelming force, which out of itself has begotten a new life of mankind, based upon a new religious and moral foundation ... He that looks at the Bible with an unprejudiced mind, can hardly believe that anyone has ever convinced himself, that dogmatic Christianity is the Christianity preached by Jesus." ([19])

„Fear not! before our eyes the received form of religious life tumbles to pieces. The old dogmatic teaching (of the Reformers), that, which in our youth we have believed with simple minds, has lost its leaves and blossoms, nay in its roots it is dried up ... The old leaven will have

([19]) Ibid. 109. 110.

to be cleared out ... True Christians will only wish to be true *men.*" ([20])

Let us hear from Lang, that his want of faith in Christian dogmas does not deprive him of the right of calling himself a Christian. „Who will prevent us from saying with the first Christians: Thou art the Christ of God, the Son of God, leaning on whom we will grow up to become children of God? May we not celebrate Christmas, because we have come to the knowledge that the evangelical tales about Christmas are only sweetsmelling flowers of the pious mind which has been kindled by Christ, growing round the fact of the desire of the world to be freed from oppression and fear through that religion which makes children of God? May we no longer celebrate Good Friday, because we no longer believe in the death of a God who came down upon this earth to propitiate his own wrath with his own blood? Jesus has never taught anything of this kind. The personal selfsacrifice for the objects of God's kingdom, which in the death of Jesus sheds its light over the entrance to the Christian period of the world ... deserves a perpetual remembrance. May we no longer celebrate Easter, because we do not believe that a dead body has returned to life again? Paul and the first Christians did not believe it!" ([21])

The orthodox party has not been idle. Tholuck and Hengstenberg, who had done their best to stem the tide of infidelity, are dead. In our own days Stöcker may be looked upon as the leader of this party, which, though not holding any longer the symbolical Lutheran books, preserves at least the Apostles' Creed and tries to defend it against the onslaughts of the Protestanten Verein. Between the two parties there is war à outrance, yet the Evangelical Church of Prussia has room for them all. The liberal Protestants consider every attempt at upholding any dogma as an attack on the „free German con-

([20]) Dr. Hanne, quoted in Hamburger Briefe p. 138.

([21]) Westermayer 112.

science". This national conscience furnishes one of the most favourite phrases. Though we do not sympathize with them in the least, we must say that, salvo meliori judicio, they have far more logic on their side, than their antagonists have, who in the long run will find it difficult, nay impossible, to maintain their position. For if the principle of private judgment is established, who will draw the line? An authority would be required, which is excluded by the very principle, and the acknowledgment of which would destroy the principle.

Bluntschli and his party are perfectly right, when they say: We are legitimate children of the Reformation. The orthodox children may not acknowledge them as their brethren; but already Erasmus had said to Luther: „You do not recognise them as your children, but they recognise you as their father." They deny the authority of the great Pope of Rome, and they are perfectly right, when they scorn the pretensions of the little Popes in the ordodox ranks who say: So far and no farther. Lessing, who need not be credited with too much orthodoxy and Hartmann, the author of the „Philosophie des Unbewussten," who is a perfect infidel, have both declared that, if any authority in religious matters had to be acknowledged, they would cling to the rock of Peter.

Erit maxima confusio! This word of Luther has been fully verified and is being more verified every day. It is not a Catholic, but a Protestant theologian, and a minister, Schüler, who perceives „Symptoms of death in the territorial Church of Prussia," and who has expressed his opinion on this subject in a pamphlet published under the above title. He points out that a Church which is doubtful and debating about its very foundation and which at last practically gives up the same, cannot possess any vitality. Lisko spoke at the 13th. general meeting of the Protestanten Verein (held in Berlin, June 1881) of the present state ot Protestantism as that of „a decomposition,

the like of which it will be difficult to find in history."([22])
On the occasion of the last meeting Zittel, one of the
founders of the Union, said: „Hardly ever has the German
Evangelical Church been interiorly so full of dissension
and so powerless in the struggles of the time, as during
the first ten years of the new German Empire."([23]) The
remedy suggested by the „Berliner Tageblatt" is worth
noticing. It consists in the realization of absolute liberty!
In other words, to heal the dissension agree to differ and
let everybody be his own Church and then you will have
the Church intended and founded by Him, who prayed
that all his disciples might be one!

Even the pomp of the Luther celebration of the year
1883 has not been sufficient to palliate the dissensions, nay
the mortal combat between Luther's disciples, who all build
up their system on his own principles. It has not been
sufficient, though on that occasion all parties agreed in at
least one point, in the cherished legacy of the Prophet of
Wittenberg: „Impleat vos Dominus odio Papae." During
the celebration and during the preparation for it this has
been the most favourite subject. The palm for coming
nearest to the master in hatred and calumny must be assigned to seven infidel ministers at Hamburg, whose lectures
would only make a Catholic smile, if the grief of seeing
his Church attacked in such an infamous way did not prevail. In either downright ignorance of the nature, doctrine and practice of the Catholic Church, or in malici-
ously distorting the same, those gentlemen stand quite
unparalleled.([24]) But we trust the Catholic Church will
survive those seven heroes. At any rate, Luther's prophecy
that Popery would not last long, has not been fulfilled.
The Catholic Church is still alive, all over the world, also
in Germany, which gave birth to the so called Reformer.
She is there alive in spite of the Culturkampf, with which

([22]) Kirche oder Protest. p. 312. a proper answer in the „Hambur-
([23]) Ap. Westermayer p. 90. ger Briefe". Berlin. Verlag der Ger-
([24]) Their attacks have met with mania.

Luther's disciples, the apostles of freedom, Bluntschli and Company, have tried to smother her for the last thirteen years, in recompense of the blood shed by the Catholics on many a battlefield for the common Fatherland. And whilst Lutheranism is in a state of decomposition and, as far as it has not arrived there as yet, on the highroad to infidelity, we find a guaranty for the Church's further existence in the words of Him, whose words shall not pass away:

Tu es Petrus, et super hanc petram aedificabo Ecclesiam meam, et portae inferi non praevalebunt adversus eam.

Index

to the abbreviations of references.

Aen. Sylv. Aeneas Sylvius, De Germania, in Schardii opus histor.

Balan. Monumenta Reformationis Lutheranae ex Tabulariis secretioribus S. Sedis. 1521—1525. Collegit P. Balan. Ratisbonae 1884.

De Wette. Dr. M. Luther's Briefe, Sendschreiben und Bedenken, Edit. De Wette. 5 voll. Berlin 1825—28. Seidemann has added a supplementary volume in 1856.

Döll. Die Reformation, ihre innere Entwicklung etc. Von J. Döllinger. 3 voll. Regensburg 1848.

Erl. Luther's sämmtliche Werke. 67 voll. Erlangen 1826—1868.

Evers. Martin Luther, Lebens- und Characterbild, von Georg G. Evers. I—IV. Mainz 1883.

Germanus. Reformatorenbilder. Historische Vorträge etc. von Dr. Konstantin Germanus (Pseudon.) Freiburg 1883.

Gröne. Tetzel und Luther, oder Lebensgeschichte und Rechtfertigung des Ablasspredigers etc. von Dr. Valentin Gröne. Soest 1860.

Hasak. Der christliche Glaube des deutschen Volkes beim Schlusse des Mittelalters, dargestellt in deutschen Sprachdenkmalen. Von Vincenz Hasak. Regensburg 1868.

Hergenröther. Handbuch der allgemeinen Kirchengeschichte. Von Cardinal J. Hergenröther. 3 voll. Freiburg, 1880.

Hermann. Joannes Tetzel, der päpstliche Ablassprediger, nach Sage und Geschichte dargestellt von Karl Wilhelm Hermann.

Hutten. Ulrici De Hutten opera quae exstant. Edidit Münch. Berolini 1823.

Janssen. Geschichte des deutschen Volkes seit dem Ausgang des Mittelalters. Von Johannes Janssen. 3 voll. Freiburg 1878—1881.

Jörg. Geschichte des Protestantismus in seiner neuesten Entwickelung. Von J. E. Jörg. Freiburg 1858.